About the author

Claude Randall was born in London, grew up in Surrey, read History at the University of Exeter, was a political lobbyist and now lives in Wales.

THE MORNING TREE

Claude Randall

THE MORNING TREE

Vanguard Press

A CIP catalogue record for this title is
available from the British Library.

ISBN 978 1 784655 69 3

*Vanguard Press is an imprint of
Pegasus Elliot MacKenzie Publishers Ltd.*
www.pegasuspublishers.com

First Published in 2019

**Vanguard Press
Sheraton House Castle Park
Cambridge England**

Printed & Bound in Great Britain

To Jess, who achieved so much

Introduction

In February 2008, Dr Daniel Clifton, lecturer in Tibetan at the School of Oriental and African Studies, University of London, came across a hand written manuscript claiming to be by a Tibetan monk of Mongolian origin called Thaza.

The manuscript was written in 1966. It describes Thaza's participation in events in Tibet in 1931-32 involving an ancient text of considerable spiritual significance called the Morning Tree. Dr Clifton's translation of Thaza's account and accompanying notes are presented in the first half of this book.

Dr Clifton's own account of discovering and translating the manuscript, and what happened thereafter, forms the second half of this book.

Claire Hoskyns
Editor

Thaza's account

Translated and edited by Dr Daniel Clifton

My name is Thaza. I am a Mongolian horseman. Although I wear the red robes of a monk, my true home is not here, in Yerlang monastery in central Tibet, but the plains and mountains of Mongolia.

How I miss my home! And how I despise these monks! They think I'm lazy or irreligious because I don't attend all the services and haven't learnt their sacred texts by heart. But these fools wouldn't recognise true religion if it stared them in their faces. They mumble their words, don't understand what they're saying, and have no grasp of the real truth that lies within Tibetan Buddhism. But I KNOW. I know because I have experienced, first hand, the esoteric knowledge that has been safeguarded for thousands of years behind the mountain walls of Tibet. I have helped to ensure that that knowledge is passed on for another thousand years. But how I have suffered for the help I have given!

I make no apology for who I am. I used to tame wild horses, find water in parched plains and look after my family and flocks. These monks just wait to be served by the local population. Even a child, where I come from, has more practical knowledge than they do.

I used to ride, ride fast, and fight. I felt joy in galloping. I excelled at horsemanship. I was the best wrestler out of all the clans we knew. But all of this was taken from me when my body was shattered and I was left dying on the scree a few miles from here. I was rescued by monks who carried me back to this place and nursed me to health. When it became clear that my broken body meant I'd never ride again, let alone walk without a limp, I knew I couldn't return home. What use is an invalid? How could I live when I couldn't live as I loved? So I stayed here, at Yerlang monastery, and I've never left. That was over thirty years ago.

I used to think I was lucky to be alive. But now I wonder if I wasn't rescued by the devil who wanted to taunt me with my disabilities. To be unable to ride – to live without the people I have loved -- to bear the disdain of my fellow monks – this is truly more painful than the complaints of my now old body. In my next life I want restitution for all that I have suffered in this one.

The monks who rescued me all those years ago were true monks. They had humility and compassion. And they knew – they knew what I had done to help their religion. Of course, we did not talk of it; as I said, they were true monks. But shortly after I arrived the then abbot, the Venerable Lama Chingdop, visited me on my sickbed. He motioned the attending monks to leave, and then said in that deep voice of his, "My son, I have heard from Lhasa. They are grateful. We are all grateful."

I didn't reply; the herbs I had been given to heal me had choked my voice. But I inclined my head. Nothing more was ever said. And I knew I was safe as long as he was head of our lamasery. So, for the first few years, I was treated with the courtesy and respect that was due to me.

But the monks today! They just view monkhood as a soft option to tilling the hard ground in the nearby villages, or earning a living by trading. They are not here to advance their souls or serve others. They go through the motions but don't mean what they say. The last Butter Festival[1] was a disgrace! The villagers would be better off paying homage to a pile of yak dung than this lot.

The thing I can't stomach is how cowardly they are. Ever since the communist Chinese invaders arrived – it was about seven years ago that they first came to Yerlang, when the Dalai Lama had to flee to India for his life[2] – the monks just let their tongues hang out and don't do anything to stand up for themselves. The Chinese have guns, the monks say, we have nothing but books. In fact, they have nothing but air-headed fear. So they let themselves be ruled by skinny men who look too weak to fire the guns they obviously have difficulty

---

[1] One of the main festivals of the Tibetan New Year celebrations held in February each year.

[2] The Fourteenth Dalai Lama fled to India in 1959 to escape the communist Chinese. Thaza says that was seven years ago, which means he is writing this account in 1966.

14

carrying. For I know the Chinese – mean and capable in their own way – but they can be beaten. I know, for I have done it.

Today, the local commander came to the monastery with a company of soldiers. We all had to turn out to see him. I spat as he passed. He glared at me. I returned the compliment. Then I was pulled back roughly by another monk who apologised, saying I was old and ignorant. The others around me murmured in agreement. I turned to assail the monk who had restrained me, only to have a spasm in my hip that caused me to stumble. I suppose the commander took this as an apology from a mad old man and he moved on. But I was livid!

"How dare you…" I began, before I was bundled backwards out of sight. A senior lama took me inside and hissed, "Be quiet, you fool, before you get us all killed!"

"You'll all be killed anyway!" I shouted before stalking off. If they didn't want the Chinese to see me then I wasn't going to hang around.

Yes, I know, we've been hearing horror stories from Lhasa and elsewhere about fanatical Chinese soldiers waving little red books, destroying monasteries, killing monks and smashing holy images.[3] And yes, I know, they could do that here. But bowing our heads won't stop them. Only fighting will. Why don't we fight?

And the worst of all this is, I knew this was going to happen. I was told oh so many years ago by a truly spiritual person about the tragedy that would overtake Tibet. I protested at the time that they should take action to stop it, but he wouldn't hear of it. Spiritual people confuse me: how can they let bad things happen? By all means let these monks suffer, but why let a whole culture be destroyed?

As if today's incident with the Chinese soldiers wasn't enough, this evening, at meal time, I was barged out of the queue by a monk who growled that we shouldn't let foreigners eat what little food there was available. Yes, said another, nor should we let outsiders put their religion at risk. Foreigners? Their religion at risk? When this 'foreigner' has done a signal service safeguarding 'their religion'? I saw red. I

---

[3] Thaza appears to be describing the start of the Cultural Revolution 1966-76 during which the majority of Tibet's monasteries were destroyed.

smashed the first monk's jaw from underneath with my elbow (a martial arts technique I once learnt) and heard it crack. That will stop him eating what little food there is available. I was about to turn to the other one when Pemba Gephal pulled me away. He is a young monk, and the only one here who still shows me any respect. He took me out of the refectory and away from the trouble that was brewing to a quiet room near the library.

But I was still angry! How dare they discriminate against me! I have sacrificed my life to save their precious knowledge – knowledge they have no inkling of. Let them all be eaten by the Chinese, but let them show due deference to an elder who is more of a man than they will ever be.

I have decided to write down everything I have done. I remember it all. How could I forget, such were the things that happened. I know I took a vow of silence, never to speak of what I was told or did, to protect the esoteric treasures of Tibet. But 'writing' isn't 'speaking', and I will let no-one see this until I am in my grave. And when I am, and when this manuscript is read and the truth finally released, then maybe people might have more understanding for me.

So, I will miss the services, the observances and the chores – it's not as if I'm wanted – and I will stay here and write my story. I will tell the TRUTH. Then perhaps I might find some peace. My hip aches so much in the cold mornings, and my body is beginning to feel distant from me. My life force is ebbing away. Curiously, I, who have held on to life, am not alarmed at the prospect of going to the Heavenly Fields. The wheel of life is turning, and I with it. May a compassionate Buddha watch over my passage.

It Begins

It all started when I killed my grandfather. I didn't mean to. It just happened.

My grandfather had brought me up after my father died. Shortly after my father's death, for reasons that were never explained to me, my mother moved back to my grandfather's family. Her return was considered a mark of great shame for my grandfather's family, especially as my father's family kept her bridal dowry of silver and furnishings.[4] As a result, when I was growing up, my father was never honoured or even talked about.

I was three when my father died, and can barely remember him. I would ask about him as a child. But my mother would not say anything. His early death had turned her religious. She would look after me, make butter and cheese, light fires, cook food and sew clothes, but she would do all this absentmindedly. She was only really interested in religion. She spent all her spare time in front of her little altar, turning her prayer wheel, nodding her head as she repeated mantras, or constantly feeding her rosary through her fingers. The most she would ever say about him was that Buddha was looking after him and he would be blessed in his next life.

My grandfather was even worse. If I ever asked about my father he would snarl, say something bad or hit me. I soon learnt not to

---

[4] In Mongolian society, a woman who married left her family with a dowry and became part of her husband's family, even if her husband pre-deceased her. The fact that Thaza's mother returned to her parents is highly unusual and explains the sense of shame felt by Thaza's grandfather.

mention his name. But I knew in my heart that he had been a good man, unjustly dealt with by the gods and others. I swore to myself that I wouldn't let life treat me the same way.

I had no brothers or sisters, although my uncle – my mother's younger brother – married and had children after my mother and I came to live with my grandfather. I came to realise that my uncle was a weak man, in mind and body, and an illness carried him away when I was ten. At this point I became, in reality, the eldest son in the family, even though I wasn't formally recognised as such.

My grandfather did teach me many important things. He had an eye for a good horse, and we earned most of our income, not from our herds, as most families did, but from trading horses. I soon discovered that I too could spot a good horse. Indeed, I discovered that I had a special way with them not given to ordinary men. Horses would obey me, even the fiercest stallion would nuzzle my hand, and when I mounted a horse, both the horse and myself would grow in stature.

Riding became my passion. By the time I was thirteen I was a much better rider than my grandfather – much better than anyone else I knew. I would practise for hours trotting, galloping, performing acrobatics and shooting arrows from the saddle. I would spend as many hours grooming them, attending to their hooves, feeding them, and just being with them. They were closer to me than my family.

My favourite was a stallion called Jarzo. He understood me, he really did. I learnt more from him than any other horse. He broke his leg when I was scooping metal discs from the ground in preparation for a local nadaam.[5] My staff rebounded off the hard earth into his legs and we both went flying. There was a crack as he fell, and a whinny of pain. I had to cut his throat minutes later. But even then he gazed into my eyes and knew that I loved him.

---

[5] Nadaam: traditional Mongolian games consisting of wrestling, horse racing and archery. Competing in local or national nadaams conferred great honour, especially on the winners.

I feel so happy, yet so frustrated, recalling my time with my horses! I felt joy with them, galloping so fast that the wind stung my face, showing the world what I could do. I found companionship I certainly never had with my grandfather. Yet, all of this has been taken from me. For so many years now I've not been able to ride. Oh, sometimes visiting lamas come on ponies, and the farmers bring me theirs if they are sick, but I never ride. The unfairness of it all! I still dream about them, you know. I feel the pull of a horse's head on the reins, or breathe in their fulsome scent, or hear the chimes of their bridle. But then I wake up and I'm not with my horses but in a dormitory of snoring, comatose monks, wrapped in their robes.

My grandfather taught me other things as well. The best way to kill a sheep or goat, how to skin an animal, how to help spring lambing, how to judge the best pasture. Of course, I was soon a better herdsman than him. And I had another knack not given to others. I could detect water. I could scan the landscape and feel where water might be. I was right so often that other families knew of my gift.

By the time I was eleven I was running my family's affairs. I was like the eldest son. My younger cousins deferred to me, as did their mother. My mother was too absentminded to realise just how important I had become. Even other families noticed me. But not my grandfather. He ordered me about, but never acknowledged or thanked me. And he'd criticise or beat me if ever he thought anything was wrong. I bore it, but I bore it darkly. I knew I was better than he was, and I knew I deserved better.

There was continual bad feeling between us. I accepted our relative roles because, after all, he was notionally the head of the family and his horse trading deals did ensure we enjoyed a better standard of living than most. I would even have liked him if he had been half fair to me. But he just resented me. I've never understood why.

When I was fifteen things went from bad to worse. I wanted to marry; it was my right, and my desire. I knew of several families who would have given their daughters to me in matrimony. But my grandfather had to give his consent. And it was clear he never would.[6] I know one family made an overture to my mother and grandfather one spring. He wouldn't even let them make their case. In a way I was relieved (their daughter was not pretty) but I wanted to fulfil myself.

Why was he so obdurate? I used to think it was because he knew how useful I was and he didn't want to lose me. I could understand that. I offered to stay with him, my mother and my cousins if he would let me marry; my only condition was that I would have my own yurt.[7] But my grandfather was furious that I was bargaining with him. He saw my betrothal as entirely his matter. Pleading with my mother to intervene was no use.

I sometimes wondered if he was reluctant to let me marry because he didn't want to give me my portion of the family's herds and horses so I could set up with my bride on my own. But that didn't make sense because, as I have said, we were well off. No, I think the real reason my grandfather refused to let me get married was spite. He didn't like me.

My teenage years were a misery. Even the goats were luckier than me; they could at least act as nature dictated. But I was forced to suffer in silence. The only good thing was that by now he'd stopped beating me. I was bigger and stronger than he was.

Then I met Sarangerel. I was seventeen, she was fourteen. We spent part of the summer together when our two families and others were sharing grazing grounds near Lake Chorcail. I didn't notice her at first. Well, I did – she was bent over her cooking pots as I rode past – but I was busy with our livestock. We met later by ourselves while collecting water. We struck up conversation. Although we'd never been introduced, it was very easy. We met two or three times after that by accident, and each time we stopped to talk to each other. From

---

[6] In Mongolian society, children could only marry with their parents' consent. In Thaza's case, it meant his grandfather's consent.

[7] When a son married, he was traditionally given some animals and a yurt so he could start a new family. Only poorer nomads stayed in larger groups. So Thaza's offer to stay with his grandfather after his marriage was a departure from tradition.

then on we were much more self-conscious. But that was only because we knew there was a strong attraction between us.

I know she liked me. She flushed when she saw me, demurely turning away, yet smiling at the same time. I certainly liked her. She was a little plump, but she was pretty and she just had this glow about her. She was also playful when she talked to me. I would normally strike anyone who teased me, but she was different. I just felt happy with her.

I knew she was the girl I wanted to marry. I was suddenly glad that my grandfather had prevented me from marrying up to that point. This entirely new feeling was wonderful and I wanted to keep it. I wanted to be with Sarangerel.

Of course, I knew my grandfather would be difficult. At the time I still thought he was against my marrying because he was reluctant to lose my valuable talents, so I still thought he could be brought round. Indeed, it was that summer that I made my proposal to stay with him and my mother if ever he would consent to me getting married.

I also knew that I had to cultivate Sarangerel's family. Oh, I was clever, positioning myself so I would pass by her family's yurts or herds so I could greet them, and helping them whenever an opportunity arose. I got to know her father, Batzorig, a chubby, jovial man. I didn't respect him – he was usually laughing and he didn't seem to pride himself on anything – but Sarangerel and the rest of her family adored him. I played my part, deferring to him, praising him, and one evening, when I was looking at a sick horse of theirs he suddenly said, "Ah Thaza, what a good son you are! Have some shimiin arkhi[8] with me." I drank with him, happy that he approved of me.

I couldn't ask him if I could marry Sarangerel – that was my grandfather's job – but at that moment I was so close to doing so. That night, in their yurt, drinking and eating with them, and feeling Sarangerel close by (we were careful not to reveal our feelings so we pretended to be distant), was the happiest moment of my life.

---

[8] Distilled fermented mare's milk that produces a clear, tasteless type of vodka that is high in alcoholic content.

21

Thinking that a life like this could soon be mine intoxicated me more than any amount of shimiin arkhi I was drinking.

But within a week everything was in ruins. Two days after my evening with Batzorig, my grandfather announced we were moving on. I didn't see why; the pasture was still good and water was nearby, but my grandfather refused to be contradicted. We had a blazing row that could have been heard from hell. Had he seen how close I was getting to Sarangerel's family, and was he spitefully spiking my happiness? I was sure of it. But then I wasn't old enough to disobey him and have my way. So, some days afterwards, we dismantled our yurt and moved on. Batzorig came to say goodbye. My grandfather waved him away without looking at him. I would have been offended, but Batzorig didn't seem to mind. He came over to slap me on my back and say he hoped we'd meet again.

So did I. I made a point of telling him which direction we were going in, but he didn't seem to take my hint. I looked for Sarangerel but couldn't see her. Risking appearing a sentimental fool I said, "Say goodbye to your family from me."

"Of course, Thaza," he replied. "I know Jorchin will miss you." Jorchin was Sarangerel's idiot of a brother, one year older than she was. At that point I really did despise Batzorig; could he honestly think no more of me than being Jorchin's friend? Couldn't he see what an ideal son-in-law I would make? But the man was still smiling, and I still thought I needed his approval, so I smiled back.

A thousand thoughts went through my head as we left our camp by Lake Chorcail. Anger at my grandfather. Joy thinking about Sarangerel. Planning what to do when we met again. And more anger, this time at the gods for placing me in this vice where I was condemned to have my hopes continually squeezed from me. Even the sunshine that morning felt cold. I think it was at that moment that I vowed to do whatever was necessary to break away from my grandfather.

So it was we headed south-west towards the Altai mountains. We kept moving for the next few months. I couldn't see why; we were just unnecessarily tiring our animals. Winter came. It was harder than usual. We lost several animals to the cold, and some to desperate wolves. My late uncle had once exchanged a number of rugs and sheep for a rifle and some ammunition. He'd rarely fired it, and my grandfather disdained such modern things. But that winter I exhausted the little ammunition we had trying to protect our herds. The rifle roared, but it was never accurate. The wolves scattered when I fired, but I never hit one. By the end of the winter I was forced to revert to my bow and arrows. I did kill one then, but had to stalk it for hours in the freezing cold. It felt good though to drag it back to our camp. I skinned it and asked my mother to make me a jacket from its fur.

I said by the end of the winter, but in truth that winter didn't seem to end. Warmer weather should have arrived, but instead, the days persisted cold with flurries of sleet. It was then that my grandfather suggested we move the herds to higher pasture in the nearby hills. I protested as loudly as I could; the idea was madness. Indeed, I'd begun to suspect that old age had unhinged his mind. Either that or he was ill. His breath had begun to smell more than it should, and I was beginning to sense a new weakness in him. If he'd been a goat I'd have singled him out for early slaughter. But he wasn't a goat (at least not outwardly) and by tradition I still had to do his bidding.

Luckily at that time we were camped near two other families. They heard of my grandfather's suggestion and they too expressed concern. Even my mother was anxious. Finally, and to my surprise, my grandfather said that we should ride to the higher pasture and inspect it. I'm sure he felt he would be vindicated. So it was agreed that my grandfather and I, and a man from one of the other families, would ride there the next day.

The fateful morning arrived. I can still remember it. My mother had lit the dung fire to make tea. I broke the film of fat from the previous night's stew and had some cold meat for breakfast. My mother handed me some tea – she always put too much salt in it because that was the way my grandfather liked it. I could tell by the low moan of the wind around the yurt that it was still cold outside.

Eventually my grandfather got up, cleared his throat and took his tea from my mother without a word. My cousins, always subdued around my grandfather, looked on.

I put on my outer coat and left the yurt to prepare the horses. The wind had an edge to it. I looked at the sky; some dark clouds were coming in from the east. Madness to go on this trip, I thought to myself, but if it was the only way to convince my grandfather of his folly then it had to be done. At that point one of the men from the other families came over to say that he wouldn't join us on our visit. I understood why: they needn't follow my grandfather if he persisted in his mad idea, so why bother making the difficult journey on a day like this? But how I have wondered since what would have happened – or not happened – if that other man had been with us that day.

My grandfather emerged from the yurt and with a grunt mounted his horse. We set off in silence. I can't remember how long it took us to get to the higher pasture – several hours, it must have been – but we didn't exchange a word the whole way. The clouds parted briefly and bathed the whole world in sunlight. I even felt the sun's warmth. But then the weather closed in again. We finally arrived as some sleet started stinging our faces.

We dismounted to inspect the pasture. Of course I was right. The ground was more frozen here than on the plains, and the grass was sparse and dead. The only advantage to being here was that no-one else would think of coming, so what little there was would be ours. But it was still absurd to think of moving here at any time apart from the summer.

"Grandfather!" I shouted above the wind. "It's no good!"

My grandfather turned away and walked on, ostensibly looking at the ground. I couldn't believe, even with all I knew about his obstinacy, that he would persist in thinking a move to the higher pasture was still a good idea. He continued towards the edge of a gully. Then he turned round and said, in a voice louder than I believed he possessed:

"We move here tomorrow!"

I felt anger then. Why should this demented goat risk our livelihoods – even our lives – with his numbing stupidity? Why should he continue to ruin *my* life? I felt real hatred. But I swear I had no idea what I was going to do next. Devils racing through the air must have whispered to me, for just then the wind whipped up and a thought crossed my mind. Why not push him over the edge of the gully and end this nonsense once and for all? I felt myself moving towards him. He had turned round to look over the gully again. In a couple of strides I was behind him. In less than an instant I had shoved him in his back. He stumbled and turned. When he saw me, an angry scowl crossed his face. He was about to say something when I shoved him again, this time far harder and from the front. He staggered backwards, slipped on some loose stones and thrust out his hands. He gripped nothing but air. I moved forward, ready to push him again, but before I could he finally fell backwards over the edge.

It was a surprisingly steep gully. I heard him yell, and saw him fall. His head dashed against an outcrop of rock, then his body spun viciously before breaking on the boulders below. I knew he must be dead.

Yes, I can remember all this in detail. I feel now as I did then. My heart was thumping and I knew I'd committed a crime. I was shocked at what had happened. But at the same time I was strangely unmoved. Truly, I had never thought of killing him. It was an act of the moment; wrong of course, but at the same time not wrong. He was old, not right in the head and no longer fit to lead our family. Who would miss him? Hadn't I suffered enough? And if he'd continued with his plan to take us to the higher pasture, wouldn't he have jeopardised us all?

I had a flash then of all his madness leading up to this trip. Argh! He had gone off his head. Standing there in the wind and sleet I felt his years of oppression and just knew, however it looked to an outsider, that there was justification. The great Genghis Khan had been forced to kill weaker people for the greater good. I didn't need to feel bad. He had been evil, and I was rid of him. I could be myself at last.

I don't know how long I stood there contemplating what had happened. But another lash of cold wind brought me to my senses. I couldn't stand there wondering; I had to take action or freeze to death.

I narrowed my eyes and scanned the gully below to calculate if I could climb down and haul his body up. I quickly saw this wasn't feasible. He would have to rot there, and good riddance to him. I caught his horse, mounted mine, and rode home. I cantered most of the way even though I knew the horses were tired and hungry. It was dusk by the time I returned. I was frozen, wet and starving.

"Mother," I cried, falling in front of her in the yurt, "Grandfather's dead!" It wasn't difficult to sound deflated, as if I mourned his death. I was tired in body and soul. Before she could say anything I continued.

"It was in the higher pasture. He was next to a gully when he slipped. He reached out, but I was too far away to catch him. He was dead before he hit the ground."

My mother clutched her rosary. She looked shocked and confused, but there was also understanding. She leant over to pick up her most treasured possession – a picture of the Thirteenth Dalai Lama.[9] She then began to rock backwards and forwards slowly.

"His body?" she asked at length, her breath rasping.

"Too far away to reach," I replied. "I couldn't retrieve it."

Just then a man from one of the other families came in. He could sense something was wrong. My mother said nothing, so I explained what had happened. "The pasture was useless anyway," I added.

The man paid his respects and offered to help collect the body. I wished he hadn't done that, but I pretended thanks, and we agreed to

---

[9] The Thirteenth Dalai Lama 1876-1933. Born Tubten Gyatso in Takpo Langdun, south-east of Lhasa, he was recognised at the age of two as the reincarnation of the deity Chenrezig and the Thirteenth Dalai Lama. He assumed religious power in 1895 and then, unlike most of his predecessors, temporal power as well. He was an able ruler, bringing much needed religious and administrative reforms. He earned the title the Great Thirteenth in recognition of his abilities. Mongolia was a devoutly Buddhist country, and its population recognised the Dalai Lama as the head of their faith as ardently as that of Tibet.

fetch it the next day. However, the weather was even fouler the next day, so it wasn't until the day after that six of us set out to recover my grandfather's corpse.

The others were silent on the way out of respect for me. I was tight lipped, not because I was in mourning, but because, try as I might, the situation was difficult. Yes, I was relieved my grandfather was gone, and his departure had been long overdue. But I had killed him. I was suddenly wondering if some vengeful god might make me pay.

When we at last reached the place, I wondered if that vengeful god wasn't already making me pay. We went up to the gully's edge and scanned the ground below for my grandfather's body. It wasn't there. It should have been, but it wasn't. Oh my god, had he somehow survived and crawled away? Would he reappear and accuse me of trying to murder him? A spasm of fear went through me.

"Look Thaza," said one of the men, pointing down. "Some clothes."

"And look," said another, "bloody bones."

We followed their gaze and saw clothes and bones and fur boots half hidden by boulders sloping away as the gully bottom descended. They were definitely my grandfather's clothes. A wave of relief washed through me.

"Probably vultures," said one of the men.

"Yes," I replied, swallowing hard. "Eating him before we can bless his body." My mother had wanted us to bring his body back so she could bless it before leaving him to the birds to consume.[10] But they had already done their bloody duty. Now all we could return to her were some stained clothes and the few belongings we might find.

We roped ourselves up and climbed down to gather what we could. We were all in a lighter frame of mind riding back. And I was in a lighter frame of mind for several weeks afterwards. My grandfather was truly gone and, although it took us some time to

---

[10] Mongolians of the period practised 'sky burials' as in Tibet where dead bodies are left naked for the vultures to dispose of.

understand the change, we did all feel freer. No-one disputed my suggestions; I was in charge to run the family as I wished. My young cousins came out of their shells; they were more lively and useful in managing our affairs than I had believed possible. Their mother, my aunt by marriage, took to singing as she did her chores. Even my mother seemed happier. Though, of course, none of us voiced the real reason for our new found spirits.

And, as if the heavens were somehow blessing what had happened, spring finally arrived. We didn't move to the higher pasture – I didn't want to see that place again – but we moved grazing grounds and life definitely improved. Lambing went well. My horses bred well too. And I fixed some good deals with travelling traders which put silver in our pockets.

Around mid-summer we were camping near several other families. One contained the famous wrestler Batsaikhan, who had competed in the national nadaam some years ago. I spent many hours with him, learning his skills, becoming a competent wrestler. I sweated more than a lactating sheep on a hot day in my bouts with him, and my body was black and bruised, but life was good and I was happy.

Before we moved from that camping ground, one of the families there approached my mother with an offer of marriage for me. The girl, Altantsetseg, looked strong and capable. Her family were not rich, and they could promise only a modest dowry. But I reasoned we did not need much as our fortunes were on the rise and I knew that, with my skills, I would be able to look after us all properly. So I asked my mother to accept the offer. Yes, I know, I had wanted to marry Sarangerel, but I didn't know where her family was, and couldn't trust her dim-witted father to offer her to me, so I took what the gods were providing. At last I would have my own yurt!

The betrothal was agreed, but I would have to wait until the following spring for Altantsetseg to join me. This was to give her family time to assemble the dowry, small though it would be. We fixed when and where we would meet the next year. I didn't want to wait – and how I have since rued that decision! – but to have accepted an even smaller dowry would not have honoured me. But still, I was at last to have a wife. I was happy.

I can't remember when the bad dreams began. Probably around the start of that winter. Certainly the weather was cold and uninviting. In the beginning the dreams weren't very distinct. Just blackness, or a dark creeping feeling that something evil was around. At the time I didn't link them with my grandfather. But after a while his image started to appear, or he would be in the background, dead but alive, and threatening. My mother began to tell me I was thrashing about in my sleep. I didn't need her to tell me that my nights were disturbed, and was angry whenever she mentioned it. During those times my cousins began to look at me as they had at my grandfather – with wariness and fear. I didn't care – they should respect me as the head of the family.

One night I was outside relieving myself. The wind was biting cold and I was trying to hurry up. I swear I heard a hiss – it wasn't the wind, it was quite distinct – and I saw his face. I don't know how I saw it in the pitch black, but I did. And it was his face. I waited to feel a blow, for ghost or not I knew it was his evil presence, but none came. That was the first haunting while I was awake.

Then there was the time my aunt was serving the evening meal. She was ladling out piping hot mutton stew when I suddenly heard my grandfather snarl out my name. I was so startled I knocked the bowl of stew over one of my cousins. "Ow, you idiot!" he exclaimed. I struck him harder than I should and glared at the others. Had they heard my grandfather too? They were all nervous… but not, I realised, because they had heard a ghost but because they were witnessing my temper. We ate our meal in silence.

Perhaps the most disturbing was when I was thrown from my horse. Something unseen startled it and I was caught unawares as it reared up and flung me off. My head banged painfully on the hard earth as I landed. I felt my grandfather's presence, felt his face close up to mine as I groaned on the ground, and felt – or more accurately smelled – a cloying sourness, like cheese gone off. Again I waited for a blow, or even some words, but nothing more happened. I finally picked myself up and shook the dust off my jacket. I am ashamed to say my knees buckled as I realised he could spook my horses anytime and kill me in what would appear simply as a freak accident.

By now I was truly fearful about what might happen to me. I didn't get the bad dreams or physical hauntings all the time, but my mind would continually conjure up some terrible event like my grandfather appearing with his leering face, or his actual denunciation of me as his killer. I became jumpy. Of course, I covered this up and told no-one. Who could I tell without condemning myself? But I became short-tempered and irritable. Laughingly, I was becoming like my grandfather.

By the end of that winter I knew I was cursed. I was being followed around by my grandfather's evil presence. I was sure it was bent on revenge. Revenge? After all he had done to me? Wasn't his death balancing the bad karma he had carried out on me? If anyone should have revenge, it should be me. But how could I fight a spirit? The worst of it was I didn't know what powers this spirit possessed. I became convinced my grandfather could kill me anytime.

Life now was not good. The dreams and hauntings continued, all the worse for being unpredictable. Sometimes days would pass with nothing, and I dared to hope my grandfather was gone. Then he'd return – a nightmare, a grotesque vision, a dangerous 'accident' – and I knew he was on the prowl again. Life was worse now than when my grandfather had been alive. At least then I could shut my ears to his torments, I knew he would never dare beat me since I was stronger than he was, and I could always escape with my horses. But now, even when I was with my horses, I couldn't get the evil thought of him out of my mind. Now he was in the spirit world, he was able to be everywhere with me in this one.

I began to look hangdog, ate little, and far from gaining in happiness as my wedding approached, I was being eaten away from within. My mother thought I was ill and began praying for me. At first I was irritated, but after a while I too began to ask Buddha for help.

Believe me, I had never turned to Buddha before, even when I'd been suffering the worst of my grandfather's oppressions. The gods had always seemed deaf to my pleas, and I in turn despised them. But my grandfather's ghost was like a wild animal that I didn't know how to handle.

The thought crossed my mind that I might need to visit a lamasery and ask the monks for their blessing. I didn't want to – I didn't want to kneel down before some idle monk (yes, they were idle in Mongolia too) and beg for his services. But then I didn't want to die either, and couldn't think of anything else to do. My mother had occasionally told me stories of miracles that some lamas had carried out. Maybe those stories were true, and maybe they could conjure a miracle for me. Of course I wouldn't tell them why I wanted a blessing, but maybe they could lift my curse.

I was still undecided when a trader I'd dealt with before sent word that he wanted to buy several yearlings from me. This deal alone would secure enough money to last the year. So I agreed to deliver the horses to his compound at Talshand. There was a lamasery there which my mother had visited years ago. When I was done with my business I would ask for a blessing. The idea still stuck in my throat, but I had no alternative.

Miraculously, once I'd made my decision, the bad dreams stopped, and so did the hauntings. Was Buddha intervening on my behalf already? I have since learnt that if Buddha helps you, he invariably wants something in return.

I Seek Help

So, a week later I set off with my horses to Talshand. I'd hired two men from other families to help. They needed the money, and would be in debt to me should I need a favour in the future. I couldn't bring my cousins; they were too young and needed to stay to look after our flocks.

It took five days to get to Talshand. We arrived late in the afternoon and camped on the outskirts. I went to scout around. I discovered the trader's compound was to the west of the settlement. Talshand itself was made up of the local lord's residence, herds and the lamasery. There was a market in front of the lamasery. The yurts of the traders and nomads, who were congregating there, were dotted around wherever there was space. It was the greatest number of people I had so far seen in one place.

Next morning I concluded my business. My contact was a rare thing – an honourable trader – and he wasn't trying to cheat me. He knew the quality of my horses. I paid the two men off (I didn't want them witnessing my visit to the lamasery) and then went to the market. I was scanning the lamasery from afar when suddenly I heard a shout.

"Thaza!"

I followed the voice and saw Jorchin, Sarangerel's brother, lounging at one of the stalls. I was surprised to see him in such unfamiliar surroundings. Then irritated that he'd interrupted my deliberations. Then aware that if he was here, maybe the rest of his family were too…

"Thaza," he said coming towards me and spitting on the ground, "what are you doing here?"

"Business," I replied. I wasn't going to tell him what business. "And you?"

"Business too," he grinned, waving his hand towards the stall he'd just come from. "My cousin trades metal tools. I'm helping him out while my father pays his respects to Lord Ambaghai. We're the same clan. Come and look."

I went to his stall. His cousin had some good things. I bought some knives and leather straps with buckles. Jorchin's eyes widened when he glimpsed the size of my purse.

"How long are you staying?" he asked.

"Not long," I replied.

"You must stay with us tonight. I know my father would be pleased to see you."

I accepted. Actually, I accepted with a wave of excitement bursting inside me. It would be good to sleep in a yurt and have hot food. But more than that, it would be wonderful to see Sarangerel again! All the happy feelings I'd had when I'd been with her returned, and they were drowning out the confusion I was suddenly feeling about my betrothal to Altantsetseg.

But first I needed to go to the monastery. Making my excuses to Jorchin, and checking he wasn't following my movements, I made my way to the double wooden doors of the lamasery. They led into a large courtyard where monks and others were milling about, and pilgrims were prostrating themselves on the ground, making their slow progress towards a hall opposite the entrance. I had never seen such a big building before. Of course, I have been in the biggest building in the world[11] since then, but up to that point I had scarcely seen a building at all.

"What do you want?" barked a monk at me.

"A blessing," I replied, taken aback by his intrusion and glaring in return.

---

[11] It is to be assumed he is talking of the Potala Palace in Lhasa.

"Can't," said the monk. "Noon day service."

Just then I heard the call of conch shells sound from within the hall, and saw some of the monks making their way towards it.

"Well then, when?" I countered.

"Tomorrow."

"What's wrong with this afternoon?"

The monk drew himself up and spat. "Tomorrow, peasant. The lamas have a special ceremony to conduct this afternoon. Now go away!"

With that he turned to leave. I grabbed his robe. He stopped in his tracks and turned round, surprised.

"What are you doing?"

"Making you give me an answer." I wasn't going to let this lowly monk mess me around. I thought they were supposed to help people and I needed my blessing.

He tried to move my arm, but I grabbed his wrist and twisted it hard. He cried out. Just then a smaller, older monk came over.

"What's going on?" he demanded. "How dare you assault a monk!"

"I want a blessing!" I replied.

"You won't get it with violence!"

I released the first monk who glared at me sullenly. The small monk was angry.

"Get out!" he said. "If you calm down, come back tomorrow."

But he wasn't as angry as I was. Useless monks! They are supposed to give help, yet all they do is to try to lord over the ordinary people who work to support them. I would have gone home there and then – only I didn't want the hauntings to start again. I could almost feel my grandfather prowling round the grasslands of the steppe beyond Talshand waiting for me to venture out unprotected by the blessing I knew I needed.

I arrived at Jorchin's family's yurt at dusk. I brought some shimiin arkhi with me as a gift, but truly I wanted it for myself. I was uncomfortable dealing with monks and asking for blessings, even though I was excited at seeing Sarangerel again. Batzorig seemed genuinely happy to see me, telling everyone they had an important guest, and getting his wife to serve me. Once everyone had shuffled into their seats and the smiling died down, I looked for Sarangerel.

"So, Thaza, how's your family? How are you?" said Batzorig raising his tea cup to me.

I told him about my grandfather.

"Yes, we heard," chipped in Jorchin. Batzorig shot him a look before turning back to face me.

"Yes, yes, sorry to hear about that, Thaza," he said in a low voice. "But then," he added after a pause, "the old devil's better off in paradise, so let's not be downcast. Let's drink to his being reincarnated to a better life!"

I drank with the rest of them but knew my grandfather wasn't in paradise. As for him being reincarnated to a better life, the runt of a litter of goats would be too good for him.

I asked Batzorig how he was. By now I could see Sarangerel wasn't in the yurt. Maybe she was outside cooking. Batzorig bored me with a detailed description of his family's fortunes. No wonder they were languishing. As far as I could tell, the man had so little sense of propriety, telling me things that should have been kept from an outsider, such as his inability to choose the right pasture or his weak bladder, that it was no wonder he wasn't prospering. When the head is not firm, how can the body be strong?

"And your sister?" I asked casually turning to Jorchin.

"Which one?" said Jorchin. "Oh, you mean Sarangerel?" he said first with surprise and then with understanding dawning in his eyes. But before he could embarrass me his father cut in.

"She's not here. Surprised you should remember her though. She's with my brother and his family. We're hoping she might marry one of his children. He's got one with a bad leg that I know is a worry to them. Then we wouldn't have to pay such a large dowry. That would be a great help to us." He stared into his tea for a moment. "Ah,

let's have some of that stuff you brought Thaza, and enjoy ourselves."
With that he broke open the shimiin arkhi and food was served.

I didn't enjoy myself that evening, but I suppose I was grateful
for the company and the food. As if dealing with monks wasn't
difficult enough, now I had to endure Batzorig's pig-headed stupidity
over Sarangerel.

The next morning I gave my thanks and, without telling them
where I was going, made my way back to the monastery. This time I
saw a line of people and ascertained that it was to see someone called
Lama Chortzig – apparently the most renowned in the area – to
receive his blessing. I joined the queue and waited. It didn't move for
hours. Rumours went down the line that the lama was deep in
meditation or casting out a devil. What did I care? I just wanted him
to get a move on. The longer we waited, the more frustrated I became.
None of the other monks came near the line, but there was one monk
guarding the door at the head of the queue. I went up to him to ask
what was going on.

"I'll deal with you when it's your turn," said the monk in a nasally
voice.

"I just want to know—"

"I'll deal with you when it's your turn!"

I would have hit him but remembered what had happened the
day before. Why do these monks give themselves such airs? I returned
to my place in the queue only to find that the person who had been
behind me wouldn't let me back in. He wasn't a monk. I soon dealt
with him.

Finally, after the noon service, people started to go through the
door at the top and the line moved forward. It still didn't move quickly
but, by late afternoon, I was three places from the head of the queue.

"The Lama Chortzig will see nobody more today!" announced
the nasally monk. The other pilgrims were disappointed but resigned,
and with a murmur the line broke up.

"What do you mean?" I cried, as the pilgrims ebbed away. "I've
waited the whole day!"

"You must come back tomorrow," said the monk looking down at me from his position on the step leading into the room behind him – the room I so wanted to be in.

"Tomorrow? I was told that yesterday!"

"You must try again – or not bother. The choice is yours."

"Then I want to come back to this place in the queue," I demanded. "I'm not going through all this again!"

Some of the other pilgrims and monks were staring at me with astonishment. But I wasn't making a scene; I was just trying to get justice done.

"We do not save places," said the nasally monk, as if talking to a child. "You abide by our rules or leave. As I've said, it's your choice."

I fumed. Why was it so hard getting what I wanted? I cursed the monk, the monastery and my grandfather. I returned to the stall with the shimiin arkhi and bought some more. I would not let them beat me.

I was back the next day earlier than before. But the line was just as long. Again we waited, but this time it started moving before the noon service. I was full of hope. But that afternoon the line halted. The lama was engaged on other business, the pilgrims started saying. Nothing happened for an age while I fought down rising frustration. The nasally monk, who had been by the door again, eventually stood up and repeated, "The Lama Chortzig will see nobody more today!"

This time I curbed my temper. I hovered near the door to the lama's room while the pilgrims dispersed and the nasally monk fussed around and then disappeared into the room itself. The door shut in front of me. I waited to hear if it was locked. I heard nothing. Other monks were watching me, so I affected nonchalance and walked away. I hung around the entrance for a while. And then, when the space around the lama's room had cleared, I hugged the lengthening shadows, doubled back and slipped through that elusive door into the room behind.

The room was dark, there were no windows, and it was stuffy – a mixture of butter lamps, old incense and dust... a smell I have come to know only too well. I waited a moment to let my eyes become accustomed to the darkness, then I moved cautiously towards what I thought was a door at the opposite end.

"Are you lost?"

The unexpected voice in the dark startled me. I looked around but could see nothing.

"Are you lost?" the voice repeated. It was a deep voice. Strange to relate, my initial agitation was subsiding and I could feel a new sense of calm in me. I was breaking into a monastery, had just been surprised by an unexpected voice, the owner of which I couldn't identify, and yet I was calm, even clear, inside.

"I'm looking for Lama Chortzig," I said to the darkness.

"Why?"

"I want… I need a blessing."

"Can't you wait with the others during the day?"

"I have waited! For three days! But still I haven't been seen! I thought holy men were supposed to help, but all I've encountered are obstacles."

"There is an order to being seen," continued the voice – I had by now located where it was coming from – "an order to everything, though no doubt you are unaware of it. If you haven't been seen by now, there will be a good reason."

"What reason?" Despite my calm, I refused to be denied again.

"Maybe it was because this way, by breaking in when you've been told to go, you have proved yourself. Maybe it was because now I can spend more time with you. And maybe it was because, without my attendants, it is more private."

I could barely take this in. He seemed to be condoning my actions.

"Are *you* Lama Chortzig?" I asked.

"Yes," said the voice. "Come forward." As he spoke he turned up a butter lamp and I could see the outline of a cross legged figure on a seat of cushions. He looked younger than the sound of his deep voice. He wore new, thick, well embroidered robes, and a large yellow

38

hat. He seemed rich, even though he had no ornaments on or around him. He was certainly a man of substance. He was the first monk I'd seen I could think of respecting.

"I see you are not familiar with the usual ways of greeting a lama," he said.

Reluctantly I prostrated myself. But I kept my eyes on the lama all the time.

"Enough." He waved a hand. "What is your name?"

"Thaza," I replied, getting up, "of the Mongshad clan."

"Thaza, what do you want?"

"As I told you, a blessing."

"Why?"

"I am being haunted by an evil presence! It wants to kill me. I'm sure of it."

"Do you know who this evil presence is?"

"Not exactly." I paused. "I mean, I don't know… it's a presence."

The lama was silent, as if waiting for something.

"I think it's my grandfather…" I continued. My heart rate quickened. Could I feel my grandfather just then? The lama considered me.

"Why would your grandfather's spirit want to kill you?"

"He… I… I could have prevented his death."

There was a long silence. I was beginning to feel uncomfortable. Finally the lama sighed heavily. "I suppose you are being truthful in your own way," he said, looking at me intently. If anything, he seemed a little sad. "So, you want me to remove this presence from you?"

"Yes, lama, please! It haunts me! It's evil! It makes my horses throw me to the ground. It'll kill me of fright if nothing else."

Lama Chortzig nodded. "Compose yourself," he said.

He closed his eyes and seemed to shut himself off from me. He started murmuring some words – I couldn't recognise them, they were in another language – and he rocked slightly back and forth. Suddenly he sat upright and opened his eyes – although he wasn't looking at me or anything in the room. His breathing altered; it became deeper,

39

stronger. He seemed very intent. He started speaking again, but not to me, and in this other language.

I searched the room. Was he talking to my grandfather? Was he here? There was nothing but the murky darkness. My heart was racing. The lama paused, talked some more, and then jerked awake – not that he'd been asleep, but there is no other way I can describe it. He seemed drawn. He waited a moment before speaking.

"I can't."

My eyes widened in alarm. "You can't what?"

"I can't lift your haunting."

"But lama—"

"Your crime is great, you know." A chill ran through me. I hadn't told him I'd killed my grandfather, but he seemed to know. Lama Chortzig, still looking drawn, gazed at me. "But we are compassionate," he continued. "And, as I have said, there is an order to everything, even if you are unaware of it. So although I cannot help you, I know someone who can."

This was unexpected. I thought any lama worth his yellow hat[12] would be able to banish a haunting. Yet this one, the much sought after Lama Chortzig, even though he seemed an impressive man, couldn't do it. Ha! Useless monks.

"Well then, who?" I asked, with a mixture of anger and frustration.

"Lama Pemba Kunchen, Chakpori lamasery, Lhasa," came his reply.

Lhasa! Lhasa was a difficult four month journey away. It was full of monks and pilgrims and Tibetans. And it was another four month journey to get back home. I could be gone for up to a year when all I wanted was to claim my bride, enjoy life and increase my family's prosperity.

"No!" I said. "Lhasa? There must be another way. Lama, I'm a horseman, at home on the steppe. I'm about to get married. I'm not a

---

[12] Lamas of, what is called, the Reformed Sect of Tibetan Buddhism wore yellow hats. Lamas of the older, unreformed, sect wore red hats.

pilgrim. Let me make a donation to you. I'm sure you can bless me. You are a powerful man. Surely I don't need to go to Lhasa!"

Lama Chortzig just looked at me. I waited to see if he would change his mind, but he seemed as settled as the Altai mountains. I've since noted these important religious types can't be made to change their minds if they believe they are following the dictates of whatever higher knowledge they say they are in touch with. But I was young then, so I tried once more.

"Lama, please! Let a man make a family and herd his animals, as Buddha intended. I'll make offerings to monasteries! I'll be good. But Lhasa is so far away. My family, they need me." I slammed my fist into my hand. "There must be another way!"

"It's your choice. If you want the hauntings to stop, if you want to make amends for what you have done, go to Lhasa. If not, go home."

My choice again.

"And after I've been to Lhasa, then can I go home?"

"I will not make bargains with you," said the lama in his deep voice. "But I can say if you do what has to be done, you will be rewarded beyond your highest expectations."

I mused for a moment. It was my choice. I didn't want to go, yet I didn't want the hauntings to continue. I had a shiver of fear at the thought of returning home at the mercy of my grandfather's evil spirit once again. It was trying to kill me, and it was an enemy to be more feared than any other because it was unseen and could strike at any time. But Lhasa – it was so far away. To hell with it all!

I sat in anger in that darkened room. It was all so unfair. Why should I have to put off my life again because of my grandfather? I swear I saw his putrid face in the darkness at that moment, and felt his glee at my discomfort. I tore at the thin air to get rid of him. That bastard wasn't going to beat me! I would banish him, forever, into the flames of hell. So, all right, I would go to Lhasa, if that was required. I would damn well win! Besides, I reasoned at last, pilgrims made the journey regularly, and I would still be young by the time I returned, so

I could still have a family and prosper. And I would be rewarded, the lama said so. I laugh now at his duplicity, having been stuck for thirty years in this hole of a monastery. But sitting there in front of the lama at that moment I thought of all that I wanted in life – to compete in the nadaam, to be with my horses, to marry, to have sons who would do me proud – I thought of all this, and then I said:

"If there is no other way, I'll go."

The lama nodded. "Come back tomorrow," he said. "I will give you a letter to take to Lama Pemba Kunchen. He will direct you as he sees fit."

I didn't think what those last words might mean. I just grunted and made my way out of the room. It was already dark when I got outside. I had to find a monk to let me out of the monastery. He was surprised I was still in there as the doors had been closed to laymen for some time.

I was back the next day, but not as early as the previous days. I'd seen the lama and didn't need to queue with the other hopefuls. I made my way to the top of the line.

"Lama Chortzig is expecting me," I announced to the nasally monk. He was about to stop me when a small acolyte hurried out of the lama's room and whispered into his ear. The monk's eyes widened in surprise.

"You may go in," he said, barely disguising his confusion.

I entered the room. There was more light this time, and I could clearly see the lama seated cross legged on his cushions. He looked serene and solid. Next to him, on a smaller cushion, was an older monk with a pen, ink on his hands and papers on a small table in front of him.

"Thaza, you have come back," said Lama Chortzig evenly looking me over. "I see you still don't know how to greet a lama."

I prostrated myself again. I hated this bowing, but a dog has to please its master if it wants to be fed.

"Here is the letter for you," he continued. His attendant leant forward and handed me a sealed parchment. "You are not to read it, do you understand?"

"I can't read." I couldn't then and didn't see the point. What could a book teach me?[13]

"Nor are you even to tell anyone else about it. Is that clear?"

"Yes lama. I won't tell anyone else about it. But—"

"Nor are you to ask me what is in this letter. You may know that it deals with your request to me last night, but again you must not breathe a word of this to anyone else."

I nodded. Why would I want to tell anyone else about it? I wasn't Batzorig, happy to tell everyone of his failings.

"Good," continued Lama Chortzig. "You are to take the letter to Lama Pemba Kunchen at Chakpori lamasery in Lhasa. The only person you may tell about this letter is the doorkeeper at Chakpori. You may tell him you have it, and you may tell him it's from me."

Again I nodded.

"And you should leave for Lhasa as soon as possible."

What?

"But lama," I protested, "I must go home and arrange my affairs. And I am to marry in a few months. Let me get married first!"

Lama Chortzig considered a moment. "You may go home," he said at length, "but don't get married. As I have said, there is an order to everything, and things must be done at the right time. Besides, travelling in summer is easier than in winter. If you delay, conditions will become more difficult. Truly, it'll be to your advantage to leave as soon as possible. And take someone with you."

"Lama," I said, "you want me to be a camel and a horse at the same time. I am to go in secret to see this Lama Kunchen. I must go now not later. Yet I should bring someone with me. Who? And how do I explain the purpose of my journey if I am not allowed to tell anyone of this letter?"

---

[13] We must assume Thaza was taught to read and write at Yerlang monastery over the years he was a monk there.

43

"I take it you haven't told anyone else of your hauntings? No? Then not telling anyone about the letter shouldn't be a problem. Who should you take? Someone who wants to go. What should you tell people about the purpose of your journey? What did you say when you first came here?"

"I came on business. A trader asked—"

"Then there is your answer."

It was possible, I suppose, to say I had business in Lhasa. But who should I take with me?

Lama Chortzig had stopped speaking. I waited, but he seemed to have no more to say.

"I will do as you say, lama," I said at last, putting the letter inside my tunic and getting up to go.

"Wait, Thaza."

What now?

"Take this," he said taking out a leather pouch from inside his robe and handing it to me. "Put the letter inside this and hang it from your neck. It'll keep the letter dry should you get wet."

I did as he said. It felt soft against my skin. It was a feeling I would come to know very well.

I left the lama and came out into the strong sunshine. I ignored the stares of the other pilgrims still standing in line. Let them wait for the definitely mixed blessings they would receive from the so-called famous Lama Chortzig. I left the monastery, relieved at least I didn't have to return, but not pleased at the turn of events. I scuffed the ground as I walked along. I cursed my grandfather again for creating this mess for me.

"Hey Thaza, why the scowl?" I looked up to see Jorchin hailing me from his market stall.

I was irritated to be interrupted. I made for his stall, ready to give him the edge of my tongue, but the fool was as ignorant as his father, for he carried on talking before I could start.

"It's such a shame we have to leave here tomorrow! Father says we have to rejoin the rest of the family. I wish I could stay here. Herding animals is not as fun as selling things."

I was still irritated at his impudent assumption that I wanted to talk to him when suddenly it hit me.

"Jorchin," I said, modulating my voice. "I have business… in Lhasa. I need an assistant. Do you want to come?"

"Lhasa!" he replied excitedly. "Lhasa? Can there be a more interesting place to visit? The Potala![14] The markets! The women! Tibetan women are very beautiful, you know. Thaza, do you mean it?"

I told him I did. I told him that I would supply his horses and pay his expenses; in return he was to help me in whatever way I asked. I added that my trip to Lhasa was connected with my business in Talshand, but it was confidential. He accepted all these conditions, just happy to be going on an adventure. But we had to ask his father first if he could go.

"Huh, you want to take my eldest son, why not one of my daughters instead?" said Batzorig when we visited him later that day.

I felt a flurry of happiness in my heart thinking of Sarangerel, and an urge to hit this man who couldn't see that I would be a better son-in-law than any he could hope for.

I could tell Batzorig didn't want to lose his eldest son. Although Jorchin was useless, Batzorig always gazed at him with a light in his eyes. But he gave his blessing. And I didn't wonder that he did. He would be losing a worker, but he had other sons, he would have one less mouth to feed, and with Jorchin gone he wouldn't have to worry about getting him married and giving him a portion of the few animals he possessed.

So it was that Jorchin left with me to rejoin my family before setting out to Lhasa. Had he known what would happen, would he have come?

---

[14] The Potala is the Dalai Lama's official residence and the seat of religious power. In Thaza's time, when the Great Thirteenth Dalai Lama ruled Tibet, it was also the seat of secular power.

To Lhasa

What turned out to be my last sojourn with my family was an uncomfortable one. As soon as the excitement of my return – and the surprise of my return with Jorchin – had died down, I had to reveal that I was going to leave again, this time to Lhasa.

Everyone was nervous. My cousins had coped well enough with the livestock during my absence, but clearly needed my experience if the family was to prosper. They were alarmed at the prospect of being left in charge. I would have jumped at the chance when I was thirteen to have run the family's affairs, and Buddha knows I would have done a good job, but they had their father's weakness in them. I was exasperated. I didn't want to leave, and I didn't want to leave my wealth in their hands, but I had no option. If I could have given them some of my spirit or knowledge, I would have done.

My mother at least was excited that I was going to the holy city. I could visit the Jokang Cathedral,[15] she said, and the Potala, and even see His Holiness himself! But I flatly lied about my reasons for going.

"I made good money in Talshand," I told her, "and an opportunity has arisen to make deals in Lhasa. I'm going for business, not religion. What do I want with monks and their kind?"

But I did promise to bring her back some religious artefacts, including a picture of the Dalai Lama, which pleased her. I swear, I made my promise in good faith, but it was one I was unable to keep.

---

[15] Jokang Cathedral is the holiest building in the Tibetan religion.

A few days after my return, I began to entertain the idea that I need not go to Lhasa after all. The bad dreams hadn't reoccurred since seeing Lama Chortzig, nor had I felt my grandfather's presence. I was in the prime of my life, and I still wanted to get married. Maybe life could return to normal. Lama Chortzig and his strictures suddenly seemed far away, and I went to sleep that night with happy thoughts of my future. Only later that same night, I was chased in my dream up a mountain and felt myself falling until I jerked awake in a cold sweat. It had been my grandfather chasing me – he hadn't gone away, the goat. I wondered if my pounding heart could be heard by the others. But then what did I care if it was? They would never ask me what the matter was – they had become too afraid of me. I felt bitter at that moment. Normally when you awake from a nightmare, you are relieved it was only a dream. In my case, I awoke and realised I was still cursed, and my cruel path still led to Lhasa. I swore at my grandfather for ruining my life when he was alive, and ruining it now he was dead.

A few days after that one of the brothers of my betrothed, Altantsetseg, arrived with news that they had assembled the dowry and could bring forward the date of the wedding. I so wanted to get married, but Lama Chortzig had ordered me not to. I had to tell her brother that my plans had changed and the wedding would have to be postponed for a year or more. He was furious. This was a slur on his family, he declared, and we would pay for it. I wasn't in the mood to deal with his outburst, angry at his rudeness, and angry with the gods for again denying me a woman. I snarled at him to go away. I swear I would have cut him with my knife if Jorchin hadn't urged me to calm down.

I realised then that I would have no happiness until I went to Lhasa and had my curse lifted. The atmosphere in the family was heavy: my cousins and aunt were wary of me, and fearful of the future. Jorchin was bored doing nothing. And I couldn't properly dedicate myself to my horses or herds. I also had nothing to look forward to now that I wasn't getting married. So, I resolved to leave for Lhasa as

47

soon as possible. I only needed to pack some clothes, a tent, provisions and money, and then we could go. I made curt farewells, unable to think happily of going to Lhasa or of my eventual return. It would have been harder if I'd known then that I would never return. Perhaps the gods are merciful in small ways after all.

It took us three weeks to get to Altai, the largest town in the region. I had never been there before. I didn't like the stink of the place. But Barkol, the next major centre, was different. It was noisy and colourful, and full of Kazaks with their weird music. But best of all, were the horses available for trading. I turned a large profit by buying some good stock from a trader who didn't know the value of what he had, and then selling it on to someone who had more money than sense. I couldn't understand the interest in the camels that were also traded there – ugly, smelly animals with no love for their human masters. But at least I was happy then, happy that I was living life, making money and free in a way that I never felt before. But we had to move on.

About six weeks after we had set out, we came to Dunhuang. This was the first time I encountered Chinese people. They struck me as duplicitous and difficult to deal with, even then. Why they felt so superior was a mystery. But Jorchin was wide eyed, claiming that Chinese girls had the softest skin in the world. He marvelled at their pagodas and food. I couldn't understand why the Chinese wanted everything to be so ornate.

We moved on from Dunhuang across the desert, the soft sand making our going difficult. It was the most awkward part of our journey so far (and one where I conceded a camel would have coped better). But at last we came to Golmud – a strange place sitting in the bottom of a great basin. Tibetans, Mongolians, Chinese and others mingled there, but there was a wariness about everyone.

Golmud, I knew, was the starting point for traders' caravans to Lhasa. Although Jorchin and I had travelled that far by ourselves, I wanted to join a caravan for the remainder of the journey. I didn't speak Tibetan then, I wasn't familiar with their customs or officials, and it would be good to have someone else to navigate for a change. I had also heard there were brigands on the Tibetan plateau, so there was safety in numbers.

I made my way to a large square near the centre of town to find a caravan we could join. It was a dirty place, and people tried to avoid looking at or talking to me if I approached them. After a while I found a group of Mongolians. They directed me to a tough looking Tibetan seated near, what I discovered was, a drinking house. He was going to Lhasa soon, I was told, so I should ask him.

His name was Lorga Cherzin. He spoke a few words of Mongolian. He was only interested in my money and not my reasons for going to Lhasa. I felt I was being robbed, but I had plenty of silver thanks to my good fortune in Barkol, so eventually we agreed a price. Jorchin and I could join his caravan of about thirty people and a hundred or so pack horses and yaks. It was the first time I'd seen a yak – a slow, ungainly animal, and as stupid as anything, but, as I witnessed later, strong and utterly dependable.

So we loitered a few days near the drinking house while we waited for Lorga's caravan to assemble. Jorchin liked it, making himself affable to people there, flirting and drinking. He would have gambled too, but I didn't give him any money for that. I didn't understand why he was willing to make a fool of himself. From the looks Lorga gave him, he didn't understand either.

Eventually we were ready to set off. The caravan was laden with goods for sale in Lhasa. There were also about ten pilgrims from Mongolia as well. I kept Jorchin and our horses towards the back of the caravan. I didn't feel comfortable being too close to Lorga. He roared at everyone, telling them to keep up or stay in line. He had a whip which he'd use on his own men, and I saw him raise it to some of the merchants too. A few days out one of the pilgrims had the audacity to question him. Lorga bawled at him for several minutes, flung some coins in front of him, and ordered him to leave the caravan. The shocked pilgrim stared after us as we moved on without him.

Despite Lorga, the first part of the journey was uneventful. The landscape became stonier and steeper as we toiled our way, seemingly forever, uphill. We passed a few other caravans heading the way we had come. After a while, despite his temper, I began to appreciate Lorga's abilities. He knew just how far to go in any one day, and was always attentive to his animals' well-being. I still didn't like him, but we were making good progress. The weather was fine too. And then one morning, after an arduous few days climb and several cramped nights camping on no more than a pathway, we crested a pass and finally emerged onto the Tibetan plateau.

"Tangjula Pass," announced Lorga. "In good time too."

I still remember his smile of satisfaction as he bared black and red teeth with a good many missing. He was ugly. He permitted the pilgrims to conduct a small ceremony to thank Buddha and placate the mountain spirits watching over the pass. I could sense he didn't put much store in their goings on, although he played his part as any sensible man of the world would do. The pilgrims fussed around, hanging even more prayer flags, flapping wildly in the breeze, over the already covered chorten,[16] while the rest of us looked on.

By now I'd become aware of Lorga's wife Bayarma. She was Mongolian, young and pretty. I wondered why she'd married Lorga, a man many years older and not Mongolian. I found out later that she'd been given to him by a Mongolian merchant as payment for a debt. Lorga seemed either to ignore her or to order her about roughly. She travelled with him at the front of the caravan, but when we camped we sometimes found ourselves near her, and we struck up conversation. She could speak Tibetan, and I asked her to teach me some of the language. I needed to know the basics to help me buy provisions as we went along, and who knows I might need it when I finally met Lama Pemba Kunchen.

---

[16] Chortens are Buddhist religious monuments in the shape of a mound. On caravan trails they would be piles of stones put there by travellers. Typically prayer flags would be flown from them as well.

She was pretty, as I've said, and good company. Actually, she was very pretty. From the start Jorchin made lewd suggestions about my interest in her. But I swear it was only some time after we'd begun our Tibetan lessons that I noticed an attachment between us. Yes, I liked her. And yes, she liked me. It wasn't like Sarangerel – Bayarma was older and more versed in the ways of the world – but she liked being close to me, and she didn't move out of the way when I brushed against her. In fact, I swear she created opportunities for us to be together. The boredom of the journey, and my uneasiness of the unknown that lay ahead, were at least partly offset by the happiness of our times together.

Lorga began to show interest in me. He would ask me questions which Bayarma would translate, translating my replies back to him. After some weeks I could make some replies in halting Tibetan, which pleased him enormously. He appreciated the quality of my horses, and the way I treated them, and I know he respected my riding ability. One day a group of horses roped together slid down a loose rocky slope. They became very nervous. I expertly traversed my horse down the steep bank, rounded up the wayward horses, soothed them, and then led them along the gully bottom until we found a firmer place to lead them back onto the path. Lorga was very grateful, that night inviting me and Jorchin to share his meal. The men who worked for him began to treat me differently too, as did the other traders and pilgrims. It was at this time that Jorchin and I rode at the front of the caravan with Lorga and Bayarma.

Jorchin, however, was becoming difficult. He resented my orders. I don't know why: he'd agreed to come along and help, I was paying his passage, and I was only asking him to prepare our sleeping arrangements and cook while I looked after the horses at the end of the day. He began to be tardy getting our bedding ready, or deliberately slow making our meals (they weren't tasty either). At one point he actually said he wasn't my slave! I had to remind him I was his master. He just glared.

I think the idiot expected me to like him. Why, I don't know. I'd never pretended to be his friend and had always acted as his better, which I was. The best we'd ever been was companions, fellow Mongolians, and I tolerated him because he was Sarangerel's brother. But friends? That was never part of the deal. No, it was his fault he became bitter. But I can see now that if I had kept him on side, maybe I would have been able to return to Mongolia instead of being incarcerated in this loathsome lamasery. I have often wondered about that. But then he was being unreasonable, so why should I make the effort to be nice to him?

It happened like this. We had stopped for our midday meal a day or so away from Gongtang. This was our immediate destination, and we were to rest there a few days while we restocked. Bayarma and I had been talking Tibetan (by now I was able to string sentences together). She laughed at something I said.

"Oh, what did pretty boy say that was so funny?" asked Jorchin sarcastically. Bayarma heard what he'd said. We both shot him dirty looks.

"She is someone's wife, you know," he said in a louder voice. Just then Lorga appeared to get his meal. "I don't think you'd like him to know what was going on."

Jorchin had been speaking Mongolian, so only Bayarma and I understood what he was saying.

"Nothing is going on, Jorchin," I hissed. "And you will be quiet!"

Lorga noticed the tenseness in my voice and looked at us.

"First Sarangerel, now this," continued Jorchin, as if to himself.

I hit him. Jorchin fell to the ground, startled. He propped himself up on his elbows and scowled at me. I dared him with my look to get up. But he wouldn't of course. I was stronger than he was, and he was friendless here in the high Tibetan plateau. He needed me for now. He spat on the dirt and rolled away. Lorga smiled. He appreciated the firm way of treating others. I think I rose in his estimation then.

Of course, Bayarma and I didn't speak about what had happened. But Jorchin and I didn't speak at all. He was surly, and I ignored him.

Then we reached Gongtang where we restocked. I had been negotiating with a local trader for provisions for ourselves and our horses for hours but had been unable to get anywhere. The prices he was asking were too high. I was about to walk away in disgust when Bayarma came up. She started bargaining on my behalf. When the trader saw I was on good terms with Lorga's wife, he instantly became more reasonable and smiled. We soon concluded a deal. I shielded my purse as I opened it. I didn't want him to see I could have afforded more money.

I followed the trader round to his storeroom at the back of the building to collect my goods. Bayarma followed me. I hadn't asked her to come. The trader left us alone for some minutes while he went to another part of the storeroom.

I don't know why I risked everything. I was young. She was pretty. She'd followed me for goodness sake. I grabbed her hand and kissed her. I remember her kissing me back. There were some bales of hay. We went behind those being as quick as we could.

I don't know how long Jorchin had been watching. I suppose he'd followed me to help with the provisions, but I doubt that. Since I'd knocked him to the ground he'd been doing as little as possible. Maybe he'd seen me with Bayarma and just wanted to create mischief. At any rate he looked, he leered and he left.

Bayarma hadn't seen him, and I didn't tell her. I wanted to finish what I was doing.

"Thaza, let's run away together!" said Bayarma still lying on the ground as I was buttoning up my tunic.

That was unexpected. I was in a flush of feelings – happiness at my success, worry about Jorchin, and now she was asking me to elope with her. No wedding dowry as she was without family, already someone's wife, and with Lorga probably seeking vengeance on us.

"Thaza?" she questioned, propping herself up.

"Bayarma, not now! I have to go to Lhasa."

"But after Lhasa?"

"Get up before the merchant returns!"

53

She got to her feet and smoothed down her dress, still looking at me intently.

"After Lhasa, yes." Well, I had to say something. I did want a wife. As far as I knew my engagement to Altantsetseg was over. Perhaps, if I had more luck with my horse trades, I could return home with Bayarma loaded with carpets, household belongings and a yurt, and pretend it was from her family. How we might escape from Lorga, though, was another matter.

Bayarma left and I waited to collect my goods. When I emerged into the sunshine I saw Jorchin, Bayarma and Lorga having an intense conversation. Oh my god, had Jorchin already told Lorga? I went over and heard, with relief, Lorga talking about moving on the next day. Jorchin shot me a dirty smirk while Bayarma didn't make eye contact.

"Jorchin, help with the provisions," I ordered. He looked disdainful but then, to my surprise, shrugged his shoulders and came to help.

"I think there should be some changes around here," he said in a loud whisper as we picked up our supplies. "Unless you want to create a dangerous enemy." He looked at Lorga while he spoke.

"You can't prove anything," I countered in a low voice.

"I don't think a man like Lorga needs proof, do you?"

I didn't want to yield to Jorchin in any way. "How will my getting into trouble help you?" I demanded.

"I'd be free from you."

"Yes, and alone."

Jorchin looked at me without speaking.

"I'm not going to be blackmailed," I said angrily.

"We'll see about that."

The next few weeks were a misery. Jorchin was alternately chippy or morose – I would have killed him too if I had the opportunity and didn't fear him haunting me later. Bayarma kept her distance; I don't know if she'd cooled towards me or was just trying to avoid suspicion.

Lorga was chummy, but in a menacing way. Once he called out, "Ha! Seems that boy of yours needs another beating!" on seeing Jorchin in another of his sulks.

Thankfully he spoke in Tibetan and Jorchin didn't understand. I would have done anything to leave that damned caravan. I kept fingering the leather pouch around my neck and wondering if I could just ride on. But that would arouse Lorga's suspicion, and I couldn't risk leaving Jorchin alone with him.

I was blind to the country we were passing through. In fact, the settlements were becoming more numerous, some of the valley floors were green with crops, and we were getting nearer Lhasa every day. People in the caravan, especially the pilgrims, were getting more excited the closer we got. Stupid fools, with their prayers and chants for a safe journey, they didn't know what their precious Buddha had in store for them.

I didn't know either. I'm not sure where we were exactly. Lorga had said we were about two weeks from Lhasa. It was the rainy season,[17] and we'd put up tents for the night. If we hadn't, we might have seen them coming. As it was, we had settled down to sleep when I heard movement outside. At first I thought it was one of the others in the caravan. But the sounds became too numerous, I heard some horses whinny, and then I caught a gruff voice I'd not heard before. I grabbed my knife and went outside. I saw countless shadowy figures and realised we were about to be attacked.

"Brigands!" I yelled.

There were shouts, mayhem and then screams. I knifed one figure and started to wrestle another. When I managed to get on top of him (all my time with Batsaikhan was not in vain) I knifed him too. I saw a group of them surrounding Lorga – they'd obviously marked him out as the leader – and saw Lorga thrashing at them with a tent pole. I was then attacked. When I'd finished him off, I saw another brigand

---

[17] July and August are the rainy months on the Tibetan plateau. The weather for the rest of the year is usually dry.

55

on top of someone else. I came up behind him, pulled his head back, and slit his throat.

"Thaza!" gasped Jorchin, kicking the juddering man away, oblivious to the blood spurting on him, "thank you!" I hadn't realised it was Jorchin. I helped him up. Then I was clubbed from behind.

I don't remember being robbed, or stripped of my possessions, and I don't know how I ended up in a ditch at the side of a walled field. I can only think that after I'd been robbed, I was pushed or rolled away and fell into the ditch. It was the ditch that must have saved me, for when I came to, just before dawn, and looked around I saw only dead bodies – everyone else, all the horses and pack animals, had been carried off.

I was almost naked – they'd taken my outer tunic and strong boots. And worst of all, the leather pouch around my neck was gone. A cold horror stole over my heart. I didn't have the letter! How would my curse be lifted now? Clearly I was out of favour with the gods. I thought of my present predicament, of Bayarma, of my grandfather, of all the obstacles that had continually been placed in my way: I clenched my fists and roared until I was hoarse. I had never been so angry.

When I stopped, I felt myself to see if I had any broken bones. Apart from an enormous bruise on the back of my head, I seemed all right. I then took some clothes from a dead pilgrim – they had been too shabby for even the brigands to take – and considered my options. I had to go on to Lhasa. I was penniless and didn't have the resources to make the long journey back home. With luck, I should be able to reach Lhasa, and then I could see what I could do.

My 'new' clothes and lack of money made me look like a pilgrim – a very poor one – and I found that people treated me that way. At the end of the day I reached a village and finally sat down. After about five minutes rest, I was astonished when a villager gave me some tsampa.[18] He must have thought I'd been begging. So I copied the

---

[18] Tsampa is the staple food of Tibet. It is roasted barley flour usually mixed with butter tea, rolled into a ball and eaten by hand.

antics of the pilgrims I had seen on the caravan: I made a silly smile and prostrated myself on the ground. But at least I had some food.

It wasn't hard to find my way to Lhasa, and it wasn't hard to get food, although I had to prostrate myself more than I cared. Tibetan peasants are soft headed, bamboozled, if you ask me, by their monk overlords. They think that giving food and shelter to the poor, especially pilgrims, will help build good karma for their future lives. They also don't seem to judge others. If I see a lazy man, I think he should suffer the consequences of his laziness. But Tibetans will be kind, even to criminals. I saw ordinary peasants give just as liberally to convicted criminals as they did to pilgrims.[19] When I first saw this, I expressed astonishment. But I was told that a criminal is just an ordinary person, like them, who has been found out. Maybe, but I wouldn't have been so generous.

I was still nervous of brigands, though I suppose a solitary and clearly penniless pilgrim wasn't going to interest them. I also kept wondering what had happened to Jorchin, Bayarma and Lorga. I hadn't seen their bodies among the dead, but I reckoned they wouldn't have lasted long with their captors. My blood boiled when I thought of what they might do to Bayarma.

I was also feeling depressed. I loathed being powerless. Even when my grandfather had been his most overbearing, I'd had more dignity and resources. I'd never been without food or shelter before. And I'd never been alone before – not like this. What's more, I didn't like pretending to be a pilgrim. I hated people thinking I was religious, I didn't know what I was doing and prostrating myself so many times was humiliating. On top of this, my clothes stank, my feet were blistered and I had dysentery – I'm not sure from what, but something I'd been given to eat had been rotten. I also didn't know what to do when I got to Lhasa. I didn't have the letter from Lama Chortzig, and

---

[19] There were very few jails in pre-communist Tibet. Often convicted criminals would have cangues or wooden yokes on them to mark them out as a criminal, but they were then free to go where they liked. Most had to rely on begging to survive.

didn't know how I was going to get to see this Pemba Kunchen without it.

I don't know what day it was when I finally shuffled into Lhasa. It was near the end of the last summer month.[20] I passed Sera Monastery,[21] where I was told thousands of monks lived together. I couldn't conceive of that number of men in the same place. Eventually, I came to the North Gate of the city. I saw officials at the gate checking people as they went in. I noticed that everyone had to have a permit or explain themselves to the guards. I moved forward in the jostling line. When it was my turn I tried to carry on walking but was roughly pulled back.

"What's your business here?" demanded a guard, still holding my filthy clothes.

"Pilgrim," I replied faintly. I was weak from the dysentery.

He looked at me, maybe noting that I didn't have the usual prayer wheel or silly look of awe on my face as I was about to enter the holy city.

"Where are you from?"

"Mongolia…"

He looked me up and down again.

"I just want to do the Circle,"[22] I pleaded.

---

[20] Thaza so far has not dated his journey. The last summer month, as he describes it, is typically taken to mean August. We know from later in this account that Thaza left Lhasa in February 1932. Therefore we can deduce that he entered Lhasa sometime in August 1931.

[21] Sera (Wild Rose Fence) was one of three great monasteries in Lhasa known as 'The Three Seats'. It numbered over 5000 monks and its abbots were a political as well as a religious force.

[22] There are three holy circuits in Lhasa which pilgrims traverse. They are the Inside Circle around the interior of the Jokang Cathedral; the Immediate Circle around the Cathedral; and the Park Circle around the city and the Potala. This is four and a half miles in length. Devout pilgrims do these Circles prostrating themselves on the ground three times, standing up, moving their feet to where their head was, and then prostrating themselves again. Dressed as a pilgrim, Thaza would be expected to want to do the Circles.

58

"Phaw, you'll need to do it a thousand times just to atone for your stink!" he replied. But he shoved me forward, and I was in Lhasa.

I followed most people going south along a main road. I had to step over countless pilgrims knocking their foreheads on the ground. I know now that I had come across the Immediate Circle around Jokang Cathedral. But at the time I just dragged myself past the prostrating pilgrims until I came to a large square with market stalls and people in front of a big building, and saw for myself the red and black walls and golden domes of the Cathedral.

I had never been in a city before, let alone one as large or important as Lhasa. I was startled by the size and number of buildings, and by the crowds of people. I followed the pilgrims around the outside of the Cathedral, spinning the long rows of huge prayer wheels as we went, until we came to the front again. Ignoring the other pilgrims prostrating themselves by the entrance, I went into the darkened interior lit only by butter lamps. I moved along a line waiting to see the Sakyamuni statue.[23] My mother had often prayed to this statue, and now I was about to see it. It wasn't as large as I'd imagined, but it was solid gold. I bet most of the monks in Yerlang – ignorant fools who've never been further than their monastery walls – would offer a limb to have seen it. Yet it was only a statue. For me, I just marvelled at the wealth it represented. I'd never seen so much gold before.

I went outside and wondered how, with so many pilgrims, I'd get fed or find a place to rest my head for the night. Just off the square, I eventually found a pilgrim house run by monks. It was a place where townspeople gave food to help with their karma, and I could sleep under cover. I made sure I was there early to get food and a place to bunk down. All the while I was thinking how I could reverse my bad fortune. I didn't know if I could still get to see Lama Pemba Kunchen

---

[23] The Sakyamuni statue is the holiest object in Tibetan Buddhism. Called Cho or 'The Lord' in Tibetan, it is a statue of the Buddha brought to Tibet in the seventh century by a Chinese princess who was the bride to Song Tsen Gampo, the warrior king of Tibet, who began building the Potala.

without my letter. And I didn't know how I could get a decent set of clothes, horses and money to enable me to return home.

I needed a miracle.

But that night, jammed between snoring pilgrims, my cursed fate continued. I had a dream – the worst yet – with my grandfather. He was looking for me in the square in front of the Jokang Cathedral. He seemed young and fit, and had a long whip. I was trying to get up from my sleeping place so I could run, but I was held down by invisible weights. Even when I managed to struggle up, I could hardly move my legs, and kept tripping over sleeping pilgrims. I also had to go to the latrines with another attack of dysentery, but I didn't know where they were and was getting more and more anxious. Every now and then I could see my grandfather, vengeful and determined to find me. I woke up sweating, and had to find the latrines quickly, this time for real.

I was tired and weak by dawn, but clear that I should find Lama Pemba Kunchen, letter or not, as soon as possible. He lived at Chakpori lamasery, I'd been told, so I asked where it was. The monk I'd asked looked at me as if I were an idiot.

"Chakpori? Opposite the Potala. You'll be asking where that is next!"

I would have done too, but after his insulting attitude I felt like hitting him. Only I was too weak from dysentery. So I asked another pilgrim how to get to the Potala. She told me.

I made my way along what I later learnt was the Barkhor Road, looking at the large houses en-route. I was impressed by their size and number. But nothing prepared me for the Potala. Even in my weakened state I was astonished. A huge white, maroon and gold palace grew out of a small mountain, towering above me and the surrounding area. It was beautiful, powerful and sublime all at once. I began to believe that its inhabitant, the Thirteenth Dalai Lama, must be divine to live in a place like that. I must have been gaping because some people from the dirty houses clustered at the foot of the Potala[24] pointed at me and laughed. They brought me back to my mission – finding Chakpori lamasery. To the west of the Potala, on a narrow peak with paintings of Buddhas, rose another, smaller and less impressive building about the same height as the Potala. That, I'd been told, was Chakpori.[25]

I sat down to rest and work out how to get there. I could see a small path where monks were coming down with buckets swinging from poles, disappearing from view, and then reappearing and going back up the steep hill with their buckets now filled with water. I made my way over to the path. None of the monks interfered with me as I started to climb. But I was soon panting – I was so weak from my illness – and the going was hard. The monks carrying water were going into a small side door about half way up. I looked over that way but it was guarded by huge monks with staves. So I forced myself on to the top of the path. Straight ahead were two large wooden doors. I went up to them and banged with my fists. I waited. I could hear movement behind the doors. I banged again. Eventually a small window in one of the doors opened.

"The dispensary is closed now. Come back at noon!" said a voice and the window slammed shut.

I banged on the door again. And again. After a while, the window opened a second time.

"I said the dispensary is closed now, come back at noon!"

"Please…" I began, but my mouth was so dry.

The window slammed shut again. This time anger gave me strength. I banged on the door several more times. The window opened more quickly and two glaring eyes looked out.

"I can see you're ill, but the dispensary is closed!"

---

[24] Despite the Potala being the seat of religion and government, there was a small village at its base called Sho. The Chinese have since cleared the village and replaced it with the large square that can be seen today.
[25] Chakpori, or Iron Mountain, was the seat of Tibetan medicine. The monastery was torn down in the Cultural Revolution and today houses a radio mast.

"I've come to see Lama Pemba Kunchen," I croaked.

"Come back at… who?"

"Lama Pemba Kunchen."

There was a pause while the eyes through the window looked me over.

"Who are you to ask to see the lama? And you're foreign!"

"I have been sent by Lama Chortzig, Talshand monastery, to see Lama Kunchen."

"I don't know any Lama Chortzig and I've never heard of Talshand. Do you have any proof?"

"I had a letter."

"Had?"

"It was stolen…"

"Pah! Don't try tricks with me!"

"Really—"

"Look, if you are ill – in your body, not your head – then come back at noon and see the ordinary medical lamas!" With that the window slammed shut.

I sank to the ground. I'd never felt so ill before. Or desperate. My mouth was parched and I needed rest. I leant against the wall and tried to get my breath back. My eyes closed, and soon I was in a troubled sleep. I was banging on the door, there was a commotion around me, and I knew my grandfather was coming up the hill. I woke up to see the last of a group of people go through the doors for what I assumed was the noon dispensary.

"Wait!" I cried weakly getting to my feet. I felt dizzy at the sudden movement. I tottered over to the door but a huge monk with a staff barred my way.[26]

"You are not allowed in!" boomed his voice. "Orders of the doorkeeper!"

I could see a monk behind him looking agitatedly at me. I pushed at the huge monk, but I was so weak it was like throwing a pebble at

---

[26] It was common for discipline in monasteries to be maintained by police monks. They usually carried wooden staffs.

the Potala. He brushed me back with a flick of his wrist. I fell to the ground as the doors closed in front of me.

Why had I been forbidden entry? I had been told at least I could go in to see the medical lamas, yet now I was being specifically barred. I couldn't understand what was going on, beyond that it was the workings of a malign fate permanently against me. I drifted in and out of sleep for the rest of the day. Ordinary people would occasionally be let out of the doors, sometimes lamas on Tibetan ponies would arrive and be let in. But no-one seemed to notice me. I thought I must be dead.

Darkness fell. Then I felt a rocking. I came to and saw four monks lifting me. I thought I was being taken to the Heavenly Fields. I wondered what my punishment would be for murdering my grandfather. No matter, it was out of my hands now. A wasted life, not my fault. Let the gods do with me what they will.

Chakpori

I came to in a darkened room. I was surprised to find myself on a comfortable mattress wrapped in warm blankets. Flickering butter lamps made dancing shadows on the walls. I didn't know where I was. I didn't feel dead. My hands and arms looked the same. But I did feel rested. I moved my head to see where I was.

"Ah, you've returned," said a mellow voice.

I twisted round to see an old lama seated on some cushions. The room was not large. There was a low table with a gold bell on it, and a mandala[27] on the wall. A small window on the other wall had begun to show pinpricks of brilliant starlight in what I took to be the early night sky.

"How are you feeling?"

"I…" But I felt queasy and couldn't go on.

"Don't speak for now," said the lama, and he rang the bell on his table. A moment later an attendant entered with cup of steaming liquid.

"Drink this," said the lama handing me the cup. "It will help you recover."

I hesitated. The drink smelled foul. How did I know what it was?

"It will help you recover," repeated the lama.

---

[27] Buddhist religious painting of intricate design used as a tool to aid enlightenment.

I eyed him warily. And then took a sip. It was bitter and hot. But I took another and then gradually drank the whole cup. It was unpleasant to taste, but surprisingly I could sense it making me whole.

Feeling some strength returning, and wanting to know where I was, I sat up slowly for a better look around. I could see nothing untoward. The lama watched me passively.

"Where am I?" I asked.

"In Chakpori monastery. You were lying outside our gates for several hours. We carried you in two nights ago."

"And who are you?"

"I am a medical lama. I've been looking after you. You were quite ill." The old man had a definite presence. Not threatening but something strong. "If I may ask," he continued, "who are you?"

I looked around the room again. "A pilgrim," I replied.

"From Mongolia, judging by your accent. And your name?"

I swallowed. I'd had a battle getting here. I still wasn't sure what was going on. I didn't want to give away too much in my weakened state. But there was something compelling about the man.

"I'm Thaza."

"Thaza—"

Just then a young lama rushed into the room.

"Honourable lama!" he panted, "I've just heard he's come round. I'm here to…" and then he saw me. "Oh, I see you are talking to him already."

"Sit down, Jigme. Have some tea," said the old lama, his mellow voice undisturbed by the sudden interruption. He rang his bell again and the attendant returned, this time with tea.[28]

"But none for you," said the old lama to me. "You have been quite ill and you need medicine not tea."

"Honourable lama," began the young lama – and he was young, no more than my age – "shall I call the police monks?"

---

[28] Tibetan tea is mixed with butter and salt to produce a thick, usually lukewarm beverage. Tibetans of all classes at this time drank twenty to thirty cups a day. Thaza will have been familiar with this tea as it was also drunk in Mongolia.

"Let's just talk for now," said the old man. "You were saying, Thaza?"

Why would he want to call the police monks? I glared at the young lama.

"I am here," I replied, "to see Lama Pemba Kunchen. I demand to see Lama Kunchen and no-one else."

"You are in no position to demand anything!" broke in the young lama hotly.

The old one chuckled. "I am Lama Pemba Kunchen," he said, his voice and face as unperturbed as ever. "Why do you want to see me?"

So he was Lama Pemba Kunchen. The aim of my quest. I looked at him again. An old man, with a definite air, but an old man. Did he have the power to help me? And would he?

"I've been sent," I said in reply to his question, "by Lama Chortzig of Talshand monastery."

"Do you have anything from Lama Chortzig by way of proof?"

"As I told the doorkeeper, I had a letter. But it got stolen by brigands. Along with my clothes, money and horses."

The old man took a sip of tea. Jigme, the young lama, was staring at me intently like a dog guarding its flock.

"That's why I turned up here like a pauper!" I continued. "I had to beg for my food on the way. That's how I got sick."

"Do you know what the letter said?" asked Lama Kunchen.

"No! I can't read! And Lama Chortzig didn't tell me what he'd written beyond that it was a request for you to help me."

The two lamas were silent for a while. I could see the young lama was agitated.

"So we have no way of knowing who you are," he blurted out. "You say you had a letter, but it was conveniently stolen. You turn up here in rags without any identification. You could be anyone asking to see Lama Kunchen."

"Could you describe Lama Chortzig?" asked Lama Kunchen.

"He is about twenty five. Clear skin, strong face. He wears rich clothes. And he has a deep voice," I replied.

"How did you meet him?"

"I broke in." I hesitated saying this, but I was with Lama Kunchen at last and wanted to ask him to lift my curse. I had to start to explain myself. "I'd been waiting days but couldn't get to see him. So I broke into his room after the other pilgrims had gone. It was the only way."

"And what did you tell him?"

"That I was being cursed by my grandfather's evil spirit and needed his help to lift it."

"Why were you being cursed?"

All these questions.

"He was an evil spirit! He never liked me when he was alive. He hated me in the afterlife."

The old man waited. We all waited.

"All right," I said weakly. "He didn't just hate me. I... I killed him."

I don't know if it was my days without food that made me confess so quickly but, as I said, I needed to ask Lama Kunchen to lift my curse. I reckoned that at some point he needed to know the truth, even though I was dicing with my own death if they decided to report me to the authorities...

To my surprise, Lama Kunchen just nodded at my confession, unmoved. The young lama Jigme was still looking at me with wary, but not condemnatory, eyes.

"I killed my grandfather. I didn't mean to, but he hated me. He wouldn't let me marry. I'd done nothing except help him and all he did was despise me. He was old, he'd lost his mind. Everyone was happier when he was gone. But he's been cursing me ever since. I can't fight a spirit! He'll kill me sooner or later, I know he will. That's why I need a blessing to lift his curse."

"What did Lama Chortzig advise?"

"To come and see you. I don't know why he couldn't lift the curse himself."

"How did he come to his decision?"

"I don't know, he just told me."

67

"Can you describe what he did?"

"What he did? Well, I told him what I wanted and he sort of drifted off and started talking to himself. I don't know what he was doing, I'm not a religious person."

The old lama closed his eyes. Jigme kept staring at me. I really didn't like him.

"Yes, yes," said Lama Kunchen after a while, opening his eyes again, "I believe your story."

"But lama!" said Jigme.

"Be calm, Jigme. This young man has accurately described Lama Chortzig and correctly relayed the, shall I say unorthodox, way in which he met him and what took place. He has also confessed to the crime for which he wants absolution. An impostor, even one that had met Lama Chortzig, is unlikely to know all these details or want to confess to murder for fear we would punish him. Besides, look at his colours.[29] They indicate he is telling the truth."

"Wait!" I cried. "You already knew what passed between me and Lama Chortzig?"

"Yes."

"How?"

"He communicated with us," said the old lama.

I sat upright. "You mean, you knew I was coming? Then why did you deny me entry? Why did you let me rot outside like a goat whose time had come to die?" I was angry now, despite my weakness.

The old lama just smiled. "Because Thaza," he replied evenly, "we had to test you. We had to see just how much you wanted to see me. An impostor probably would have given up, especially in your condition. But you persevered."

---

[29] This is a strange phrase, but Thaza writes it clearly in his account. I am grateful to Lama Sonam Prasang who suggests that Lama Kunchen was talking about Thaza's aura – a band of energy seen as swirls and colours that is said to surround the body and which indicates a person's physical, emotional and mental states.

I was feeling dizzy. No food for days and now this strange information. "But why would an impostor want to see you? And why are you being so secretive?"

The two lamas glanced at each other. I swear Lama Kunchen looked sad. Jigme was about to say something when Lama Kunchen spoke.

"These are difficult times, Thaza. Although we are simple men of religion, there are those who oppose everything we do. It is difficult sometimes to know whom to trust. We knew you were coming, but we didn't know when you would arrive. That's why the letter was so important, for Lama Chortzig would have described you and told us what you wanted and why you wanted it. It wouldn't have mattered if you had read the letter – or if anyone else had – for it was written in code and would appear just a letter between two lamas. We would have tested you, even if you had the letter. As it was, when you arrived and said you wanted to see me but didn't have the letter, well, we had to be careful. There are some people who, shall we say, don't have the best intentions, who would like to harm or even kill me. We had to see how determined you were to see me. That's why we barred you entry to the lamasery at first. That's why we're questioning you now."

"You thought I wanted to kill you?"

"I think Jigme still does," chuckled Lama Kunchen. Jigme barely disguised a grimace.

"Lama!" he broke in, "are you sure this is wise? So much information?"

Lama Kunchen paused. "Perhaps you're right Jigme, this is enough for now. We need Thaza to agree to what we want him to do before we tell him more. But for now, it is time for you," he said looking at me, "to rest." Conches sounded in the distance. "We need to go to evening services. Do not leave this room. If you need anything, ring the bell and the attendant will see to you." With that he and Jigme stood up. But I had one more question.

"My curse. Can you lift it?"

Lama Kunchen stopped at the door. "Yes," he said slowly, "but there will be payment."

Payment? How could I pay him? Were my trials never to end? Before I could protest, he had gone.

I lay there angry. I disliked being questioned. Disliked not being believed. And I disliked that young lama. As for Lama Kunchen, how did I know if he had the wherewithal to help me? And here I was a prisoner in this room, too weak to leave. I drifted off to an uneasy sleep with the sound of chanting and cymbals and drums from below. I had strange dreams that night of monks sitting in a circle around me, plucking at my bedclothes trying to uncover me. I didn't get much rest.

The next morning Jigme returned. I could tell he still didn't trust me. But that was fine because I didn't trust him. He examined me, held my hand, tapped my stomach and looked into my mouth. Then he said I was on the mend and could eat solids. He left, returning shortly afterwards with the robes of a chela[30] and another monk armed with a scalpel. Before I knew what was happening, the monk began scraping my head while Jigme measured the robes on me. I tried to protest, but my head was held in an arm lock and I was too weak to resist. When my hair was shaved and I had put on the robes (they'd obviously burnt the rags I'd arrived in), Jigme explained, to my discomfort, that while I was at Chakpori I had to pretend to be a chela from Mongolia. I was here to have special study with Lama Kunchen in herbs and their healing properties. I didn't need to attend the normal classes for chelas, but I had to sleep in their dormitory, do my share of chores and attend the services.

"And you are *never* to breathe a word to anyone about the real reason you are here!" he warned. "If you do, we cannot lift your curse." He stared at me hard to make sure I understood. I felt he'd curse me worse than my grandfather if I broke his command.

---

[30] A chela is a monk in training to become a lama. Chelas were often apprenticed to particular lamas. The rank of lama was usually attained by examination.

With that he threw me out of the room and told me to find the refectory. I was smouldering. Masquerading as a monk in my ill-fitting second hand robes was the last thing I wanted to do. Why couldn't Lama Kunchen simply lift my curse and let me get on with the rest of my life? I had to accept my poor grazing grounds for the time being, thinking I might still be gone within weeks. How I laugh now at the cruelty of the gods. Thirty years later and I'm still a monk. If I'd have known that then, I might have chosen to live with my grandfather's curse.

My robes itched. Monks going about their business gave me curious stares. No-one was around to help. Common sense told me the refectory would be on the ground floor, so I made my way there. A police monk barred my entrance to a room and asked what I was about. When I told him, he directed me to the refectory. Much good it did because the kitchen monks refused to serve me. It wasn't meal time, they said. I remonstrated with them, but it was no use. Glaring, I turned round and bumped into a small but richly dressed lama.

"What's the matter?" he asked.

"These monks won't feed me when I've been sent by Lama Kunchen to get a meal!"

He looked understanding. He patted me on my shoulder and spoke to the kitchen monks. Moments later I had a bowl of hot tsampa in front of me. He smiled and left before I could thank him.

Mind you, I still wasn't pleased. I'd had nothing but tsampa since begging for my food. It's doughy, tasteless, bungs you up and never satisfies. Give me meat any day. Meat is good for you. But these Tibetans bleat on about how they can't kill animals because they might be the soul of their departed mother or some such rubbish. All I know is that meat tastes good and makes you strong. Mongols eat meat, and Mongols have built empires. Tibetans eat tsampa, and all they have built are monasteries. I didn't know on that first day in Chakpori that I would seldom eat meat again. No wonder most monks are lazy and inert – it's because they're all constipated and under-nourished.

Later a novice appeared by my side – sent by Lama Jigme, he said – to conduct me around. He showed me the dormitory for chelas where I was to sleep. Explained about the services I had to attend. Told me about meal times. And then took me to the Master of Chelas so I could be detailed my chores. The Master gave me extra ones since, he said with some satisfaction, as I wasn't to attend the normal classes, I must have a great deal of extra time on my hands.

So I began the daily round of chores, services and meals. There was precious little spare time. I know now that the monks at Chakpori were mostly diligent and a credit to their calling – quite unlike these ailing dogs here at Yerlang. The monks at Chakpori worked hard learning scriptures and medicine, took the services seriously and were largely considerate of each other. I still didn't want to be a monk though, hated following all these rules and didn't understand why I had to play this game.

Of course, I tried to see Lama Kunchen. But as a chela I was forbidden to go to the lamas' quarters. He was on a podium the other side of the main hall for the services. And meals had to be eaten in silence – you were beaten if you talked. So I was reduced to hanging about the main areas in what little free time I had hoping to catch sight of him.

I did see Jigme a couple of times. But he just brushed me off angrily when I caught hold of him. After the second attempt, as I was staring at Jigme's departing figure, I heard a chuckle behind me. I turned round to see the small, richly dressed lama again.

"The wolf gets his prey by being patient," he said.

I couldn't say anything in reply – hadn't Jigme warned me about talking to others? – but I was grateful for one touch of kindness.

Lama Kunchen left me alone for *three* weeks. During that time, I formed a loose friendship with some of the other chelas, so at least I had some company. They accepted my story without question, and didn't seem to think it odd that my 'master', Lama Kunchen, was ignoring me. In fact, they seemed to think I was somehow blessed to have him as my tutor.

In the little free time we chelas had, we would play tag or fly kites. Once we climbed up onto the roof to drop stones on unsuspecting monks below. Suddenly everyone ducked down and was silent, not breathing. I stayed standing trying to see what had made them act like this. They pulled me down and squawked, "the Dalai Lama!" I peeked over the parapet and saw a lonely figure in rich clothes walking on the rooftop[31] across at the Potala. If we had been discovered we would have been thrashed.[32] I didn't know that at the time, so I took a moment to watch him, much to the consternation of the others. I noticed he had a stoop. I had never understood the adulation shown by everyone, including my mother, to this god-king. I was curious to see him for myself. His head was bowed deep in thought as he paced up and down.

Among the chelas I mixed with, I became friendly with one called Norchen. He was a nomad's son from Amdo in the east of Tibet, and he missed his home life. We spent many hours talking about herding animals, yurts and daily life on the plains. He told me a great deal about yaks, while I told him about riding. His family had been so poor that they were forced to send him to a local lamasery.[33] From there, he'd been chosen by a medical lama from Chakpori, who was visiting his lamasery, to accompany him back to Chakpori to become a medical lama himself. It was a great honour, Norchen said. But I could see the sadness in his eyes. Like me, he really wanted to return to his family and his true way of life.

My friendship with Norchen helped keep me sane in those first weeks. I hadn't had any more bad dreams, but I still felt my curse hanging over me. I was like a sheep on a dark night as far as my future was concerned. I felt betrayed by these outwardly learned monks

---

[31] The Dalai Lama's personal quarters were the highest point of the Potala, hence Thaza's comment that he was walking on the rooftop.

[32] No-one is supposed to stand higher than the Dalai Lama and Chakpori, by virtue of its peak, was marginally higher than the Potala. There was a strict rule in Chakpori that no-one was allowed on the roof.

[33] About a quarter of the male population in Tibet at the time were monks. Most families sent at least one son. It was a way out of poverty for many.

Jigme and Kunchen who were supposed to be helping me but who had in fact deserted me. What was the point of coming here?

Most of my time was taken up with water carrying duties. Twice a day I was part of a party shuffling down the inner recesses of the monastery, out of a small door and down the narrow path I had seen when I first saw Chakpori. The path led to a well at the bottom of the peak on which the monastery was built. There we had our buckets filled which we then had to carry back up the path, into the monastery, and all the way to the kitchens to pour into a large vat. It was arm aching, back aching work that made my lungs rasp. I cursed the Master of Chelas for picking on me in this way. I noticed that monks found transgressing one of the many rules were often punished by being put on water carrying duties. I wondered, resentfully, what I had done to merit such treatment, and what worse punishment I would receive if I stepped out of line.

I soon found out. A crotchety monk was usually in charge of the party. He'd snarl out his commands and beat people with a stick whenever he felt like it. Norchen was with me that day. We'd been chatting and been beaten for it. I was angry, but sensible enough not to cross the monk directly. But when I was on the path above the well with a full bucket of water, I leant out to let a monk go by. He pushed me as he passed. My bucket wobbled. I could have caught it, but didn't, and it fell with a crack on the crotchety monk's head, drenching him as well. An accident, I claimed. Norchen supported me. But the crotchety monk strode up to me, rained blows on my head, and dragged me and Norchen into the Master of Chelas' office.

Words I'd never heard before were hurled at us by the Master of Chelas. Norchen winced, but I was unrepentant. At least he didn't hit us. I found out later he didn't dare be too hard on Lama Kunchen's pupil. But we were ordered to clean out the latrines for three days. In the end I'd rather have been beaten than have the punishment we had to endure.

Norchen was downcast, but this ordeal did strengthen our friendship. In fact, he was the first real friend I'd ever had. On the evening of the third day of our latrine duties, after we'd washed ourselves clean, Norchen told me to follow him. To my astonishment he led me to the lamas' quarters, knocked softly on a door and ushered me in.

The richly dressed lama who'd been nice to me before was seated on a magnificent throne of cushions. Around him were books and objects. And on the floor was a deep, intricately embroidered carpet. A thick stick of incense was filling the room with heavenly smelling smoke. He had a welcoming smile on his face.

"Come in," he said putting down a sheath of papers. "Norchen, pull up some cushions for our friend."

I swear the room felt warm, even though there was no heating. I was amazed at the furnishings. The lama was clucking to Norchen directing him to arrange the cushions for me just so.

"No need to worry, Thaza, isn't it?" said the lama. "Norchen has told me all about you. I'm glad you're such good friends. Would you like some tea? I'm Lama Neto, Norchen's master."

Norchen was subdued in his master's presence even though Lama Neto was very friendly. Tea was brought. And then – a big surprise – bowls of hot noodles! He motioned to us to eat. It was the nicest food I'd had since arriving in Tibet. We talked. I noticed his accent and Norchen's were similar. I suddenly realised that they were from the same part of the country. Lama Neto must be the lama who had taken Norchen to Lhasa.

"So, you're in Lama Kunchen's charge," said Lama Neto.

"Yes," I replied with a mouthful of noodles. "But he doesn't seem to be taking much interest in me."

Lama Neto laughed. "Lama Kunchen is a great man. You mustn't judge him by ordinary standards. Winter has to come before spring. I'm sure he has everything in hand."

At that point I didn't care. I was just happy to be eating delicious food in a warm room in good company.

Lama Neto showed me some of his possessions. He had lots of gold objects, most of them religious. I looked around the room again and then at him. It was clear he was very rich. The food we had just eaten was another sign of that.

"I hear you and Norchen have been royally punished," he said with a twinkle in his eye. "Cleaning the latrines. Our favoured punishment. Don't worry. You can work off bad karma and show yourselves to be of service at the same time."

I wondered about the crotchety monk. When was he going to pay off his bad karma?

Conches sounded for the evening service. We started to get up to go but Lama Neto waved us back down. "Let's stay here for now," he said. "I think you two have worked hard enough for today. I'll vouch for your absence."

So we stayed in his room for several hours talking and drinking tea. We tiptoed over snoring chelas as we finally reached our dormitory in the early hours of the morning, sleepy but very happy.

Testing Times

The next day, feeling tired but warm from my time with Norchen and Lama Neto, I was leaving breakfast when, to my surprise, Lama Kunchen came up to me. He told me a novice would take me to his room that evening. Before I could say anything he had moved away.

At last! Finally, I could get justice. That evening I was taken back to Lama Kunchen's room. He was seated on his cushions, and Jigme was next to him, cross legged on the floor.

"Ah, Thaza, I hope you are settling in. I hear you have incurred the displeasure of the Master of Chelas." He chuckled. "Please sit down." He motioned me to sit opposite him. An attendant came in with tea. The lama looked at me serenely. "Hmm, you seem better. Good."

"Lama," – I couldn't contain myself – "why haven't you seen me? It's been weeks!"

Jigme started. "It is not up to you to say when we see you!"

Lama Kunchen was silent for a moment. "A novice doesn't know why he has to learn letters first," he said, "but when he can read he understands there was no other way. It will become clear."

"But I'm not even learning letters!" I protested.

"You are doing more than you think," came Lama Kunchen's reply.

Yes, cleaning the latrines. Is this what he wanted me to do? And for how long?

"I will see you again Thaza," he continued, "in another three weeks. In that time, think how you might best help yourself."

With that, I was dismissed.

I was flabbergasted. I had waited so long only to be told I had to wait longer! What game were these manipulative monks playing? I wanted to protest, but my words were strangled by my surprise and despair. I sat dumbfounded, and Jigme had to handle me out of the room. As soon I was in the corridor, he slammed the door in my face.

I was sullen for days. I hated being so powerless. Why can't religious people be straightforward? Norchen asked what was eating me. I snapped that my master wasn't being helpful.

"Are they supposed to be?" he asked.

"How should I know," I replied. But I couldn't say more for fear of having Lama Kunchen's promise of help withdrawn.

By now I was used to life in the lamasery. I still didn't understand why a man would choose to be a monk – unless he were lazy and wanted to be looked after. But the monks at Chakpori were, for the most part, hard working. Maybe their prayers did have an effect. I don't know. I was just trying to make sense of it all. My temper wasn't improved when I heard that Lama Kunchen had left on business and might be away for months. Yet he'd promised to see me in three weeks!

Then it happened. I had a bad dream about my grandfather. The first since coming to Chakpori. He was tiptoeing over the sleeping monks with a knife in his hand. He hadn't seen me but knew I was nearby. I wriggled around with a knot of fear in my stomach. I had to get out! Confused, I stumbled over the other monks. Some cried out. The idiots! They'd attract my grandfather's attention! I started running, but then fell with a blinding crash. I woke up having fallen over prone monks and banged my head against a wall. I was roundly cursed and pushed out of the way. I spent the rest of the night awake, fearful my grandfather would return.

Later the next day, I was following a group of monks down a corridor. I saw a piece of paper escape from a monk's hand and zigzag to the floor without him noticing. I picked it up and called out, "Hey!" The group turned round and I saw, to my surprise, it was the abbot and his officials. I should have bowed but I still wasn't used to the normal procedures. I received angry stares worthy of Jigme. The abbot looked at me with pursed lips for a moment. Then he snatched the paper from my hand and walked on. Why do so-called religious men treat you like the runt that deserves to die?

A few days later I was on water carrying duties again. An elderly man was in the party. He was having difficulty carrying his pails. I had my own to carry and didn't pity him. But then he slipped. I was behind him, caught his pole and managed to prevent his water spilling out. He would have been punished if he'd lost his load. He was very grateful.

"What's going on up there?" growled the monk in charge.

"Nothing!" I shouted back. We carried on.

I forgot about it. But that evening, as I was leaving the refectory after supper, there was a tap on my back. I turned round to see this large, simple looking monk – clearly a farmer plucked from his fields. He was one of the kitchen monks.

"You helped Noyzen today," he said, "come with me."

He took me to the back of the kitchens. It was warm from the fires. And there, in a corner, was a pile of freshly baked flatbread. The monk said it was for me. Well, if they wanted to reward me I wasn't going to complain. The monk explained that Noyzen had been unfairly punished and sent on water carrying duties. His friends had tried to take his place but they had been punished for questioning Noyzen's treatment. For some reason they were very protective of the old man, and so were very grateful I had helped him.

Some days later I was relaxing in the sun outside. I had no chores that hour, and no classes to attend. There were some novices throwing stones and playing tag. One young novice careered into a group of chelas making their way across the courtyard. At the same time, a stone thrown by another novice hit the leading chela in his face. The chela was outraged and made to hit the novice.

I don't know why, but I called out, "They were only playing. It was a mistake."

The chelas looked in my direction. The first chela wanted to make a meal of the incident but I moved forward with a set look on my face. Really, I just wanted a fight to get some frustration out of me; I didn't mind taking them all on. But they backed away, made some facetious comment and left. The young novice looked at me with frightened eyes and scarpered. I didn't care if I made enemies among my peers; I didn't want to stay any longer in Chakpori than I had to.

Then there was the bird incident. One afternoon, a monk raced in to say that a white stork had landed on the roof above the abbot's apartments. The initial reaction was that this was a good omen,[34] until it was noticed that the stork was injured. Then there was real consternation. If the stork died in the monastery, it would bring bad luck. It had obviously come to Chakpori to get healed (as if it knew the difference between this roof and another!). But the monks truly believed they had to save it or else suffer misfortune.

But how could they get the stork? It was perched on a remote ledge, obviously injured and frightened. It couldn't be reached from a window, and throwing something was likely to hurt it or cause it to fall.

The monks were quite distressed. They really did care about this bird's well-being. There was an urgent discussion about how to rescue it. Some said it was too dangerous to climb up. Others insisted a way had to be found. Someone even suggested holding a service for the bird!

"I'll go," I said.

Everyone looked at me. What did I care? I was bored. And I knew I was a better climber than those monks. I also knew that I could lasso the injured bird just as I had caught so many bucking horses back home in Mongolia. The senior monk present pondered what I'd said and then gave his approval. So, half an hour later, when I'd made a lasso from some rope I'd asked to be fetched, I started to climb onto the roof. I pulled myself up above the overhang, and moved along the

---

[34] The behaviour of animals was often interpreted as foretelling good or bad luck. White storks were particularly venerated in Tibet.

tiles. It wasn't too difficult. The bird edged back nervously as I approached. I lay still for a while to soothe it. Then I slowly started to swing the lasso. The bird stood up when I began before crumpling down in obvious pain, its wing limp by its side. I continued swinging the lasso to accustom the bird to it and to judge the distance. The bird seemed hypnotised. Then I let it fly. The lasso closed around the bird's upper body. I pulled, and swung the bird from the ledge down to the excited monks below. They gathered the bird and rushed it to the infirmary. I climbed down alone. A few of the remaining onlookers slapped me on the back as I regained the ground.

The bird died three days later – frightened to death by the foolish monks twittering over it, I bet – but for a brief period I had earned the others' respect.

Despite my short-lived fame, I was still angry at kicking my heels in that place when all I wanted was for my curse to be lifted so I could go home. And I was still frightened in case I saw my grandfather's spirit again. Moreover, there was no sign of Lama Kunchen (or, thankfully, Jigme). I had complained to Norchen several times about my master's absence. Then one evening, before a service, I passed by Lama Neto and Norchen.

"Thaza," called Lama Neto, "how are you? I hear you are missing your master." He looked at me sympathetically. "I know I am not your master, but can I help in any way? I too am a lama, though not of Lama Kunchen's level, but I know the holy texts as well as another."

I was tempted. Why not confess to him and ask for his help? He'd been kind to me so far, and might be able to lift my curse. But I held back. I seemed to have this man's respect, yet, if I told him about killing my grandfather, he might withdraw it, and Norchen surely would look at me in a different light.

"Thank you," I said to Lama Neto, "I should wait for Lama Kunchen."

Lama Neto looked hurt. He moved on. I thought Norchen shot me a disapproving look as he followed his master. Oh god, had I made the right decision?

I was still wondering this the next day when a novice appeared and told me to follow him. He took me to Lama Kunchen's room and ushered me in. There was Lama Kunchen and Jigme. I hadn't known they were back.

Lama Kunchen studied me for a while. I felt like a horse being looked over by a buyer. Then he nodded and I sat down. An attendant came in with tea. There was silence while I drank mine – so much better than the burnt stuff they gave us in the refectory.

"Thaza," said Lama Kunchen at last, "we have been watching you."

How? They hadn't been around. Perhaps they'd set spies on me.

"You've done well. And I'm not just talking about the incident with the stork. You have been helping others. That is good. And you have kept your word and not spoken about why you are really here. We are ready now to keep our word and help you."

At last! I didn't wait.

"Lama," I started, "my curse. Can you lift it?"

Jigme frowned. No doubt he thought I shouldn't be speaking. Well, he wanted to be at Chakpori, I didn't. And he didn't have a malevolent spirit after him. But Lama Kunchen smiled.

"Yes Thaza, I can lift it."

"And I'll be free?"

"Yes."

Relief flooded through me. Buddha knows I didn't hold with monks and their ways, but for some reason I did believe this man could do what he'd said. I mean, he couldn't wrestle a lamb, but I had to admit he had a palpable inner strength. He could lift my curse.

"But, as I've said, there will be payment."

My spirits sank. "Payment?" I asked slowly.

"We'd like you to deliver something..."

"Lama," broke in Jigme in an anxious whisper, "are you sure?"

Lama Kunchen sighed. "Yes Jigme, I am."

"But he's so... *young*."

Young? We were the same age!

"I mean," Jigme continued, "can you trust him?"

"Yes," replied Lama Kunchen. "We have to give him the opportunity to win, the opportunity to demonstrate what he can do."

None of this made any sense to me. Why do religious men always have to complicate things?

"Deliver what?" I cut in.

Jigme was now really nervous. Lama Kunchen raised a hand to still his colleague.

"A book," he said quietly.

Jigme dropped his shoulders. Lama Kunchen seemed sad. There was silence in the room.

"A book? What book?"

"I can tell you that if you agree to deliver it."

"Deliver it where?"

"India."

India! That fabled land of heat and colour. But heaven forfend, it was so far away! It'd take me months to go there and could be a year before I got home. Another year without getting married, without my horses, without my life.

"Lama! I've already made the journey to Lhasa! India is so far away! I don't want to take a book there. I'm not interested in books or India. I want to go home! Get one of your monks to take it. At least they can read the damn thing."

"You need to pay if you want your curse lifted," said Lama Kunchen.

"But this is payment indeed!"

"Your crime is not negligible."

"I didn't mean to kill my grandfather!"

"But you did. You took away his chance to live."

"He was going to die soon anyway."

"You have a debt to repay. You can either return in a future life and serve your grandfather, or you can help us now and we'll settle accounts for you."

83

I was stunned. The idea of coming back in another life and serving my grandfather, when he had so harshly oppressed me, was as cruel as it was astonishing. Words died on my lips. I thrashed around in my mind trying to find an alternative. This was a morsel too bitter to swallow.

"Can we have your answer, please?" asked Lama Kunchen.

My mouth was glued shut. I was desperately searching for a solution.

"Thaza?"

I looked around the room for inspiration. Jigme glanced at Lama Kunchen. In despair I shut my eyes.

I couldn't agree, but if I didn't...?

I heard a sigh, and someone shifting in their seat.

I stayed silent thinking hard.

"Lama," said Jigme at last with irritation, "shall I—"

"I agree," I swallowed.

I had to force the words out. But what else could I say? I didn't want to be cursed by my grandfather for lives to come, so I had to agree to their demands. I opened my eyes and saw them both looking at me.

"You agree?" repeated Lama Kunchen. "You agree to deliver a book for us to India at a time of our specifying?"

"Yes," I said, "and you will lift my curse."

"We will."

A stillness filled the room. I didn't want to speak, and nor did either of the lamas. I felt defeated. Nauseous. I just wanted to leave. As if reading my thoughts, Lama Kunchen said, "That's enough for now. You may go. But Thaza – you have made the right choice. You'll see."

I couldn't see anything beyond the manifest unfairness of life. I'd done nothing to merit my grandfather's bad treatment, I'd killed him because he was endangering the whole family and he'd have died soon enough anyway. I'd already made the long journey to Lhasa, nearly been killed doing it, yet now I had to undergo another arduous journey just to placate his spirit – and if I didn't, the evil bastard would probably kill me and I'd have to return in a future life to serve him!

I was making my way to the door, sullen with bad thoughts, when Lama Kunchen stopped me.

"Look over there," he said, directing my gaze to a low table under a window. There were some wooden bowls on it. "Pick one." I didn't understand at first, and stared at him. "Please, pick one."

"But I already have one,"[35] I said.

He looked insistent, so I went to the table and peered at them. Then chose one. They were all old; in fact, they were all older than the bowl I already had. The one I'd chosen was smaller than the others and very worn. Lama Kunchen held out his hand to take it. He and Jigme inspected it and then looked at each other. Jigme was surprised. He nodded to Lama Kunchen who then said:

"You may use this bowl, Thaza. Leave your old one there." I fished it out of my robes and dropped it on the table. Jigme got up to hand me my 'new' bowl.

Monks and their silly games.

---

[35] All monks carried a wooden bowl in a pouch in the front of their robes. They used it to drink tea and eat their meals. It was part of their uniform.

Martial Arts and Other Matters

After our talk, I expected to be handed this blessed book and be told to go to India. I was certainly willing because I wanted to get on with my life. I especially wanted to find Sarangerel. I had been thinking about her recently. I knew she was the girl I wanted to marry. I felt disdain for the monks around me because they meekly accepted they would be without women. I have always been puzzled by this. They are worse than neutered rams. At least the ram fights to preserve his maleness (I know; I've been kicked many times castrating them). But most monks just timidly accept their enfeebled state, and many are even relieved about it. I still don't know why we have to be celibate. How I have suffered because of this rule! You can still focus on Buddha if you have a family. In fact, I'd wager most monks would more happily carry out their religious duties if they were allowed to marry.

But for days after Lama Kunchen had revealed what I needed to do in return for having my curse lifted, nothing happened. I was left kicking my heels, carrying water, getting what food I could and trying not to get irritated with the other monks. I waited for a summons to Lama Kunchen's room, but none came. I was like a tethered sheep with no grass to graze.

Then one day, a novice approached me and asked me to follow him. At last, I thought, I'm going to see Lama Kunchen. But instead of going to the upper storeys we headed down to a part of the lamasery I'd never been to before. We entered a windowless room lit by butter lamps, and there the novice left me – rather quickly, I thought. The air smelled down here.

"So, you're Thaza," said a gruff voice. I spun round to see an old man. He spat on the ground leisurely.

"Yes," I replied pulling myself to my full height. "Who are you?"

"Who I am doesn't matter," he said matter-of-factly. "I must say, I didn't think you'd be so flabby." He jabbed me with a finger. "And weak," he added, squeezing my arm.

"What are you talking about?" I said angrily, pushing him away.

"Flabby, weak and angry – what a sorry specimen…"

I scanned the room quickly to see if anyone else was there. There wasn't.

"I don't care for what you're saying," I said, advancing on him.

"What are you going to do about it?"

I moved to put my arm around his neck. Suddenly I felt a yank, a pain in my back and I was slammed to the floor. The old man was standing over me, smirking. I saw red. I grabbed his feet, only to be kicked away by what felt like an iron bar. I rolled back to be kicked again. I got up and charged, only to have a thudding pain in my chest and find myself twisted with ease and slammed to the floor a second time. I lay there panting.

"Who are you?" I asked again.

"Mingyar," said the old man. "Your martial arts teacher."

I was in too much pain to move. Just then the door opened and Lama Kunchen walked in. Mingyar gave a deep bow and then kicked me as if to say I should do the same. I just groaned.

"Leave him there," said Lama Kunchen. He almost sounded amused. "I see you've met Mingyar, Thaza. He is to teach you martial arts."

"I don't need to be taught," I said, struggling to get up. "I can wrestle."

"So I can see," said Lama Kunchen. "But martial arts are useful, especially considering some of the people you might encounter when you leave here. Besides, I thought you'd like to be taught a new way of fighting."

He was right. I loved to wrestle, and loved to know I could beat any man I met. I was angry that I'd been made to look a fool by such an old man, but at the same time I realised Mingyar might have something to teach me. He had used techniques I had never come across before. I thought if I could learn his form of martial arts, then I'd easily win the nadaam when I returned to Mongolia. I'd shown patience and humility with Batsaikhan; maybe I could do the same with Mingyar.

So it was, I learnt Tibetan martial arts.[36] It is the best form of fighting. Mingyar showed me that it not only uses the strength of the opponent against him, but it also relies on detailed knowledge of the pressure points in the body. As such, the art was practised in its highest form at Chakpori, the medical lamasery of Tibet. It is also ruthless. Tibetan martial arts aims to break bones, sever joints and make an opponent unconscious in the quickest time. I had never encountered anything like it before. Mongolian wrestling was like a new born lamb compared to this.

I soon learnt to respect Mingyar. He was tough – I was never allowed to complain – but he was fair. Above all, he was genuinely committed to helping me. I don't know what his orders were, but he made clear his great respect for Lama Kunchen, and his absolute determination to make me as proficient as possible, in as short a time as possible.

I had lessons with Mingyar in his airless room for several hours a day. Sometimes I trained with other monks, but mostly I was alone with him. I ached, I was bruised, but I was happy. I was truly interested in what I was learning, and longed to return to Mongolia to show off my expertise. At last I could see a reason for being in Chakpori and pretending to be a monk.

---

[36] Tibetan martial arts are sometimes referred to by the terms Gar Tak or Tescao among others. As these are not readily known, and as phrases like kung fu or judo do not accurately describe the Tibetan martial art form, I have simply used the term martial arts.

Some weeks after my martial arts had started, a novice came to me one evening and said Lama Kunchen wanted me. He led me, not to the lama's quarters, but to a lower storey in the lamasery. I was shown into a small room. Lama Kunchen, Jigme and an ancient lama with wizened skin were there. There was flickering light from a few butter lamps.

"Thaza," began Lama Kunchen, "I promised I would lift your curse. I would like to do so now. Please sit down."

I sat on the floor. How were they going to do it? The three lamas formed a circle around me and held hands. Lama Kunchen began murmuring very quickly. Then Jigme did the same. The butter lamps cast dancing shadows on the wall; to me they looked like demons. Suddenly, the ancient lama let out a shrieking howl. It made me jump out of my skin. The others raised their voices. I shivered, and felt like throwing up. Then I felt a wrench – I can't describe it any better – a jerking wrench, and then suddenly the three lamas were silent but breathing heavily. My breath was unsteady, my heart hammering in the sudden silence, and I felt even more nauseous than before. Then Lama Kunchen, in a quiet but firm voice, said:

"The first stick of incense is lit to placate the malcontent spirit."

I could smell the incense as it began to waft through the room.

Then Jigme said, "The second stick of incense is lit to light the spirit's way." Again, more incense wafted into the room.

Then the ancient lama said, "The third stick of incense is lit to help the spirit over to the Heavenly Fields."

The three lamas were staring at a spot above my head while holding their sticks of incense. All three were concentrating hard; I could see beads of sweat on Lama Kunchen's forehead. Then, in a moment, they jerked their heads simultaneously and brought their focus back to the room. They looked tired.

"How do you feel Thaza?" asked Lama Kunchen, clearing his throat.

"Is he gone?" I asked.

"Yes. He didn't want to go, but he is gone. How do you feel?"

"Sick… but lighter." And I did feel lighter. As if I had taken off a layer of wet, soiled clothes I didn't even know I'd been wearing.

"He was determined," chuckled Lama Kunchen, "but he will bother you no more."

"Where is he now?" I wanted to make sure he really was gone.

"Your grandfather's spirit was earthbound but has now gone to the Heavenly Fields. He will rest there awhile, review his past life, and then choose the circumstances of his next incarnation."

"Without me?"

"If you fulfil your promise to us then, yes, without you – certainly without you being bothered by him."

I stared at the floor. My grandfather was gone. At least that was one thing I'd achieved from this trip.

The ancient lama suddenly coughed and slumped forward. Lama Kunchen rushed to his side, with a look of concern on his face. Jigme dismissed me with a fierce glare. So I left and made my way to the main part of the lamasery. Everything looked the same. Everyone looked the same. But I felt elated. My curse had gone! My grandfather sent packing! He might even now be looking to be reincarnated – as a dog, if there was any justice – but whatever, it was going to be without me. All my life he had exerted an evil hold over me, but now he was gone. I really did feel happy. And best of all, that night I had a dream about Sarangerel.

I was elated for days afterwards. I would have whistled on water carrying duties if that were allowed. I looked Mingyar straight in the eye. And I didn't even fidget in the services. There was a purpose to this place after all. Norchen noticed my happiness, and asked me about it one morning. We were sitting outside trying to get some sun. I just told him things were going well. As I was talking, he suddenly became quiet. I turned round to see his master, Lama Neto, coming towards us.

"Thaza, it's good to see you so well," said Lama Neto. "You must be making progress."

I told him I was.

"I think you deserve a treat, then," he said. "Come with me." Norchen and I exchanged glances and followed him. He took us into the lamas' private courtyard and there, tethered to the wall, was a horse.

"Norchen has told me you like horses. I've got to go to the Potala shortly, that's why one of my horses is here. It's not much, but you can ride him round if you like."

I hadn't seen a horse for months, let alone been near one. I looked at Lama Neto to make sure I could approach it. He smiled. So I went up, holding out my hand. The horse moved away; I could sense it was frightened. But it was nothing I couldn't handle. I soon had the horse nuzzling my hand, and then I led it round the courtyard. It would be wrong to ride the horse in such a confined space, so I didn't. But just to smooth its coat and breathe in its smell was a godsend.

"Thank you lama, for this and all your kindnesses," I said. "You have been good to me. But I am just a chela, I cannot repay you."

Lama Neto laughed. "A gift is meant to be received, not repaid," he said. "But if you want, one day, if I need your help, you can repay me then."

"Anything," I replied.

Lama Neto smiled in return.

The next evening I was summoned to Lama Kunchen's room. He was seated on cushions and Jigme was on the hard floor as usual. As I came in Lama Kunchen rang his gold bell and asked the attendant to bring refreshments.

"Thaza, have some tea," said Lama Kunchen. "How are you feeling? You look better. As I say, your grandfather didn't want to leave, but he has gone now. A very interesting exorcism. Now that his curse has been lifted, and you have agreed to transport this book, we thought we should tell you more about it and why it is so important."

Jigme was looking uneasy. This time Lama Kunchen pre-empted his expected complaint that I shouldn't be told so much by saying, "He has promised not to divulge what we tell him, haven't you Thaza?

91

Since he is going to risk his life for us, it is only fair that he knows why."

Risk my life? What was he talking about? I was about to remonstrate when Lama Kunchen continued, "Or would you rather not know, Thaza?"

"No. I mean, yes. I would like to know."

Lama Kunchen was pleased. Jigme frowned, but stayed silent. I took some tea.

"Tibet is a special country," Lama Kunchen began. "We live apart from the rest of the world, protected by our mountains, where we are free to live our way of life. As a people, we are dedicated to religion. We don't always practise it well," here he chuckled, "but we are mostly sincere. Foreigners see our lamaseries and way of life and think we are devoted to Buddhism. We are," he paused, "and yet we are something more.

"Our religion is also the protector of an ancient knowledge. A knowledge which gives consciousness, understanding and almost unlimited abilities. There was a time when this knowledge was widely known, but it was abused, so the knowledge was taken away and only a small group of people were left who knew it. These people have to be pure so as not to use the knowledge for their own advantage. They have to be strong for they cannot tell others what they know or else darker forces would try to prise this knowledge from them.

"So a secret order grew up in Tibet dedicated to safeguarding this ancient knowledge, to keeping the flame alive for future generations, and to release that knowledge when humanity had earned the right to benefit from it again. There are not many of us in this order. Most lamas know nothing of it. But we exist, and we safeguard this knowledge, with no thought for ourselves, doing what needs to be done.

"This knowledge has been written down in a book – the Morning Tree – and it is this book that we are asking you to deliver for us."

"The what?" I queried.

"The Morning Tree. The title need not bother you, Thaza. There is a meaning behind it, but we need not reveal it now. The title in fact is deliberately unassuming so that if anyone did come across it, it would not arouse their suspicions.

"The Morning Tree is a very closely guarded secret, and only a handful of people know of its existence. The book must remain inviolate and unseen for now, for it details the secrets of life and the future course of humanity."

He smiled. "We call this knowledge secret, but when you know it, it is not so much secret as wonderful. If you know the basic laws governing life, then what happens is not so difficult or surprising, and you can change the way you live to make your life better. Indeed, you understand that the universe only operates for our benefit. But humanity's spiritual evolution is not yet at a stage where people would appreciate or accept this knowledge. In fact, in the wrong hands it could be used to dominate or corrupt others. That has happened before, and we have all suffered for it."

"Before?" I asked.

"Oh yes, but a long time ago. So long in fact that the world looked different. Tibet, for example, was under the sea."

I wasn't sure I was following what Lama Kunchen was saying, but now I was certain he was mad. Tibet, the highest country in the world, under the sea?

"Humanity then had a chance to go up, but instead they chose to tamper with the laws of life in a negative way. All this happened in the time of the Atlantean root race.[37] They brought destruction upon themselves and ushered in darker times.

"We are in those times today. We are in the Age of Kali, a time of division, when man is the furthest from God he has ever been. However, although it might not seem so, we are nearing the end of these darker times. The wheel of life has turned, and mankind is paying off its karma. Indeed, the wars and turmoil are evidence of that. In time, a new, golden age will dawn. This will happen in stages. The Year

---

[37] I am grateful to Lama Sonam Prasang for translating this phrase.

of the Fire-Rabbit,[38] and the next but one Year of the Earth-Ox,[39] for example, are important staging posts. It won't be noticed at first, but gradually consciousness will shift, people will look at things in a new way, and old problems will dissolve. It will be up to mankind how quickly this happens. If people resist, then there will be natural disasters, and economic and political upheavals too. But if mankind cooperates then change can happen quickly. A new human race will be born. And there will be three thousand years of peace and harmony, and a completely new way of doing things. A great many high beings are working today to ensure that this happens."

Lama Kunchen chuckled. "Actually, when I say a completely new way of doing things, I mean a completely new way. People will become telepathic, they will recognise their souls, and they will begin to see God in all forms and themselves. There will be no need for religion because people will have direct experience of the divine and they will know, for a fact, that reincarnation is real. Work will not be the drudgery or necessity it is today, but a means of fulfilling oneself. Earth will in fact return to the purpose for which it was intended: a finishing school for souls. Earth was always meant to be a place for evolved souls, a planet where they can live in a physical body, but in harmony and in a spiritual way. Humanity took a wrong turn in the past, and today the planet is mostly filled with young souls. In fact, because most souls are young, with all their fear and struggle, it has become difficult for many evolved souls to come down – the energies are too gross. All this will change however, and eventually Earth will be restored to its true purpose.

"The knowledge we are safeguarding can help to wake people up to their true inheritance. It can help speed the dawn of this golden age. If we can keep the knowledge for now, and then plant its seeds in the future, we will have done a great service for mankind. We may even

---

[38] Tibetan calendars at the time operated on a 60 year cycle of five elements and 12 animals. The year of the Fire-Rabbit that Lama Kunchen refers to would be 1987.
[39] The Year of the Earth-Ox would be 2009.

94

be able to bring forward the golden age that is coming. That is where you come in."

"Me?"

I wasn't interested in a golden age that would happen long after I was dead. I just wanted to go home and enjoy my life now.

"How am I involved?"

"Because Thaza," said Lama Kunchen, "there are forces seeking to destroy the Morning Tree and prevent the golden age. Forces that, even now, are closing in on us. That is why we need the book taken out of Tibet – before they succeed."

"Who are these 'forces'?"

"We call them the dark. A principle of dark light that informs certain people, and makes them dedicated to foiling mankind's evolution to higher consciousness, preferably for their own profit."

"You mean evil people."

"It's not as obvious as that, Thaza. Yes, the dark kills and lies, but that does not mean they are oafs. Some of them are very sophisticated. In fact, the biggest barrier to humanity evolving is not evil, as most people perceive it, but misinformation. The dark sows misinformation that keeps people confused and anxious. Then exercising power over them is easy."

"And they are after this book?"

"Yes. Once it is released, and people have access to this knowledge again, the dark's grip on humanity will dissolve. That is why they are desperate to get hold of the Morning Tree. In fact, the closer we get to the dawn of the new age, the more desperate the dark becomes."

"So taking this book will be dangerous."

"It could be. As I've said, the dark will kill to fulfil their ends. But we hope to wrong foot them by choosing you."

I accepted his concealed compliment – I was competent and could do the job – but still I'd rather not. Hadn't I just spent several months toiling across Tibet's trackless wastes? Surely they could find some inaccessible mountain cave and deposit their precious book there? Why have me go out of my way to India? I said as much to Lama Kunchen.

"If only it were that simple," he replied. "Let's just say that the dark know the book is in Tibet, and that is where they are looking."

"But Tibet is a huge country. You can easily—"

"What he means," interjected Jigme angrily, "is that Tibet will be invaded and our ancient knowledge crushed underfoot!"

I looked at Jigme, surprised at his sudden outburst, and then at Lama Kunchen. The old man was sad. He nodded.

"Yes, Thaza, a select few of us know the future. It is covered in the Morning Tree. A great war is about to engulf the world. The Land of the Rising Sun will invade China. That once great country will be plunged into civil war. At the same time in Europe, people will rise up and fight each other. The British, the Russians and men from the lands of the Red Indian, will eventually prevail. But a new darkness will cover half the world. It will be coloured red. They will proclaim the freedom of the downtrodden, but in fact, as is the way with the dark, they will twist the truth and use fine sounding words to control and imprison millions of people."[40]

Lama Kunchen paused. It was the first time I had detected any disturbance in his otherwise balanced poise. He helped himself to more tea.

"The darkness that will cover half the world will cover China. Under direction of the forces of darkness, China will claim Tibet as part of its territory, and it will invade."[41]

China will invade Tibet? I didn't like the Chinese even then.

"But lama," I protested, "if you know China will invade then you can take precautions. You can build defences, train your army. Why, you can even invade China first!"

Lama Kunchen laughed. "Thaza, we are not allowed to use the secret knowledge for our own benefit. Even if we were, we are few

---

[40] It seems that Lama Kunchen is predicting the Second World War and the spread of communism.
[41] Communist China invaded Tibet in 1950 and claimed the country as part of its territory.

and they are millions. We have a handful of ancient guns, they have modern weapons. Besides, we are not supposed to take other people's lives."

"But you must fight!" I said. "Are you men or sheep?"

"It's no good Thaza," said Jigme, on my side for once. "I have had this conversation with him many times. He is determined to let the dark rule Tibet."

"The dark will invade Tibet," continued Lama Kunchen. "It will crush our religion, burn our monasteries, kill monks and nuns. A great many Tibetans will be forced into exile. The Chinese soldiers will not respect any part of our life. They will in fact be pawns used by the dark to seek out and destroy the secret knowledge. But that is why we are taking steps to safeguard that knowledge."

I still wasn't satisfied. "Lama, there must be another way. You cannot allow bad people to beat you. Or if you do, surely it is better to die trying!" I couldn't understand how he could be so accepting of Tibet's tragic fate.

"We must not avoid what needs to be done, even if it is bad for us. But Thaza, we must also remember that it is sometimes difficult to distinguish between light and dark. Yes, the dark will cause untold suffering. But, if we are steadfast, the light will win. Then we will be able to see that the dark has served a useful purpose: it will have strengthened us, and cleared out old butter at the bottom of the lamp. The new butter that goes in will burn more brightly. So, yes, Tibet will have to suffer. But as a result of that suffering Tibet will be stronger."

He paused and looked at me slowly. I didn't follow his reasoning, but I kept my mouth shut. Lama Kunchen continued.

"Not only will Tibet be stronger, but the knowledge we have protected these thousands of years will be known to everyone else. For if we are successful, then the dark's very attempt to get hold of the Morning Tree will have helped the book to reach the wider world. Then the Morning Tree might be released sooner rather than later. That will be a true blessing, for it will mean the golden age mankind has been working towards, can finally be realised. Of course, we must

97

be resolute, we must make sure the dark do not win, as they did in Atlantean times. The darkest hour is before the dawn. We are now in that darkest hour. As such, the forces that oppose us are more anxious than ever to crush us before the wheel of life turns from them. That is why we need to take the secret knowledge out of Tibet and seed it elsewhere so it can bloom in the future."

We were all silent for a while. I was trying to take in everything I was being told. All right, they had this special book. Apparently Tibet wasn't a big enough place to hide it in. And they really wanted me to take it to India before the Chinese or the dark, or whoever, invaded and found it. I know Lama Kunchen had said I needed to atone for my grandfather (though, truly, he should atone for what he did to me), but I wasn't interested in all this. Surely I could do some sort of other penance.

"Why can't Jigme take it?" I asked. "Why me?"

"Why you, Thaza? Because the dark will be looking for a Tibetan, not a Mongolian, for a monk, not a layman. And because we need someone, how shall I put it, resourceful, able to look after themselves, should others try to stop him…"

"I still think it's foolish," said Jigme, angry again. "Our whole order depending on someone we hardly know! It's too big a risk." I wondered how he dared to openly oppose his master. Lama Kunchen, however, was unmoved.

"Dalai Lamas can be born to uneducated peasants; we cannot judge by external appearances alone. Thaza wants to repay his debt; we must let him help us."

Jigme fumed.

"Don't forget," added Lama Kunchen to Jigme, "we know the Morning Tree has to be taken out of Tibet, so it can be safe from the dark, resting in a place until a future time when its treasures can be revealed."

The lamas were talking to themselves. I felt a sudden surge of anger. Once again I seemed like a sheep herded against its will by a dog with bared teeth. I just wanted to be with my horses and woman,

I didn't want to be ordered around by lamas I didn't know and get involved in protecting a book that had nothing to do with me. I was being used. If I had to do this job, then I wanted more than just the lifting of my grandfather's curse.

"Lama," I butted in. "If I do this for you, will you guarantee that I'll be able to live in peace and marry the woman I want?"

"But... but you've already agreed to do this!" Jigme spluttered. "You can't make a new bargain now! Don't you realise the importance of what we're doing? Lama, I told you we couldn't trust him!"

I stood my ground. This was more than just taking a book to India. I needed more in return. Lama Kunchen looked at me with his deep black eyes. It was the first time I'd noticed the light in them. He looked stern.

"Thaza, we have fulfilled our side of the bargain – we have lifted your grandfather's curse. You must fulfil your side. If you don't, I can't tell you what will happen."

"To me or your order?"

"To the world."

We were silent for a while.

"But will I be able to live in peace and marry the woman I want?"

Lama Kunchen softened. "Yes," he said quietly.

"And will I be able to marry Sarangerel?" The dream I'd had about her recently was still fresh in my mind. I had decided that, as soon as I returned home, I'd seek her out and marry her, if her fool of a father hadn't given her to someone else by then. That's why I needed the lama's promise that she'd be mine.

Lama Kunchen looked disappointed, as if let down by his own son. "Thaza," he said, "you should fulfil your promise to us. We can't make you, but I think you will. But if you insist on me answering your question, then let me just say that, after you have carried out your task, yes, you can marry the person you call Sarangerel. I see it."

This made me very happy, even if the two lamas were looking distinctly unhappy. At last I had something concrete I could look forward to. A promise from a religious man of power that I could be with Sarangerel. We said no more. We'd all had enough. Moments later I was back in the main part of the lamasery making my way to my dormitory. I know now what great truths were divulged to me that night – truths that have since become painfully real – truths I admit I didn't appreciate at the time – but what of the great mistruth told to me? I have been eaten up with that ever since.

Different Directions

Life was now good, believe it or not. My grandfather's curse was lifted. I was going to marry Sarangerel (or so I thought). And I was getting better at martial arts. I didn't pay much attention to the esoteric information Lama Kunchen was giving me, and was now resigned to taking this secret book to India. I didn't want to, but I could do it, and the sooner I started the sooner I could go home and marry. But this good state didn't last long.

One day, while on water duty, I heard another monk make a sly remark about how lazy Mongolians were. I was surprised, as monks at Chakpori were generally well behaved. But I wasn't having any of his nonsense. So I challenged him, hoping secretly to have a fight. I barged him with my water carrying pole, he hit me back, and I flung myself at him. Easily dodging his whirling pole I jabbed him twice – once under his arm, which fell nerveless to his side, and once in his kidneys, which made him double up in pain. I was about to stand triumphantly over him when I felt myself lifted by a staff. It was one of the police monks – a huge man – who'd picked me up and then crashed me to the ground. I got up, angry, thinking about applying my skills to him, when there was a sickening crack. I cried out in pain as my arm now hung limply by my side. He had smashed me with his staff. The police monk then grabbed me and carried me none too gently to the infirmary where I was left. Eventually, a medical lama came to see me. I'd broken my arm. He put it in a splint and told me to go. I ached, and was unhappy. How could I let myself be beaten so easily? And how could I now practise more martial arts?

Once again the Master of Chelas set about me. But no punishment this time. That, he said ruefully, would be left to my master.

That evening I was summoned to Lama Kunchen's room. He and Jigme were there. He shook his head while Jigme scowled.

"Thaza, we heard what happened today," Lama Kunchen began. "Didn't Mingyar tell you that the martial art form you are being taught is never to be used to attack anyone – it is only for self-defence?"

"But that man was rude to me," I said.

"Should we attack every man who is rude to us? By your reckoning Thaza, I should have attacked you several times."

"He insulted me!"

"And you must learn to recognise that you don't always have to avenge insults or protect your honour. What would have happened if you'd ignored him?"

"He would have thought I was weak."

"And?"

"He'd have bullied me again!"

"Would he have been able to force you to do something you didn't want to do?"

"Of course not! I would never have let him."

"Exactly. If he had tried to force you to do something you didn't want to do, then you would have resisted him. If he had used physical force against you, then you can use martial arts on him – and then the police monk would have intervened to help you. But as it was, that monk, so I'm told, was only verbally rude to you. If you had ignored him, the incident would have passed and you would not now be laid up with a broken arm."

I was still angry – at being injured and being told off. I couldn't live according to their religious standards. I'd already suffered so much with my grandfather that I wasn't going to be pushed around anymore.

"I told you he couldn't be trusted," put in Jigme.

I glared at him – a man worse than grit carried in the wind that stings your face – and thought of replying, but I didn't want another lecture from Lama Kunchen. So, with a pain in my stomach, I let his remark go.

"He has his failings," sighed Lama Kunchen, "but we are here to help. Come Thaza, let me look at your arm." He inspected it, and then gave Jigme a list of herbs. "We'll put them on as a compress twice a day to aid healing. We need you fit, Thaza."

With that, I was dismissed. At least I hadn't been punished beyond a telling off. Mingyar came to see me the next day. He gave me a torrent of abuse at how stupid I'd been to try to show off my skills, and how he'd had a dressing down for failing to impress upon me that the advanced form of martial arts I was being taught was only ever for self-defence. He couldn't be held responsible for my foolishness, he shouted. When I was better, he promised I'd learn properly or he'd personally make sure I never left the monastery. I hadn't expected Mingyar to be like this.

I was dejected. My broken arm surely meant I would rot as a monk for several weeks longer than necessary. Lama Kunchen was as good as his word, and my arm was dressed twice a day in a herb compress. One morning it was done by an oaf of a lama in the infirmary who either didn't know what he was doing or deliberately wanted to hurt me. He reapplied my splint far too tightly, so it was really painful. I complained but was told to shut up. I bore it for some hours, but when I slipped on some spilt butter wax and banged my arm, I cried out in agony. I wondered if I hadn't broken it again. I didn't want my stay in Chakpori further delayed, so, with tears of pain and frustration in my eyes, and a disregard of the lamasery's rules, I made my way to Lama Kunchen's room to get it seen to.

I swear I knocked, but hearing no answer, I pushed the door open. Lama Kunchen was in his usual place; Jigme was seated in front of him with his back to the door. Between them was a large open book.[42] Lama Kunchen was surprised. A horrified Jigme quickly threw a cloth over the pages.

"Thaza, what are you doing here?" asked Lama Kunchen.

I began to tell him about my arm.

"Shut the door!" cut in Jigme.

I did so.

"This is most irregular Thaza," said Lama Kunchen. "You should have gone to the infirmary. We are busy."

I told him the lama in the infirmary had been the problem in the first place. I really needed my arm seeing to.

"Well, bring it here then," relented Lama Kunchen. As he was looking at my arm, Jigme made sure he was standing between me and the book.

"There," said Lama Kunchen, having redressed the splint, this time properly. "That should be better. Well, I wonder if that lama didn't do you a favour after all. Thaza, do you know what we have here?" He indicated the book Jigme was still shielding from me. "It's the book we want you to deliver for us."

He pulled the cloth cover off to reveal pages of densely packed script and strange drawings. I squatted down to have a look. Of course, the words and drawings meant nothing to me, but I feigned an interest. So this was their Morning Tree. The book I had to deliver to India before dark forces snatched it from them and snuffed it out. The book I had to risk my life for.

Jigme was clearly uneasy at my seeing so much, even though he knew I couldn't read. Without being asked, he put the pages back and lowered a dark wooden cover over them. The cover, I noticed, was carved. The relief showed some mountains, and a sun breaking over them, shedding its light on the slopes. I ran my hands over the carving. It was very smooth, very pleasant to touch.

---

[42] Tibetan books were not like western ones. They were typically oblong in shape, and the pages were not always bound by a book spine but could be loose-leafed.

"It's nice, isn't it," said Lama Kunchen. "Sometimes a picture can say more than words."

I studied the carving for some moments. I don't know, there was something about it that took me. Some illumination in the sunlight, some power in the mountains, a happy blending of light and dark.

"Sit down, Thaza," said Lama Kunchen. I did so, the three of us forming a triangle around the book. "Scarcely more than a dozen people alive today have seen the Morning Tree as you are seeing it now," he continued. "A handful of us are allowed to study it; most of those who know of the Morning Tree's existence are there to protect it – and that is not many more. As I have said, the knowledge in this book can lead to untold powers. That is why the book must never fall into the wrong hands. But more than that, the knowledge in the book can help speed humanity on its way to much better times. If the Morning Tree does not survive, humanity could be set back."

I wasn't really listening. Yes, the book was important – he'd said that enough. But I was still staring at it. Bizarrely, I couldn't shift my eyes from it. It seemed to have its own insistent hold over me. Suddenly, and without expecting it, I was gripped by the book and couldn't shake myself away.

"This information, handed to us thousands of years ago, has been safeguarded here since before Buddhism came to Tibet," he continued. "It has been incorporated into the Buddhism we practise today. It is, in a way, the purpose of our religion, although the vast majority of monks know nothing of it. I would add that although Tibet has been the guardian of this secret knowledge for some thousands of years, we will not be the guardians of it forever. That mantle will pass to others. What we are doing now, by preparing to deliver the Morning Tree outside Tibet, is the first step in that process. Eventually, another country, another group of people, will be guardians of the knowledge, and they will be responsible for releasing it to humanity.

"The East, which today is spiritually focussed, will over time become more materialistic, whilst the West, which is excessively materialistic, will become more spiritual. This is merely a necessary balancing which will benefit both East and West. There will be greater unity in spiritual – and material – matters in the future. So, today, if you want a spiritual life, it is common to be born in the East. But tomorrow, if you want a spiritual life, you can choose the West. Indeed, the West will become the spiritual leader in the world. This is because change is needed, and the West has specialised in change; so, high beings in the future will incarnate in western bodies to bring about important spiritual developments. Of course, materialistic power will, at the same time, pass to the East. It's quite amusing when you think about it."

He carried on talking for some time. About how higher consciousness will come. How the answers humanity needs will appear. And how life will become so much more fulfilling than it is today. He gave me treasures whose worth I couldn't grasp then and can only marvel at now. I just sat with him, and the Morning Tree, taking in what I could. Eventually, after I suspect he'd told me much more than he should, I left.

Over the next few weeks my arm was still painful, so I was excused from water carrying duties. This gave me more time to while away. For some reason I can't remember, Norchen was free some of that time too. He showed me a back entrance into the refectory where, if we waited for the kitchen monks to be distracted, we could snatch extra food. As this was usually tsampa, I wasn't that excited, but sometimes we stole cheese. We were never given cheese – I think it was reserved for senior lamas – but I really missed it. Tibetan cheese though is nothing to Mongolian cheese. Yak milk is not really suitable for cheese.

We spent some of our time on the roof. Since most of the monks were in classes, we were unlikely to be discovered, but we did have to be aware of the police monks. They could be anywhere anytime.

We also explored the lower reaches of the monastery. I came to realise that there was as much of Chakpori below the peak on which it was built as there was on top of it. My martial arts lessons, when I had had them, I knew now were below ground.

I don't know how Norchen knew his way around so well, or why he felt so confident moving about the lower reaches. Perhaps he'd just explored by himself. One afternoon he led me down to a room at a deeper level than we'd been to before. He'd brought two butter lamps which he lit.

"Where are we going?" I whispered.

"A special place," Norchen replied. "Wait and see."

He seemed to get lost, but eventually, down a long narrow corridor, reached by a flight of steep steps cut out of the rock, he pushed open a heavy, oval shaped door. It led into a room – I couldn't judge its size because of the darkness – but it was filled with objects on tables and on the floor. Norchen began picking them up and examining them. I did the same. There were lots of strange things I'd never seen before. Then Norchen giggled.

"Come and look at this Thaza!" He handed me a heavy object slightly bigger than my hands that had two cylinders joined together. There were discs of glass at either end. He put one end to my eye. I yelped. At the other end was Norchen's face, but very small, grinning at me.

"Turn it the other way," he said.

I did, and suddenly dimly lit objects further in the room were close up.

"What is it?" I marvelled.

"I don't know."

We carried on looking around. Then I found a crystal ball. It was about ten times the size of my hands, cold to touch, but flawless as far as I could see in the dancing darkness. I felt an urge to pick it up. It was heavy, and its weight made me fold cross legged onto the floor. It hurt my broken arm, and nearly spilled out of my grasp, but with an effort I steadied it. For some reason, I was in a cold sweat. I looked into the ball. Strangely, I felt a wrench in my stomach, and then it was as if two strong hands had gripped my shoulders making my body rigid. The ball suddenly filled with brilliant white light. I saw a woman – not Mongolian, completely different, with wavy brown hair wearing

107

a white tunic – in some sort of garden with water in a paved concourse. She seemed happy, but then a man, dressed in a similar tunic, came up behind her and slashed her throat with a knife. I shuddered as he did so. Then I was on the plains riding a horse, with armour and a lance. I was in Genghis Khan's army. Then, just as abruptly, I was a man with a big nose and low brown shoes tied with laces in some large, cold building. There was a woman there – she was learned, important – but at the same time I felt some passion for her. Only she was pushing me away.

I pulled myself from the ball. These visions were strange, and I didn't understand what was going on. But I was fascinated. I looked for Norchen and saw he was engrossed with something further into the room. He wasn't looking for me, so I turned to the ball again. There was another swirl of light and I felt myself being pulled inside the ball, and yet at the same time felt that the ball was inside me. Then I saw Jigme, only it wasn't him because he was an old man. I knew I was around too, but I couldn't see myself. Suddenly I saw a skinny man with hardly any clothes flash a knife and kill him. I felt a pang of guilt because I was sure I could have stopped Jigme being killed. But I still couldn't see myself. None of this made any sense either.

"Thaza." It was Norchen.

I jerked away from the ball, feeling sick, my pulse racing.

"We better go," he said. "It's time for the evening meal. We don't want to be missed."

I stood up and gingerly put the ball back on its stand. I didn't know what had happened. It was a bit like the times my grandfather's spirit had cursed me, only this time it did not feel evil. I was shaken from the weirdness of it all. As we heaved the oval door shut and made our way up the stairs, Norchen said:

"Don't tell anyone about this Thaza, or we'll be punished."

I certainly wasn't going to tell anyone, but what had just happened perturbed me. Truly, there were strange forces in this place.

Apart from my time with Lama Kunchen and the Morning Tree, he and Jigme ignored me for days after my dressing down for fighting that monk. I had guessed they would. But honestly, I didn't mind not trekking to his room for more lectures. But one evening, to my surprise, I was summoned. They had incense burning as I walked in. It smelled heavenly, quite unlike that muck they sprayed around in services to cover the smell of butter lamps and the lump of unwashed monks.

"Ah, Thaza, sit down," said Lama Kunchen, as I entered. He rang his gold bell and asked the attendant to bring me tea and sweetmeats. I drank the tea and then tried one of the sugared cubes on a plate beside me. It was the nicest thing I had ever eaten. It was worth being in his room just for this.

"I see you like sweetmeats," said Lama Kunchen. "They're from India. A gift for the Dalai Lama from senior officials there. Sometimes he gives me some. I thought I'd share them with you."

May he give you more, I thought.

"Now Thaza," continued Lama Kunchen, "we've been thinking what to do with you. Your arm is healing, but it will be some weeks before you are fit again. However, we must continue your lessons."

But how? If my arm was unusable, how could I carry on with martial arts? I had another sweetmeat. Truly they are the tastiest food in the world.

"You've done well with your martial arts, despite your lack of respect for what you are being taught," said Lama Kunchen. "I've tried to explain that we're teaching you martial arts only to help you with your task. The dark will try to stop you, but if you can look after yourself physically, you will stand a greater chance of succeeding." He paused to see if I was listening. "We're going to teach you other techniques to help you beat the dark."

This meant nothing to me, but it was exercising Jigme as usual.

"Lama!" he said, "we've seen how he is with martial arts. Why entrust him with greater powers?"

He was becoming like a dog who can only whine and snap. They are unhelpful and should be kicked. But Lama Kunchen seemed to have infinite patience.

"We will entrust him with greater powers, Jigme, in order to safeguard the Morning Tree. We act only for this purpose."

"What do you mean?" I asked. "Greater powers? Are they like martial arts?"

Jigme turned away in disgust.

"Like martial arts, but using your senses," Lama Kunchen said. "Thaza, I've told you we are the keepers of the secret knowledge. Man is really greater than he knows. He has powers and abilities that are as yet untapped. People used to have some of these abilities in the past but, because they were abused, they were taken away. Man is not yet ready to have these abilities again. But certain people – if they are pure in mind – can learn these abilities. We have some of them," here he gestured to include Jigme, "but we can never use them for our personal advantage. Do you understand, Thaza? We can never use them for our personal advantage."

I nodded.

"Do you trust Jigme?"

This was a strange question. I toyed with saying yes but decided to tell the truth.

"No," I replied.

"Why do you say that?"

"Because I don't like him!"

"I didn't ask if you liked him, I asked if you trusted him."

"No," I repeated, "because he doesn't like me!"

"And yet Jigme is part of our order and, whatever his personal thoughts, he too is dedicated to helping you."

I glared at Jigme. I didn't care if he was helping me or not. I still didn't like him.

"You are letting anger and bias distort your judgement, Thaza," continued Lama Kunchen. "We will teach you how to discern a man's true intentions so that you can take the right decisions at the right time." This still wasn't making sense to me. I think Lama Kunchen realised this too.

"Thaza," he said suddenly, "what would you do with a rogue horse?"

"A rogue horse? I would study it."

"Go on."

"I would observe the horse. I would be very quiet – a horse doesn't attack a still man. I would sense what it was feeling, then I would connect with it in my mind. When I felt connected I would send it calming thoughts. I would also tell it I was its master." I was thinking of all the times I'd calmed an angry stallion, all the times I'd been one with a horse. For a moment I was back home on the plains and happy.

Both the lamas were silent.

"It's not nonsense!" I said hotly. "It's what I do, and it works."

Lama Kunchen smiled. "We never said it was nonsense. On the contrary, we understand what you are saying. I would even go so far as to say you are a natural."

Jigme was smiling too, and for the first time almost looked pleasant.

"What you do with a horse, we would teach you to do with a man," continued Lama Kunchen. "But first I must give you some background to help you understand. Have some more tea and sweetmeats."

I stared at my empty plate. Lama Kunchen rang his bell and the attendant came in to replenish us.

"Everything has its own frequency or energy," he began. "Think of stone. It is hard and dense and you can't pass your hand through it. We can say that the particles that make up the stone are vibrating slowly. Think of water. You can pass your hand through water with some resistance, and we can say that the particles that make up water are vibrating more quickly. Now think of air. You can pass your hand through air easily and we can say the particles that make up air are vibrating even more quickly."

He was labouring the point, but I was following what he was saying.

111

"All objects have their particular rate of vibration; it determines what they are," he continued. "As with objects, so with thoughts and emotions. We quite unconsciously say that we're up or down, happy or depressed. We even colour our emotions, saying we've seen red or are green with envy. All of this is an instinctive recognition that thoughts and emotions have their own frequency or rate of vibration. Generally, the happier and more excited we are, the higher our thoughts and emotions, and vice versa.

"In fact, we are surrounded by mental and emotional networks, or grids, of these different thoughts and emotions. You can be feeling quite happy but then you can meet someone who is worried or depressed. He might not even say anything, but if his energy system is stronger than yours, you might suddenly find yourself worrying about something when moments earlier you were happy. You think this is your worry when in fact it is his. It works the other way round too: someone who is higher can wash your system clean without you knowing it."

I understood what he was saying. I'd always known that my grandfather had given off miserable feelings – even outsiders would feel morose in his presence. Just as I had always given off good feelings towards horses, which is why they liked me. Lama Kunchen was calling this energy. All right then, but really it was common sense. For the first time since meeting these so-called holy people, I was interested in what they were saying. Mercifully, it was free from endless references to 'the Buddha said this' and 'the saint did that' and 'the eight steps of this and that are something else'. Anyone with half a mind would know what Lama Kunchen was saying was obvious. It explained so much: why I might dislike someone, or how I could track the mood of a horse, or why (as I was beginning to notice) I usually felt good in Lama Kunchen's presence.

"I take it you are following what I'm saying?" Lama Kunchen asked. "Good. I thought as much. Now Thaza, this energy that exists in objects and our thoughts and emotions also exists in situations. When you wake up in the morning, there will be an energy pattern that affects you that will unfold throughout the day. It explains why some days go well whilst others can be difficult and fraught. This energy also exists more generally. You can walk into a room, for instance, and the energy will be directed in a certain way. It accounts for why a group of monks here might be happy one day and surly the next. As with small situations, so with larger ones. Indeed, a country will also have its own energy currents. Tibet, for example, is now running down as we are pressed on three sides,[43] and I have already told you that one day, not many years from now, we will be invaded. The important point to remember is that everything has its own energy.

"So, a bowl of tsampa will have its energy – from the ground the barley grew in, through the farmer who harvested it to the man who cooked it. A person will have his own energy depending on his thoughts and emotions or the thoughts and emotions of the dominant person in their space. A building will have its own energy depending on the ground energy and the energy of all the people who've ever been in it. And an institution, like a lamasery, will have its own energy depending on the thoughts and emotions that have gone into creating and sustaining it." Here he laughed. "People think that lamaseries must be good places because religion is practised in them, but in fact the opposite is usually the case. People go to lamaseries with all their problems, and the monks are not always at peace with themselves, so often the energy in a monastery is low and turbulent.

"We would teach you to sense this energy, be it in a person, a building or a situation, and use that awareness to help you make the right decision. Look back at that incident when you had the fight which broke your arm. What do you think about the energy of that situation?"

I was blank.

Lama Kunchen continued, "Feel into it as you feel into a horse."

I did so. It was funny at first, but gradually impressions came to me.

---

[43] British India, China and Russia were all competing for influence in Tibet at the time.

113

"There wasn't much behind the monk's remark," I began. "He didn't really mean it. But... well, it feels like black energy, it washed over me and I got angry."

Lama Kunchen beamed. "Exactly! Quite right. I told you he was a natural," he said to Jigme. Even Jigme looked pleased. "Thaza, you have ability. We will increase that ability. For now, I only ask you to start assessing the energy as you go about your day."

With that I was dismissed. Oh, I admit I was pleased I had been praised. I was even more pleased that what I had done naturally with horses was some sort of esoteric power. But I couldn't really be bothered to assess the energy all the time. I was still too preoccupied with thinking about how and when I might get out of Chakpori and return home to claim Sarangerel and my herds.

The next day, Norchen came up to me urgently and pulled me to one side. "Thaza, I have to go into Lhasa. Do you want to come?"

Of course I said yes. I had many hours of free time and longed for distraction. What's more, I realised, with a start, that I'd been confined in Chakpori for more than three months; I needed to get out. It turned out that Norchen had been asked by a lama to deliver a package to a jeweller. We slipped out of the door used for water carrying and raced down the hill. It was a bright sunny day and even the wind, for the time of year, was muted. We made our way eastwards into the town. I hadn't asked where we were going, and didn't ask when we turned down an alley and then pushed through a cloth covered entrance into some sort of hostelry. It was dark inside, and there were knots of men talking in subdued voices around low tables. Norchen moved to the back of the room and said something to a woman. She disappeared into another room and returned with two beakers, giving one to each of us.

"Cheers," said Norchen raising his beaker to his lips. I did the same. It was a fiery liquid, far stronger than shimiin arkhi.

"Is this what you came into Lhasa for?" I asked.

"Of course not," he replied. "But there's no harm, now we're here, in having some fun."

"But we're monks, or dressed as some, and we're not supposed to drink! Why are they serving us?"

"You can always get what you want if you know where to look," was his reply.

Just then, two swarthy men came over. They pulled Norchen to one side and spoke to him. Norchen jerked himself away from them, and made towards me. I was about to ask him what was going on when he quickly drained his cup and told me we were leaving. I followed him out into the bright sunshine, my head fuzzy from the drink. We rejoined the main road and then started to look for this jeweller. It was clear Norchen hadn't been there before. He kept looking up and down the street, doubling back, then going forward again, until at last he went into a house. Again it was dark inside, in contrast to the bright sunshine. He went up to a man behind a counter and gave him a package he'd been carrying in his robe. The man opened it and took out a little gold figure encrusted with jewels. He also took out a piece of paper and read it. He grunted and went into the next room. A few minutes later a Chinese man came out with the little figure and an expectant look on his face. As soon as he saw us he smiled and nodded and spoke in Chinese.

"Mr Hu says he is very pleased to meet such honourable lamas and asks that his compliments be presented to the honourable Lama Neto." It was the first man who was translating.

"Mr Hu requests that you join him in some refreshment," continued the man, as Mr Hu bowed and opened the curtain for us to enter an inner room. Then he barked some orders to people in a kitchen beyond and we heard the sound of cooking. In a short time, a servant came out with a jar and little cups. It was rice wine. I didn't want another drink but felt I couldn't refuse. It was more refined than our first drink, but still strong. The servant reappeared with cold pickles and, joy of joys, noodles. They were hot, contained meat and were delicious. Norchen and I put the chopsticks to one side and, using our fingers, ate with alacrity. Compared to tsampa this was heavenly.

"Mr Hu apologises for the humble meal and trusts that the honourable lamas will not think badly of him."

I didn't understand this needless flattery or indeed why Mr Hu was treating us this way, but I didn't care. I did love the food. A little later Mr Hu slipped Norchen a piece of paper which he stuffed into his robe.

"Mr Hu says that he will make the repairs to the gold figure and will contact the honourable Lama Neto when it is ready." And then, with more smiles and bows, we were shown outside.

I felt sick but content. Sick from the alcohol and the odd company, but content from the food and my trip to Lhasa. Norchen was elated. We climbed up the path to Chakpori and entered at the side door.

"There you are!" roared a voice as a staff crashed down on us. It was a police monk. "You!" he said jabbing Norchen with his staff, "have missed classes without permission! And you are required by Lama Kunchen at once!"

I am Given Instruction

I made my way to Lama Kunchen's room with a sense of foreboding. Did he know about my trip into town? Would he smell the alcohol on my breath? And would he sense the weird places I'd visited? But when I arrived the room was calm, he was alone and he greeted me with a smile.

"Ah Thaza, sit down," he said. "I wanted to see how your arm was healing. Let me take a look."

It seemed strange to be in his room during the day. He took off the splint and herb compress and examined my arm.

"Yes," he said. "In a couple of weeks you can resume light martial arts training." This raised my spirits. "But for now," he continued, as he reapplied the splint and dressing, "we can carry on with your other training."

I groaned. I wasn't in the mood for lessons. But he surprised me with his next question.

"What makes you happy?"

I thought for a moment. "Horses," I said. "Riding them. Looking after them. Herding my animals with them. Just being with them." In that moment I was back on the plains again with my horses oblivious to Lama Kunchen, the monastery and Lhasa.

"And what do you feel right now thinking about horses?"

I forced myself back to the present. "A wellness…" I replied.

"Where do you feel this wellness?"

I looked at him.

"In your body," he continued, "where do you feel this wellness?"

117

"Here." I pointed to the centre of my chest.

Lama Kunchen rang his bell and the attendant came in with some tea. We sat for a moment while we drank it. Then Jigme came rushing in.

"Honourable lama!" he panted, "I have bad news!"

Lama Kunchen looked shocked.

"It's Thaza," Jigme continued, glaring at me. "He's stolen a gold Buddha from one of the side temples!"

I froze. It wasn't true – I'd stolen nothing! But Norchen had had a gold figure, and I'd been with him. Oh god, now I stood accused as a thief!

"Thaza, is this true?"

"It wasn't me!"

"Don't listen to him, lama!" said Jigme. "He was seen. We have witnesses."

Lama Kunchen looked at me confused. I found I had a horror of letting this man down. I don't know how this feeling came to me, but for the first time in my life I was ashamed at disappointing another person. And yet I hadn't stolen anything! All those times when I'd felt powerless with my grandfather came flooding back to me. I knew no-one would believe me. I'd probably be cast out and left penniless in this stinking town months away from home. My stomach was churning. I wished to heaven I hadn't been drinking.

Lama Kunchen was still looking at me. "What do you feel now?" he asked.

"Hopeless!" I cried. I hate to admit it but I was close to tears.

"No, what do you feel in your body?"

"Sick. But I swear to you I didn't—"

"Where do you feel sick?"

I pointed to my stomach.

He nodded. "Thank you Jigme, you may go." Jigme left. I still felt as if demons were racing around my insides.

"Lama, I didn't steal anything!" I protested. I couldn't let Jigme frame me. If that bastard succeeded…

118

"I know, Thaza. Don't worry." Lama Kunchen paused a moment. I could hear my blood pounding in my ears. "It's all an exercise to show you something."

"An exercise?" I swallowed. "To show me what?"

"I told you last time about energy. How every thought, person and situation has its own energy. Well, this energy interacts with us through energy centres we have in our bodies. They're called chakras. Just now, when I asked what made you happy, you experienced good energy in your heart centre. The heart centre is the seat of the soul, the place of love. It's the main one we have. When Jigme accused you of being a thief, the energy went straight to your solar plexus – that's why you felt sick in your stomach. The solar plexus is the chakra where you feel emotions, and too often low emotions like domination. It's usually unsettled, difficult energy. Most of the time people operate from this chakra instead of the heart.

"If you are to get a true understanding of energy, you need to not only sense it – as you did last time – but to see which chakra it is in. That way you will be better able to handle the energy."

"Wait," I interjected. "Jigme rushing in was all a set up so that I could be alarmed?"

"Yes," said Lama Kunchen.

"So you don't think I'm a thief?"

"Of course not."

Relief flooded through me. "So you're not making any accusations?"

"No," he repeated.

Well then, he didn't know about my trip with Norchen to Lhasa, and I wasn't going to tell him. He waited until he saw I was ready to listen to what he was saying, and then continued.

"Chakras are very important. They determine how we experience energy. Just as we have organs in our body that process the air we breathe and the food we eat, so we have chakras in our energy bodies that deal with the energy we have or receive. So, in your dealings with another person, if your energy is coming from your solar plexus, then your relationship with that person is likely to be contested, or one of domination or being dominated. The energy in your relationship with your grandfather, for example, was mostly coming from his solar plexus to you and from yours to him. It was always difficult. But if you are coming from your heart centre, then the feeling is very different. You have mentioned someone called Sarangerel. With her you were a different person because you were more open, trusting, happy. That is because your energy with her was coming from your heart centre.

"Now, if you can learn to block bad energy from going into your centres, then you will have taken an important step in strengthening yourself, for you will no longer be drawn into difficulties. For example, when Jigme came in and accused you of being a thief, you could have blocked the bad energy coming from him and you wouldn't have felt unsettled. Similarly, if you have a problem, or someone is being difficult, you can send light or good energy from your heart centre to theirs – or to the problem generally – and there will be a change for the better."

He paused to see if I was taking this in. It seemed to make sense, although it was all new to me.

"All right," I said, "but where are these chakras? I've never seen them."

He leant over to get a roll of paper which he unfurled in front of me. It was a picture of a seated man with circles going from the base of his spine to the top of his head.

"Most texts you read will say a human has seven chakras. In fact, there are many more. You will see in this diagram that there are twelve. We start at the bottom." He pointed to the circle at the base of the man's spine. "This is the base centre. The next is the sexual centre. The third is the solar plexus. The fourth is the lower heart centre. The fifth is the higher heart centre. And the sixth is the throat centre. The other six chakras are in the head. The most important of these are the third eye behind the forehead and the crown at the top of the head."

I peered at the drawing. Then I looked at Lama Kunchen. "But I still can't see them."

He smiled. "You can't see them because your inner sight is not developed enough. Nevertheless, they are there, in your energy body. They are vortexes of light that receive, interpret and transmit energy. I can see them in you. Your base, sexual and solar plexus centres are all strong. Your base centre deals with survival and animal instinct, your sexual centre with procreation and creativity, and your solar plexus, as I've indicated, with the strength, or otherwise, of your personality and emotions. Your heart centre is quite large too, which you may find unexpected."

I certainly did. Apart from Sarangerel and now Norchen, I don't think I ever really liked anyone. But then Lama Kunchen corrected my thoughts.

"When you are with your horses, you are operating from your base but also from your heart centre. It's one of the reasons you are so successful with them. When you sense the energy in a horse, you are using your third eye which deals with intuition. Now, over the coming years, with the changes I have already described to you, the energy in mankind's chakra system will move up from the solar plexus to the lower heart centre, and then to the higher heart centre. This will transform human relationships, and mankind's relationship with the planet.

"Actually, as the Morning Tree describes, eventually mankind will have additional chakras. As consciousness grows, the bodies that make up humanity will need more advanced energy centres to handle the new light coming in. These new centres will receive, and also create, higher levels of consciousness. I can see one day there will be twenty five, then a hundred, and then many more than that." He paused, smiling. "Those extra centres will increase consciousness, and a much, much better way of living will be possible as a result. The divine will be more present in people. But for now, I want to hone your awareness and understanding of the chakras we currently have."

He paused again, this time to take some tea. "Now Thaza, look at me and see what you can sense about my chakras."

I had no idea what to do, so I just opened up and felt into his energy system, if you see what I mean. I got a lot of light from his chest and head. I told him so.

"Very good Thaza! Exactly right. My heart centre, third eye and occasionally my crown are my largest centres. This is not to say my centres are 'better' than yours. They are more developed because of the work I do. I would not make a good police monk because I am not physically big enough. Similarly, on an energy level, to be in our order, I do need to develop my heart and third eye chakras especially."

That made sense.

"I should add," he said, "that not just humans, but every living being has chakras. Animals, fish, insects, plants. Of course, they are not as developed as they are in humans, but they are still there. In fact, even mountains, countries and this planet have their own chakra systems."

That didn't make sense.

"What, you mean those mountains have a chakra system?" I said, gesturing to the peaks we could see outside the room.

"Yes," replied Lama Kunchen.

"And... Tibet? Mongolia?"

"Yes."

"How?"

"Although you might not think so, the mineral kingdom has consciousness. You recognise consciousness in plants because you can see if they are alive or dead. If you were a farmer, you'd also know that plants grow better if they are loved by the people who tend them. Well, minerals have consciousness too but it is hard to see because time for them is so stretched compared to time for us that we can't really sense it. So, those mountains do indeed have consciousness: they are young, they grow and they become old, albeit over millions of years. As they have consciousness, they also have chakra systems.

"As for countries, any part of the Earth that has focussed energy as a result of humans living there, starts to develop a consciousness of its own too. It might sound odd but it isn't. You accept that

Mongolians have their own traits, as do Tibetans, as do people all over the world. These traits are a collective consciousness that has its own intelligence and its own evolution. It forms part of the overall collective consciousness of humanity which is a being in its own right. That being will have its own chakra system too. Indeed, certain countries represent the planet's different chakras. India, for example, is currently the solar plexus centre, and that is where the energy is focussed today."

"But what about Britain, Russia and America?" I asked. "They are such powerful countries. Aren't they part of the chakra system?"

"Some are," he replied, "but you have to understand that military or material strength are not important in this context. Spirituality is. This world exists because there is a spiritual reason for it to exist. That is why God created form and all that you see around you. So the reasons why a country might or might not represent a chakra are not the typical ones most humans might think of."

Lama Kunchen went over this information again to see how much I was taking in. It was all new to me, but I could grasp the essence of what he was saying. He then made me review occasions in my past and asked me to say what centre the energy had been coming from. This was more difficult, but I was getting some of the answers right. He showed me a book with photographs and asked me to say where the energy was coming from in the people in the photographs. This was even more difficult (although I marvelled at how exact likenesses of people could be put on paper). Finally – I was tired by now and it was late – he dismissed me. But before I went he had one more exercise for me to do.

"Thaza, close your eyes," he said. "Visualise your chakras. Close and lock them from the top downwards. Now see them encased in black light – not 'bad' black light, but good, warming, reassuring black light."

I did as he suggested, wondering if I was doing it correctly. I began to feel relaxed, at peace – almost for the first time.

"Good," said Lama Kunchen. "Now you may go to bed – and remember keep your centres locked."

As I say, all this made a sort of sense to me, much to my surprise. I didn't think these monks had anything to teach me. But then, as I have also said, most of this was common sense too – they were just using fancy phrases to describe it all.

For the next two weeks I was summoned to Lama Kunchen's room in the daytime to practise energy exercises. This involved sensing the energy in people, objects and situations, and locating the energy in the chakra system. He also blindfolded me and made me stumble about to see if I could sense where he'd placed furniture. I banged my shins several times and had to stifle oaths. But over time I developed some skill at this – I just opened myself up as I had done when I was with my horses and became one with the situation. However, I seldom practised these exercises outside my lessons. I know Lama Kunchen kept saying I needed these skills to help me when I delivered the Morning Tree, but I just didn't pay proper attention.

I was busy during these weeks, so didn't see much of Norchen. He was different in some way, but he was still the only friend I had in that place, so I did take time to see him. He didn't want to talk much, and only lit up when we chatted about his life as a nomad. In an effort to cheer him up – and to get some diversion myself – I suggested we watch the enthronement procession of one of the abbots at Sera monastery. Ordinarily I wouldn't be interested in a bunch of monks and their ceremonies, but we had been given the time off and a party from Chakpori was due to leave for Lhasa that afternoon. Norchen agreed, so we joined the others – about fifty strong – escorted by a senior lama and police monks.

The streets of Lhasa were busy and full of people. Several noble families were out to pay their respects to the new abbot. Traders were everywhere, making the most of the event. About halfway to the Jokang Cathedral, Norchen stopped to bargain with a stall holder for some refreshment. A dispute arose and I had to pull Norchen away.

By now we had become separated from our group, and Norchen had no desire to catch them up. We idled away the time going down a side street, looking at the stalls and the people. The women, with their brightly coloured skirts, were pretty. But I was becoming bored with no money to buy anything (though Norchen seemed to have some), and no chance of getting to know any of the women. By now we had rejoined the main road and got mixed up in a large party of monks from Drepung.[44] They seemed in an agitated mood, and there was jostling and cursing as we forced our way through to the other side of the road. Some horns, cymbals and drums were heard, and the first of the abbot's party from Sera began making its way down the road. A low jeer went up from the Drepung monks, but the townspeople and pilgrims on our side of the road seemed happy.

"Let's go," I said to Norchen, but he pulled himself from my grasp and walked on head bowed. I followed him down another side street where he found a restaurant of sorts. He ordered two beakers of chang[45] and I joined him in a drink. And then we had two more. I think he'd run out of money by then or else he might have carried on, but as it was, this time he did agree to find the rest of our party.

When we re-emerged onto the main road there seemed to be a confrontation between the monks from Sera and Drepung. At any rate, the procession had stopped, there was some confusion, and police monks were shouting and shoving people aside. I wanted to see what was going on (in fact, I wanted to see if there was going to be a fight), but a wedge of police monks, with their long staves, were forcing the two bodies of monks apart, so it appeared that nothing would happen. I was feeling unsteady as a result of our chang, and our way ahead was blocked by onlookers, so I shouted to Norchen that we should just return to Chakpori.

When we got back there was still nothing to do. We were hungry, so we stole into the kitchen in search of food. We found some

---

[44] Drepung, along with Sera and Ganden, were the so-called Three Seats: the largest and most important monasteries in Lhasa and Tibet. There was always intense rivalry between them.
[45] Tibetan barley beer.

flatbread, but just as we were about to take it there was a shout. We turned to see a kitchen monk running after us. We raced out and up several levels until we reached a small room above the empty prayer hall. We waited, stifling our panting breath, to see if we were still being pursued. When we were sure we were safe, we started to look around. I don't know what possessed me – Norchen's strange mood, the aggression of the monks from Drepung or the chang – but I just decided to walk across this narrow beam in front of me to see if I could get to the other side. A few steps across I slipped on butter wax encrusted on the beam.[46] I caught the beam with my now mending arm, and winced in pain.

"Norchen!" I cried, swinging over the deserted hall. He quickly stretched out along the beam and grabbed the back of my robes. He pulled me with surprising strength back to the ledge. I gripped it with my two hands and hauled myself up.

"Thank you," I said, my heart beating wildly. I hadn't expected a near death experience. But before I could say more there was another shout. A police monk from below was roaring at us. We couldn't run this time – we'd been seen, and a colleague of his was rushing away to reach us. So we stayed put. The second police monk soon appeared and jabbed us with his staff.

"Get down!" he growled. He pushed us down several ladders[47] to the first police monk who was waiting outside the prayer hall. The first thing he did was club us as we covered our faces with our hands. He was shouting that he was going to report us to the Master of Chelas when suddenly he stopped. Lama Neto had appeared.

"What's going on?" he asked, barely concealing his anger.

"Honourable lama," said the police monk bowing, "these chelas were out-of-bounds in the room above the prayer hall, and we have a

---

[46] The only form of light in 1930s Tibet was butter lamps. They used a wax from yak butter to burn a flame. After years of use, residue from the butter wax would be deposited on the walls and furniture.
[47] Most Tibetan buildings did not have stairs but wooden ladders to get to different storeys. They were not wooden ladders as in the West. Rather, they were one central pole with lateral slats to climb on.

report from the head of the kitchen that they were trying to steal food."

Lama Neto, although small, was haughty. "Are you sure these were the ones stealing food?" he asked.

"We've had reports—"

"But are you sure?"

"We can't be certain—"

"You can't be certain... As for them being out-of-bounds, I'll take care of that. Now go about your duties."

"But lama..." The police monk was silenced by a withering stare from Lama Neto. "Yes, lama," he said at last, bowing stiffly.

"Follow me," snapped Lama Neto without looking at us. We traipsed after him to his room.

"Why are you drawing attention to yourself?" he said, turning on Norchen as soon as the door was closed.

Norchen prostrated himself. "Honourable lama, we were just larking about. I didn't mean—"

"If you're going to work for me, you have to be less conspicuous! If you can't follow simple instructions... And you," he said to me, his voice harsher than I'd heard it, "we can talk later. For now, I need to instruct Norchen. Leave us."

I made my way back to the main hall. I saw the party that had gone to Lhasa returning. They were talking excitedly about the stand-off between the Drepung and Sera monks. I was suddenly feeling tired and dejected.

"What is it, Thaza?" said a voice from behind.

"Lama Kunchen!" I said, spinning around. I was relieved to see him. He was studying me closely.

"Your centres are quite muddied," he said. "Come with me."

I followed him to his room. I felt calmer in his presence. We sat down and had tea. All the while he was looking at me. Eventually he said:

"Thaza, I trust that you are practising the energy exercises we are teaching you?"

127

"It's difficult. Outside this room there are so many distractions, so many people. I can't focus."

"It is precisely outside this room, as you say, that you need to practise the exercises because out there is real life. I would not be much of a medical monk if I could only pass exams and not remember what I had learnt when I was called to a patient. You need to constantly be aware of the energy first. It is more important than the words people say or the actions they take. Surely you know that someone might say honeyed words but their intention – the energy behind the words – might be completely different?"

I slumped forward.

Lama Kunchen continued, "Perhaps it's my fault. Perhaps I haven't taught you enough. Yes, Thaza, I need to teach you more." He rang his bell and asked his attendant to bring sweetmeats and more tea. "Let me teach you about handling the energy so you are more in control of what happens to you."

I was tired, and not keen to study, but I said nothing and waited for the sweetmeats.

He went over the chakras again and how they interpreted and transmitted the energy that we experience. He explained we had a choice: we could be unconscious of the energy or we could open up, assess it and take action. Again, he made me think of things or incidents and see which centre I was operating from. Again, he made me look at photographs and analyse the energy in them. He made me recall painful memories, he made me imagine unhappy futures, and then he asked me to describe how I felt, and where in my body I felt it.

"Now Thaza," he said, "instead of feeling discomfort, I want you to block the energy from interacting with you."

He made me visualise the energy as a stream, like a snake winding into me. Then he made me visualise a shield – big, black and powerful – that could block this snake from entering me anywhere. I succeeded sometimes, and instantly felt better, calmer and more balanced.

"That is one way of handling the energy, Thaza. There are other ways. If you suddenly find the energy inside you, you can see it again as a stream of energy, but see it flowing through you without it touching you." I practised that and found again I could be unaffected by what I was experiencing.

"There is a third way," he continued. "But you need to be more advanced to do that." I asked him what he meant. "It is possible to transmute the energy," he said. "But you need to have proper guidance or else you might burn yourself and cause harm to others. Far better to practise blocking the energy or letting it flow through you. If you are in any doubt about what to do, just smile at the energy and let it move on."

Then he fixed me with a serious stare I'd not seen before. "Thaza, you might not think what we've been doing is important, but it is – very important. Life is energy. We are tossed around by this energy, negative and positive. We act without thinking. Most of us are ridden by this energy and are in truth unconscious. And so life continues in this chaotic way. Think of your anger towards your grandfather, your lust with women, your desire to fight others. All of these feelings are natural and yet, at some point, we need to be able to rise above them and chart our way more clearly.

"We can still love and hate. But crucially if we no longer let the energy dominate us, we can begin to choose how we love and hate. We can, for example, begin to love more and hate less. We can begin to enjoy life more, and not create such mayhem as we go through it. Just think, if you had been able to block your grandfather's bad energy, how much more you would have enjoyed your life up till now. In that clearer state, other options would have appeared for you to have fulfilled yourself, in spite of your grandfather's obduracy. And think of when you met Sarangerel – you would have seen more clearly what was going on, you would have been less daunted by what you saw as obstacles in your way, and you may have opened a door that would have led you to a very different place from where you are now.

"I'm not saying you've done something wrong. One of the immutable laws of life is that we learn through experience. In this Age of Kali, experience usually means failure, though in the future we may learn through success instead. But this failure shows us where we are going wrong and it will lead to eventual success. Another immutable law of life is that we are always led upwards, we are always given another chance, and we will always get to experience success in the end.

"I haven't told you all this just so that you can live your life more productively in the future. I've also told you this because you are about to embark on a difficult journey. You will need all your wits about you. By telling you about energy, helping you sense and control it, you will be able to make better decisions and increase your chances of success – a success that will help all of mankind."

By now it was dark. The attendant had lit some butter lamps, and we had missed the evening service. I hadn't even noticed the attendant or heard the conches calling us to prayer. Our tea had long grown cold. We sat in silence for some while. Suddenly I felt a great burst of happiness. I saw Lama Kunchen bathed in this brilliant yet soft white light. A white light that sparkled and cleaned the energy in my system. A white light that put to rest any doubts or unhappiness in me. A white light that healed and made me feel one with something greater.

"You may go, Thaza," he said. A huge, expanding feeling filled my heart centre, and I left.

The Potala

I started practising the energy exercises Lama Kunchen was teaching me. I began to see so much more. I could see that Norchen was in his base chakra a lot of the time. Concern with survival, Lama Kunchen said. He certainly was unhappy – I didn't know why.

I saw there was a great difference between the lamas in the monastery. Some were truly peaceful and in their heart centres. But many were in their solar plexus or base centres. That surprised me. Lama Kunchen laughed when I asked him about it. He said that those lamas were concerned with status and gaining power over others. I was not to judge them harshly; although they might not be spiritually evolved, they were gaining experience and they were learning.

I saw that most of the monks were in their lower centres. Again, Lama Kunchen told me not to judge them harshly. They were having useful lives as monks, and no-one can reach the top of the ladder without starting at the bottom rung. He added that I was in my lower centres most of the time too.

I even saw that the tsampa we were eating was happy – I know that sounds odd, but that was the message I got. I wasn't happy eating it, but that dull, boring stuff felt right. I suppose this was because it was grown and cooked by spiritually content people (unlike the tsampa at Yerlang which is definitely cooked by unhappy people).

Lama Kunchen kept reminding me that none of this was for my diversion; rather, it was deadly serious training for when I took the Morning Tree to India. Dark forces were after it, and although he felt we were one step ahead of them, he could never be quite sure. If I could perceive energy and people more clearly, I would be better able to carry out my task. I understood what he was saying, but surely I'd recognise a cut-throat when I saw one.

Although I was opening up, I still had some doubts. Surely there was more to it? I couldn't be gaining secret knowledge this easily? Lama Kunchen put me right.

"Thaza," he said, "humans have many more abilities than they are aware of. But just because they don't currently use them doesn't mean that they are difficult to acquire. Think of your five senses. Do you have to 'try' to see or smell or taste? No, these happen naturally. So it is with these higher abilities. One day it will be as natural for people to sense energy, or communicate telepathically, as it is for you to feel the warmth of your tea cup as you hold it or experience the taste of the tea as you drink it. Under my guidance, you are becoming many years in advance of the human race. But one day everyone will be like you, and a great deal more."

Despite all my time with Lama Kunchen, I still wanted to return home, marry Sarangerel and prosper. But I was becoming more interested in what Lama Kunchen was teaching me. And I was feeling increasingly good in his presence. Even Jigme, who sometimes helped with the energy exercises, was less irritating. Then, joy of joys, my martial arts training started again.

Mingyar was distant at first. He still hadn't forgiven me for letting him down. He was also harder. I sometimes thought he was deliberately trying to break more bones. But then I could be harder in return. Yes, I was bruised and always ached somewhere. But I derived genuine pleasure from learning what Mingyar had to teach me. And I always felt calmer after a session in that airless room below ground.

Even Norchen began to cheer up. He had a new kite – where from, I don't know – and we had a good time flying it from the rooftops. He entered a debating competition for chelas and won. I hadn't realised he was so knowledgeable in the scriptures. I didn't understand half of what he said, but everyone reckoned he'd be a lama in a few years.

Then one afternoon Norchen grabbed me excitedly and told me to follow him. We went to Lama Neto's room. Inside was a series of low tables laden with dishes filled with hot food. Lama Neto was there. He bade us to sit down and eat whatever we liked. I couldn't believe my eyes. There was actually some meat – yak, as it turned out. Lama Neto waved away my astonished look and, after a moment's hesitation, Norchen and I dug in. We both went for the meat. It was delicious.

I didn't dare ask where the meat came from – I'd thought it was strictly forbidden – but in that moment I didn't care. Norchen explained that his master, Lama Neto, had laid on the feast as a reward for winning the debating competition. Seeing Norchen so happy, and thinking he might one day be a lama, I reckoned that his life was not so bad after all.

Lama Neto was pleasant, making jokes and conversation. He was very nice to me, saying how much Norchen appreciated my friendship, and how well I must be doing to be studying at Chakpori. He asked me many questions about my family and life back home. He too had an appreciation of herding and riding. He even said how much he missed horses, and he was knowledgeable about them as well.

We had chang to drink too – something else I'd thought was forbidden – and I began to feel warm and fuzzy.

"So Thaza," said Lama Neto, "how long are you to remain with us?"

"I don't know – until Lama Kunchen says I can go," I replied.

"Ah yes, Lama Kunchen. A great man. How do you find him?"

"Very honourable."

Lama Neto gave a big smile. "Oh, I remember, there was something I wanted to ask you." He reached for a piece of paper. It was a drawing of a plant with writing. "This plant – what is it used for?"

I didn't recognise the plant, and couldn't read the writing. "I don't know," I said.

"You don't? Oh what a shame. I thought you were studying herbs and medicine."

"Among other things."

"I see. Not to worry. I'll ask someone else. Please, have some more to eat."

That meal was one of the best I have ever eaten. I don't know where the food came from, or even if it was allowed. I knew that Lama Neto was rich – he had silk underclothes, many gold objects in his room, and I knew that he gave Norchen money. Maybe the rules were different for rich lamas. That afternoon I didn't care. And that evening, with my belly fuller than a goat's in high summer, I was certainly content.

One morning, some days later, I was sent for by Lama Kunchen. When I arrived in his room, he was standing up and had a leather bag in his hand.

"Thaza," he said, "we are going to do some more energy work, but not here. Let me look at you." He rearranged my robes (I never could get the hang of them) and ran his hand across my head. "Hmm, it needs shaving but there's no time. You'll have to do."

I followed him down to the main reception area and then, to my surprise, out of the monastery.

"Where are we going?"

"To the Potala."

My heart missed a beat. Although I had seen it every day from the monastery, and although the building was now as familiar a sight as a yurt, I had never been inside it.

"Why?"

"I told you, energy work."

We climbed down the many steps to the plain below. We crossed the chorten in front of the Western Gate, two simple monks amongst the traders, villagers and government officials, and made our way towards the Potala which rose like a giant being in front of us. We didn't go in through the main entrance but a side one which I was told later was reserved for senior lamas. We climbed up some steps and went through a door near the base of the Potala. Despite his age, Lama Kunchen was surprisingly fit and took the steps at as fast a pace as me. Once inside, we entered a side chapel where Lama Kunchen bowed in front of a Buddha. We then made our way up several stairs to a long corridor. A party, led by a man in a dark costume with a fur collar and fur hat, was approaching from the other direction. As soon as the man saw us, he bowed and said:

"His Excellency Kunsangtse[48] recognises the Honourable Lama Kunchen and gives way." With that his party pressed themselves to the wall.

"Lama Kunchen recognises His Excellency Kunsangtse and prays that the Buddha guides him for the benefit of all," replied Lama Kunchen as we passed them.

"Lama," called the man as we went by, "when the rain falls the barley drinks. Since you are here, could I ask your advice?" The two men went a little way down the corridor and started talking. I was behind Lama Kunchen and couldn't catch what they were saying. Eventually they bowed to each other and Lama Kunchen moved on. I hurried behind.

We came to a big hall. Monks and officials were going about their business. Some bowed to Lama Kunchen. No-one questioned our presence. Lama Kunchen then turned and we started climbing down again. At last we came to a large darkened hall – sometime before we reached it my pulse quickened. I could smell horses. When we got there I could hear their whinnying as well.

"These horses are used by the officials in the Potala to go about their business," said Lama Kunchen, as our eyes grew accustomed to the low level of light. "But a number are sick. I have herbs here to cure them, but first I would like you to find out what ails them."

I needed no urging. I'd already sensed a sadness, and wanted to find out more. I felt into the energy and followed it to a horse standing by the far wall. It was a revelation. When I'd been with my horses at home I'd felt certain things, but now it was as if we were having a

---

[48] Someone of this name was a cabinet minister at the time.

conversation together. I immediately had a picture of its hooves and pain. I made my way to the horse. I put out good energy from my heart centre and then put out my hand. The horse whinnied quietly as I rubbed its nose. I then picked up its legs and felt its hooves. The horse shuddered but didn't back away. Its hooves were inflamed. I had an image of bad hay and felt a pain in its stomach.

"Lama," I said, "this horse's hooves are inflamed. It is in pain whenever it walks. It comes from its food which is bad and which has upset its stomach."

Lama Kunchen nodded and then looked into his sack. He pulled out some herbs and began to administer them to the horse.

"Please check the other horses," he said.

I did so. It was obvious that many had been affected by the rotten feed. The horses also made clear to me that they wanted to be in the open air during the day. I passed this on to Lama Kunchen. As I say, it was a revelation. I was picking up messages from the horses as clearly as if they had been talking to me. I hadn't realised how beneficial my energy exercises had been.

When we left, Lama Kunchen told the attendants looking after the horses to change their feed and to let the horses out during the day in the pasture to the north of the Potala. I was reluctant to leave, and felt the horses were reluctant for me to go, but I followed Lama Kunchen back up to the halls above.

"Thaza," he said, when we reached the upper levels, "you have done well. I have one more piece of business to transact here. Please take my bag and follow me."

We went through more halls, past more chapels and rooms full of officials, to a quiet, airy set of apartments somewhere near the top of the building. We entered a room filled with sunlight. Three other lamas were already seated on cushions.

"Ah, Pemba," said one of the lamas, "we've been waiting for you." Lama Kunchen sat on the fourth cushion.

"Your attendant?" asked the lama.

"He is with me," said Lama Kunchen, not asking me to leave. The other lamas accepted his word without demur.

I hung back by the wall. The four lamas started a prayer chant – first one, then another, then a third, then all four. Suddenly they stopped. Then one began intoning what I took to be another prayer. Eventually he was silent. All four shut their eyes. I could see dust particles dancing in the sunshine coming through the window and falling on the meditating monks. A great harmony filled the room – I could feel it filling my heart centre. These four men appeared to be truly at peace with themselves and each other. This peace continued for some time until, as if on cue, they opened their eyes. Then one of the lamas spoke.

"Is everything in hand?"

Lama Kunchen inclined his head.

"And you are satisfied?" asked another.

"There is always a risk," said Lama Kunchen, "but I feel now our chances of success are greater."

There was a pause while all four were silent.

"I hear you met Kunsangtse this morning," said one of the lamas. "What did you tell him?"

"What I had to," sighed Lama Kunchen. "That we should continue negotiations with the Chinese."

"And they'll repay us through invasion."

The four lamas fell silent again. You could feel the sadness and resignation in the room. Then again, as if on cue, they sat up, said something in a language that wasn't Tibetan, and rose to leave.

I followed Lama Kunchen out. Without a word he led me to the western side of the building. Here there were what looked like giant chortens. One was huge – at least ten times my height – and covered with gold. There were large jars around it. I never thought the world contained such treasures. Its value was incalculable. As we approached it, a monk moved to block our way. Then he recognised Lama Kunchen and bowed to let us pass. Lama Kunchen sat in meditation in front of the chorten for some minutes. I waited behind him. Then he rose and I followed him, this time out of the building. We made our way back to Chakpori.[49]

"Don't tell anyone what went on," he said.

The next few weeks were spent visiting Lama Kunchen almost every day. We would practise energy exercises and he told me something about his secret order. Apparently, I had been very fortunate to witness one of their meetings in the Potala. I had come to like this old man; I wish he had been my grandfather. But Lama Kunchen was often called away on business, so sometimes our meetings were cancelled. On one of these days Norchen, looking flushed, found me and pulled me to one side.

"Thaza," he said, "do you want to ride a horse?"

"What do you mean?" I asked.

"Follow me!"

He led me out of the monastery to the plain below. A chilly wind was blowing and the sky was darkening. Stamping their hooves in the cold were three horses being held by shivering attendants. I acquainted myself with the horses, still not sure what was happening.

"What's going on?" I asked above the wind.

"Wait and see!" Norchen replied. The horses were impatient, as was I, to get moving to keep warm.

Eventually, Lama Neto emerged from the monastery. Taking the horse with the most elaborate saddle he motioned us to mount. It was so good to be on a horse again, despite the weather. We set off at a trot. People parted for us as we went down the streets, making way for a high lama and his two attendants. I didn't pay attention to where we were going; I was just enjoying the ride. We trotted across town and at length drew up outside another monastery. We dismounted, led our horses inside and handed them to waiting attendants. They all

---

[49] Thaza appears to be describing the mausoleums of previous Dalai Lamas. The Fifth Dalai Lama onwards are buried in tombs kept in the western part of the Potala. Each Dalai Lama accumulated gold and other treasures during his lifetime for his mausoleum. It appears that Lama Kunchen went to meditate at the tomb of one of the previous Dalai Lamas.

bowed deeply to Lama Neto. We followed Lama Neto into a great hall where a group of senior lamas were waiting for him.

"Welcome, honourable Lama Neto," said a man in gorgeous robes and a hat.

"Thank you, your holiness," replied Lama Neto. "We are grateful for your hospitality."

These pleasantries continued for a while before we went off to a smaller room where we were given refreshments. Lama Neto and the other lamas then withdrew into an inner room.

"Where are we?" I whispered.

"Tengyeling monastery,"[50] replied Norchen. "When I heard we were going to ride here, I asked Lama Neto if you could come along."

"Thank you," I said, "I appreciate it." But as I spoke, I felt uneasy. I started to scan the energy. It felt underhand, wrong. I focussed on the abbot I had seen. He was black energetically, but in a sophisticated way, and flaring from his solar plexus. I focussed on Norchen. He seemed innocent. I didn't understand what was going on.

Eventually Lama Neto reappeared with the others. They were laughing and in good humour.

"Come Norchen, come Thaza," said Lama Neto, "let us eat." He led the way to another room where food was laid out. He and the other lamas filled their bowls first, then Norchen and I followed. No meat, and no chang, but still very good food, including flatbread and cheese. I was happy too. Another welcome relief from tsampa.

---

[50] Tengyeling monastery was not large but it was exclusive. Its monks tended to come from Amdo, in the east of Tibet, on the borders of China. Thaza says that Norchen and Lama Neto came from the east as well. Tengyeling was one of only seven monasteries in Tibet whose abbot was a tulku (a recognised incarnation) and eligible to be the Regent during a Dalai Lama's minority before he reached 18 years of age. A previous head, who was the Regent during the Thirteenth Dalai Lama's minority, was suspected of trying to poison the young Dalai Lama. He was dismissed and died shortly afterwards. Thereafter, Tengyeling opposed the Thirteenth Dalai Lama and even fought with Chinese soldiers against their countrymen during the uprising against the Chinese occupation of Lhasa in 1912.

Eventually, the lamas from Tengyeling left and we were alone. I thought we would go too, but Lama Neto offered us more food. I didn't need a second invitation. I filled my bowl again.

"Do you like the food?" Lama Neto asked.

I nodded.

"And the ride here?"

I told him it was a treat.

"I am glad you are here Thaza," said Lama Neto. "There are so few people nowadays one can trust. Norchen has always spoken highly of you."

I had finished eating by now and again thought we would go. But Lama Neto seemed keen to linger.

"These are difficult times Thaza," he continued. "Tibet is a small country, the world is a big place. We need to be certain who our friends are. Mongolia, of course, is a loyal friend, but we need other friends if we are to survive. The Russians are godless, the English untrustworthy, but the Chinese – they are like our brothers. Have you seen the Sakyamuni statue in the Jokang Cathedral? A present from the Chinese and now the most sacred object in Tibet. We can live in harmony with our Chinese neighbours; they can guarantee our way of life against the outside world. They have been the only foreign power to show a consistent interest in us. And yet most people here think the Chinese are our enemies. From the Peak[51] downwards, all think we should resist our brothers. There are only a few of us who see the folly of this way."

I said nothing. Lama Kunchen had told me something quite different. The energy was uneasy.

"Perhaps you don't understand what I'm saying," carried on Lama Neto, "and perhaps I shouldn't say so much, but I feel I am among friends." He smiled at me. "But I needn't trouble you with politics. Have you eaten enough? Good. Well, maybe we should go."

With that at last we did make a move. I kept my eyes on the floor. But before we got to the door, Lama Neto stopped and said:

---

[51] The Peak is the usual Tibetan term for the Potala.

"Do you remember you promised you would help me one day? There is something you could do for me. It's nothing much, but I think it would be a great help."

I felt a lurch in my solar plexus.

"Could you tell me Lama Kunchen's movements, especially when he visits the Potala or another monastery? As I said, it's nothing much…"

"Lama Kunchen?" I replied, slowly looking up. "But he never tells me what he's going to do. I don't know where he goes."

"But you accompanied him to the Potala recently, did you not? What happened?"

I looked at Norchen; had he told Lama Neto I'd gone? Norchen was looking absent.

"We tended to some sick horses," I said, dismayed that I'd spoken about something I'd promised not to reveal.

"And you met no-one?"

"Some people. But I don't know who they were or what they said…"

Lama Neto looked at me closely. "Thaza, listen: we're friends, aren't we? I have looked after you, helped you. I would like to continue helping you, giving you good things like the food today. All I ask is that you tell me what your master is doing."

I was silent.

"You wouldn't want me to get angry? Norchen would certainly suffer if I were angry."

The tone of Lama Neto's voice hadn't changed but I could see now the energy behind it. It was black. Very black. A chill went through me.

I stayed silent. Lama Neto was regarding me. Like his voice, his physical manner hadn't altered – he still looked to all the world a high lama – but I could see now how dark was the place he was coming from.

Lama Neto was expecting a reply. I didn't know what to do. I felt myself nod my head slowly.

141

"Do we understand each other, Thaza?"

I nodded again. I knew now I wanted to cut his throat, but I had to get out of there, and making a scene I guessed wouldn't help.

I was glad to get outside. Even though the winter wind cut through me, it was still warmer than the icy feeling coming from Lama Neto. Our horses were retrieved and we rode back to Chakpori. I kept as far apart from Lama Neto as I could. I scanned him energetically and was shocked to see a large, black snake coiled around his solar plexus. I was in an unexpected bind. I certainly didn't want Norchen to suffer. But I didn't now want to break my oaths to Lama Kunchen. I thought religion was supposed to comfort, but here I was being tortured by a clash between two lamas. What was going on?

I still didn't know what to do when I was summoned to Lama Kunchen's room the following evening. Jigme was there as well. Lama Kunchen picked up my disquiet immediately.

"Thaza, is something bothering you?"

"Lama, I...." and I told him everything. About how Lama Neto had befriended me, given me treats, had now asked me to spy on Lama Kunchen in return, and if I didn't, Norchen would likely suffer. I added that I'd begun to see how dark he really was.

Jigme grimaced. "Argh, he thinks he's so clever, Lama Neto, but in fact he is so obvious," he said.

"He is to us," said Lama Kunchen, "but to most people he is suave and persuasive. Thaza has done well to assess him energetically rather than just on his words and external appearance."

"You mean, you know about him?" I interjected.

"Yes, Thaza," said Lama Kunchen. "I told you about how the dark want to destroy the Morning Tree? Well, it appears that Lama Neto is one of them."

"He wants to destroy your book?"

"Yes."

"And he knows you have it?" Lama Kunchen inclined his head. "And that I'm to take it for you to India?"

142

"We hope not. Not unless you've told him something you shouldn't."

"I've told him nothing!" Well, nothing about the Morning Tree. "But... but if you know who he is, why don't you do something? Why have you let me befriend him?"

"Why have we let you befriend him? You have free will, Thaza; we can't circumscribe your every move. We need to see what decisions you make, for your decisions tell us more about you than your words."

"But what if I told him everything? About your book, what you want me to do with it?"

"But you haven't. And in not telling him you have proved yourself to us once more."

"But what if I had?"

Jigme broke in. "If you had, then we would have given you a different book to deliver, one which wouldn't have mattered if Lama Neto had captured it."

I was taken aback. I was being played like an ignorant goat about to be slaughtered! I felt a familiar surge of anger in me. "But what if I had told him, and you didn't know about it?" I persisted.

Lama Kunchen spread his hands. "Then the dark would have won. But you didn't tell him Thaza, and you didn't because you have a spark in you for the truth that we would fan into a flame."

I was silent for a moment, letting my anger flow through me. It still didn't make sense. "Well, if you know about him, why don't you stop him?"

"First of all, we don't have any concrete evidence against him," said Lama Kunchen. "And if we stop him, another will take his place. It might take us some time to identify his successor. It is far better to know whom we are dealing with and ensure he does not prevent us doing our work."

Lama Kunchen could see I still wasn't satisfied. "You have to remember Thaza that we judge people not by worldly standards but spiritual ones," he said. "Lama Neto has free will too. He has chosen the dark side. As I respect your free will, so I respect his. We are not of the dark, but we recognise that the dark has an important role to play. The dark exists to help people towards the light. If Jigme and I were not challenged by the dark – as we are by Lama Neto and others – then we would not have the opportunity to make decisions to show that we are on the light path. If you attack me, for example, I can retaliate or let it pass. If I retaliate, then I show I am at a certain level of evolution. If I let it pass, then I show I am at a higher stage of evolution. The dark is an important element in helping us all move forward."

"You mean, people like Lama Neto are good?"

"He is not good as we judge it, but he is necessary. The dark helps us see the light. The important thing now is not to let the dark win again. They won in Atlantean times, and mankind has had difficulties ever since. Now there is an opportunity to regain the higher consciousness humanity once had – in fact, to exceed what was ever present in the past. The dark still prefer we fail again, for then they enjoy another period of hegemony. If they get hold of the Morning Tree, they have the chance to stop mankind moving forward. That is why your task is so vital. But, unlike the dark, who would extinguish us if they could, we cannot extinguish them – in fact, we cannot even hate them – for if we do we become like them. So we must tolerate their existence."

"So… to help us move to the light, as you put it, people like Lama Neto are allowed to harm us and others?" I said.

"Don't forget karma," replied Lama Kunchen. "People who harm others have to repay their debts. Look at you with your grandfather. You are making amends by helping us. You were 'dark' if you like, but it has helped you become light. One day Lama Neto will have to make amends too. He will be quite light at this rate."

"But all this pain and suffering? It doesn't seem worth it. I'd much rather my father had stayed alive and that I'd never met my grandfather! I wouldn't have committed my crime then."

"You still need to be tested, Thaza, to know where you stand on the path of spiritual evolution. You might not have killed your

144

grandfather, but problems would still have been sent your way so your response could show how light or dark you are. But in one sense you are right: as mankind evolves, as higher light comes into the planet, so the need for so much suffering will diminish. But you will never escape tests. However high you go, you will still be tested."

None of this was helping me with my immediate predicament. I asked Lama Kunchen what I should do.

"You have rejected Lama Neto? Then, for the sake of Norchen, tell him what you know."

"But won't that endanger you?"

"I'll make sure you know nothing that will endanger me. Besides, if you don't tell him anything, you might endanger yourself."

"Shall I," – an idea had occurred to me which I was suddenly eager to share – "shall I tell him something that will lead him onto the wrong scent?"

"No Thaza," laughed Lama Kunchen, "we should always try to tell the truth. If you start to mislead him, and he begins to suspect what you are doing, then you could well endanger yourself and Norchen."

I had to accept his advice but still couldn't see why Lama Kunchen didn't just despatch Lama Neto to his next life. But then Lama Kunchen was the most extraordinary man I'd ever met. I couldn't match his equanimity or forgiveness, and normally I wouldn't have respected it in a man, but he was different.

So, I was to go along with Lama Neto's plan, even though I didn't want to. I hoped to avoid him, but the very next day there he was after the morning service asking me, in that rich voice of his, to follow him. We went to his room where he asked me what Lama Kunchen's plans were.

"Lama Kunchen will not be seeing me today; he told me so yesterday evening. I don't know where he will be."

"Thank you Thaza," said Lama Neto. "I know he has business today with the abbot. Keep telling the truth. You and Norchen won't regret it."

What was it about his voice? So soothing but really so threatening. At that moment I felt into his energy. It turned my stomach. And to think only a few weeks before I wouldn't have noticed any of this. I left his room, disgusted at my powerlessness, and shocked at what I was discovering.

The Potala Again

It was hailing. My robe wrapped round me, I was hauling water from the well when the monk in charge came up and, with obvious irritation, gestured to me to follow the novice by his side. The novice pulled away from the water carrying party and told me in his squeaky voice above the drumming of the hail that Lama Kunchen wanted to see me immediately. I ran back up the path into the monastery.

"We're going to the Potala," said Lama Kunchen, when I entered his room. My face must have lit up for he continued, "Don't look so happy, we're not going to tend to the horses. I have other business."

He seemed sombre, so I made no comment. Lama Kunchen looked me over, said nothing, and turned to go. I wanted to ask why I was needed but kept my counsel. Whatever it was, it was better than carrying water.

We left the monastery by the same path as the water carrying party, crossed over the chorten, passed the village of Sho and went up the side path reserved for senior lamas into the Potala. There were few people about. The bad weather had cleared the streets, and I for one was getting stung and soaked by the hail. Lama Kunchen was giving no notice to the weather however, so I attempted to do the same.

We entered the Potala, shook our robes and waited for our eyes to become accustomed to the darker interior. Lama Kunchen then led the way to the upper floors. It is impossible to convey how large and rich the Potala is. I've heard there are buildings that reach to the sky in America, but even they can't be as big as the Potala. It truly is a wonder. Eventually we reached a gold door with a monk attendant standing outside it. He bowed when he saw Lama Kunchen and stepped back so we could go through. We made our way into a small but well furnished room. Lama Kunchen sat down on some cushions while I stood behind him.

"The rain falls as it must, giving life to some and destruction to others," he said. "We must accept the rain for what it is."

I didn't know what he was talking about, but he did sound sad.

Just then the door opened and the three lamas he had met before came in, each with a serious expression on their face. They looked at me, and then at Lama Kunchen, who simply said, "He is with me."

The three lamas sat down. Lama Kunchen reached into his robe and took out a small bronze object I didn't know he'd been carrying. He handed it to one of the lamas who looked at it closely, then nodded towards Lama Kunchen in acknowledgement of something, and put it in his robe. There was a heavy silence for a few minutes before they started talking.

"The State Oracle[52] has told the Dalai Lama that the storm clouds from the East are gathering faster than predicted," said one.

"We need to move more quickly than planned," said another.

"Are you ready Pemba?" asked the third.

Lama Kunchen considered the other three lamas. "I too have received intelligence that the danger is greater than perceived. I haven't told Thaza," – I jumped: what had this to do with me? – "but he is here now. I had hoped to have more time with him, but if he has to leave sooner than planned, so be it."

The three lamas looked at me. Why was I spooked by three old men? I could break all three without even using the techniques that Mingyar was teaching me. Yet these ancient, seemingly harmless monks unnerved me.

"Is this still the right course of action?" asked one of the lamas.

---

[52] The State Oracle at Nechung was regularly consulted on matters of state by the Dalai Lama and the Tibetan government. Its pronouncements were always followed.

"Yes," replied Lama Kunchen. "We must honour our commitment to pass the knowledge on. We must take it out of Tibet to ensure it is given to mankind at a later date. We don't want the treasures we have to die with us; they must live with others. We must continue what we have planned."

"But taking this knowledge out of our hands, giving it to this… this man… what if he doesn't succeed?"

"Then at best we are no worse off than if we don't try. At worst, the dark will have got hold of the knowledge they have been seeking for centuries."

"And then Pemba?"

"The dark always has a chance to win. But so do we. What if Thaza is successful? Then everything we've hoped for can unfold and the dark will be in retreat."

There was silence for a while. At last one of the lamas spoke. "I agree with Pemba. We must try. And we must be hopeful. The light is building. It might not seem so, but we can succeed."

The other two lamas said nothing.

"So we're agreed. Pemba is to continue with his plan. We will hold a special service of protection and power to help Thaza succeed in his mission. Thank you for your time."

The other lamas left. Lama Kunchen was calm and relaxed. "Sit down, Thaza. You will have gathered from that meeting that you are to leave us soon."

Strange to say, I was ambivalent. I so wanted to return home, but I was not so keen now to leave Lama Kunchen.

"Let me give you some more information about your journey," he continued. "As you know, you are to transport the Morning Tree out of Tibet. You will take it to India. We will roll up the pages and put them in watertight containers, and we will wrap the wooden cover separately. It will not then look like a book to any cursory inspection. We will also give you silks, handicrafts and some religious artefacts – nothing too valuable – as your goods which people will assume you are taking to India to trade. Once you have delivered the Morning Tree, you can return home."

"But lama," I said, "I will need horses, provisions, money."

"Yes Thaza, we will give you those. And yaks to carry your goods."

"I'll need someone to help me too."

"We can arrange that as well."

It all seemed feasible. I would have what I needed. Thankfully, winter would end soon, so my journey would be taken in the summer months. But where in India was I to go? And who was I to give the Morning Tree to?

"I will tell you more later," said Lama Kunchen. "For now, have the idea that your journey will begin soon."

We left the room and made our way out of the Potala. It had stopped hailing, but it was still overcast, and a vicious wind cut through our robes. There were more people about now. My head was down and I was busy thinking about everything that I'd been told. If I hadn't been, I might have been able to act sooner and save Lama Kunchen.

As it was, we were pushing our way through a small crowd when I suddenly felt my third eye throb and the hairs on the back of my head rise. At the same time, my stomach turned over. I looked up and saw a hooded figure moving quickly towards us. The figure raised his right arm and there was the glint of a knife. Immediately I grabbed Lama Kunchen's robes and jerked him backwards. The hooded man plunged the knife into the retreating Lama Kunchen who collapsed into my arms. The man moved forward to strike again, but I dropped Lama Kunchen, grabbed the man's arm, and in one move cracked his forearm. He cried in pain and dropped the knife. I was about to seize him when I was clubbed by another man I hadn't noticed. I recovered my balance and smashed my elbow into the second man's chin. Both took off in different directions as people around us started shouting and gesticulating. I spun round to check there were no more assassins. Sensing the danger had passed, I rushed to Lama Kunchen's side.

He was bleeding. There was a dark, warm stain on his maroon robes around his chest. Shouting to the people who had gathered that the lama had been injured, I asked for help carrying him to Chakpori. A dozen rough hands lifted him and followed me at a trot to the base of the Iron Mountain. Lama Kunchen was conscious. He was clearly in pain, but was that a half smile on his face? We went up the hill as fast as we could. When we got to the main gate I shouted to the startled doorkeeper that Lama Kunchen was wounded and he was to fetch Lama Jigme at once.

There was commotion inside. Horrified monks rushing to look at Lama Kunchen, then at me, and wondering. All the while something was nagging at the back of my mind. That second man – the one who prevented me from catching the assassin – I'd seen him somewhere before. Then it came to me. It was the man at the Chinese jewellers that I'd visited with Norchen. Not the jeweller, Mr Hu, but his Tibetan assistant.

At last Jigme arrived. He was shocked but calm. Detailing some monks to carry Lama Kunchen, he led them to the lama's room. I followed but was barred entry. I was furious.

"The lama needs my protection!" I shouted. But Jigme just shut the door in my face. I spun round to see the abbot and some more lamas arriving.

"Out of my way, son," said the abbot.

"I know who did it!" I cried. But the party paid no attention and went into Lama Kunchen's room.

I stayed outside Lama Kunchen's room until Mingyar came. He took hold of my arm and propelled me away. We went to the kitchen for refreshment. Neither of us spoke; the enormity of the crime was still sinking in. Who would want to kill a senior lama? Who would want to kill Lama Kunchen? And in a religious country like Tibet where the taking of life – any life, even an animal's – was viewed with horror? Then I remembered what Lama Kunchen had said at our first meeting: that people wanted to kill him. It had to be the dark! It had to be Lama Neto! I suddenly shuddered and felt sick. These were the people I had to deal with when I took the Morning Tree to India. My martial arts lessons, the energy exercises, they weren't just mildly useful diversions – they were deadly serious after all.

Just then an agitated novice came and told me that Lama Kunchen wanted to see me. He was still alive then, but for how long? I raced to his room, knocking down some chelas in the narrow corridors. As I approached, I saw Lama Neto leave Lama Kunchen's room. I banged into him too, earning a nasty look, and rushed in. Lama Kunchen was sitting up, with Jigme by his side. Jigme glared at me for my noisy entrance.

"Lama!" I cried. "Are you all right?"

"My lung is punctured. I'll need an operation and rest. But I will live," he said weakly.

I saw he had a dressing on his chest and smelt herbal poultices. He looked drawn and was breathing fitfully.

"I have to thank you, Thaza," Lama Kunchen continued. "You saved my life."

"Lama, I was inattentive. I noticed the assassin too late."

"You noticed in time. If you hadn't pulled me back, the stabbing would have been fatal."

"What did you notice?" asked Jigme.

"I felt bad energy. It was very strong. That's what made me look up. It was then that I saw this hooded figure with a knife. I just knew he was going to attack Lama Kunchen, so I pulled him backwards."

Jigme nodded. "You did well Thaza."

"I would have caught the assassin too," I said, "but another man prevented me. But lama, I know who that other man was!" I told them about my visit with Norchen to the jewellers, and our meeting with Mr Hu and his assistant. "It was the assistant!"

Jigme looked angry. "Are you sure, Thaza?"

"Yes!"

"We knew about Mr Hu but you wouldn't let us act!" said Jigme to Lama Kunchen. "I will go and deal with it!" With that he stalked out of the room.

152

"Jigme is so angry," said Lama Kunchen, when the young lama had left. "But I am still alive. All is well."

"But you knew about Mr Hu?" I asked. "Then why didn't you act?"

"What did we know? That he was a Chinese agent? So is practically every Chinese person in Lhasa. That he was working for the dark? Yes, and he's not the only one. But if we had expelled him from Lhasa, another agent would have been sent. We would only have angered the Chinese government further."

"But I went to Mr Hu's with Norchen. I'm sure Norchen is innocent. But his master is dark! Why did you let him visit you just now? Why don't you arrest him?"

"I've tried to explain before, Thaza. If we arrest Lama Neto, he will know that we know he is dark – we will have lost a valuable advantage. If we arrest him, his influential friends will make our life difficult. It is far better not to arouse his suspicions, to watch him, and to make sure he causes no real harm."

"But he nearly killed you!"

"But he didn't. You saved me."

"I..." then it hit me. "Lama, did you know someone was going to try to kill you today?"

Lama Kunchen looked thoughtful and paused before replying. "I could sense a great black light." He sounded frail. "It made me feel sick. But I also knew there was a probability all would be well."

"You mean, you thought I would be able to sense the danger too? What if I hadn't?"

He shut his eyes. "I need rest now, Thaza. Please leave me. We can talk later."

The whole monastery was abuzz with the news of the attempt on Lama Kunchen's life. The fact that I had saved him wasn't widely known, just that I had been with him at the time. Most wore worried looks. A few foolish ones either thought the affair was overblown or were ready to march to the village of Sho to take their revenge. More than once during the evening meal the proctors had to beat monks caught whispering to each other. No-one mentioned that the Chinese were behind the attempted assassination. Lama Neto looked as concerned as his colleagues, but he was just like a snake camouflaged in the grass. Eventually, the abbot had to make a special announcement to calm things down. This didn't work, of course, and the gossip continued.

Norchen was like everyone else: agog at what had happened. He showed no signs of knowing more than the general facts. I was convinced he was innocent. I didn't tell him about Mr Hu's Tibetan assistant – I didn't tell anyone – but I just knew Lama Neto was involved.

I wasn't sent for the next day, nor the day after that, and I couldn't find Jigme. A rumour ran round that Lama Kunchen had died, but the deputy abbot assured everyone he hadn't. Then I was cornered by Lama Neto. He wore a concerned smile and almost bowed to me.

"Ah Thaza," he said, "you were with Lama Kunchen at the fateful moment were you not? I understand you saved his life by beating off three assailants."

"Just two," I replied.

"Two, I see. But what were you doing outside the monastery?"

"We'd been to the Potala."

"Who did you see there?"

"Monks."

"You know what I mean."

"I don't know their names."

He frowned. "But why would anyone want to kill a lama, and one as respected as your master? They say it was people from the village of Sho."

"I don't know that it was."

"Really? Did you catch sight of the attackers?"

"A bit."

His eyes narrowed. "Have you told the authorities?"

"Sort of."

"Speak plainly! This is a grave matter!"

154

I felt like hitting the man, but knew Lama Kunchen wouldn't want me to, so I stayed silent.

"Thaza, I've been good to you haven't I?" Lama Neto continued. "This is a serious affair. There is interest in it from the highest quarters. You wouldn't want any suspicion falling on you, would you?"

"What? Lama Kunchen knows what happened!"

"But it was a confused situation. A man's recollection can be faulty."

"Lama Kunchen will testify to what occurred!"

"If he's well enough… or alive."

"He'll live," I growled.

"It's a serious wound Thaza, I've seen it. If he dies, his testimony won't matter. Finding the killer will. I really don't think the authorities know who they are after. But they'll want to bring someone to justice, to reassure the population that everything is under control. Finding someone – anyone – will be more important than finding the true culprit. And you are, after all, a foreigner who arrived here in suspicious circumstances who was with Lama Kunchen at the time."

"But I saved him!"

"I know, Thaza. But in these difficult times, all sorts of accusations can be made."

I was too angry to speak.

"Make sure you have the right friends," he concluded before turning to go. I stayed rooted to the spot until he left.

I had to see Lama Kunchen. I hadn't been summoned, but this was an emergency. I went to his room. His attendant barred me entry, so I started pleading with him. In a moment, Jigme's head appeared around the door.

"What are you doing here Thaza?"

"I have to see the lama!"

"He needs rest."

"I need to see him! I can't say why out here!" I heard a mumble from within and Jigme put his head back inside. A moment later he opened the door and I entered.

155

Lama Kunchen was lying on a mattress. He looked pale, but I could sense his spirit was strong. Jigme helped him sit up.

"What is it, Thaza?" Lama Kunchen asked.

I recounted my conversation with Lama Neto and how he had threatened me. Jigme was cross, but Lama Kunchen merely sighed.

"Thaza, don't worry. I can guarantee no suspicion will fall on you. The authorities are fully aware of what happened. The highest authorities are fully aware. Besides, I am not going to die – not yet anyway. I may look weak, but my wound is healing. I will resume my duties in a couple of weeks."

"Why don't you arrest Lama Neto!" I said. "He as good as tried to murder you!"

"Yes, he was linked. But as I've already told you, arresting him won't stop the dark. We have a better idea."

"The Dalai Lama will ask him to help organise the Great Prayer Festival,"[53] said Jigme. "He'll think it's a promotion. He'll be kept occupied, but he won't be in a position to do much harm."

"But why give that dog a better life?" I asked.

"Thaza, how many times do I have to explain?" said Lama Kunchen. "If we arrest him, he will know he's been uncovered. His allies will step up their campaign against us. Instead, we will appeal to his vanity and distract him from his path. It is by far the best way. Benevolence to counter evil – this is our path."

"But he doesn't deserve this!" I thundered.

"He is still a soul, one that is experiencing the dark so that he might one day become light. You are not cruel to a stone because it is not water; they both serve their purpose. We must not let him beat us, for if he and his kind do, then humanity will be plunged into another dark age. But we needn't be too harsh on him either."

---

[53] The Great Prayer Festival was the biggest event of the year. It took place in February at the start of the Tibetan New Year and involved several days of services, processions, religious debates, plays and the Butter Lantern Festival. The Dalai Lama was intimately involved in all aspects of the Festival and it required intensive planning.

I couldn't accept this. This old monk, nearly killed, if not by Lama Neto directly then at least by his associates, was preaching kindness towards that odious man.

"But what am I to do about Lama Neto?" I asked.

"As I said before, do nothing to arouse his suspicion. Tell him nothing of importance. And keep out of his way."

"But Norchen is my friend! I must still see him, and help him escape Lama Neto's clutches."

"Still see Norchen, for if you didn't that would look odd. But don't try to rescue him. If he asks you for help, then help him. If he doesn't, let him walk his path."

"But he's trapped! It's not his fault. It would be dishonourable not to help him escape. Hell, he'd help me if our positions were reversed."

"You cannot know why a soul has chosen the path it has. You cannot know what good he is doing by walking his path. Norchen could, for example, be serving an apprenticeship with the light. He could be a more advanced soul than Lama Neto, come down to help him from the dark. If you try to save him, as you put it, then you might be interfering, and you might not be helping him at all."

None of this made sense, but by now I respected Lama Kunchen, so I tried to accept what he was saying – while all the time inwardly resolved to help Norchen when I could. Lama Kunchen was looking drained, and Jigme told me to leave. I did, even though I was still confused at how these men were playing this dangerous game. To me it was like keeping a wolf in a sheep's pen and feeding it in the hope that it won't pounce on the sheep. Thankfully though, I did manage to avoid Lama Neto over the next few days and it was not long afterwards that Lama Kunchen reappeared, just as he had said, in the services and about the monastery as before. A rumour went round that the authorities had arrested two men for the attack. I didn't think it was true, but it helped to lay the affair to rest. For my part, I paid extra attention to my martial arts training.

One night, about a week after Lama Kunchen had reappeared, I was asleep in the dormitory when I was rudely kicked awake by a chela I'd never seen before. I was about to grab his ankle and make him pay for his unwarranted actions when he grunted that Lama Kunchen wanted me. Putting on my robe, I followed the chela out and then, not to Lama Kunchen's room as I'd expected, but to an upper storey in another part of the monastery.

I was fully awake by now, sensing the energy, and ready in case this was a trap. The chela looked feeble enough – I could deal with him – but the energy didn't feel bad. At last we reached a small room lit by butter lamps. I don't know if I'd been there before. But there was Lama Kunchen, Jigme and the ancient lama who'd helped banish my grandfather's spirit.

"Thaza," said Lama Kunchen clearing his throat, "as you know, the danger facing us is greater than expected. The attempted assassination on me is proof of that. We had hoped that you would leave in the spring – the normal time for traders to go to India. But we will have you leave in a few weeks time instead. It will be more dangerous, but it is the only way."

I understood.

"But before you go, we would like to give you added powers. Look upon it as a reward for saving my life."

I had no idea what he was talking about. The ancient lama was looking at me strangely. Jigme seemed on edge. There was a strong smell of herbs too.

"Sit down and let us examine you."

Lama Kunchen and the ancient lama began prodding me, pushing back my head and looking at me. I was aware of a certain excitement. It didn't show in their faces but it was present in the room. After a while the old man nodded at Lama Kunchen and they both sat down again.

"Thaza, we're going to open your third eye," said Lama Kunchen.

My third eye? I knew it was one of my chakras. I knew it was in the middle of my forehead just above the top of my nose. But I didn't really know what it was.

"Of course," continued Lama Kunchen, "your third eye is already partially open, for it is where you sense the energy I've been talking to you about, it's where your intuition comes from, without which I for one wouldn't be here." He smiled. "In fact," he continued, "we have been surprised at just how developed your third eye is. It's been a bonus for us. And because you took the action you did in saving my life, it's created the opportunity for us to do more for you."

Lama Kunchen seemed pleased, but I wasn't so sure. "What does it mean?" I asked. "Opening my third eye?"

"You will see new levels of reality. Your ability to sense energy and divine people's true intentions will be greatly enhanced. Normally, we wouldn't do this, for it is not allowed to speed someone's development before they are ready. And normally, when one is ready, then the third eye opens of its own accord. But in your case, because the task you will perform for us is so important, and because you saved my life a few weeks ago, we feel we are justified in opening it more now."

"How do you open it?"

"We need to stimulate your third eye chakra physically. Don't worry about how we do it. Now look over there please."

Lama Kunchen directed my gaze to a mandala on the wall. He asked me to focus on the Buddha in the middle. At the same time Jigme started rubbing a foul-smelling liquid on my forehead.

"Keep your eyes on the mandala," instructed Lama Kunchen.

I did, but couldn't help noticing the ancient lama moving just out of my line of sight. Suddenly he shrieked and I was stunned by a sharp, hard object slamming into my forehead. I couldn't see, blood ran down my face and my breath was stopped by the pain in my head. Then Jigme pushed me to the floor and Lama Kunchen leapt on me. He started vigorously massaging the wound that I now realised I had on my forehead. It made my nerves dance, my nose run and my stomach turn. Lama Kunchen kept pressing on the wound, grinding it into the bone underneath, as if he were torturing me. I couldn't even cry out. Then at last he stopped – but the pain didn't. It carried on unfolding, as if Lama Kunchen had started something that wouldn't cease. At the same time, I felt pricks as Lama Kunchen now seemed to be closing the wound in my forehead with what I glimpsed looked like a needle and thread. Then a bandage was wrapped around my forehead and eyes. It was tightly bound and I couldn't see a thing.

I was catching my breath fitfully. The pain was bewildering. The others pulled me upright. As they did so, lights flashed in my inner eye and the agony danced. A cup was pressed against my lips.

"Drink this," said Lama Kunchen, "it will help you sleep."

I don't know what it was, but soon there was a merciful release from consciousness.

I awoke with a pain in my head like no other. It was a thousand times worse than drinking too much shimiin arkhi, for I had not only a thumping headache but also a swollen bruise on my forehead that made me nauseous every time I moved. At the same time, through my pain, I could sense that there was a huge space in front of me, although my eyes remained bandaged.

I didn't know where I was. I heard a rustle and a door open and close. Then silence. A little later I heard someone come in.

"How are you feeling?" It was Jigme.

"Awful," I croaked.

"You're not to eat," he said. "But drink this." He closed my hands round a warm cup. It was another bitter tasting herbal liquid.

"Where am I?"

"In the lamas' quarters, in a spare room. No-one knows you're here. We're telling others that you're sick."

"What... what happened?"

"You were hit in your third eye with a stone. It was stimulated further by Lama Kunchen pressing on it. It may have looked crude, but it required great skill."

"What about my bandages?"

160

"They will stay on for some days. The energy that normally goes to your physical eyes needs to go to your third eye – to build it up."

"But what am I to do?"

"Rest. And get used to your new abilities. You're very lucky, Thaza. Most of us have to endure many lives to become as clairvoyant as you are now. You've done it all in one."

Yes, but with such pain!

But Jigme was right. I did have new powers. As he was speaking I could hear a new dimension behind his words. I could sense that he was telling the truth. I had a vision of the room I was in, and had an awareness of my surroundings that, despite not seeing with my physical eyes, I had never had before. Later, I started seeing things. At first I thought I was dreaming. I could see my home, I saw my mother and cousins in their yurt and knew they were all right. I saw the horses I'd seen in the Potala; they were happy. I saw the blue sky outside – only it was a deeper, more vibrant blue than I'd ever seen. And I saw Lama Kunchen, this time with a swirl of very bright colours around him. I noticed that when I had these visions, the thumping in my third eye grew, only this time it wasn't painful.

I mentioned all this to Lama Kunchen when he came to visit me. He told me this was normal when someone's third eye opens more fully. He explained he would teach me how to close my third eye so that I could have some respite from the information streaming into me. But for now I was to rest.

So I stayed bandaged for seven more days. On the seventh day, Lama Kunchen, Jigme and the ancient lama came to remove them. The cool air on my face felt wonderful. The old lama looked at my forehead and said everything was healing very well. They made me walk round the room – it was surprisingly difficult using my physical eyes again to balance. And very difficult combining what my physical eyes were seeing with what my third eye was showing me. Lama Kunchen was a blaze of brilliant colours, the ancient monk wasn't ancient at all but a young, active man looking at me keenly, and even Jigme, I was surprised to discover, had a glow of goodness about him

161

that I'd never seen before. I even felt a strong bond of friendship between us – most peculiar.

At length, after stumbling round the room, they said I could rejoin daily life in the monastery. Only Lama Kunchen ordered me to see him every morning and afternoon for intensive lessons in mastering my new powers.

It was strange seeing the world through new eyes. I staggered around those first days, trying to cope with all that was happening. It made people think I had been really ill. Norchen was doubly concerned when he saw the cut on my forehead. He touched it once and I yelped in pain.

Colours or images or messages would flash into my head. When I saw Norchen I felt his mother dying (I don't know if she was, I just felt her pain). I saw Lama Neto and could see the blackness around him – a very refined blackness, even an intriguing blackness, but a blackness all the same. I saw a young novice and at the same time saw him as a distinguished lama. I saw colours around people's bodies, and could sense if they were healthy or going to be sick. I saw people together, not as the monks they were today, but as different people in different lives. And I saw Lama Kunchen and sensed his many lives walking the true path. I saw how much he had suffered for the truth, and I saw him as a small boy before he became a monk. It was all very confusing.

Perhaps best of all, I could sense animals even more clearly than before. I knew that a bird flying overhead had just eaten a rodent. I knew the temple cats were actually guarding the Buddhas they prowled around or slept on. And I knew that most of the horses I could see in the streets below were cold, overworked and underfed. I found I was able to reach out and give them some comfort.

And it wasn't just living beings. I could see swirls of dark energy in corners and inevitably these were the places where people slipped or fell. I could see some of the rows in the refectory where we sat were more 'up' than others, and the monks sitting in those rows would look happier. Perhaps most weird were the creatures I saw darting around,

162

usually just out of the corner of my eye. They seemed mischievous. And when I looked out over the Kyi river[54] and the willow trees on its banks, I could see calmer, almost see-through beings that seemed to be tending to the plants and the water.

Of course I didn't tell anyone else what I was experiencing. They would think I was mad – as indeed I thought I was some of the time.

"Several things are happening," explained Lama Kunchen. "You can see or sense auras now. These are energy fields around every human that appear as moving colours. They reflect who we are and what might happen to us. You are developing telepathy. This doesn't just mean picking up other people's thoughts. It means tapping into their energy and feelings as well. And you are getting glimpses of people's Akashic records,[55] past and future by the sound of it. One day everyone will have these powers. But for now, you are far in advance of the human race.

"You are also seeing patterns of energy that build up in places, unseen by the humans who pass through them, but which nevertheless are active and can affect human behaviour. I believe you are also seeing what are called fairies or sprites."

Then he warned me. "Because you haven't had previous training, these powers may not stay with you for long. There is only so much we can do to open your third eye artificially. You will find your powers diminishing over time. But diminish or not, you are better equipped now to carry out your immediate task."

He was right. I now had another awareness that gave me an advantage. I could see and sense people more clearly. I could even wake up in the morning and know in advance what sort of day it was going to be. And a thumping foreboding always told me when Lama Neto was near.

He was also right about my powers diminishing. I still have the scar on my forehead, and I can still read the energy, but the lights,

---

[54] The Kyi river, a tributary of the Brahmaputra river, flows through Lhasa.
[55] The Akashic records are said to be the complete history of a soul detailing all its past lives.

colours, images and information went long ago. I can't say I mind – I'm sure all I'd see is the misery of the monks here at Yerlang and our Chinese oppressors – but sometimes I wish I could talk to Lama Kunchen again. He knew nothing about riding, animals or fighting, but he truly was the father I never had.

A Surprise

Some days later Lama Kunchen told me, "We have to fix a day for your departure."

I was disconcerted. I know he'd already indicated that I would be leaving soon, but I was still finding my feet with my new powers, I hadn't resumed my martial arts training, and I didn't feel up to an arduous journey.

"When should it be?" I asked uneasily.

He had an astrological table in his hands which he consulted. "On the offerings of the 15th during the Great Prayer Festival. A doubly auspicious day for your soul day is Sunday, is it not?" He was still looking at his table when he added, "People should be much too busy with the festivities to notice a simple trader leaving town."

The Great Prayer Festival was three weeks away. I was about to ask details of my journey when Lama Kunchen carried on. "We will get everything ready. We will prepare the sacks into which we will put the Morning Tree. Do not open the sacks. We will also assemble the other goods which you will trade, and your provisions. And we'll arrange the ponies and yaks. Now, Jigme has found two men to accompany you. They know nothing about the Morning Tree or the true reason for your mission. Under no circumstances should you tell them. They are trustworthy, but for their sake it is better if they do not know the truth.

"You will need some clothes. Jigme will organise those as well. And I will give you money – enough for you to reach your destination and get home again."

"But where am I to go? And who will I give the Morning Tree to?" I asked.

"You will go to Darjeeling. It is a major town in Bengal. You will set up your stall in the main market and wait to be approached. The person will not make it obvious that he is there to collect the Morning Tree, but you will know."

"Know?"

"Yes. It is the main reason we have practised the energy exercises and opened your third eye. You will know." It seemed tenuous, but Lama Kunchen said no more. I had to trust him.

"One more thing Thaza," he continued. "You will say nothing of these arrangements or your impending departure to anyone. And you will not say goodbye to anyone here."

He looked at me closely. I know he was seeing if I would mention anything to Norchen. I wouldn't. The less he knew, the less likely he was to be punished by Lama Neto.

"I will inform people some days after you have left that you have returned to Mongolia. Which, in a roundabout way, will be true."

So, my destination was at last known. I asked Lama Kunchen how I was to get to Darjeeling. He gave me the details which I committed to memory. As I did so, I caught images of the route. I also had an uneasy feeling. Lama Kunchen was staring at me; had he picked it up too? He started to intone a prayer of protection for my journey. I wanted to ask him about the feeling, but I got the message that it was for me to work out. I have since wondered why I didn't then just think of returning straight home to Mongolia with the goods and money they were going to give me and to hell with Darjeeling. How different my life would have been! But the thought never crossed my mind. Uneasy feeling or not, I genuinely wanted to help Lama Kunchen. What he knew was true and real, and I wanted to repay his trust in me.

I was curious about something though. "The Morning Tree – where will it go once I've delivered it?" I asked.

"I can only say it will be kept safe," he replied.

"Where?"

166

"It has been arranged."

"Will the dark be able to get hold of it?"

"I trust not. It will be hidden."

"Where?"

"I can't tell you Thaza."

"But you do know?"

Lama Kunchen laughed. "Yes, I do know." He was thoughtful for a while. "I can give you a clue. If you had to hide a pebble, where would you hide it?"

"A pebble? I don't know. Anywhere. In my bowl. In my pouch."

"And anyone finding your bowl or going through your pouch would see the pebble at once, for it would stand out."

"Well, where would you hide it?"

"With other pebbles. In the bottom of a stream perhaps."

"But isn't that too obvious?"

"Not at all. How would you find one pebble amongst hundreds? It could rest there safely."

This didn't tell me much. I tried to feel into where the Morning Tree might be hidden, but it felt blocked. But then it didn't matter. My job was just to deliver it and go home.

I had mixed emotions those next few days. I was anxious about the journey ahead and wondered how strong I was to undertake it. I was also sad I wouldn't see Lama Kunchen again. But at the same time I was happy at the prospect of returning home and finding Sarangerel. In fact, I was very happy about that. It seems cruel, now that I've rotted thirty years in this monastery, to recall how happy I felt about the future then.

As promised, Jigme delivered some clothes to me. They were a set of fine trader's clothes, and in the Mongolian style. I really would look the part. We kept the clothes in Lama Kunchen's room. I admit, seeing the clothes made me feel excited. I would return home looking smart, and with the extra benefits of my martial arts skills and new powers.

About a week before the Great Prayer Festival Lama Kunchen told me to report to his room before dawn the next day. I turned up at the appointed time, and he led me to the main gate where two ponies were waiting. We mounted them and were let out by the night watchman. We rode down to the chorten and then headed out of Lhasa. The sky was beginning to lighten, and I was curious about where we were going.

Eventually we reached the gate to a park. I realised with a start – why hadn't I twigged before, especially with my new powers – that we were at the Norbu Linka.[56] I mouthed a silent question to Lama Kunchen, but he was already talking to the khaki dressed soldiers on guard outside.

We were let into the park and trotted through the grounds. There were plenty of trees, and a low white wooden building. The energy felt calm, high and good. We came to some tall walls where we dismounted. We were greeted by some monks who took our horses and led us through a gate into a large compound. There was an amazing glass house filled with plants on one side. I had never seen anything like it – all glass, the size of a small yurt. I wondered how it stood up. There was a tiger and a leopard in cages, and some monkeys, deer and dogs in the grounds. And a camel – I smelled it at once. There was also a temple, a lake with geese and ducks, and a pavilion on stilts in the lake joined to the land by a small bridge. We walked across this bridge and into the pavilion. I was amazed at the sights I was seeing. The Heavenly Fields must look like this, I thought.

We continued into an inner room. There were gold, silver and porcelain objects, and some tall backed chairs. We sat down. I wanted to ask Lama Kunchen a hundred questions, but he was silent so I remained silent too. The energy felt stronger and calmer than I'd ever experienced. I could see Lama Kunchen flaring with strong, bright colours – quite a contrast to his frail body (I suppose he still hadn't

[56] Norbu Linka, Jewel Park, was the Dalai Lama's summer residence just outside Lhasa also called the Summer Palace. The Thirteenth Dalai Lama preferred the Norbu Linka to the Potala and lived there for as much of the year as he could.

fully recovered from his wound). Suddenly there was a rustle and a simply, but beautifully, dressed figure came into the room.

"Ah, Pemba, sorry to have kept you waiting."

It was the Precious Sovereign![57]

I jumped to my feet, heart pounding. I never suspected I would feel like this at meeting the Dalai Lama. I sank to my knees and put out my hands, deeply ashamed I didn't have a scarf to give him,[58] and wondering why Lama Kunchen wasn't doing the same.

"My son," said the Dalai Lama, "you may get up. We have no need to be formal here. These are my private quarters. Only my friends come to this pavilion. I don't want ceremony with my friends here. I have enough of that outside."

I stood up, heart still pounding, and looked at him more closely. He was so clean and strong, although he was not a young man anymore, and he definitely had that stoop I'd first seen from the rooftops all those months ago. I got a flash in my inner sight of a great white light, yet one facing a great black light too. He was truly in selfless service for his country and religion. At last I understood why my mother and so many more worshipped him.

He too looked at me. "So this is the one, eh Pemba? He looks fit. Mongolian, you say? I have always admired Mongolian horsemen. I wish I'd had the chance to do more riding."

He sat down and poured three cups of tea, one of which he gave to me. "It's so nice to relax here. Sadly I shall be leaving soon. Official duties.[59] But at least I have a few hours today." He took a sip of tea. "I trust everything is in hand?"

"Yes, Tubten,[60] I believe we are ready," said Lama Kunchen.

---

[57] One of the many terms used to refer to the Dalai Lama.

[58] It is normal to give the Dalai Lama or any high personage in Tibet a white scarf when meeting them.

[59] The Dalai Lama typically left the Norbu Linka to live in the Potala at the beginning of the Great Prayer Festival at the start of the Tibetan New Year in February.

[60] Tubten Gyatso was the Thirteenth Dalai Lama's given name. It appears that Lama Kunchen is on very good terms with the Dalai Lama to address him by his given name.

"And he understands the task in front of him?"

"He does."

There was silence. A spreading peace filled the room. All thought left me. Then he spoke again.

"We owe you our thanks, Thaza," he said. "The greatest jewels of our religion – the ones that perversely are the least known – are to be entrusted into your hands. Your success or failure will not only affect us but the future course of humanity. I have complete confidence in your master, so I have complete confidence in you."

I didn't know what to say. But I suddenly saw how well Lama Kunchen had prepared me. The martial arts, the energy exercises, my increased powers, and above all a gradual but complete transformation to his cause. What did I care about these secrets? Now that I knew Lama Kunchen, the answer was everything.

"You say he has had his eye opened?" continued the Dalai Lama.

"Yes."

"Then I wonder if he can help me." He led us back outside and over to the cage with the Bengal tiger. "A present from the Maharaja of Sikkim," said the Dalai Lama to me. "But he is not happy. Can you tell me why?"

The tiger was pacing around his cage; he had a thick winter coat and was making a low growl. A magnificent beast. I got quiet and put myself into the tiger's energy. Immediately I felt a constricting blackness, a strong animal presence, and then unhappiness. I had a searing image of the leopard in the next cage.

"The tiger is unsettled by the leopard, Your Holiness," I said. "He can't relax with another predator so close to him. He asks to be moved, and asks for the shelter of trees."

The Dalai Lama was nodding his head. "I will give orders for him to be moved at once," he said. "Thank you."

The Inmost One then showed me around the grounds. All the other animals were happy to be there. He told me of the flowers he was preparing to plant, and how the garden came alive in the summer. I could contain myself no longer.

"Your Holiness, what's that?" I asked, pointing to the glass house.

"It's for my plants," he replied. "It shelters them from the cold wind and allows me to plant seeds earlier than would otherwise be the case. That way I can get flowers to bloom sooner and for longer. I had it shipped from India."

I still couldn't believe how something that fragile or astonishing could exist.

He led us back to the pavilion where food had been laid out. Tsampa. I admit, I was disappointed. But also impressed to see the head of the country eating as a simple monk.

I was helping myself to some food when the image came to me. I saw the Dalai Lama looking much as he did at that moment but he was lying down and surrounded by monks intoning prayers over his prone body. But here's the strange thing, I saw him at the same time walking away from his body into a great light. Then there was a swirl of energy which parted to reveal a small boy. But a small boy surrounded by hardship and misery, especially the misery of not being able to live in his own country. I saw this small boy as the Dalai Lama but hiding away. I looked up to see Lama Kunchen peering at me intently.

"What is it, Pemba?" asked the Dalai Lama.

"I believe Thaza has just looked into your Akashic record," said Lama Kunchen.

I hadn't done anything; I'd just received a vision.

"Don't look so worried, Thaza," said Lama Kunchen. "Now your third eye is open, things like this can happen. The Akashic record is normally barred to others, but it seems in your case you have been granted access to the Inmost One's path."

"But I didn't ask to see, and I didn't understand what I saw," I said blushing.

"What did you see?" asked the Dalai Lama.

I told him.

He just laughed. "You really are gifted," he said. "Since you were given that vision, and since you are Pemba's pupil, I will tell you what

171

it means. You saw my passing from this life in the near future,[61] and my rebirth some two years later. You also saw the difficulties I will face, and how I will have to leave Tibet."

He seemed perfectly calm as he spoke to me about his death, and about the tribulations he would face in his next life. I was astonished how he accepted his fate so evenly. He and Lama Kunchen – they had a level of acceptance equalling Buddha's. I still don't understand why they were both so composed about the destruction of their country and religion. Some things I never will understand.

We stayed for some time longer, the Precious Sovereign and Lama Kunchen talking. I won't tell what they said – I wouldn't be believed. And then it was time for us to leave. As we parted the Dalai Lama put his hand into his overcoat and took out a small Buddha on a chain.

"This is for you," he said handing it to me. "To protect you on your journey. I have blessed it."

I was speechless. It was a simple bronze Buddha, like many you could pick up in the market. It didn't look expensive, but it warmed the palm of my hand as I clutched it, and to me was more valuable than a sack of gold. I felt a strength flooding my inner body and knew that that little object was truly blessed with goodness. With my gift in my hand, we were out of the pavilion and heading towards the gate where our horses were waiting.

Do you know, I've never spoken about my visit with the Great Thirteenth to anyone. I've wanted to. I've wanted to break open the heads of these idiot monks here and tell them *I've had a private audience in the Norbu Linka with the Dalai Lama!* A man ten thousand times greater than any of them. And he treated me as an equal. But they wouldn't believe me. I sometimes wonder if it happened myself. But it did, word for word as I have written here, Buddha strike me down.

I wanted to tell Norchen too, for I was bursting with excitement at my visit. But I didn't need Lama Kunchen to remind me not to

---

[61] The Thirteenth Dalai Lama died on 17th December 1933. The Fourteenth Dalai Lama was born 6th July 1935.

speak to anyone of what had happened, not even Jigme (I wonder if he ever had a private audience with the Great Thirteenth). So we returned to Chakpori as just two monks who had been out on business.

The next day Jigme and I went through the preparations for my departure. Everything was ready. He took me out of the monastery to inspect the ponies and yaks that would form our caravan. They were being kept at a guest house in Lhasa. And I met the two men Jigme had found – Tsang and Lobsang – who were to accompany me. They were simple, honest people who felt honoured to be helping Jigme, whom they clearly held in high regard.

The next night I was in Lama Kunchen's room. I had been going there every evening in those last days. We sat in silence for a while. He was contemplating; I was eating sweetmeats. I knew then with all my being that he was a truly great man. Without thinking, I blurted out, "Lama, are you a tulku?"[62] I knew the abbot of Chakpori was, and I knew that several other high lamas were, but I had never heard it mentioned that Lama Kunchen was. Yet surely he must be.

"Why do you ask?" he said.

"Great monks are," I replied, "so you must be."

He seemed surprised and touched. "The answer to your question is yes and no. Yes, I am a tulku in the sense that everyone is a reincarnation, and I have certainly been a lama in previous lives. But no, I am not an official tulku. It was decided that I would be better able to carry out my work if I were not so prominent. So I came down as an ordinary peasant and joined a monastery in the west of Tibet before coming here as a chela. Our order is supposed to be secret, so it is best not to draw attention to ourselves."

"Are you the head of your order?"

"I cannot say."

"But the Dalai Lama, he is a tulku?"

"Oh yes, he is as we believe him to be: a reincarnation of previous Dalai Lamas. But, you know, he won't continue reincarnating as the

---

[62] A tulku is a recognised incarnation of a high lama.

173

Dalai Lama – it wouldn't serve his soul to come back again and again in the same position. Besides, if he is successful spiritually – and I think he will be successful spiritually – he'll be able to move on, perhaps getting off the wheel of reincarnation altogether and moving up into divinity. So the soul that is currently the Dalai Lama will one day stop being the Dalai Lama."

"Does that mean the Dalai Lama will cease to exist?"

"As long as there is a need for the Dalai Lama, there will be a Dalai Lama. But, as I've said, the soul that is the current Dalai Lama will one day move on. And, well, yes, I can say that one day, not so far hence from now, there will be no more Dalai Lamas."

I thought of my visit to the Norbu Linka and of how truly great the Great Thirteenth was.

"Is the Dalai Lama the greatest soul on earth? He is so good. Surely there can't be another like him."

"He is a great soul, Thaza, and we are blessed to have him governing our country and religion in these difficult times. But he is not the greatest soul." He sighed. "Terms like great imply that others are less. It is not true. But some souls are more evolved than others. Highly evolved souls, if they wish and if they earn the right, become members of the spiritual hierarchy. It is this hierarchy that is responsible for creation. I say hierarchy, but you are not to think in terms of worldly power and money, of a lord who is more important than his subjects. No, the spiritual hierarchy serve those in creation; they have a contract of work on behalf of others. Some members may have worldly power and wealth, but most are modest people, and all carry out their work without the bulk of humanity having any idea who they are."

I didn't need to ask if Lama Kunchen was a member of the spiritual hierarchy.

"What work do they do?"

He spread his hands. "If you were my pupil for a dozen years I still would not be able to fully explain what they do. Suffice it to say, they control everything that happens. Kings and governments think that they determine the affairs of men, but in fact, the spiritual hierarchy do. They also make the winds blow and the rain fall. In truth, they regulate creation."

"But why then do they let bad things happen? Why will they let Tibet be invaded? Why did they let me be persecuted by my grandfather?"

"I told you Thaza, if I had a dozen years I still would not be able to explain everything fully. Suffice it to say, the spiritual hierarchy carry out the Father's plan. You may think the destruction of Tibet is wrong – and in many ways it is – but there will be benefits. Tibet will be opened to the world. That will help the world and Tibet. People might not see the benefits at first, but they will be there. It is the same with the war that will engulf most of the world in a few years. There will be much destruction and suffering, but it will offer great opportunities for souls to demonstrate courage and self-sacrifice. Old spirit can also be broken, and there will be many social and technological advances as a result of the conflict. Remember, all this turmoil will be balanced by a golden age that is coming."

We sat in silence for a while. I was still thinking of my visit to the Dalai Lama.

"If the Inmost One isn't the greatest soul, who is?"

"There is one soul," replied Lama Kunchen, "greater than others. It is the Father who returns to Earth again and again to help His creation along. He is God in human form. He came as Krishna, Buddha, Jesus, Mohammad and several other personalities. He comes every 400 to 700 years. And He is here today."

I sat bolt upright. The Buddha, here today? The Buddha who was also Jesus and other great figures? How could this be? And if it was true, where was he and why hadn't I heard of him?

"Don't look so surprised," said Lama Kunchen. "The Father comes down again and again to help creation when it is needed. Each time He comes, He comes as a different figure because He has a different job of work to do. As the Buddha, He showed how we can achieve peace and harmony through guiding our thoughts and actions.

175

As Jesus, He demonstrated the power of love. Each time He adds something, and so helps creation evolve."

"You mean," I put in, "this soul, the Father as you call him – this same soul – has founded all the different religions?"

"Yes."

"Then the arguments between religions…"

"Are a waste of time because they are all aspects of the Father's teaching. It is amusing – but also sad – to hear that one religion is superior or the only one when in reality all religions come from the same source. Of course, the minds of men have woven a great deal of mischief into the original teachings of the Father as Buddha or Christ or whoever. But that is what men have a tendency to do."

"But… but isn't Buddhism still the best?"

"As I've said, it demonstrates one aspect of the Father's teachings. It suits us here and now. But in other lives you will experience other religions. And, as Buddhism is one of the older religions on earth, the initial energy charge behind the religion is fading. In time, not long actually, it will fade altogether."

First he talks about the destruction of Tibet, now he talks about the ending of Buddhism. Lama Kunchen constantly surprised me.

"So will there be a new religion?" I asked.

"The Father doesn't always come to create a new religion. In many ways, humanity has had enough of religions now. In His present incarnation, He will instead usher in a new era of spirituality. Don't look so confused Thaza. Religion is not the same as spirituality. Religion may contain spirituality, but a great deal of religion is simply men exerting control over each other. In Tibet, many lamas use their religious status to extract tithes from peasants and obedience from landowners. When laymen come to ask for spiritual blessings, many lamas know in their hearts they have nothing to give, but they do not admit this. Instead, they go through the motions, for it encourages others to look up to them and so cements their power over the laity."

True, so true. Just as I always thought. And definitely true of the monks here at Yerlang.

176

"It is the same elsewhere," continued Lama Kunchen. "Priests of whatever religion will not think of their prime task – giving spiritual guidance – but instead will look to secure power and wealth over others. They are no different to governments, landowners, soldiers, brigands, bullies and dominant people anywhere."

"But if we are not to have a new religion, what will happen?"

Lama Kunchen laughed. "A very good question, Thaza. This time God has come not to teach but to awaken. He will move creation along by working directly with every soul. No more religion. No more authorities, with one person set above another. Instead, an awakening. New consciousness. Direct experience of the divinity that really exists. Higher frequencies available to all. A new light body for everyone. And when I say everyone, I mean every soul in creation – including the mineral, plant and animal kingdoms. I've already told you a new golden age is coming. One of peace, understanding and harmony. One where the powers once lost by humanity will be returned. Well, that golden age will be the result of what the Father is doing now. Assuming humanity can accept what is on offer. I think this time they will. But we still have our part to play. The Father is both light and dark – He is obviously everything, as He is creation. So He is also the dark, testing us to see if we are ready for more light.

"Part of what we are doing now – safeguarding the secret knowledge, protecting it from the dark – is to see if we can rise above the old fear, the old way of doing things. How we act today – how you perform in the coming months, Thaza – will help to decide what sort of future we will enjoy. It is the same for everyone: their way of acting now will influence what unfolds. As I've said, I think this time humanity will make the right choice. But the Father has to operate respecting, among other things, our free will according to our level of development. So, although this golden age is coming, exactly how and when it comes is partly chosen by us. There are always choices."

"But you say the Father is incarnated on Earth now. I haven't heard of Him. Surely, if God is here as a man among us, we would recognise Him and He would have a huge following?"

"You would think that would be the case, but it rarely is. When the Father walks among us as a man, His light is very strong. Too strong in fact for most people to accept. So people look to the Father's past incarnations, as Buddha or Christ and so on, rather than the Father in the present. But in many ways this is for the best. The Father can work more freely if he is not universally recognised. Again, this will change in the future when people can accept more light and recognise divinity. But for now, only a few thousand out of the many millions present in any divine incarnation recognise that God is among us as a man."

"Is he Tibetan?"

"No," laughed Lama Kunchen. "He is currently in India. Some of those with Him today know Him for who He is. But even though He says clearly and with authority that He is God, very few accept Him as that."[63]

"Will I see Him in India?"

Lama Kunchen looked impressed. "No Thaza, you won't see Him. But you will most likely give the Morning Tree to one of His agents, if I can put it that way. Who that will be, I cannot say. But you will recognise him when you see him."

"But all this you are telling me, why doesn't everyone know it?"

"Another good question, Thaza. I've already told you that humanity had the chance to go up during the Atlantean root race. They voted to go down instead. That ushered in a time – a very long time, a period in fact that we are still in – where the dark was in dominance. The dark is above all misinformation and disempowerment. So truths that we are immortal, we do not die, there is abundance, no-one is above another, we are all here to gain experience, and experience will help us learn to love and recognise we are each of us in fact divine – these truths are lost or distorted. Instead, fear and worry, and consequent aggression and competition, rule. That

---

[63] I am grateful to Professor Thurgood for suggesting the person Lama Kunchen is talking about is Avatar Meher Baba 1894-1969. See avatarmeherbaba.org.

is how the dark like it. So what I am telling you now would not be understood. But times are changing, and the dark will have to give way to the light. We are part of that change. One day everything I'm telling you will be known and understood. Everything and a lot more."

Silence descended again. A deep silence as I took in everything I'd been told. And a contented silence as a flame of knowledge burned inside me. Conches sounded in the distance, bringing us back to the here and now. Time for the evening service. As I went down to the main hall, I wondered how many others knew that the Buddha – this being they worshipped – was also the founder of the other religions. And how He was on Earth today to do things I frankly didn't understand but which would transform everything.

I Depart

A few days later it was the Great Prayer Festival. The beginning of the Year of the Water-Monkey.[64] We crowded round the windows overlooking the road to see the Dalai Lama enter Lhasa. Soldiers lined the route. Aristocratic families with their fine clothes stood at the foot of the Potala. Then a long procession appeared. A throng of high lamas in their red robes rode ahead of a yellow sedan chair carried by a dozen or more men. Behind the chair rode government officials in their colourful ceremonial robes of office. Immediately behind the chair was the man who'd asked Lama Kunchen's advice on my first visit to the Potala. The colours in his aura showed him to be a sincere man. But most of the other lamas – they were black or grey and yet they were supposed to be holy.

In the chair, but covered by veils, was the Inmost One. Everyone bowed their heads as he passed. The monks withdrew from the windows for fear of being seen. But I stayed staring at the spectacle until it left my line of sight.

The monastery was a hive of activity. Monks from Chakpori were involved in every aspect of the Great Prayer Festival – blessings from the Dalai Lama, formal dances to cast out the evil of the old year, sermons, debates – I couldn't follow it all. The town was heaving with monks and pilgrims who had come for the Festival. I understood now

---

[64] This is the only time Thaza gives a clear date. The Year of the Water-Monkey is 1932. Thaza arrived in Lhasa in August 1931 and left in February 1932, a stay of six to seven months.

why Lama Kunchen suggested I leave at this time. There was so much going on I could definitely slip away unnoticed.

Lama Neto wasn't in the monastery. He was attending the Dalai Lama and helping with arrangements for the festivities. Norchen was one of those preparing Chakpori's entry to the Butter Festival.[65] So I could leave now without either of them noticing. In the late afternoon Jigme came for me. He took me out of the lamasery – my home for these last several months – to the guest house where Tsang and Lobsang were staying. Outside was a string of yaks laden with goods and provisions and three horses. Jigme led me inside to an upstairs room. There I changed out of my robes and into my new clothes. I felt a surge of excitement.

Jigme took out three pouches and handed them to me.

"Money for the trip," he said. "More than enough I think. But make it last. We won't be able to give you any more." From the weight, it was certainly a considerable sum.

"Delay your departure until the Butter Festival has started, then make your way out of Lhasa. It will be dark then. No-one will notice you. Remember everything we've told you." Jigme looked me straight in the eye. In the moment of silence that followed I felt a depth of fellowship with him.

"Lama Kunchen?" I asked.

"He can't be with you now. The Inmost One has asked him to help judge the Butter Festival."

I felt alarmed and dejected. Jigme shook his head.

"Thaza, remember the work is of the utmost importance, not your personal preferences. But also remember your powers."

I understood. I opened up and felt for Lama Kunchen. Immediately his presence and blessings streamed into me. I was ready to go.

---

[65] The Butter Festival takes place on the fifteenth of the month. It is one of the main festivals of the New Year celebrations and involves monasteries making large painted religious figures out of butter wax.

Jigme left us. Wait until dark, he'd said. It wasn't yet dusk. So I made my way to the Muslim quarter. If I was to go on a long journey I wanted to fortify myself with some meat after all these months without.[66] I had coin enough to pay, so I ordered a handsome meal with chang. The meat was good (although with my powers I felt not only the goat's life but also its death), but the chang was a mistake. One mouthful gave me a severe pain in my third eye. I had to pour the rest away.

On my way back, pushing through the crowds, I suddenly felt a confusion and tugging. I turned round and stared at a group of beggars propped up against a building. One was covered with rags. My heart was racing. I knew I had to uncover those rags. I did – and there was Jorchin.

He was filthy, drunk (small black entities were dancing around him, if only he knew it), and he had little life force. In fact, his aura looked shredded. He turned over angrily to see who was disturbing him. I suppose all he saw was a well-dressed man looking down at him. At any rate, his scowl turned into a whimpering smile.

"Honourable sir, for the love of Buddha, please spare a few coins," he said in broken Tibetan.

"Jorchin, it's me, Thaza!" I said in Mongolian, shaking him.

He blinked.

"It's me, Thaza!" I repeated.

"Thaza? But you're dead," he croaked.

"I'm alive. I thought you were dead."

"Thaza? Is it really you? It can't be. I'm seeing things."

"It's me! Come, come, you can't stay here."

I pulled him up. He stank.

"Thaza?" He was still confused.

---

[66] There was a small Muslim population in Lhasa located near the Jokang Cathedral. They specialised in the butcher's trade as dealing with dead meat was frowned upon in this intensely Buddhist country.

"You're drunk, Jorchin. I don't know how, as you're a beggar. But when you sober up you'll understand. Come with me. I'm going to take you home."

I half supported, half dragged him back to the guest house. I don't know, I guess the meat and the crowds and Jorchin's dismal energy had blurred my senses. I felt sick all the time I was with him, and had a pain in my head – signs, if I were in my right mind, that something was wrong. But all I knew then was that this beggar had once been my companion and was the brother of the woman I wanted to marry. I had the wherewithal to help him, so I should. That's why I decided to take him with me.

Back at the guest house, Tsang and Lobsang were surprised to see me return with this bedraggled man. I broke open some fresh clothes and put them on Jorchin. I told them we were going to tie him to one of the horses and leave. They were alarmed – this wasn't in the plan Jigme had explained to them – but I snapped at them to be quiet. They did my bidding. So it was a little later our small caravan was ready to move off.

My hand went to the bronze Buddha the Dalai Lama had given me which I was now wearing round my neck. I rubbed it for good luck. I was on my way.

I led the horse with Jorchin, now asleep, strapped to it. Tsang and Lobsang, unwilling to ride if I couldn't, led their horses too. Our yaks, strung together, followed. Lama Kunchen was right. No-one noticed us. There was much revelry, and many people, including many monks, were beginning to get drunk. I noticed strange coils of black energy around the drunks; it was unpleasant. We made our way past the Potala, past Chakpori, and across the small bridge over the Kyi river just as I had seen so many other traders do in my months in Lhasa. The night sky was clear, and the moon lit our way. My journey had begun.

I wanted to put as much distance between myself and Lhasa as possible, so we ploughed on even though the going was slow. Eventually we stopped and rested the few hours till dawn. Then we set off again. By now, Jorchin had woken up. I helped him to some water.

"Thaza, I can't believe it's you!" he said. "When I saw your face looming over me in the dark, I thought it was the drink. But it's you, it's really you!" He seemed happy, his surliness from the road to Lhasa all those months ago had gone.

"I thought you were dead," he continued. "I thought everyone apart from the handful of people the brigands dragged back to their camp was dead. What happened?"

I told him how I'd been knocked unconscious, stripped of everything and then pushed into a ditch. I presumed they'd thought I was dead.

"Lucky you," said Jorchin. "I was a prisoner in their camp for weeks. They tortured us, were worse to Bayarma, and treated us like slaves. It was dreadful. I didn't care if I lived or died. Then one night they were out on another raid. I just slipped away when the few guards weren't looking. I ran so fast I cut myself on the rocks. I didn't know where I was going. I wandered for days until I came across a small settlement. They fed me and told me Lhasa was not far off. So I went there as a beggar. And stayed as a beggar until you found me."

"So Bayarma was alive?" I asked.

"Yes, but Thaza, I don't think she can be now. They treated her very badly." Jorchin dropped his head. I felt a sharp pain in mine. I didn't need to know any more. I shut out the nasty visions that were appearing to me.

"And Lorga? I didn't see his body when I came to."

"He was with me. Quite broken. He didn't seem to care about anything. The way they treated Bayarma, he didn't say a word. I don't know what was going on inside his head. But Thaza, what happened to you? How come you have this caravan? And where are we going?"

I told him that I too had begged my way to Lhasa, and there rendezvoused with the person I was planning to meet all along. He had helped me. I was now working for him – the caravan was his – but that after selling these goods in India I was free to return home.

All true, expect I omitted the most important details. Jorchin didn't ask any awkward questions. Instead he just asked if I would take him home with me.

"Of course. That's why I rescued you." That and hoping to do his father such a good turn that he would consent to me marrying Sarangerel.

We were making good progress now. We journeyed through several settlements, but hardly anyone noticed us. It was still winter and no-one was working in the fields. I kept scanning the faces of the few people we passed, but they were all simple peasants or wandering monks. None excited my third eye. Jorchin was gaining strength. He was the cheerful person he had been in Mongolia, before our difficult journey to Tibet. Tsang and Lobsang were excellent at marshalling the animals and setting up camp. On the evening of the second day I had a surge of joy that everything was going my way.

The next morning was squally and bitterly cold. We forged a crossing of the Tsangpo river. It was miserable going. I don't think I have ever felt water that cold. After the crossing I felt sick. I wondered if I was coming down with an illness, but my nausea had a different quality. I couldn't shake this feeling of sickness. I remember trying to get to sleep that night feeling like death.

I still felt ill the next morning. I had an image come to me – venal monks prostrating themselves – but it didn't make sense. A few hours after setting out, as we were passing Yamdrok Tso, we came across a group of monks. Only they had a wild look about them. I suddenly identified my nauseous feeling, and the image I'd had earlier, with them. They peered intently at us as we passed. I pretended not to notice – until I realised with a start that I recognised one of them. Their leader was one of the monks I had seen consorting with Lama Neto in Tengyeling monastery.

Had he recognised me? We passed each other by, my heart thumping. After a few more yards I stupidly turned back to look at them – and saw him staring at me. There was no doubt about it. He was one of the monks from Tengyeling, they were in cabal with Lama

Neto and the Chinese, and they must be looking for me. I didn't need to reason anything out. I just knew, my third eye thudding in agreement.

I was startled. I'd assumed my departure hadn't been noticed. We'd been at pains to time my leaving when Lama Neto and even Norchen wouldn't be around. I'd reckoned that Lama Kunchen's plan of using me, a Mongolian and a layman, would have fooled the dark who would be looking for a member of the secret order to be transporting the Morning Tree to safety. But only two days out and already I was being pursued.

Why hadn't they attacked us? Perhaps they weren't certain it was me. But then I was sure their leader had recognised me. Maybe it was because there were only four of them and they didn't think they could overpower the four of us. Maybe they were going to get reinforcements.

I thought of the Morning Tree in the saddlebags on the yaks. I thought of Lama Kunchen and his order. I thought how alarming it was that I had been discovered so quickly. Was there a spy near Lama Kunchen? Could it be Jigme, for surely no-one else knew of my plans? And he'd never liked me. But then I thought of all my training. Jigme or not, I would beat these people. I would deliver the Morning Tree. But how?

I didn't know how to explain to the others about the Tengyeling monks pursuing us without revealing information about the Morning Tree, so we just rode on for a while. Jorchin was trying out his Tibetan on Tsang and Lobsang. They were smiling but I could see they didn't understand a word he was saying. Then he hailed a pretty woman in a colourful dress as we passed her on the road. She understood his meaning at least and turned away. We seemed a contented group as we went along. But I knew a cloud of death hung over us.

"We're not going to Gyangste!" I announced.

This surprised the others. Gyangste was our next destination, part of the main route to India, and an important town where we could get more provisions. But I knew the Tengyeling monks would know we were heading there, and I didn't want them waiting for me.

"There's a quicker way," I said. "We take that." I spoke so decidedly no-one questioned me.

There was a quicker way – a track some thirty miles to the east of Gyangste – Jigme had mentioned it to me. The terrible thought crossed my mind that Jigme had told me about it in order to trap me. But I had to do something. I tested the energy of the track, and it felt open. I tested the energy of continuing on the main road, and it felt dangerous. The track it was then. If it was a trap, to hell with Buddha and the Morning Tree and everything Lama Kunchen had told me. But if it worked, we'd be ahead of our pursuers.

We found the track with some difficulty, and entered it as night was falling. I didn't want to stop even though the light was failing. We pressed on. That was my mistake. At a narrow point, in almost total darkness, one of the yaks missed its footing. It fell sideways, its full weight on Tsang who happened to be next to it. He collapsed, his leg snapping on a rock he couldn't see in the blackness. There was screaming and commotion. When I understood what had happened I cursed. Why was life always so difficult?

We strapped Tsang's leg as best we could. He was in agony. There was nothing we could do but corral the animals and wait for dawn. I could feel the animals' fear. They disliked being in a confined, narrow place. Dark swirls of energy, distinct even in the blackness, hovered around us. I soothed the horses, and then tried to soothe the yaks. They are much less sensitive than horses and much less willing to recognise a human's presence. My aim had been for speed, but now we had an injured man to carry. I was furious.

The going was hard the next day. The weather was foul, the path narrow and rocky, and Tsang was in considerable pain. His leg was hanging at an unnatural angle. Jorchin didn't understand why we had chosen such a difficult route. I wondered that too. But at the same time I could sense Lama Kunchen's approval at my choice. That was a help.

As the day wore on, Tsang subsided into unconsciousness. That was a blessing for us all. Jorchin kept asking if I knew where we were, and how far we had to go. After some sharp words from me, he stopped his questioning. In truth, I wasn't sure how far we had to go; I just knew we wouldn't get there that day. By the next morning we had fallen into a silent routine: all our effort going into negotiating the path, no strength for other thought. So it was with some surprise when, in the late afternoon, we found the path broadening into a large valley.

Our spirits rose – but we were cruelly misled. Although we were now traversing a plain, it started to snow. The fierce wind whipped it into drifts that blinded our eyes and made the yaks and horses stumble. It felt like we were being pierced by a thousand knives. We passed another sleepless night – it's a wonder no-one died – and pressed on at first light.

I knew where I was going. Lama Kunchen had advised me to stop at Chatsa monastery on the lower slopes of Chomolhari. We would have passed it if we had taken the main route from Gyangtse. Now it was where we would rejoin the road to India. It was also where I hoped we could leave Tsang to heal his leg. He was in a bad way and I feared for his life. Thankfully, by dusk that day, we finally reached the monastery. I banged on the main door and shouted for assistance. The monks who let us in were shocked at the state of our party.

We crowded into a small stable towards the back of the monastery, the snow still on our clothes and pack animals. But at least we were out of that wind. I pointed to Tsang, seemingly frozen on his horse, and told the monks he needed medical help urgently. A monk ran off. Minutes later he reappeared with two lamas. One briefly examined Tsang, wincing when he saw his broken leg. He gave orders to carry him away. The second lama asked who we were and where we were going.

"Traders," I replied. "Going to India with our skins and Tibetan crafts."

"At this time of year?" asked the lama.

"We were caught out by the bad weather. We will continue on our way. But for now we would like to rest here."

"For how long?"

I estimated we should be two days ahead of the monks from Tengyeling, maybe more if they had been delayed by the bad weather.

"One day. We will leave at first light the day after tomorrow." I knew this was the right decision. Anyway, the journey from here to India would now follow an established road, according to Lama Kunchen's directions, so the going should be easier. We should be able to press on more quickly once we'd regained our strength.

The lama agreed to my request. He detailed a monk to show us to the visitors' quarters. And then to show us to the refectory. So it was not long afterwards that we had the first warm food for days. Of course it was tsampa, but by now I was used to it. Some minutes later an ancient monk made his way to where we were sitting. He gave us a cursory glance, and then noticed the bowl I was using – the one Lama Kunchen had given me.

"That bowl is worn with age," he commented. "Where did you get it?"

"This? From a lama. A very learned lama," I replied.

Jorchin hadn't followed what had happened – his Tibetan wasn't good enough – so he was still eating away. The old monk peered at me in a strange way, and then smiled. I assessed him in the way I'd been taught... and then smiled too. Because in that moment I'd had the strange but happy experience of seeing Lama Kunchen in the old man. His image had appeared, merged with the old man, smiled at me, and then left.

"I see we have friends in common," said the ancient monk. "It is an honour to meet you."

I bowed my head, determined not to give anything away.

"I won't bother you," continued the monk, "for I'm sure you don't want to draw attention to yourself. But you should know there is a detachment of Chinese troops in Pari." With that he shuffled off.

"What'd he want?" asked Jorchin, still eating.

"I think just to look at some strangers," I said, helping myself to more tsampa. But all the while I was thinking hard.

That ancient monk was clearly part of Lama Kunchen's order. He'd recognised me – how, I don't know: maybe his third eye was open too. I half suspected Lama Kunchen had made sure someone from his order was present in Chatsa in case we'd needed assistance. That was why he'd advised me to stop here. Certainly the monk's information was vital. We had to go through Pari. If there were Chinese soldiers there, if the Tengyeling monks were in concert with them, then danger lay ahead rather than behind, as I had assumed. I had to trust that we were safe for now in the monastery. But I felt as if we were being tracked by wolves on two sides.

We saw to our animals as soon as we'd finished eating. And then I made Jorchin and Lobsang carry everything to our quarters. They complained, but I told them we couldn't risk having anything stolen. When everything was assembled, I barred the door with a cupboard. That would ensure we weren't taken unawares in the night. Then I settled down for the first proper sleep in days.

The next morning I got up early to go to the morning service. Jorchin was surprised, but I told him we needed to appear devout in the eyes of our hosts. Afterwards, I asked to see the abbot and made an offering. I gave more than I needed, but I wanted to make sure he viewed us in a good light. The energy in the monastery, and the abbot himself, still felt good, but I did not want to be betrayed.

I then sought out the lama who had seen to our needs the day before. I asked if we could buy provisions from the monastery. That way we could avoid having to make a stop in Pari. But he said the monastery had little and he couldn't help. Masking my disappointment I went to see Tsang. He was still in a bad way. If he had been at Chakpori he would have been much better looked after. But the monks were doing what they could, and at least he was more comfortable. I could see he was in no shape to continue with us. I didn't want to be held back by him, so I paid for his board and keep for two months and told him Lobsang would pick him up on the return trip. I wasn't sure if he understood me but I couldn't waste any more time with him.

I spent the afternoon with the doorkeeper asking about the route from Chatsa to Pari and beyond. I didn't want to give away our plans, but I guessed that the Tengyeling monks must have known, from the direction we were travelling in, our likely destination. Even so, I asked particularly about Bhutan. If ever the doorkeeper was interrogated about our conversation, he might be able to confuse our pursuers to some degree.[67]

Later, I checked our animals. They were in good condition considering our journey to Chatsa. The yaks disliked being in a stable and wanted to move on. I spent time with each of the yaks and horses, telling them I appreciated their strength, as I knew our success depended on their ability to make good going over the next days. Again, I was struck by the difference between the horses – who responded positively – and the yaks who seemed to ignore me.

As I was leaving the stables, I froze inside. The wind was still icily cold, but it wasn't the weather that had made me freeze. I knew it was an evil presence. I hung back in the shadow of the stables and looked around to see what was making me feel this way. A few monks were walking briskly from building to building in the cold wind. It wasn't them; their auras and energy were unexceptional. I edged forwards and peered round the side of the wall. I saw an official looking man in rich robes talking to some lamas near the entrance. The lamas were waving their hands. They were clearly getting agitated about something. But the rich looking man remained calm. My pulse was racing.

The rich looking man, so calm on the outside, had streams of dark colours coming from him. I could even see with my third eye a small black figure crouched on his shoulder darting its eyes around. The rich looking man was a bigger being than the lamas, but the lamas at least were honest and doing their best to resist him. I knew, without

---

[67] Bhutan is the closest country to Chatsa monastery. Traders went there as well as India.

191

being told, that he was a senior member of the dark. I also knew he must be looking for me.

I offered up a silent prayer to Lama Kunchen. What should I do? I felt his voice immediately saying "Nothing". I waited, feeling warmer. And then suddenly the rich man turned and left through the main gate, a spray of dark colours following him. The group of lamas went into the main hall looking wrought. I caught up with them and overheard one saying, "These aristocrats do not show proper consideration to religion! I don't care how rich he is, he cannot barge in here and do what he likes!"

Now I needed some luck. I went round the monastery looking for the ancient monk whom I presumed was part of the secret order. I found him bent over a walking stick making his slow way from the library. He acknowledged me but kept walking. I went up to him.

"Venerable one," I said, glancing round to make sure no-one else could hear. The monk stopped, scanned me, and recognised I was in a predicament. He stood up straight.

"How can I help?" he asked.

"I need three sets of monks robes. Can you get them for me?"

"Meet me in the stables before the evening service," he replied, "I will have what you need." He then reverted to his stoop and walked off.

I was at the stables at the appointed time. He had the three sets of robes. I stuffed them into a saddle bag and bowed to him. He inclined his head and left. I attended the evening service. The lama who had been overseeing us asked if we were leaving the next day. I told him we were planning to leave after breakfast and to spend the next night in Pari. I thanked him for his hospitality. I then returned to our room.

"We're leaving before dawn," I told Jorchin and Lobsang.

"Eh? Why so early?" complained Jorchin. "We don't have a snow leopard on our tail."

"The sooner we can get this over, the sooner we can go home," I replied in an irritated voice. Why did Jorchin have this tendency to be obstructive? He looked annoyed, but he didn't argue for now.

So, two hours before dawn, we assembled the animals and stole out of the monastery. The yaks' clanking bells made a terrible noise, but we managed to leave without anyone coming to see what was happening. A large bribe to the night watchman helped open the monastery's gates.

An hour later I halted the caravan.

"Get changed into these," I ordered, throwing down the monks robes.

"Was there any chang in the monastery?" asked Jorchin. "Or have you really taken leave of your senses?"

"Jorchin," I said trying to control my anger, "I rescued you and I will take you home. Just do as I say!"

Looking sour, he began to put on the robes, shivering as he did so in the cold wind. I had to help him put them on correctly as he'd never worn such robes before. I wanted us to look, for all the world, as a small party of monks, not traders. That way we might have a chance to sneak through Pari without the Chinese soldiers recognising us for who we really were.

Lobsang though had great problems disguising himself as a monk. He was abusing Buddha, he said, he didn't want to be reincarnated as a dog in his next life. I soothed him with a handful of gold. If Jigme had betrayed me, at least he had also helped by being so generous with the amount of money he'd given me.

We reached Pari a little after dawn. Although it wasn't snowing, it was still bitterly cold. I located the merchant's shop, to get the provisions we needed, but there was no sign of life. I made my way round the back. Still no sign of life. When I regained the main street I felt a lurch in my solar plexus. Our animals were where I had left them, but Jorchin and Lobsang were gone. The lurch wasn't just my shock at not seeing them, it was something worse. Something sickly and menacing.

Just then I saw a figure emerge from a house. The richly dressed man I'd seen yesterday. He stopped when he saw me. Smiling and bowing in the hope this might disorientate him, I moved quickly up to him. He seemed to be trying to work out who I was – monk, or the man he was looking for? Still smiling, I grabbed his wrist and twisted his arm behind his back before he knew what was happening. Just as I suspected: he was as weak as a child. I then marched him back into the house he'd just left to the stifled sounds of his obvious pain.

It was crammed full of people. Jorchin and Lobsang were in the centre surrounded by the monks from Tengyeling. Although I was one and they were eight, I felt in command of the situation. The monks were startled when they saw me. Some of them edged backwards. But their leader grabbed Jorchin and put a knife to his throat.

"Let Lord Tensering go!" he said in an ugly voice.

I put my hands around Tensering's head and snapped his neck. Easier than killing a lamb. He collapsed to the floor to looks of shock from the others. That man was evil, he'd abused his position as an aristocrat, and when he came back as a worm in his next life, I'd happily squash it too.

The lead monk suddenly looked doubtful. He tightened his grip on Jorchin and ordered the others to attack me. No-one moved. I knew I was going to get out of there alive.

"If you take one step more, I'll kill him!" said the monk in a loud, nervous voice.

I opened the door. "Get out!" I growled to the others. "Get out now or I'll kill you too!"

Four of them made a move to the door. Their leader screamed at them to seize me, but they paid no attention and fled. Lobsang, looking terrified, followed. A fifth moved to the door to leave and then, almost as an afterthought, made a half-hearted attempt to grab me. I smashed him and threw him back into the room. He was unconscious before he hit the floor. Actually, I felt sorry for him. He wasn't evil; I could feel that. He was just weak, doing what he'd been told rather than following his inner advice. The remaining two monks leapt out when they saw what had happened to their colleague. That just left the lead monk with his knife to Jorchin's throat.

"Give me what I want and I'll let him live!" said the monk. I knew he was in no position to demand anything. But Jorchin didn't. He was petrified.

"Give it to him, Thaza!" he pleaded.

"I'll give you nothing," I said to the monk.

"Where is it?" demanded the monk above Jorchin's whimpers.

"I don't know what you're talking about."

"It's in his saddlebag!"

It was Jorchin. To this day I don't know if he knew about the Morning Tree or if he was just guessing that whatever the monk wanted was likely to be in one of my saddlebags.

Clearly the monk believed him. He started edging round to get to the door so he could go outside and search my saddlebags. As he moved, he kept Jorchin in front of him, knife to his throat. I could see it had scrapped his skin and there was a trickle of blood. But I wasn't going to let the monk get outside. I moved to bar his way.

"Get out of the way Thaza!" shouted Jorchin.

I was taken aback by Jorchin's vehemence. He actually pushed me to make his point. Had fear unhinged him or was he really siding with the Tengyeling monk?

I had no compunction now in doing what was needed. Jorchin had chosen to side with the Tengyeling monk rather than trust me. And I was not going to let the Tengyeling monk get anywhere near my saddlebags. His companions might be harmless, but he was clearly out to stop me.

"You can go to hell," I said in a low voice, advancing on the pair.

The monk's eyes flashed between me and Jorchin who was now trying to twist away from me. The monk, sensing he couldn't hold Jorchin and fight me, slashed his knife across Jorchin's throat and thrust him aside. I kept my eyes on the monk. Dodging his swinging knife, I elbowed him under his chin, spun him round and cracked the back of his neck. He fell to the floor and writhed for some moments, making anguished, gurgling sounds. Despite the commotion, I knew his life force had gone. That left Jorchin gibbering on the ground.

I bent down to look at him. I swear, I was going to help him, but he just spat in my face. Why? He was crying now, blood spurting from his throat. Clearly he was going to die. It was miserable. So I put him out of his misery.

I tell you, I had no regrets about killing the monk and the richly dressed man. They were evil, the world was better without them. Besides, they would have killed me and taken the Morning Tree if I hadn't. But Jorchin… I was sad. It's true, I'd never liked him. Too weak as a personality, never my equal. But he should have been my brother-in-law. We should have been friends. I did forgive him in my heart in that moment, but I didn't have time to dwell on this now.

I knew the monks who had fled would not trouble me anymore. Their hearts had never been in it. I smoothed my robes and left the house. The cold wind sharpened my senses. My pack animals were where I'd left them, and there were beginning to be signs of life from the other houses, but still nobody else in the street. I knew I had to leave immediately before the bodies were discovered. Gathering myself, and looking as calm as possible, I goaded the animals forward and we made our slow way out of town. I didn't dare stop for provisions now. We'd have to make do with what we had. I felt sorry for the animals, but vowed to see them right later. I looked for Lobsang, but he'd gone too.

So, I was on my own. But in truth, I was elated. I had faced the Tengyeling monks and their accomplice – one against eight – and I had won. I had been balanced and in the moment. And I had used everything Lama Kunchen and Mingyar had taught me. It had all worked. I felt good.

What's more, my pursuers had gone. The last stage of the way to India lay open. I had the Morning Tree, and I was going to deliver it.

I Succeed

I made good progress despite the snow. The sun had come out and the path at this point was relatively easy. Although I kept looking over my shoulder, I knew I wasn't being pursued. The remaining Tengyeling monks were not after me, nor was anyone from Pari. I reckoned if someone had by now found the dead bodies, they would as soon as offer them to the vultures as try to find out what had happened. There had been no sign of the Chinese soldiers either. No, I was free from what had taken place in Pari. What's more, I couldn't sense any danger ahead.

In fact, I was enjoying myself. It was much easier to be alone. Tsang and Lobsang were worthy enough, but I'd had to look after them as much as they had helped me. And Jorchin had been a problem really from the time we'd left Mongolia. I was freer without them. I felt sharp, awake and alive.

The yaks didn't seem to mind the conditions and the fact that they hadn't been fed for a while. But the horses were more fragile. I sensed their distress and stopped at noon to give them a good feed. I groomed them while they ate to reassure them. All the while I was connecting with them and telling them we made a good team. I also changed back into my trader's clothes. They were warmer.

I pushed on as soon as I could because I wasn't sure the weather would hold and I wanted to get to Yatung before nightfall. In the event, I didn't make it. But as it wasn't snowing, I pulled off the path and found shelter from the wind in a small hollow of rocks. I corralled the animals, fed the horses and buried myself under a pile of clothes.

I was grateful for the fine clothes Jigme had provided, and for the extra monks robes which I heaped on top of me.

I made Yatung early next morning. It seemed friendly. I knew the animals needed to rest, so I found lodgings and bought extra feed. There were few travellers at this time of year, so everything was easy. No-one questioned why I was there either. I slept most of that day with my animals and belongings in a stable. At dusk I had my evening meal and then settled down for the night. I hadn't realised how tired I was.

I awoke at four, or so I judged the time. I thought of Lama Kunchen. And suddenly felt his presence. It was as if he was with me in the stable, only of course he wasn't. But he looked concerned. I mean, I felt a deep warmth inside me – Lama Kunchen really was paying me a visit – but he definitely looked concerned. That's funny, I thought, he should be happy at the progress I was making. The vision was vivid, although it didn't last long. I couldn't sleep after that for thinking what it meant.

I left as soon as dawn came. I continued down the valley before the long and arduous climb to the Dzelep Pass. It started snowing near the top. Mercifully the horses and yaks were in good condition, and we made the pass without mishap. The yaks would have done it even if the snow had been twice as deep. But I was really pleased with the horses: they were working hard for me now.

An hour after dark we reached Gnatong. The last hour had been very difficult. The path was narrow, and almost impossible to see. I had tied the animals together and was leading my horse from the front. I couldn't see, but I sensed my way forward. I understood now why Lama Kunchen had blindfolded me all those weeks before. I wondered if he hadn't foreseen exactly this moment and, out of his love for me, taught me that exercise simply to help me now.

On our arrival, two men came out of the largest building there. They had been alerted by the clanking bells around the yaks and came to see what was happening. They turned out to be servants of the local official. They pulled me to the veranda of the official's house, where there was more light to look at my face. They asked where I'd come from and where I was going. They counted the number of animals I had. They couldn't believe I'd made the last hour in the dark, and kept asking where I'd come from and what time I'd left Pari. I was getting irritated at their behaviour. I demanded shelter for myself and my animals. At last they directed me to an outbuilding and left me to it.

I suppose I should have been more aware. Hadn't I been trained by Lama Kunchen to sense energy? Hadn't he visited me the night before in a clearly anxious state? And didn't I know that the servants who'd just interrogated me were somehow suspicious? Well, yes. But I was tired. I thought I'd seen off my pursuers at Pari. And I knew I was just days from India and the end of my task. The fact is, I wasn't checking the energy. I was irritated and couldn't be bothered. Like a lazy goat I was unaware of the wolf lurking nearby.

I slept badly that night – another sign, if only I'd been aware – and the animals were restless too. When I awoke next morning I was dimly conscious of some movement around me. I sat up. Three grey coated figures were poking around at the back of the outbuilding. They appeared nervous to see me stir. A man barked at them in a foreign language. The figures rushed me. Before I could get up, they were on me: Chinese soldiers as I now saw. I rolled free and flipped up, ready to fight. But suddenly I was jabbed painfully from behind and almost fell. More soldiers to my rear were prodding me with rifles. They pushed me towards the door of the outbuilding. I could see other soldiers were waiting in the courtyard.

I moved warily outside into the light of an overcast morning. I wanted to fight, but was now surrounded by chattering Chinese soldiers, waving and stabbing their rifles at me. They looked more scared than I was. But they had loaded weapons. Even a child can be dangerous with a gun. They forced me in the direction of a small hut. I moved slowly towards it. I knew without anything being said that my fate would be decided inside that hut.

My hand went to my chest where I felt a hard object under my clothes – the bronze Buddha the Dalai Lama had given me. I would beat these bastards! The soldiers pushed me roughly into the hut. I tripped down some steps and fell onto the floor.

"Ah, Thaza," came a well-known voice, "what a surprise to see you here."

I scrambled up only to be grabbed by two more soldiers and thrust down onto a small stool. Lama Neto leered over me. Behind him was Norchen. My arms were bent double behind my back and I was suddenly in too much pain to speak. But my heart and third eye were thumping. My heart from nerves, my third eye from an oppressive sourness.

"As I say," continued Lama Neto, "what a surprise to see you here. I had been told you were returning to Mongolia. But here you are heading towards… India? Either your geography is very bad, or I've been lied to."

His voice, although even, had a depth of darkness to it. He looked me over disdainfully. "Now, why would you be heading towards India?"

I caught my breath. Shock and anger were beginning to give me strength. "What business is it of yours?" I spat, all the while trying to open up to the energy to find a way out.

"Oh come, come," said Lama Neto, nodding curtly to the soldiers behind me. They jerked my arms harder behind my back. I bit my tongue to make sure I didn't cry out. "We both know what is going on," he continued. "There's no need to pretend anymore."

I stayed silent, breathing heavily. Norchen was looking at me with concern. Lama Neto raised his eyebrows.

"The Morning Tree?" he said quietly, but with menace.

I looked at him as if I didn't understand. In truth, my heart had missed a beat. I felt barbs of icy energy twist themselves around me. Just then the Chinese soldiers started throwing my saddlebags into a pile in the middle of the room.

"The Morning Tree," repeated Lama Neto chillingly, as more saddlebags were thrown in.

"I don't know—"

There was a thud from behind as a soldier crashed his rifle butt into my head. My senses swam. Lama Neto bent down and looked straight into my face.

"We can do this the easy way or the hard way," he said. "Which is it to be?"

"Why do you want it?" I said between breaths.

"Why? Why? It is part of our religion, our culture! It should stay in Tibet! Why should it leave? What right do you have to say that thousands of years of secret knowledge should pass into the hands of just anyone?"

"But this knowledge should be given *to* everyone."

"Who says so? That old fool Kunchen? He's worse than a child. People don't want knowledge. They want to be looked after. They want security. Do you really think the peasants in this village want to be given all this fancy knowledge? They wouldn't know what to do with it."

"You mean you want to keep this knowledge to yourself."

"Of course," said Lama Neto. "It should be restricted to as few as possible."

"So you can use it to make yourself more powerful."

"How naïve you are. We may or may not use the knowledge for ourselves. That's not the point. The point is to prevent it reaching other people. That way we can maintain the status quo."

"Of keeping people in ignorance."

"Exactly. Ignorance robs people of their own power. But it is a happy ignorance. Tell me Thaza, would you rather have stayed in Mongolia and not known anything about all this, or are you happier that you know what you do and that you are now my prisoner?"

He seemed pleased with himself. The Chinese soldiers, not understanding Tibetan, were looking uncertain. In a strange way, I was suddenly feeling uncertain too. Maybe it wouldn't matter if everything stayed the same, if this book never reached anyone else. Life wasn't so bad, why make all the effort to change? The sour energy had momentarily lifted and I was beginning to feel better. But then I

201

thought of everything that Lama Kunchen had done to protect the Morning Tree, about how the dark were clearly after it and how mankind could have a much better life if it reached the outside world. I felt Lama Kunchen's presence – I saw him talking to me back at Chakpori – and a lovely energy passed over me. This was real. There was a better life we could have. I knew in a way I could not describe that I had to get the Morning Tree out. It couldn't fall into the dark's hands.

"But the Chinese—"

"The Chinese are our friends! If only the Dalai Lama would stop being so stubborn and antagonising them, we would all be much safer. The Chinese will let us live as we want as long as we recognise their overlordship. Their friendship is the best way to protect our way of life." Then Lama Neto laughed. "Oh I see. You've been told that the Chinese want to destroy our culture. Those fools! If we accept the Chinese they will be able to preserve our religion. Surely that's what you want too."

"I don't care about your religion!" I snapped.

"Good," said Lama Neto, looking at me intently. "Good. Then perhaps we can make a deal. You give me the Morning Tree, and I'll let you return to Mongolia. It is what you want, isn't it? To return home and marry some woman? It's what Norchen tells me."

"I don't care about your religion," I repeated. "But I do care about Lama Kunchen. I won't let him down!"

Lama Neto sighed. "He really has wormed his way into your affections. I'm surprised. Do you really want to sacrifice your future happiness to the whims of that old man?"

I didn't want to reply. An oppressive silence filled the room. Vivid, dark colours swirled around Lama Neto's head. I didn't know what to do. But I didn't want to give up.

"What do you know about Lama Kunchen," I said at last.

Lama Neto laughed. "Everything I need. He thinks he's so holy, and so clever, but we were watching him all the time."

"Then… then why didn't you just take the Morning Tree?"

"Do you think a thing like that is just lying about? And do you think I wouldn't be spotted taking it? No, we had to wait until it was in the open – until you had it – then we could make our move."

"So you knew about me all along?"

"I knew that old fool Kunchen was going to use you. I thought he was mad. You – you're just a herdsman! But I see now what he saw in you. You're really quite developed."

"How did you know I'd left Chakpori?" I braced myself to hear of Jigme's treachery.

"Norchen," said Lama Neto.

"Thaza, honestly, I didn't tell him anything!" cried Norchen hoarsely. He was looking miserable.

"No, the silly pup didn't *tell* me. How could he? You didn't tell him." Lama Neto sneered. "But he does love you, not that he'd express it that way. He was miserable not seeing you, and knew on a subconscious level that you'd left. I tapped into that and realised you'd gone. I am developed in my own way too, you know."

"So you used Norchen. Just like you always have."

Lama Neto raised his eyebrows. "I had hoped for more from him. But he's always disappointed me. No matter, I'll find another better suited to my needs."

Norchen looked up. For the first time I saw a flame in his eyes that had not been there before.

"What about the monks from Tengyeling?" I asked.

"I'd sent them ahead of me to apprehend you. I had to be in Lhasa to attend the Dalai Lama – silly man, he's called on me a great deal recently – but I left as soon as I could. But I see you dealt with them."

He didn't seem distressed that some of his accomplices were dead and the rest Buddha knows where.

"Thankfully the Amban[68] lent me some troops," he continued. "We had to travel night and day, but here we are."

---

[68] The Amban was China's representative in Tibet. The Chinese always had some troops in Lhasa and elsewhere.

He puffed himself up. Always a small man, he didn't look impressive. But he did have a type of power.

"So Thaza, give me what you are carrying."

I clammed my mouth shut. He looked at me hard, and then sighed.

"All right, enough of these games. I've given you the opportunity to cooperate. Had you given me the book, even under duress, we would have won a significant victory. We'd have won you over to us, even though you might still despise us."

I shot him a dirty look.

"Oh yes Thaza, it's the incidental moments that are most important. You think battling against the weather and the Tengyeling monks to get this far makes you a hero for the light. In fact, all would have been undone by one moment of weakness. One yes to me, even though you might have spent the rest of your life railing against what I stand for, would have weakened the light and strengthened us immeasurably. But no matter. Since you refuse to cooperate, you'll lose twice: I'm going to take the Morning Tree, and then I'm going to kill you."

For some reason, I thought of the time I had broken my promise to Lama Kunchen and bargained with him about marrying Sarangerel. It seemed a little thing at the time, to bargain with him. But I remembered the look of sadness on his face. I understood now that I'd failed him. Probably that I'd thrown everything into the balance. It's strange how the incidental things, as Lama Neto said, can be the most important.

It was getting hot in that small room. Lama Neto was getting more agitated. His eyes were flashing over my sacks and bags now piled up inside.

"That one!" he said pointing to the saddlebag with the Morning Tree. How had he known? "Bring it to me!"

He smacked the face of the nearest soldier to make them hurry up. He ripped open the saddlebag, hands feverishly searching inside. Then stopped. A big smile spread across his face. I knew he'd found the Morning Tree. I could feel Lama Kunchen's sadness. The failure of everything he'd worked for. But I also felt rage. The words 'not again!' for some reason rang in my ears. An energy seized me.

In an instant I twisted free from the two soldiers holding me – their attention had been distracted by Lama Neto's antics. I smashed one with my elbow and broke the other's arm. A third soldier backed away terrified.

I made towards Lama Neto. He reached inside his robe. I knew he'd take out a pistol. I couldn't get to him first as all my bags were in the way. But then, amazingly, Norchen seized Lama Neto's wrist and smashed it down on his knee. The pistol fell to the floor. Norchen grabbed it and pointed it at Lama Neto.

"You idiot!" gasped Lama Neto. "You don't even know how to use that!"

It was true. Norchen was shaking uncontrollably. He'd never have fired. Lama Neto moved slowly to Norchen.

"Give it to me," said Lama Neto menacingly. Norchen stood there shaking.

"Pull the trigger, Norchen," I said as firmly and calmly as I could.

"I would have spared your life," hissed Lama Neto, still advancing on Norchen and nursing his wrist. "But now I'm going to kill you too!"

"Norchen, pull the trigger!"

There was a loud bang, a bright flash and a musty smell. Lama Neto looked in amazement. Norchen had fired the gun but merely blasted a hole in the hut. But Lama Neto was disorientated. I flew over the bags and wrestled him to the floor. He was small and not used to fighting. He bit me – the coward's way. But I jerked his neck as Mingyar had taught me. He let out a stream of black breath while his body convulsed. Then he was gone.

It felt as if a sickly sourness had left the world.

"Norchen—"

But my words were cut off by another roar. The third Chinese soldier had fired his rifle. The bullet lifted Norchen into the air, ripped open a bloody cavity in his chest and flung him against the wall all in one moment.

I spun round. The other two soldiers had already scarpered. The third – a soft and very frightened man – dropped his smoking rifle and fled.

I went to Norchen. Blood was pouring from his quivering body, his head was at a strange angle and his open eyes were looking up to the roof. He was showing me he was going to the Heavenly Fields. I held his hand while his body shuddered its last movements. His hand was still warm. I hadn't been given the chance to thank him for saving me. But there was a glow in my heart. We had been friends. He was off to a better life for helping me and Lama Kunchen. And he wouldn't have to suffer Lama Neto's bullying anymore. Thanks to him, we would win.

I felt a fluttering go past as Norchen's body let out a final gurgle. I knew it was his spirit leaving for a better place.

I didn't have time to break my friend's bones for the vultures, or even to take in all that had happened. Coming back to myself, I realised I had to get out of there quickly. I was annoyed I had been ambushed by Lama Neto, and needed to act decisively. I opened up to the energy. I sensed dark forces but, at the same time, there was a more powerful stream of light. My next steps were clear. I gathered the saddlebag with the Morning Tree and stepped out of the door. A small group of locals were staring nervously at the hut. They backed away when they saw me come out.

"The Chinese soldiers were going to rob me!" I shouted, my voice shaking at the same time. "The lamas tried to intervene, but the soldiers shot them!" I flung open the door so the bodies of Lama Neto and Norchen could be seen. The people were shocked. At that moment the local official marched up and barked that I was to be arrested.

"What for?" I cried. "So you can hand me over to your Chinese friends?" The official stopped in his tracks. I could see he wasn't used to being challenged. "Your Chinese friends who kill monks and want to imprison the Dalai Lama?" The locals were getting agitated now. I could see there was no love lost between them and the official.

"It's true!" shouted a man. "I saw the soldiers push him into that hut and throw in his belongings. He didn't have a gun. Then there were shots and the soldiers ran out!"

"Leaving two lamas dead," added another man, peering more closely into the hut.

This was too much for the by now middling sized crowd. They turned on the official. He tried shouting at them, but had to cover his face as he was pelted with rocks. He shuffled backwards and then turned and fled.

I sat on the ground. Someone asked me if I was all right. I told them to fetch lamas from the nearest monastery. While we were waiting, I re-saddled my animals. I made a point of paying those who helped me. I wanted to ensure their good opinion by the time the local monks arrived.

About an hour later they turned up. The lamas were genuinely shocked and outraged when they saw the bodies of their dead companions. I needn't have worried about them believing my story. They had been told what had happened by the villagers who'd fetched them. It was clear they'd never liked the official either. I hoped his days were numbered.

I didn't want to stay in Gnatong – it still felt slimy, and seemed to be shrouded in this permanent damp mist – but I needed new supplies and by the time everything had settled down it was too late to set off. So I stayed another uncomfortable night in that outbuilding. But at least this time I regularly scanned the energy. Despite the griminess, everything was clear.

Then at dawn I resumed my journey. I still felt the stain of what had happened, but at the same time there was a current of clean energy. I sensed it was growing. I sensed I had crossed an abyss and the way was clear now to accomplish my task.

Shortly after Gnatong the path descended abruptly into Sikkim – India at last. I followed the wire lines down the valley.[69] It definitely was a different world. Thickly wooded hills, steep green valleys and so much warmer. But this was nothing to Kalimpong. It wasn't as big as Lhasa, but it was so crowded and busy. And it had cars. I'd heard of them, but never seen one. They are truly miraculous. Wheeled vehicles that move by themselves. I've tried telling the monks here about them, but they don't believe I've ever seen one. What do they know! Of course, they can never replace horses – you can't herd animals with them – but I would have loved to have experienced riding in one.

But the horses were also a thing to excite wonder. Of course, there were Tibetan ponies ridden by the locals. But there were also taller, less sturdy horses ridden by foreigners. I doubted they'd survive a Mongolian winter, but all the same, they had a beauty about them I'd never have appreciated if I hadn't seen them for myself. They were intelligent too.

And the people – I saw my first Europeans, including a girl with white hair and a man with a red beard. Truly astonishing. I stared at them as they passed me by and I'd never have believed it if I hadn't seen them with my own eyes. There was such a mix of people too – Bhutanese, Nepalese and so many different kinds of Indians, as well as a handful of Europeans. There was a lot to marvel at.

However, I kept a low profile. I lodged in a small stable and kept myself to myself. The next day I sold my yaks – they were uncomfortable at these lower altitudes and wanted to go home. I bought some horses instead (Tibetan, not European – I didn't know how to work with them and didn't want to add to my burdens by finding out), and stocked up on feed and provisions. The day after I continued my journey to Darjeeling.

The journey was uneventful. By now I was accustomed to the different and very green scenery. And I saw my first tea plantations. Unimaginable rows of tea bushes with workers drifting through them.

---

[69] There was a British run telegraph station at Gnatong. Presumably Thaza was following the telegraph wires.

I had never wondered where my tea came from before. I was continually checking the energy, but it always felt clear. I knew at a deeper level inside me that I was safe, but after Gnatong, I wasn't going to take anything for granted.

I arrived in Darjeeling three days later. It was amazing! Such a big city. So full of people, noise, buildings and smells. I couldn't believe the number of shops and restaurants, nor the fiery food on offer. But at least I could have my fill of meat. My belly complained in the beginning, but I had never had such tasty food before – or since. I was astonished that food could taste like that.

But this was nothing to my astonishment at seeing the steam beasts! They were so loud and travelled on iron rails. I had heard of them, as I had heard of cars, but had never seen one. They are terrifying when you first see them. But I'm told they can do a journey in days that would take weeks or months. They say Europeans have no religion, but truly they have other wonders to compare with anything we have in Tibet.

I admit I found my first afternoon in the city difficult. After so many days on my own, to be pressed on all sides by so many people was bewildering. My third eye was also hurting. I wondered if these powers come out best in peace and quiet. But at least I had arrived at my destination with the Morning Tree intact. And it had taken no more than a month after leaving Lhasa. Spring was definitely in the air, and the first flowers were coming out too.

I lodged in a Tibetan monastery. It's what other traders from Tibet did. I took the opportunity of selling all but three of my horses. I would need them for my return journey. I then took a few days to acclimatise myself to the city. I scouted out the main market, and checked the prices of the Tibetan goods on sale. I didn't need to secure the best prices for my furs and silverware (I still had a sizeable amount of money left), but I didn't want to stand out by selling too cheaply. Another Tibetan trader told me where I could get my certificate for having a market stall. This took several days and more money than I anticipated. But at last I was ready.

Lama Kunchen said I would know who to give the Morning Tree to. He didn't tell me how I'd know. I had to trust. So I set out my goods and waited. Most of the people who came were other traders curious to check what I was selling. But eventually buyers came. This went on for three days. Every evening I would pack up my goods and return to the monastery. And every morning I would go back to the market.

It was a good opportunity to study the people who came to the stall. I could sense the honest and the dishonest ones, the serious buyers and those with no intention of buying. With my powers, it was easy. I had an altercation with one man who tried to lift some goods without paying for them. A small crowd gathered while we sorted things out.

Then, in the afternoon of the third day, suddenly there he was. An Indian. Quite skinny. Wearing a mixture of Indian and European clothes. He didn't stand out from the crowd. But when I saw him, I just saw this tremendous light around him. He came up to my pitch and spoke to me. I gestured that I didn't understand his language. He nodded and went away, returning a little later with two Tibetans. He spoke to one of the Tibetans who then spoke to me.

"Is this all you have for sale?"

I spread my hands over my remaining stock. The Indian man looked puzzled. He peered at everything I had and then spoke again to the interpreter.

"Do you have anything else? Anything especially Tibetan?" said the interpreter.

I knew I had to give the Morning Tree to this Indian, but still my mind wanted reassurance.

"Does he have anything in particular he is looking for?" I asked the interpreter. More conversation between the Indian and the interpreter and then the answer:

"A book."

I felt as if the sun had come out inside me. Everything was just right. I didn't speak for a moment – the feeling was too great – but the Indian mistook my silence for a negative answer.

"He says he was told by his master to ask you for a special book," said the interpreter. "He doesn't understand that you don't have it."

I stood up and opened the two saddlebags that were next to me – one with the book, the other with the cover. The Indian smiled when he saw what was there. I handed the bags to him. There was a feeling of complete rightness and success. And, as if to confirm it all, I felt Lama Kunchen beside me then, deeply happy at what was happening. The Indian, so unassuming, and bending now under the weight of the saddlebags, was bathed in beautiful colours as I sensed his honesty and his master's love. The saddlebags were too heavy for him to carry, and he had to ask one of the Tibetans to help. The Indian bowed to me, and I to him. And then he left.

"Hey," said the other Tibetan, "he didn't pay you for it!"

"He didn't have to," I replied, as I felt a warm glow in my heart centre.

I had accomplished my mission.

Against all the odds, and ending up in a place I would never have imagined (and, if I'm honest, showing traits I never thought I possessed), I had succeeded in my task.

I felt so good. At the same time, I felt so calm. I thought of my long journey from Mongolia and realised how much I had achieved. Now I was free. Free to return home and marry Sarangerel.

I spent the next few days feeling calm and detached. I wondered if I'd achieved some heightened meditative state that most monks would give their right arm to experience. Nothing bothered me and, curiously, although I wanted to return home and pick up the reins of my life, I didn't feel the urge to leave Darjeeling at once. Even the noise and crush of the city, that had irked me and hurt my third eye when I'd first arrived, didn't unsettle me. I remember one of the monks in the lamasery where I was staying asking if I'd just made a lot of money or else why was I so at peace. I didn't tell him. I just didn't feel the need to explain myself or anything to anyone.

And I didn't feel the need to communicate with Lama Kunchen either. He'd appeared to me at the moment I'd handed the Morning Tree over. He knew. I knew he knew. There was nothing more to be done.

This detachment gradually subsided, and I found myself eventually longing to return home again. So I sold my remaining stock at rock bottom prices to another trader, and bought provisions for my return journey. I also bought silks, gold ornaments and some modern tools. They would serve well when I got home. Finally, I had the best meal I could find. I was growing used to the powerfully flavoured food and wanted as much of it as I could before I left.

Then I set off on my return journey.

Epilogue

I went due north to Shigatse, then Ganden and on across the Tibetan plateau. It was the most direct route home, and it avoided Lhasa. I didn't want to return there. It would delay my journey, and I wasn't sure if any of Lama Neto's accomplices wouldn't be looking for me. Yes, I would like to have seen Lama Kunchen again, but he knew I had been successful and hadn't asked me to return. Now it was my time to go home and resume my life.

I made good progress. I had chosen my horses well. And the weather was improving all the time. My mind was already on what I would do when I returned. I knew where to look for Batzorig and his family – they usually rotated among the same pastures, and my powers confirmed that I would find them there. Of course, I would have to tell him that Jorchin had died; I'd have to make up a story that showed him in a good light. But Batzorig's sadness should be matched by his joy at my marrying Sarangerel. I would tell him that I was the head of my family now and able to ask for his daughter's hand. I would also absolve him of the need for a large dowry. I didn't want anything to delay my nuptials.

I was maybe eight weeks from home when I passed through the small village at Yerlang. I had noticed that my powers had been declining. Lama Kunchen had said that they would. And I suppose I wasn't bothering as much to use them. But as I was negotiating for food and water for the horses, I was seized by alarm. I knew it must mean something bad, but I didn't know what. I transacted my business. And then I saw him.

Lorga.

He was squatting on the ground, some henchmen around him. I moved on, hoping he hadn't seen me. But then he looked my way. A moment, and then recognition crossed his face. He stood up, staring at me, his mouth open. I pretended not to notice, mounted my horse and carried on my way.

He didn't follow me. Gradually my heart stopped beating so wildly. So, he was still alive. I pressed on that day and camped late. I still felt uneasy, but didn't know why. Seeing Lorga had unsettled me, and I was puzzled by how much. That night, sitting by my camp fire in a rocky hollow, the horses started whinnying. I picked up their distress, and was feeling uncomfortable in myself. Then I heard a scrabbling noise, loose stones fell around me and I was rushed by three men. I struggled, but they pinned me to the ground and started beating me. I recognised the biggest as Lorga. As he punched me, he drew breath and roared:

"You cuckolding bastard! Stealing my wife from me! No-one steals my property!"

I lost consciousness. Before I did, the sour thought passed through my mind that maybe Jorchin had done for me after all. I bet that lily-livered fool had babbled to Lorga about what had happened between me and Bayarma.

I guess Lorga thought I was dead and left me there, broken and beyond recognition. At any rate, I wasn't dead. But I was too injured and in too much pain to move. I just waited to die. And that is how the monks from Yerlang found me. I wish now they had let me die. But for thirty years I have lived here, an invalid, cursed to live out my days in a place and in a manner not to my liking.[70]

So that is my story. I did deliver the Morning Tree to high beings outside Tibet. I did study with one of the greatest lamas in Tibet. I did

---

[70] Thaza says here and elsewhere that he has been at Yerlang for thirty years. We know he left Lhasa for India in February 1932. He says he started for Mongolia as soon as he delivered the Morning Tree to Darjeeling, so he was probably attacked by Lorga sometime in the summer of 1932. Thaza starts his account in 1966 (see note 2) so Thaza must have been at Yerlang for around 34 years.

have my third eye opened. I did meet the Dalai Lama. And I did do a real service for mankind.

It's been six days now since I started writing. Curiously I haven't been bothered by anyone asking what I am doing. Perhaps the monks are happier I'm out of the way instead of mocking them for their cowardice. Pemba Gephal has been bringing me food; I've sort of told him what I am doing. But oh, my legs are stiff. I wish for death now like I once wished for life. Curiously, an old monk who had been a hermit until recently, but is now living out his days here like me, came up to me this morning. He saw my pile of papers but just said gruffly that my work wasn't finished. What did he mean? For I have finished. And I now sign my name.

Thaza.

Dr Clifton's account

Edited by Claire Hoskyns BA, MPhil

Chapter One

The captain has just announced that take-off is being delayed for an hour. That means I'll be jammed in this cramped seat for more than ten hours before landing in Delhi. I don't know why airlines make their seats so small. Or why Indians have so little sense of personal space. The man next to me is spreading his ample arm halfway into my ribs. It's making typing on my laptop difficult. But at least I have some time to get my thoughts in order before I arrive in India.

I should have done this months ago. I must publish my findings – not just for my academic career but for mankind in general – I need to have proper notes. So much has gone on, I mustn't forget a thing.

So, what am I doing on this plane? Have I managed to evade the people following me? Is my life still in danger? And what awaits me when I get to Dharamsala?

I would never have guessed I'd ever be in a situation like this. Being pursued by people who will stop at nothing to get what they want – I don't know that I'm strong enough to cope. But I must try. So much depends on this trip to Dharamsala.

And will I really be able to find the Morning Tree? This sacred text that can help mankind enter a new and better life. That it should fall to me to look for it is astonishing enough. But actually finding it would be more astonishing still.

It all began the year before last in November 2007. It was my first term as Reader in Tibetan at the School of Oriental and African Studies in London – my first job since getting my PhD from Northwestern University in Chicago. I had enjoyed my time at

Northwestern but was glad to be back at SOAS where I'd graduated five years before. I'd just finished my final tutorial of the day (with Steve Perleman, a lanky, serious boy from Manchester who never failed to wear his Free Tibet badge). I was sitting in my room watching the darkness fall on Russell Square when Professor Thurgood's large head appeared around my door.

"Daniel," he said in that sonorous voice of his, "do you have a moment?"

As head of department, he knew exactly how light my teaching load was, so I couldn't pretend I was busy. I followed him to his office. I had known it well from my time as an undergraduate. Professor Thurgood sat down heavily in his chair and tossed over a piece of paper.

It was a letter from an Indian firm of solicitors, Chandra and Sons, in New Delhi. It was written on airmail paper, a delightful relic from a pre-email age. Professor Thurgood nodded curtly, inviting me to read the letter. It announced in somewhat old fashioned English that their late client, Dr Ram Das Ram, was bequeathing his collection of Tibetan memorabilia to his old college the School of Oriental and African Studies in London. This amounted to several boxes of papers, artefacts and paintings gathered over the years when he was a civil servant in the Indian government's Department of Tibetan Affairs. Apparently Dr Ram so admired SOAS that he wanted it to house his 'considerable' collection. The boxes were currently being shipped to London, paid for by their late client's estate. I looked at Professor Thurgood when I finished.

"I've checked the records," said Professor Thurgood. "It seems that someone called Ram Das Ram did study here in the 1950s. I wonder I didn't know him. And now he's sending us his collection of Tibetan memorabilia. It's a bore Daniel, but we need to sift through it to see if there's anything of value. As you are, ah, the newest member of department, we thought you might like to have a crack at it."

What he meant was that I was under-employed. And it was true. My teaching load was light because there were so few students studying Tibetan. I had been far busier when getting my PhD and even when I'd been an undergraduate at SOAS. I had joked with Professor Thurgood that, with our falling numbers, we ought to be closed down. But he'd replied quite seriously that the Foreign Office and 'others' in government would never allow it. They needed people who speak Tibetan, he said, so we could know what was going on inside that country. I'd never realised the spooks were keeping us going.

Not only was my teaching load light, but I hadn't started my research. I was planning to study 'The conflation of dialect in modern Tibetan: linguistic development or political pressure?' It had been agreed by the department as part of my employment. But I hadn't submitted an outline (due six weeks ago at the beginning of term) let alone done any work on it. I knew Professor Thurgood had been protecting me from criticism from others for what they saw as my laziness. So I was in no position to refuse his request.

Professor Thurgood told me the boxes would be arriving in the next few weeks. I was to make an interim assessment of their contents, pending final recommendations, to the department heads of the East Asia Faculty.

"As I said Daniel, it's a bore. We should just toss the lot on a bonfire, if you ask me. But as this bequest comes with a sizeable donation – it seems Dr Ram never married or if he did he didn't want to leave it all to his family – I suppose we should go through the motions."

With that I was dismissed. I didn't think any more about it until the first week in December when Ann, our departmental secretary, told me that Ian Gervois, the head librarian, wanted to see me urgently. Ian ushered me into a storeroom under the library and showed me a mountain of boxes with shipping manifests taped on their sides.

"I'm told you're responsible for these," he said a shade too tartly for my liking. "We simply don't have the space to keep them here. Can you sort them out and get them removed?"

I remember seeing the dim lights in the ceiling reflecting on his glasses as he moved his head agitatedly. I told him equally tartly that I would have to take my time as it was an important collection of Tibetan memorabilia that needed to be catalogued properly. He fumed. But in truth, I was daunted by the size of the task and reluctant to begin. So reluctant that I didn't start my work until the students had left for the Christmas break.

There were fifty six boxes in all. Dr Ram turned out to have been a very methodical man. He'd been so pleased with his collection that he'd written a lengthy commentary on each item it contained. I was tempted to use that as the basis of my interim report without opening any box. But I had to sound knowledgeable about the contents, so I had to look at some of them. That was when I discovered that the people who'd packed the boxes had helpfully mixed everything up. Documents from different times and dealing with different subjects had been stuffed together, and artefacts and paintings shoved in wherever there was space, so there was no clear way of seeing what was actually there or if it had any value.

This meant I had to go through each box, comparing the contents against Dr Ram's commentary and collating them into the correct piles. All this before I could make an assessment of the collection overall. I decided to go through the artefacts and paintings first as they were the easiest to do. Thankfully Dr Ram had been meticulous in recording the age and subject of the many mandalas and religious objects he'd collected. Once I had the complete list (some of the gold vessels were missing, taken presumably by the people who'd packed the boxes), I sent it to the curator of East Asian Collection around the corner at the British Museum. She replied with some useful and enthusiastic notes on the collection, asking for some of the items for the Museum.

I then had no option but to start on the papers. It was tedious, mostly because the papers were tedious – notes of meetings, policy statements, reports of work carried out etc. Fine if you were going to write a history of the Indian civil service, but worthless to anyone else.

There were some treatises on Tibetan religion and government that I suppose were useful. And there were some nuggets, such as conversations with senior Tibetan officials and their reaction to what was happening in Tibet during the 1960s and 1970s. But overall it was largely uninteresting.

This task took time. I had precarious piles of papers on the floor of the storeroom for months. I know Ian Gervois was tempted to accidentally knock them over when he came to check up on me. Only his mania for tidiness prevented him from being so daring. His visits were annoying me, and I indicated as much. Why didn't I say so earlier, he said; instead of visiting he would view me on the CCTV system, and pointed to a hitherto unnoticed camera in the corner of the ceiling. I shivered. I hated the idea of being spied on. But at least this helped me get a move on, and finally, around March, I completed my assignment.

I was about three quarters the way through when I came across Thaza's manuscript. The first thing that struck me was the roughness of the paper as I picked it up. Then I noticed it was hand cut, of a unique size and quite different from most of the other paper (which must have been Indian civil service standard issue). Then I saw the thick black ink of the parchment wrapped round the manuscript. It read "I Pemba Gephal, formerly a chela at Yerlang monastery, hereby testify that the account of Thaza the monk is true and has been affirmed by His Excellency Nawang Lingar". The whole bundle was tied together by a thin, frayed black strap with a small bronze Buddha dangling incongruously from it. It was clear this was not in keeping with most of the other material in the collection, but I was too dispirited from the drudgery of the work to pay proper attention to it then. I put it in the miscellaneous pile to be dealt with at the end.

Finally, I looked it over again and located the item in Dr Ram's commentary. He'd written that this manuscript and some other papers had come from a house loaned by the Indian government to the Tibetan government-in-exile between March 1974 and April 1975. It had been used by one of the Dalai Lama's private secretaries. When the Indian government took the house back, the papers were found by Dr Ram in a wardrobe, presumably left behind by the private secretary in the move. Dr Ram took the papers and added them to his collection.

Curiously he said nothing more about it. Had he written a brief description I might have left it at that. But because he was silent I was compelled to examine it further. The manuscript was around 200 oblong pages of densely packed handwritten text. A cursory glance showed it to be a largely uneducated hand in colloquial rather than formal Tibetan.[71]

I started reading it. It wasn't easy. The handwriting and Tibetan were both difficult. It would clearly take a long time to look over the whole document. So, in my interim recommendations for Professor Thurgood and his colleagues, I simply labelled it as 'First-hand account of life in a monastery in pre-communist Tibet'.

However, I was intrigued by what I'd read. The first few pages had been vivid, different and interesting. But my priority at the time was to finish collating Dr Ram's collection. So I presented my findings to Professor Thurgood. He said he'd circulate them and come back once the department heads had had their meeting, probably early in the summer term. I re-packed the boxes so that relevant papers and artefacts could be found more easily. And Ian Gervois at last had his storeroom back, almost as neat and tidy as when he'd lent it to me. But before I left that room for what I hoped was the last time, I slipped Thaza's manuscript into my briefcase without Ian Gervois – still prowling around – noticing.

Why? I hadn't planned to do it. But as soon as I had shut my briefcase a hundred justifications sprang to mind. It would be useful in studying dialect. It would help my translation skills. It would be academically worthwhile to have a first-hand account of life in a monastery. And so on. But in truth I wanted to know what happened.

---

[71] Written Tibetan, especially in pre-communist Tibet, was very different from spoken Tibetan.

I marvel now at how cavalier I was to take the manuscript, and how informal I was when translating it. I didn't make a copy; instead I spread the original over my kitchen table, shuffled the papers around and even rested cups of coffee on them. But this was the first time I'd had an original text to work on, and at the time I had no idea of its significance.

I encountered a number of difficulties translating the text. I gradually got used to the handwriting, but the spelling was all over the place. It was a mixture of Lhasan and central Tibetan dialects. Some of the terminology was not in any reference work, not even the more obscure religious dictionaries. And the top right of the pages in last quarter of the manuscript seem to have been washed lighter by water at some point, making some of the words indistinct. It wasn't easy, but by now I was enjoying the challenge.

I needed help translating some of the more esoteric words and passages, so I consulted Lama Sonam Prasang. Sonam was a young man whom I'd met over the years since I was an undergraduate. He was originally from Kagyu Samye Ling monastery at Esk in Scotland but was now involved in a project with the Theology and Religious Studies Department at King's College. He also had spiritual duties for the Tibetan community in London. He was very knowledgeable about esoteric matters and translated a number of the more difficult passages for me.

At last I had the manuscript translated. I had had to tidy up the grammar and style, but I was pleased with my efforts, and it made a coherent and very interesting whole. By now it was May and exam time, so I was doubly busy. My girlfriend Karen had complained over the months about the amount of the time I'd spent on it, especially at weekends, but I was happy. It turned out to be a dramatic account of a Mongolian horseman called Thaza. In brief:

• As a young man, Thaza murders his grandfather, sometime in 1930 or 1931.

• He then believes he is being cursed by his grandfather's spirit, and seeks protection from local monks.

225

- They tell him to journey to Lhasa to meet Lama Pemba Kunchen of Chakpori monastery who will be able to help him. He travels to Lhasa in the summer of 1931.

- Lama Kunchen agrees to help if Thaza agrees to transport a sacred text – the Morning Tree – out of Tibet.

- The Morning Tree contains esoteric knowledge safeguarded by a secret order – knowledge that can help humanity but which darker forces want to destroy.

- Thaza is trained in martial and esoteric arts. He has an audience with the Dalai Lama at the beginning of 1932.

- He finally sets off with the Morning Tree to India but is pursued by the dark forces.

- He succeeds in delivering the Morning Tree to India.

- On his return to Mongolia he is waylaid by someone he had crossed earlier. Thaza is beaten and left for dead.

- He is rescued by monks from nearby Yerlang monastery in central Tibet. He lives, but is an invalid due to his beating, so he stays a monk at Yerlang.

- At the end of his life in 1966, he writes down his account of events over thirty years earlier.

It seemed clear how the manuscript had got out of Tibet. Thaza actually mentions Pemba Gephal as one of his only friends in Yerlang. Thaza either gave the manuscript to Pemba Gephal, or the latter took it after Thaza's death, which seems to have been imminent at the time Thaza wrote his account. In the 1960s there was a steady stream of Tibetans escaping to India to join the Dalai Lama, Pemba Gephal was obviously one of them, and he must have taken Thaza's manuscript with him. Pemba Gephal had most likely read it and believed, like Thaza, that information about the so-called Morning Tree should not reach the wrong hands. At any rate, he seems to have given the manuscript to Nawang Lingar, an official in the Tibetan government-in-exile. Nawang Lingar, or one of his colleagues, then left the manuscript with other papers when they vacated the house loaned to them by the Indian government in 1975. And that is where Dr Ram found it.

I should point out that the manuscript was not scholarly in anyway. As I said, it was written in colloquial rather than formal Tibetan. A great deal of it appeared to be direct conversations between Thaza (or whoever the author was) and the people he met. Nor was the manuscript sober. Thaza wrote strongly, directly and without pulling his punches. All this meant that Thaza's text was quite different from most, if not all, Tibetan texts of the period, including the scant number of fictional pieces that have come down to us today.[72]

But was Thaza's story true? I admit I was excited. If Thaza's account was true, then not only would it throw valuable light on life in Tibet during the 1930s, it would also reveal the existence of a sacred text, hitherto unknown to scholars. If I could publish the manuscript and a paper on its provenance and what it taught us about Tibetan religion, it would certainly help my career.

But there was something more. There was a wisdom in the manuscript that appealed to me, especially as the information seemed diametrically different from the usual (and frankly often turgid) Tibetan teachings. I was impressed how Thaza – an angry, proud man – was won over by his master and did risk his life for him. And then there was the Morning Tree itself. What did it actually say? And could it really help humanity?

By now it was July. Exam papers had been marked, and the department was winding down for the summer break. Professor Thurgood was asking awkward questions about when I was going to start my research. So I decided to risk appearing unprofessional and told him that I wanted to pursue a new line. I told him about Thaza's manuscript, the work I had done on it, and how I would now like to prove it was genuine.

---

[72] Most Tibetan texts of the period are religious texts written according to a formula that stresses how holy monks are, rather than more realistically describing day to day life as it actually was in Tibet.

Professor Thurgood was surprised. He said taking the university's property without permission was highly irregular. Sensing the worst, I showed him the manuscript and my translation. He took the latter away to study. He called me into his office on the last day of term. He repeated how irregular I had been and said my actions could be a case for a formal warning. I told him I had been too excited by the manuscript to think straight. Could he not see its academic potential? No, he could not; it was original, certainly, but unorthodox and potentially a giant hoax. He had never in all his years come across any references to a Morning Tree or an order safeguarding it. I reasoned with him that it came via an impeccable source, without any claims, it was strikingly different to the standard religious texts, and it must be worthy of further study. At the very least, I contended, I could undertake preliminary research to see if it was likely to be authentic.

I was wondering whether I should add that there was something genuine, even compelling, about the information in the text, which made it important to see if it was true or not, but I wasn't sure how Professor Thurgood would react.

He breathed heavily and looked at me with that large head of his. "All right Daniel," he said finally. "You see if it looks authentic. Present your findings to me. If there is something in it, we can take it from there. But if there isn't, you drop it and return to some serious research. Lord knows how I'm going to justify this to the Review Board."

I felt great relief. I was about to thank him when he added, "And don't be tardy. Work hard, do you hear?" He waved me away.

I don't know what had made him change his mind. I think somehow he had always liked me: he had been good to me as an undergraduate, and he had chosen me over two better qualified candidates for this post. But I was happy. At last I could work on Thaza's account openly. And it was so much more interesting and fulfilling than my original research.

Over the course of the summer break I mapped out how I was going to proceed. In essence, I was going to subject the manuscript to a number of tests.

1. Can the names, places and dates mentioned be verified from existing sources?

2. Does the life Thaza describes in Mongolia match what is known about the country and people at the time?

3. Does Thaza's account of Chakpori match what is known about that lamasery and lamaseries in general?

4. Are there references to the Morning Tree in religious sources?

5. Where were the paper and ink manufactured, and how old were they?

6. What reason would the author have to write his account unless it were true?

I know the last point was speculative, but it was worthwhile asking the question. All fakes have a motive, otherwise they wouldn't be produced. The Hitler Diaries, for example, were endorsed by the eminent historian Hugh Trevor-Roper in 1983, and sold for ten million German marks. They created a worldwide media storm and duped several experts. The fakers clearly achieved their aim of hoodwinking the great and the good (even if they had to give the money back). But there appeared to be no such motive for Thaza's account. It wasn't being sold; it wasn't debunking any historical figure or religion; it wasn't likely to receive any publicity. Above all, there was nothing in it for Dr Ram. If he had been the perpetrator, surely he would have done something about it during his lifetime? No, it seemed to me there was no reason to write the account other than the one given by Thaza himself: that he wanted to record what he had done. True, the account could have been the delusions of an old man. But having pored over every word, and struggled with the uneducated Tibetan, it seemed hard to believe that a delusional man would bother with the effort of writing so much – and so much so clearly – without it having some basis in truth.

Besides, would a delusional old man have been able to make up the spiritual truths, as relayed by Lama Kunchen? I doubted it. The more I read Thaza's account, the more I was struck by the uniqueness of so much of what Lama Kunchen is quoted as saying. The uniqueness and the depth. To me this was another reason why Thaza's account had to be true – he couldn't have made up most of what he'd written.

So, when the next academic year began that September, I resumed my work. I knew from my year in Lhasa as an undergraduate that much of what Thaza had written about the Potala and the town was true. Of course, Chakpori didn't exist anymore; it had been destroyed by the Chinese and now housed a radio mast. And the village at the bottom of the Peak had been cleared away to make the large square in front of the Potala. However, there were many details I didn't know, so with Professor Thurgood's assistance, I co-opted the help of two historians in the East Asia department.

The first, Michel Lacroix, was an expert on Mongolian history. He read Thaza's account and promptly returned a report. It was impossible to verify the people and even some of the places mentioned by Thaza, he said, but that was to be expected. A nomadic, semi-literate society would simply not have the records. However, the names of the people were accurate. The descriptions of Mongolian life rang true. The marriage customs (whereby Thaza had to wait for the head of the family to make a match, and the bride's family had to give a dowry) were certainly true. And the route from Thaza's part of Mongolia to Lhasa seemed plausible. On balance, he concluded, Thaza's account appeared to be written by a Mongolian of the period.

I had to badger the other historian, Dr Charles Dunleavy. He was an expert on pre-communist Tibet, especially its forms of government. It was nearing the end of November and he still hadn't got back to me. He seemed irritated when I approached him and usually didn't answer emails. But when his report finally arrived, he was gracious, even excited. I'll repeat his conclusions here:

In summary, then, with the exception of the Dalai Lama, we cannot corroborate any of the religious personae because the monastic records have long been destroyed. However, the lay officials mentioned by Thaza did exist. With regard to the 13th Dalai Lama, he was in Lhasa when Thaza said he met him, and he did favour the Norbu Linka, certainly when he wanted to relax.

Many of the other details are true. As I have mentioned, Tengyeling monastery in Lhasa was staffed by people from Amdo – the place where Thaza indicates Lama Neto originated – and they did favour strong links with the Chinese. Indeed, the monks in the monastery rebelled against the Dalai Lama in 1912, and they fermented trouble for several years after.

Above all, Thaza's account offers a fascinating insight into daily life in a lamasery. No existing record to my knowledge offers such an insight. When one observes monastic life today (especially in Tibetan monasteries in India where the old routines are observed more rigidly than in modern Tibet), one can see how the human side, the daily need to get on with hundreds of one's fellows, can predominate over the religious side. Yet Tibetan accounts almost universally ignore this human side. Thankfully Thaza brings this to life. For this alone, the text is valuable for any student of Tibet before communism.

As for the Morning Tree, the secret order protecting it, and the other esoteric information, I cannot comment authoritatively. Tibetan Buddhism has long contained elements of Bonism – the shamanistic religion that pre-dated Buddhism – and powers such as telepathy, levitation and out-of-body travel are referred to in some Tibetan texts. Certainly, some Tibetan monasteries were held to be centres for such learning. I assume that if such a secret order did exist, then references to it in the sources would be extremely limited.

As far as I am concerned, the text does accurately describe life in 1930s Tibet. The author clearly has an intimate knowledge of monastic rituals, and his uniquely earthy description of life in a lamasery, so contrary to standard accounts, makes his description even more believable.

I was having difficulty finding a laboratory to test the paper and ink. In the end, I sent samples to a private forensic science lab that admitted they weren't experts in this field. They concluded that the paper was clearly hand-made from a type of tree they could not identify, it seemed to be between 30-50 years old and the ink was made from vegetables mixed with a mineral compound. This showed at least that the paper didn't come from a normal source, and there was nothing at this stage to contradict that it came from Tibet in the early to mid-1960s.

By now it was the Christmas break. I had three particular questions left to answer. These were (1) Does Thaza's journey to Darjeeling stand up? (2) Can we identify His Excellency Nawang Lingar? (3) Are there any references to the Morning Tree in the existing sources?

A close study of maps of the region, and the lucky discovery of some maps produced for the British Indian government in the 1920s, showed that Thaza's account of the journey was in fact extremely accurate. There is a path around thirty miles to the east of Gyangtse that Thaza could have taken to avoid his pursuers. The route from Chatsa monastery to India does go to Pari, Yatung and through the Dzelep Pass. And the town of Gnatong, which I couldn't find on modern maps, was on the old Indian government maps just where Thaza had said it was. It was marked as having a government run telegraph post, which probably accounts for Thaza's strange line *I followed the wire lines down the valley.*

To help answer the second question, I contacted a post-graduate student Claire Hoskyns. She was writing her PhD on the Tibetan government-in-exile 1959-1976 (the end of the Cultural Revolution). She didn't speak Tibetan; her aim was to study governments in exile and then try to join the UN or the Foreign Office. She was happy to help. She said she hadn't come across the name Nawang Lingar, but she would ask her contact in the Tibetan government's London office. A few days before Christmas she called to say that her contact had told her Nawang Lingar was one of those rare officials who had been on both the political and religious sides, but he was now an old man and retired and we couldn't get in touch with him. Indeed, she said her contact had hinted she shouldn't ask about Nawang Lingar again.

What did this mean? I asked Claire to pursue the matter, but she didn't want to jeopardise her research. I was upset we couldn't get more, but at least it proved that Nawang Lingar existed.

This just left me with a more in-depth search of existing sources to see if there were any references to the Morning Tree and the order guarding it. By now it was nearly Christmas. I was pleased with what I'd managed to achieve so far. I needed a break, so I put everything to one side with a view to starting again in the New Year.

Chapter Two

But something happened over Christmas that kept Thaza's account in the front of my mind. I'd gone to my parents, and we went to the midnight Christmas Eve service in the local church. The vicar was young, evangelical and keen on following a stream of consciousness, rather than the Church of England order of service. He was going on about how Jesus' birth two thousand years ago brought hope to mankind, and we needed hope today.

I sat up. Hope. Wasn't that something the Morning Tree promised? A key to help us lead better lives in a new era of peace and harmony? The book wasn't a figure like Jesus, but hadn't Lama Kunchen said religion would fade and the divine would work directly in each person? Maybe the next step forward would be through a shift of consciousness brought about by knowledge contained in the Morning Tree. If that was the case, then this book was more of a spiritual than an academic one.

I didn't know how to take this insight. My first motive in studying Thaza's manuscript had been to find a more interesting line of research, especially one that might help secure my tenure at SOAS. But if half of what Lama Kunchen had told Thaza about the Morning Tree was true, then really it was a spiritual text with the power to change humanity. What then of my role? Academic or guru? I felt uncomfortable. I wasn't holy, but at the same time, I could sense the Morning Tree's spiritual importance.

I was so engrossed in thought that my sister had to nudge me to stand for the next carol. I sang the words but was fixated on this fresh understanding of the Morning Tree. It was a thought I couldn't get out of my head all Christmas.

Then it was early January. The students were still away, and we'd just had a departmental meeting. The usual boring stuff. At the end I got up to go but Professor Thurgood pulled me back.

"Your research, Daniel," he said, "let's talk about it."

I wasn't prepared, but I acceded to his request. I told him that so far everything tended to the manuscript's authenticity. I was expecting Professor Thurgood to challenge my analysis, but to my surprise he just said, "Good, good, you're doing a good job."

He then surprised me further by saying, "You know, Daniel, unearthing the Morning Tree would be a tremendous discovery. Do you think you could locate it?"

I caught my breath. "You mean *find* it?" I asked. Bizarrely, I'd never thought of tracking it down and seeing it for myself. But hadn't Professor Thurgood dismissed all this as a potential hoax?

"What do you mean?" I continued. "Do you think the Morning Tree exists?" If I didn't know him better, I'd swear he blushed.

"It could do, yes," he blustered. "There's a lot about Tibetan Buddhism we don't know. I mean, why write such a detailed account if there were no basis in truth? But Daniel, I'm just thinking about you. If you could find this text, well, it would make your name in this field."

I agreed it would.

"So you'll see if you can unearth it?"

I hesitated. I certainly believed Thaza's account was true, and I was coming to realise the Morning Tree might be spiritually important. But could I find it? And if I were to find it, where would I begin? I said as much to Professor Thurgood.

He breathed out heavily and looked disappointed. He looked, if truth be told, as if he thought I was being lazy. But I wasn't: he was more than doubling my workload, and I wasn't the best qualified person. I told him I had no knowledge of this part of Tibetan lore and there were other, more competent people. Indeed, I'd had to ask Lama Sonam Prasang to help translate the esoteric passages.

Professor Thurgood sat bolt upright. "Sonam Prasang?" he said. "*He* knows about Thaza's manuscript?"

"Not exactly," I replied, a little confused. "I merely sent him the words and passages I couldn't understand. I mean, how could I ever have translated—"

"Sonam Prasang?" Professor Thurgood interrupted. "I wouldn't trust him necessarily. He has his own agenda, you know, and he's not quite the scholar he portrays."

"I had no idea."

What I meant was, I had no idea what Professor Thurgood was talking about. Sonam Prasang had kindly translated everything I'd sent him. He'd been polite, helpful and timely. He had asked where those particular phrases and passages had come from. I remember I hadn't actually replied to that email, but he hadn't pressed the point. Had he and Professor Thurgood had a falling out?

"I wouldn't… I wouldn't involve him again, Daniel. I can give you the name of someone much better qualified in this area – a Mr Ravensburg. I've already spoken to him on your behalf. I've got his contact details here. Now, where did I put them?"

He started searching his desk. This was unlike him: normally Professor Thurgood was extremely well organised.

"No, I can't find them. Look, Daniel, I'll send you the details when I've turned them up. This chap specialises in these sorts of things. If anyone can help you track this book down, he can. And I do urge you to track this book down. I think it would benefit you tremendously."

I left, several thoughts going through my head. Finding the Morning Tree wasn't likely to be easy; how would I do it?. But more than that, I was puzzled by Professor Thurgood's behaviour. He now seemed to believe the Morning Tree existed and was insisting I track it down. What had caused him to change his mind? There was something else too. If I hadn't known him so well, I might not have noticed. But he was clearly agitated about something, and I had never known him to be agitated before.

On my way out I bumped into Claire Hoskyns. She was looking good. She asked how I was. I know I shouldn't have said anything, but I was bothered by my meeting with Professor Thurgood and indicated as much. She suggested we go for a cup of coffee. In the end we went to Sidoli's Buttery for an early and, as it turned out, long lunch. I told her the full story about Thaza's manuscript. I had already told her something of it when I asked if she could track down Nawang Lingar, but now I filled in the details. I shouldn't have divulged so much, but she wasn't a rival, and I just wanted someone to talk things over with. I couldn't do it with Karen as she'd never been interested.

But Claire was interested. "A sacred text," she said. "About the return of man's powers. That contains the answers to our problems. That is worth finding. You'll be famous!"

"I don't want to be famous," I replied. "And anyway, I've got to find it first. But how do I find a book shipped out of Tibet over seventy years ago? It could be anywhere."

"Did Thaza give any clues about where it might be?"

"No. He gave it to an Indian in Darjeeling. He doesn't record the Indian saying anything about where the book was going. And Thaza's master doesn't say where the book would be kept either."

"Well, perhaps there are clues in other religious texts."

"I haven't come across any. Nor has Professor Thurgood or Charles Dunleavy. I mean, this book's supposed to be secret, so the people who have it – if there are such people and if they do still have it – aren't going to telegraph the Morning Tree's location, are they?"

Claire stirred her pasta. "But there are some people who know about it," she persisted. "Nawang Lingar."

"How do you know he knows?"

"I don't for sure. But at least we know he exists, and from what you've told me he was given Thaza's manuscript, so it's a fair assumption that he'll know something."

"Well, yes. But didn't you say your contact warned you off trying to reach him?"

"He did, but don't you think that's an extra reason to track him down?"

Claire was right. There was something here. I smiled, and she gave a lovely smile in return. I asked if she could find another way to get to Nawang Lingar. She agreed to try. Now, was there anyone else who might know anything about the Morning Tree?

Obviously I could ask Sonam Prasang. He was clearly knowledgeable about this part of Tibetan Buddhism. But Professor Thurgood had shut that door – and bolted it too, judging by his reaction earlier. I made my way back to SOAS, turning people's names over in my mind. But I just didn't know anyone else like Sonam.

I spent the next week waiting for Claire to get back to me, whilst ploughing through as many obscure religious texts as I could find. Karen started complaining again because I was working all hours. Still, Professor Thurgood seemed to approve.

"Ah Daniel, working late eh?" he said on more than one occasion.

Mind you, I was beginning to wish I could spend more time with Karen as these texts were hard going. I've never thrilled to Tibetan Buddhism (unlike most of my colleagues).

Then, one afternoon in mid-January, Ann was dropping off some papers in my office when she exclaimed, "Oh, Daniel, your Christmas cards! Such bad luck." I looked up, confused. "You're supposed to take all Christmas decorations down by the twelfth day of Christmas… the 6th January. Today's the 15th!"

I looked at the few cards I'd received wilting in the warmth of my over-heated office. Suitably admonished, I started to take them down. It was then that I came across the one from Professor Jim McField, my PhD supervisor at Northwestern. We'd been friendly during my time in Chicago. Of course! Why hadn't I thought of him before? Jim was an expert on Tibetan Buddhism, and he believed categorically in all psychic, spiritual and other-worldly phenomena. We'd often argued over what I saw as his too eager acceptance of the supernatural.

"There are more things in heaven and earth, Daniel," he'd say wagging his finger at me.

He'd scribbled in his card 'Give me a call', so I thought I'd take him at his word and phone him. It should be early morning in Chicago.

"Hey Danny, what a nice surprise! Happy New Year to you," came his voice over the clear line. "What are you doing nowadays? How's SOAS? You know Millie still misses you."

He was as exuberant as ever, and as bad at marshalling his thoughts. I told him I wasn't really enjoying teaching but was interested in my research. I said I was trying to find references to a book called the Morning Tree. I used its Tibetan title.

The line went silent.

"Hello?" I said. I thought we'd been cut off.

"No, Danny, I'm still here," said Jim. "You want to know about what?"

"The Morning Tree."

"I thought that's what you said. Where did you pick *that* up?"

"From a manuscript in some papers donated to SOAS. I thought this might be in your line of expertise."

"Really Danny," he breathed, "the Morning Tree. Shoot, I never thought I'd hear that mentioned. You really want to know? Look, I don't know what to say. I'll send you an email. I've got to go now. I'll pass on your wishes to Millie." With that he put the phone down.

Here was something else to think about. Jim had never been anything other than friendly and helpful, but here he was cutting me off. I should have thought about this for longer but Karen was being difficult. She had been complaining for days and that night she started an argument. She said I never bought her flowers or something like that. Words were spoken, things escalated, and she spent the night at a friend's house. I spent the next few days, when I wasn't teaching, trying to placate her. I just didn't have the energy at that time to concentrate on the Morning Tree. I didn't even take on the full meaning of Jim's promised email which came the next day.

Danny:

239

Great to hear from you. Sorry I had to rush off. I have to admit I was kind of surprised when you asked me about the Morning Tree. I never thought you would be interested in this sort of thing. After all the arguments we had! You accusing me of suspending belief and accepting everything that is written in Buddhist texts. But Danny, some things I just know are true. And this doesn't make me un-academic. The greatest scientists all had hunches they knew were right even if they couldn't prove them at the time. It's the same with me and psychic phenomena.

But I digress. You want to know about the Morning Tree. I don't know whether I should be excited or worried. But I'll tell you what I know.

When I'd finished my degree, and before I started my PhD, I toured northern India, Ladakh and Nepal, visiting Tibetan monasteries. It was 1972. At that time I was wondering if I shouldn't be a monk rather than an academic. There's not as much difference between the two as you suppose: for most of history they've been about the same. I would join in the services of the monasteries I lodged in. In one – Alchi, on the banks of the Indus in Ladakh – I met an old monk who was curious that a westerner was so interested in Buddhism. We talked, and he soon discovered I was interested not just in Buddhism, but the esoteric side of it too. He showed me amazing things – things you wouldn't believe. He levitated. He moved objects just by his thoughts. And he could appear in and disappear from locked rooms. You don't have to believe what I'm telling you, because that is not the point of this story. I told him that his powers were impressive, but they were tricks compared to man's true psychic abilities. He asked me what I meant. I told him true psychic abilities would help manifest understanding and compassion between people and the other life forms we share our planet with. It's what I believed then, and it's what I believe now. I was expecting him to be angry at my dismissal of his abilities, but instead he broke into a radiating smile, he embraced me, and he told me I had earned the right to hear the truth – a truth that very few others on the planet knew.

He told me that man's powers – his psychic powers, his higher level of consciousness – had been taken away but soon they would be returned. And when they were returned mankind would indeed have a better understanding of life, they would be able to see the divine in all life forms, and they would have a knowledge that would simply dispel most of the problems we have today. He admitted that his tricks, as I called them, were just that: party games to impress people for now, for *the time was not yet right for the deeper esoteric truths to be released. But maybe, he said, I could know some of these truths now. Danny, you had to be there, in this man's presence, and then you would know for yourself that what he was saying was TRUE. We talked for many hours. He explained how Tibetan Buddhism had long been the home of these truths. And when I began to fret that these truths might disappear (after all, Tibet was being destroyed by the communists), he told me not to worry. He said everything was written down, in the <u>Morning Tree</u>, a book that had been safeguarded oh, I don't know, for centuries, and those with responsibility for the book would release it at the right time.*

Well, I was young and eager. When I left Alchi, I started to make enquiries about the Morning Tree. I wanted to find it then and release it myself. I guess I didn't trust "those with responsibility for the book" – whoever they were – to come to humanity's aid. I mean, the world was falling apart with Vietnam, economic problems, the destruction of the environment, and I wanted to release the divine knowledge that could save us before we destroyed ourselves. I admit I also wanted to see this divine knowledge for myself too; it was my lifelong passion, as you know. But I got nowhere. No-one knew anything. I began to wonder if that monk hadn't just spun me a yarn. Until one night in Dharamsala. I'd been pestering this senior lama to tell me if he knew anything about the Morning Tree. I was getting desperate because my money was running out and I had to return to the States soon. I just didn't want to go home empty handed. I swear the lama flickered when I mentioned the book, and although he denied any knowledge, I was sure he was hiding something. I was in a bar that night drinking when I felt burly presences surround me. Three men escorted me outside where the ugliest man I've ever seen put a knife to my throat. "Leave alone what you don't understand," he growled. "No more about this book."

I was shocked. But as I said I was young. So I wasn't as scared as I should have been. The next day I went in search of the lama again. He wasn't there, but the ugly man was. Only then did I back off. So I returned to the States without anything beyond my notes of my time with the monk in Alchi.

I guess that would have been it. But a few years later, in 1975, as I was nearing the end of my PhD, I went to a Tantric Buddhist meeting near where I lived at the time in San Francisco. A visiting Tibetan lama conducted a service. He used a strange phrase. He said "May the power be returned as written in the book of daybreak". I was sure he was talking about the Morning Tree. After the service I cornered him. I told him I knew about the Morning Tree, and asked him what he knew about it. He was surprised – I don't think he'd realised I could speak Tibetan. And I guess he wasn't expecting anyone to mention the Morning Tree. I don't know if I caught him off-guard, or if he was a genuinely helpful guy. At any rate he took me to one side and told me very earnestly that the book held the key to mankind's future well-being, it was being guarded from evil forces seeking to destroy it, but it would be released at the right time to usher in a new age. How would it be released, I asked. Through the right people, he replied. Where was it? At this he clammed up and waved his finger at me. I persisted with my question. He whispered it was safe. I suppose I must have looked disbelieving for then he added "With the Keeper". He looked shocked at that point, as if he'd said too much, and moved off. I was convinced we were talking about the same Morning Tree.

My interest had been reignited. I couldn't stop thinking about it. Again, I wanted to find it, read it, and tell others about it. So I tried to contact the lama a few days later. But he was gone. At any rate, I couldn't raise him. So I took three days out to travel to his centre in Oregon and confront him. He looked alarmed when he saw me. And I swear he was sweating when I spoke to him. I told him he must tell me more about the Morning Tree – humanity needed it now. He told me to go away at once. I insisted he tell me what he knew. He said he couldn't, for my own benefit: the book was guarded, and only those at the right time could know more. I demanded that he revealed everything. By now, some of the other monks and guests there had started to look concerned. I guess I was agitated, and Buddhist retreats aren't known for people having stand up arguments. Some of them approached us and asked the lama if he was all right. Yes, he told them. But I was escorted out and that was it.

What could I do? I returned to San Francisco. But I returned with a plan. I would circulate a letter to Buddhists and new age people asking if anyone knew about the Morning Tree. It might not lead anywhere, but at least it would raise awareness and there might be someone who knew something. But the day after formulating this plan I got sick. It was a vicious virus, unidentified by the doctors who treated me, and after about a week I actually had to be put on life support. They reckoned I could die. Call me superstitious, but I know that bug was sent to stop me searching for the book. When I realised this, the illness started to recede. I'd been warned in Dharamsala and in Oregon, and then made sick. I reckoned if I persisted something worse would happen. So, reluctantly, I gave up my search.

I've still forensically dissected every text I have read for any references to the Morning Tree, but haven't found any that I can conclusively say point to its existence. Except one. A commentary written in 1580 by one of Tashi Namgyal's disciples on the Mahamudra sutra.[73] In a discussion on the five paths to enlightenment, he comments: "The true meaning of all the texts is to cover the true meaning of our Buddhism. The enlightened priests are but the guardians of greater truths that one day will be realised by all. These truths are in one book that will be hidden until the time comes when it will be released at daybreak." Most scholars think that the word 'cover' means describe, but I think it means conceal. That is the only way to explain the third sentence of the passage I've just quoted. At any rate, its meaning is clear to me. And what the hell does "until the time comes when it will be released at daybreak" mean, if not a reference to 'morning'? Tashi Namgyal was known for his esoteric teachings, as was his lamasery, Nalanda Sakypa, north of Lhasa. Yes, I know, many lamas are credited with such powers, especially ones that lived hundreds of years ago. But to me it all fits together.

I've never stopped wondering about the Morning Tree. But I've never met anyone else, apart from the two monks I've mentioned, who knew anything about it – until your call. Danny please, tell me what you know and how you know it. I am desperate to find out. I hope what I have written has helped you. Please help me now.

Truly, Jim.

I was surprised and pleased that Jim knew about the Morning Tree. This was a lucky break. He had conveyed the essence of Thaza's information – that man's powers had been taken away and would be returned in a golden age. And he'd identified at least one reference and some monks who had known something about the Morning Tree. Here was proof that the book described by Thaza actually existed.

---

[73] Tashi Namgyal (1511-1587) was a great Tibetan teacher of his time who transcribed many sacred oral texts. A centre of learning grew up around him.

And yet how much had he helped me? There was nothing I could use in my research. The reference by Tashi Namgyal's disciple was too vague to be convincing. The two monks had not been identified by Jim, and would have to be tracked down and interviewed (if they were still alive and willing). They would have to admit that the Morning Tree existed, and even then it would only be their word. There was nothing, in short, that would convince the review board of an academic publication that the Morning Tree was real. And nothing to help me find it.

I replied to Jim, thanking him for his email, and telling him about Thaza's text. I wondered how much I should tell him. But then Jim was a friend, a man I could trust, so I told him all I knew. I even sent him a copy of my translation.

Jim was jubilant. He must have read it in a couple of hours, for he got back to me almost immediately. He said Thaza's manuscript was as important as the Dead Sea Scrolls – in his view, more important. It confirmed everything he'd ever believed. And he was sure the book would serve humanity as much, or more than, any religion. He bombarded me with questions about Dr Ram, his collection and the manuscript itself. He asked if he could see it. I eventually emailed him a scanned copy of the original text, and added in my message that I needed his help too. Did he have any idea how I could actually locate the Morning Tree?

He replied he was working on it. In fact, he said he'd pretty much do nothing else but help me find the Morning Tree and that we had to meet up. He had teaching commitments he couldn't get out of, but he could clear his diary and come over to London the last weekend in February. I wasn't to tell anyone he was coming, but could he stay with me when he came? I was used to his breathless ways, so I acceded to his requests. But would he actually have something useful beyond what he had already told me?

At the same time Professor Thurgood asked how things were going. I was pursuing two leads, I told him.

"Anything promising?"

I mentioned I'd been in touch with my old tutor Jim who was proving helpful. Professor Thurgood seemed pleased.

As for the second lead – finding Nawang Lingar – Claire got back to me at last. With bad news. She had been told Nawang Lingar was old and ill, and there was no way we could contact him. She had persisted, and even mentioned the Morning Tree, but she had met a brick wall.

"Was there any response when you mentioned the book?" I asked.

"No," she replied. "I don't think they knew what I was talking about."

Two steps forward, one step back. I still had Jim's information, and hopefully he was coming with more. But I needed to find someone who actually knew something concrete about the Morning Tree and where it might be.

Chapter Three

By now it was the end of January. Professor Thurgood had at last sent me details of his contact. He was an elderly man called John Ravensburg. He didn't use email but I could call to arrange a meeting. I didn't want to – he didn't seem to be an academic – but as Professor Thurgood was my boss I had to make a show of pleasing him. So I called. A thin voice answered the phone. It brightened considerably when I told him who I was. We agreed to meet at tea time the next day. So it was, I turned up at this large house in Kensington the following afternoon.

The door was opened by a Tibetan manservant. I was led into a dimly lit hall hung with mandalas and a thanka[74] draped from the top of the staircase. I was immediately assailed by the smell of incense. The manservant took me, without a word, into a room to the left of the hall (I guessed the library of the house in its more conventional days). A slender old man in a well-cut suit was sitting in an armchair beside a table. He didn't get up when I entered.

"Ah, Dr Clifton, do come in," he said in the thin voice I recognised from the phone. "Please sit down."

I did so in an upright chair across from Mr Ravensburg. His manservant reappeared with a trolley and poured tea into exquisite, and I assumed, antique porcelain cups. I half thought it'd be butter tea but thankfully it was very refined Chinese tea.

---

[74] Thanka is a large Tibetan religious banner usually hung over the sides of monasteries or mountains on special occasions.

"Professor Thurgood has been telling me that you're interested in, ah, the Morning Tree, is it? Tell me, how did you come across mention of this work?"

"I can tell you," I replied. "But first can you tell me who you are? Professor Thurgood hasn't given me any information."

"Ah, there's not much to tell," said the old man. "I'm a Tibetan scholar. I have been all my life. But I don't publish or go to meetings. I prefer working on my own."

"So you're not attached to a university?"

"Why would I want the bother of a university? I don't want to teach anyone. And I don't want the tedium of departmental politics. I know all about that from my family firm. No, as you can see, I don't need a job; I have enough money of my own. Far better that I pursue my interests without having to answer to anyone else."

"And what are your interests?"

"The same as yours, by the sound of it. The Morning Tree. I never thought some young academic would be asking about it. But then I never thought anyone would be asking about it."

"And you know Professor Thurgood?"

"Yes. He is one of the few contacts I have. He helped me once. I have repaid his kindness. And now it seems he is asking me a favour."

"Well, I don't know about a favour—"

"Please, no games. I know what you are after. Give me the manuscript that talks about the Morning Tree. If I am to help you, you must help me."

I hesitated. I didn't want to hand over Thaza's account to this strange man. If it had been up to me, I'd have left. But Professor Thurgood had asked me to consult him. So, reluctantly, I dug into my briefcase and handed a copy of the manuscript into his bony hands.

"Not this one!" he snapped. "The original Tibetan!"

Even more reluctantly I handed over a copy of Thaza's original manuscript. His eyes lit up as he caressed it. He skipped through the pages with an intent look on his face.

247

"Ah!" he said glowingly. "Indeed, indeed. Chakpori... and the Great Thirteenth. How interesting!" He was as animated as a little boy with his favourite comic book. "Most remarkable," he kept repeating to himself as he leafed through the pages. "Most remarkable."

"What can you tell me about the Morning Tree," I broke in, keen to get a move on so I could leave that place.

"What can I tell you?" he said looking at me when he had at last glanced through the pages. "Or what am I willing to tell you? Let me see." He rang a little bell on the table beside him. His manservant entered. He spoke softly to him in Tibetan. I couldn't catch what he said. The manservant nodded impassively and left. Mr Ravensburg sat in silence clutching my manuscript. I shifted uncomfortably in my seat and drained my now lukewarm tea.

Eventually, the manservant returned with a tray covered by a cloth. The tray seemed heavy, and the manservant lowered it slowly onto Mr Ravensburg's lap. He then left. Mr Ravensburg looked at the cloth covered tray and then at me. He rested his hands, still gripping my manuscript, on the tray.

"What I'm about to tell you," he began at last, "must not be revealed to anyone. Do you understand?"

"But my research. If there are extant references to the Morning Tree I need to mention them. To prove the authenticity of Thaza's account."

"There aren't any references! At least, not in the conventional sources."

"But if we find the Morning Tree—"

"Then you will be covered in glory, but you will not mention my name or divulge any information I give you."

"Why not?"

"You really don't know what you are dealing with, do you? This book – it is more important than you can imagine. There are forces... let me just say I know what I'm talking about and you don't. I don't want my name nor any information I give you to be passed on to anyone. Is that clear?" His thin voice was very agitated now.

I spread my hands. These were ridiculous conditions. If he did give me anything useful, I'd have to mention it. I could only let this pass for now. Besides, I wasn't sure if he did have anything useful. Better let him ramble on, I thought, then I can get back to the real world. Mr Ravensburg must have taken my silence as an acceptance of his conditions for he cleared his throat and started talking.

"You will have heard of Colonel Younghusband's expedition to Lhasa in 1904?[75] The British government in India wanted to negotiate with the Tibetans who were refusing to do so, so a column of troops was sent to force them into talks. As you may know, when Younghusband got to Lhasa, he was shown a prophecy that had foretold the short war between Britain and Tibet and Younghusband's subsequent occupation of the city. It was widely publicised at the time.[76] But that prophecy wasn't the only thing he was shown. He was in fact told a great deal more about Tibet's esoteric powers, and he had several meetings with senior religious officials. When he returned to India, he gave a full account of his meetings to the head of Indian Intelligence, a Brigadier Massingberd. Massingberd ordered Younghusband not to reveal anything he had been told. He shouldn't even have mentioned the prophecy relating to himself, but that slipped out. Suffice to say, Massingberd ensured that the rest of the information was known only to himself.

"You know too that the Dalai Lama had to flee Tibet in 1910 when a Chinese force occupied Lhasa?[77] Although the British had invaded Tibet just six years earlier, the Dalai Lama went to India in the hope that the British would help Tibet fight the Chinese. The

---

[75] Colonel (later Sir) Francis Younghusband led a British force to Lhasa in 1904 to compel the Tibetans to recognise British control over Sikkim, establish trade and agree to limit the influence of Russia and China over Tibet.

[76] Colonel Younghusband said that while in Lhasa he had been shown the Tibetan prophecy foretelling his invasion. His comments were reported in the press.

[77] The Chinese had invaded Tibet in 1909 and moved to occupy Lhasa in February 1910. The Dalai Lama and his senior officials fled only hours ahead of the invasion force.

Indian government housed him in Darjeeling, and also invited him to Calcutta.[78] The British were some help, although not as much as the Dalai Lama wanted, but he was able to return to a Chinese free Lhasa two years later.[79] Whilst he was in Calcutta, Brigadier Massingberd visited the Dalai Lama and his party. He had a number of questions he wanted to ask relating to the information that had been divulged to Colonel Younghusband.

"Brigadier Massingberd was a man ahead of his time. He was convinced that psychic powers were real, and he had spent time in India studying the ancient texts. He could read Sanskrit and was well versed in Hinduism. He was intrigued by what Younghusband had told him, and wanted to know more. It wasn't just personal interest that drove him. He was a patriotic man who believed that if Britain was to maintain its position in the world, then just as we should be in the forefront of science, so too we should be in the forefront of exploring the psychic potential existing in mankind.

"The Dalai Lama and his officials were happy to cooperate with Massingberd. They were heartened that a people they had regarded as uninterested in spiritual matters should be so eager to find out more. And I think they calculated that if they helped Massingberd, he could encourage his superiors to help the Tibetans in return. At any rate, one of the Dalai Lama's party – a Lama Kunchen – was asked to tell Massingberd whatever he wanted to know."

He looked at me to make sure I was following his narrative.

"Massingberd asked particularly about the State Oracle at Nechung," he continued. "He wanted to know how it worked, what other predictions it was making, and if its predictions meant they would inevitably occur. His great idea was to use divination to help guide Britain through an increasingly troubled world. He also asked about the unseen forces that govern the world and how they impacted the affairs of men. I repeat, he was an honest public servant trying to

[78] Calcutta was the seat of the British government in India.
[79] The 1911 revolution in China, which ended the Qing dynasty, created a political vacuum which resulted in the Chinese force in Lhasa returning home.

help Britain maintain its position. It's not as daft as it sounds. Many governments have secretly looked into these things.

"In the course of all his questions, he was told about the First and Second World Wars, the likely invasion of Tibet and the turmoil that communism would cause. He was also told deeper spiritual truths about mankind and its developing path. He asked what Tibetan texts existed that described all this. He was told of records made by the State Oracle. And he was told of a book called the Morning Tree. A book that described the true powers that were available to mankind. His contact, Lama Kunchen, said that man had built great cities and industries, but that man was to build even greater things of the spirit in the future.

"Massingberd returned to his office in Calcutta and kept the notes of his meetings safe. He never presented them to his superiors. He knew they'd be greeted with scepticism. But he persisted in his investigations in the hope of proving that psychic abilities existed and could be used to help Britain. He didn't find much more after his meetings with Lama Kunchen. He simply didn't meet anyone of the same calibre. The Hindu fakirs and others he interviewed in the following years were mostly unreliable. Massingberd didn't give up, but he wasn't able to substantiate his belief that psychic powers were real and could help guide governments, and he eventually retired from government service in 1916.

"But his notes were still on file. And they were handed to a young staff officer in 1926. He was intrigued by Massingberd's work, and even tracked him down the following year while on leave in England. Massingberd took to the young man and gave him his personal diary which contained some information that even Massingberd had considered too secret to put on file. The young staff officer made his own investigations. But in 1930 he was ordered to cease. Ghandi was fermenting civil unrest in pursuit of Indian independence, and the Intelligence branch of the colonial government had better things to do than investigate the "poppycock" – that was the word used by the then head of Intelligence – of Massingberd's project. In fact, the staff officer was ordered to destroy all of Massingberd's files.

"That staff officer was my father. Did you know I was born in India? Lived there for the first eight years of my life before being sent to boarding school in England. My father was a punctilious man. But in an act of disobedience that I don't think even he could explain, he took Massingberd's files rather than destroying them and kept them for himself. He didn't pursue his investigations then – he was too busy with his other work – but he did study all of Massingberd's papers and wrote his own account of the information. He retired from military service in 1947 when India became independent. He returned to England shipping his papers with him.

"Three years later, I left school being excused National Service on account of my health. I wanted to study oriental languages at Oxford, but my father insisted I join the family firm. I did so under protest. I wasn't happy in business."

He closed his eyes for a moment and his brow creased. He then rang his bell loudly. The manservant reappeared and poured more tea. After taking a sip, he continued.

"My father could see I wasn't happy. He said he needed me in the business, but that if I wished I could reduce my hours and take private tuition in whatever I wanted. So I started learning Chinese. I think my father was watching to see how committed I was to my studies. I had been indifferent academically at school, but studying Chinese was something that truly interested me. When he saw how serious I was, he approached me with a proposal. He told me I could give up my day-to-day duties with the firm if I learned Tibetan. When I asked him why, he replied to help him with a special project.

"It was a strange proposal. But then I can't say I really knew my father. Brought up by Indian nannies and then sent to school in England and staying with uncles in the holidays, I had never really spent time with him. Furthermore, he was accustomed to being obeyed. So I agreed to his proposal. At least it got me out of the firm.

And I found that, as with Chinese, I had a natural interest in the subject.

"In 1955, on my father's 60th birthday, he called me into his study. I was now proficient in both Tibetan and Chinese. He asked if I remembered the special project he'd like help with. Then he showed me this notebook."

Mr Ravensburg removed the cloth from the tray and held up a large hardcover notebook.

"Massingberd's notes?" I ventured.

"My father's account. It includes Massingberd's notes. But the originals were destroyed by my father – I'm not sure why – maybe he didn't want any evidence that he had purloined Massingberd's files in the first place. But knowing my father, I am completely sure all of Massingberd's information is here."

I waited to be handed the notebook, but Mr Ravensburg returned it to his lap. He then shuffled his hands and produced another, fatter notebook with extra pages stuffed in at either end. I didn't want to guess this time.

"The results of my research," he said. "For when my father told me about Younghusband, Massingberd and his own work, he commanded me to take the project forward. In secrecy, of course. But if I could prove what Massingberd had set out to find, well then, my father, who was also a patriotic man, would pass it on to the contacts he still had in Whitehall. God knows, in the mid-1950s, Britain needed all the help she could get. Economically weak, with her empire fraying, dwarfed by an arrogant America and a seemingly all powerful Soviet Union, we were slipping down the international top table.

"I didn't need any prompting. Unlike my father and his generation, I'm not that patriotic, but I am hungry for knowledge, especially esoteric knowledge. I want power over myself and my life. I had spent so much of my life not in control of my destiny, and I was desperate to change that, so I was eager to understand the unseen forces that govern the universe. So I readily agreed to his proposal. For the first time in my life I was excited.

"I immediately travelled to India and made arrangements to enter Tibet. I had to do it in disguise. The Tibetans weren't letting anyone in. I managed to visit several monasteries, and even the State Oracle at Nechung. Of course, I couldn't stay long in Tibet on any of my visits. My lungs coped badly with the thin air, and most lamaseries were hostile to talking to outsiders. But I was making progress. Then the Tibetan uprising took place, the Chinese retaliated and the Dalai Lama had to escape to India. I tried one more time after that. But the Chinese thought I was a spy and I had to flee for my life.[80]

"I returned to London, frustrated that I couldn't make more progress. But I carried on my work, spending large sums of money to obtain what little documents and information were coming out of Tibet. Even my father's death in 1965 – he had had malaria three times when in India and that had fatally weakened him – didn't stop me. By now I was hooked. I have made more discoveries over the years. In fact, I am sure I am the most knowledgeable person on the Morning Tree outside the order protecting it – if it still exists. But I have an incomplete jigsaw puzzle. That is why we might have information that is useful to us both."

He paused, with a serious – or was it haggard? – look on his face. I said nothing.

"I have information," he continued heavily, "that would help you locate the Morning Tree. I'm sure you'd be interested in that. But you need to help me. You need to let me read this account that talks about the Morning Tree."

"I…" I wasn't sure what to say. This man claimed he knew about the Morning Tree, and I had no reason to doubt him. But he was odd. "It's not my property to give away," I said at last. "It was a bequest to

---

[80] The Chinese invaded Tibet in 1950 and forced Tibet to accept their suzerainty. The Dalai Lama was allowed to continue to administer Tibet except for Amdo in the east. However, growing Tibetan resistance to Chinese occupation in the east led to fighting which spread to Lhasa in 1959. The Chinese repression forced the Dalai Lama to flee to India, and China took over the government of Tibet.

the university. I'll need to check with my head of department and get back to you."

Mr Ravensburg looked derisory. "Ask. But if you really want to find the Morning Tree, you'll agree to my request."

I retrieved Thaza's manuscript from his reluctant hands and was about to go when Mr Ravensburg stopped me.

"One more thing," he said. "Don't tell anyone what you're doing. This book is dangerous. I can't tell you in what way, but it is dangerous. If others know you are after it…"

I made my way out of that house as fast as possible. I rushed back to SOAS and bumped into Professor Thurgood who was leaving for the evening. It must have been around six thirty.

"Daniel, you look busy," he said. I nodded and carried on to my office. I shut the door, threw off my coat and briefcase, and sank into my chair. What was going on?

For some reason, Mr Ravensburg unsettled me. In fact, this whole business was beginning to unsettle me. I was a minor academic trying to pursue an unusual line of research but I seemed to be entering murky waters. And uncovering frankly unbelievable things. But were they unbelievable? A part of me knew they weren't – there was something real about the Morning Tree – but another part wanted to ditch the whole thing. Professor Thurgood was acting oddly, Jim – happy go lucky Jim – seemed to have been burned by this book, and now this strange man Mr Ravensburg was hinting darkly about danger. And what chance did I have of finding it anyway? It seemed impossible. What should I do? Carry on or call it off as a bad idea? I wrestled with these thoughts for some time but couldn't see a way out. My head was aching. Time to go home and have a rest.

I let myself out of my office and walked down the corridor. I heard laughter coming from Milo Andretti's room.[81] As I passed his open door I saw a group of people with glasses in their hands and

---

[81] Milo Andretti, senior reader in Tibetan, School of Oriental and African Studies.

bottles of wine on the desk. I caught sight of a lama's robes and recognised Sonam Prasang. I also saw Claire.

"Ah Daniel, come in," said Milo in that Italian accent of his. "We're just having a drink."

I hesitated. I didn't want a drink, but I did want to see Claire. Milo thrust a glass of warm white wine into my hand, and Sonam Prasang inclined his head gracefully to me. Claire was talking to someone else, so I waited before approaching her. Sonam came up and asked how I was. He said he hoped the passages he'd translated for me had been useful.

"By the way," he added, "where did you come across those passages? They were quite unusual."

Claire was still talking. I told him they were from a manuscript that had come into SOAS's hands.

"A religious one?"

"No, no," I replied. "Quite secular. Look, I am grateful for your help, but I can't say more at the moment because we might publish and I can't pre-empt anything."

Sonam looked serious. I could see Claire had stopped talking now. Raising my hand to Sonam, I started to make my way over to her. But he reached out to stop me.

"Daniel, is it to do with an esoteric book?"

"I told you, it's a secular text—"

"The Morning Tree?"

People were still talking in the room – in fact the wine was making them raise their voices – but all I heard was silence.

He was still looking serious. "Daniel," he said, "involving yourself with a power you don't understand is dangerous. If you want to talk…"

Chapter Four

I pretended not to hear him. I carried on across the room and started talking to Claire. But all the while I was trying to process what Sonam had said. Another person talking about the Morning Tree, another person talking about danger. Claire paused because I wasn't paying attention to her. I shook myself. Best to think Sonam hadn't said what he had and act as if nothing had happened. I could feel Sonam peering at my back but resisted the temptation to turn round. Soon, out of the corner of my eye, I saw him leave.

"So, how's your research coming along?" asked Claire eventually.

"Actually, I wanted to talk to you about that," I replied quickly. "When would you be free?"

"How about now?"

I was agitated, but didn't want to pass up her offer, so I agreed. We made our excuses to Milo and left. Once outside, we walked to an Italian restaurant near Charlotte Street. Although it was January, it wasn't cold, and the walk cleared my head.

I told Claire about my contact with Jim, and my meeting with Mr Ravensburg, both confirming that they had come across references to the Morning Tree, and both promising to help locate it. I added that Jim had not been himself at first, and Mr Ravensburg, well, he'd been strange from the start. Claire laughed.

"It's like Lord of the Rings," she said. "Whenever people come across the One-Ring-To-Bind-Them-All, they go mad."

"Except this is real," I replied. "And these people are making me feel uncomfortable." Then I told her about Sonam Prasang that evening.

"Are you sure that's what he said?" she asked.

"Yes. The Morning Tree. He mentioned it. He implied I could be in danger."

"Why didn't you talk to him?"

"I've been told not to by Professor Thurgood. For some reason, he thinks Sonam is not to be trusted." Actually, I'd been alarmed by Sonam and didn't want my fears that this book was dangerous to be confirmed.

"But you trust him?"

"I think so. We're friends. At least, I've known him for years. And he was very helpful translating the obscure passages in Thaza's account."

"Then you must ask him what he meant," said Claire.

She was right. I had to ask Sonam how I could be in danger. Jim and Mr Ravensburg had said the Morning Tree had teeth and I didn't want to be bitten. Why were things becoming so difficult? Claire and I ordered grappa. Sometime later we left the restaurant and I was at last feeling happier than when we'd entered.

Happier, but not settled. I got home late, still in confusion about what to do with the Morning Tree. Continue my research or drop it because of the difficulties I was encountering? Karen was already in bed, but I didn't feel like sleeping, so I tiptoed into the sitting room and took out Thaza's manuscript. I was going to read it, but instead just held it in my hands. I wasn't even turning my dilemma over in my mind. Rather, I lapsed into quietness. And then it happened. A light in the corner of the room. A feeling of love welling up inside me. And there was Lama Kunchen with the Morning Tree. I mean, I knew it was Lama Kunchen even though I obviously had never seen him, and he was holding the Morning Tree, even though it didn't look like the book described by Thaza. He wasn't talking to me but I had the distinct message that he was showing me the Morning Tree, the

Morning Tree was all that he'd said it was, and it was vitally important for mankind's future.

I then had an image of two routes the world could go down: one was the path of pain and difficulty we were on; the other was one of peace and fulfilment. I say I had this image. It wasn't a picture exactly, or some words, but it was a definite understanding that there were two routes open to mankind, and that the Morning Tree could lead us to the better one. Then I had a feeling of rightness – just that it was right that I should be involved with the Morning Tree, and that I should try to find it. It wasn't a question of being special; it was just something that had to be done.

I don't know how long this lasted. It felt like minutes but it might have been seconds. But gradually it faded – the messages, the feeling of love, the keenness of it all – and I became aware of my surroundings again.

I shook myself. I would have doubted it but for the fact that it had been so real. I wondered if I'd made it up, but knew I hadn't. I couldn't make up what had just happened; it wasn't in the way I thought. Hadn't I always ridiculed Jim for his beliefs? How could I now be thinking like him? No, this was nothing my mind had produced; it was something else. But what was it then? Part of me was willing to let it go as an inexplicable event best not recalled if it didn't fit into my normal beliefs. But another part knew something different. The depth of feeling, that amazing love, the insights – they were the most real things I had experienced. I couldn't convey this to anyone else, but I knew in myself that what had happened was unmistakably authentic.

But what did it mean? As soon as I asked the question, I had the answer. I had to find the Morning Tree. For some unfathomable reason, I had been shown the book's real importance. I wasn't religious, or even worked up about the state of the world, but I knew now that this book held the key to our future, and this key could be turned sooner rather than later. So, I was to find the Morning Tree, then humanity could step into its golden inheritance. I let out a whistle as this realisation dawned within me. It was bizarre. That it should fall to me to do this. I was a most unlikely candidate.

I put Thaza's manuscript away. As I did so, I realised that everything now felt right. I was going to find the Morning Tree. This was the answer to my dilemma earlier in the evening. Danger or not, I had to continue in my quest for the book. And this was another bizarre thing. I normally avoid danger wherever possible (even turning down invitations to go skiing in case I break a leg). But now I was calm as I contemplated an uncertain future. I yawned and suddenly felt ready for bed. Remarkably, I didn't think about a thing and went straight to sleep.

Over the next few days, I had new energy. My immediate concern was how to contact Sonam Prasang, without making Professor Thurgood think I had approached him. I couldn't work this out, so put it to one side for the time being. Then there was Mr Ravensburg. Of course, I didn't ask Professor Thurgood if I could have permission to show him Thaza's manuscript. Instead, I phoned and fixed an appointment for the following Monday to call on him.

So, that Monday I returned to his large house in Kensington. Stepping between the expensive cars parked on the street I made my way to his door. I wondered if his banker and diplomat neighbours had any idea who was living next to them.

His manservant opened the door, and led me into the same room as before. A little table with a lamp had been set up near Mr Ravensburg's chair. He seemed impatient and held out his hands for the manuscript.

"Before we begin," I said, "I need a promise from you not to publish anything you might find in the manuscript."

"You just don't get it!" he replied acerbically. "I don't want to publish anything! I don't want my name associated with it."

"Are you sure?"

"Yes! This book is dangerous. It is protected. And there are dark forces after it. These forces will stop at nothing to find out what you know. I have suffered from this."

"When—"

He waved his hand. "I don't want to suffer again. I don't want anyone to know I'm involved. I'm certainly not going to publish anything. And you will keep my name and any information I give you a secret. I just want the Morning Tree. I'm too old to track it down myself. But you can help me. We can help each other. Why can't you see that?"

He held out his hands again. I opened my briefcase and gave him a copy of Thaza's Tibetan manuscript. He handed me his two notebooks. I put them in my briefcase.

"What are you doing?" he snapped. "Those notebooks don't leave this house."

"Then how—"

"You study them on that desk," he said jabbing at the small table.

"Then I will take Thaza's manuscript away with me when I leave," I replied, annoyed at his antics. I didn't want to stay in that house longer than I needed, but it seemed I was trapped. He shrugged his shoulders. I had no alternative but to study the notebooks next to him in that darkened room.

The first notebook was written in pale blue ink and in an ornate hand. His father's notes. The second was in scrawlly black ink: Mr Ravensburg's work. Mr Ravensburg was right about one thing. His father was a punctilious man. His notes were elegant, clear and written with authority. I started reading. He had helpfully arranged everything by subject. So we started with Younghusband's expedition to Lhasa, and the secrets he was told. Amazingly, the Tibetans told him the Chinese would one day occupy Tibet, there would be two world wars, and the British Empire would disappear. Something to do with misusing their authority in India. There was a great deal of comment on this last point from Massingberd and Mr Ravensburg's father.

Then we had the Dalai Lama's flight to Darjeeling in 1910 and his visit to Calcutta. And there it was – the reference to Lama Kunchen:

Introduced to Lama Kunchen, a middle aged monk, of diminutive stature, with a pleasing smile, were the exact words. Other comments were *Lama K on excellent terms with DL. Not a tulku or high ranking abbot but respected by others and relied on by DL. Lama K detailed to liaise with me [Massingberd] on esoteric matters. Lama K very helpful.* And finally *Lama K is like St Francis of Assisi: unpretentious, not bothered with show, at one with himself and his God, far sighted, yet with a deceptive strength.*

I pushed back my chair, my heart beating fast. Was this the same Lama Kunchen? Thaza doesn't mention that Lama Kunchen accompanied the Dalai Lama on his flight to India. Yet Thaza makes clear that Lama Kunchen is not a tulku or abbot, he is a close friend of the Dalai Lama, he is well versed in esoteric matters and he is a spiritual man. His age also tallied: middle aged in 1910 would be old (certainly by Tibetan standards) by 1931 or 1932. I was sure this was the same man. This was a breakthrough.

By now it was early evening. I'd had enough for the day. But I had to admit, I was pleased with what I'd read so far. Mr Ravensburg, studying Thaza's manuscript next to me, was pleased as well.

"I trust you will return as soon as possible?" he asked in an unexpectedly warm voice, as I exchanged his notebooks for my manuscript. "This account is more than I anticipated."

I did return. In fact I spent all my non-teaching time over the next two weeks going through both notebooks. There was a great deal in Massingberd/Ravensburg senior's notebook. Most, as Mr Ravensburg had said, was about divination and how it could be used to help states maintain their position in the world. I admit on closer inspection it wasn't as silly as it sounded. Assuming psychic powers existed – and there was ample evidence of that in these notebooks – then it was merely another form of information to be used by the intelligence services. Of course, there were all sorts of unanswerable questions (such as, can such powers be relied upon, can they be used for personal advantage, and can the future be altered from the prediction made about it?), but these questions didn't fall within my purview. As far as the Morning Tree was concerned, there were three important pieces of information in Ravensburg senior's notebook.

The first was when Massingberd asks if there are any texts that describe psychic powers and how to acquire them. Massingberd records that *Lama K referred to a book called the Morning Tree (meaning?) listing powers mankind is heir to. A collation of esoteric knowledge centuries old. Lost powers soon to be returned, new consciousness coming to solve conflict. Lama K coy on when powers and consciousness will be present. Book's contents and existence a state secret known only to a handful of initiates. Lama K politely refused to say where the Morning Tree was. Even the Abbots of the Great Seats are ignorant of the book.*

This was striking gold. An extant reference to the Morning Tree. It was a shame that Mr Ravensburg senior had destroyed Massingberd's files. If he hadn't, then I could have shown incontrovertibly that there was a corroborative reference proving the book's existence. But at least this notebook was a written source that talked about the Morning Tree, and in the same terms as Thaza's account.

The second important piece of information was an underlined passage later in Massingberd's notes. He'd written *Lama K says Tibet's guardianship to be passed on to other countries, Great Britain among them. Spiritual awakening in the western world. Part of cycle of change.*

I suspected Massingberd had considered this important, because it told him that the esoteric powers he was so interested in would one day be recognised in his own country. But I found this passage important because it was a novel idea – Tibet's role as a guardian of spiritual truths being passed on to the West – and it was an idea that Thaza records Lama Kunchen telling him. Further proof that the two Lama Kunchens were the same man.

The third piece of information was in many ways the most exciting. Massingberd is pressing Lama Kunchen with questions about how to acquire psychic abilities. Lama Kunchen tells him that it is really a question of waiting until higher frequencies are present, then people will find themselves becoming more aware of other levels of reality.

When will that be? asks Massingberd.

In the years to come, replies Lama Kunchen. But then he adds, *Maybe sooner if the Morning Tree can be released ahead of time.*

Two things made me sit up. The first was that this tallied with all that Lama Kunchen told Thaza about the book and how crucial it was for mankind's future. The second was that it recalled the vision I'd had in my flat. Again, I felt the truth of the Morning Tree, and could feel its power.

As for Mr Ravensburg's notebook, that was harder going. It was difficult to decipher, not well laid out and his writing betrayed a certain anger. He seemed to take his failure to make all but the slowest progress personally. Either that or he was desperate to prove to his father that he was worthwhile. Whatever, his notebook just wasn't very readable. But I ploughed on. I have to admit, I admired his tenacity, especially as travelling in Tibet in the late 1950s was perilous. He did squeeze out nuggets of information. The man got into the State Oracle at Nechung, for goodness sake, and interviewed the State Oracle himself. Mr Ravensburg's notes of the meeting were almost unintelligible, but I had no doubt he had done what he claimed.

And then, as he had said, the Chinese declared him a spy and he had to flee for his life. He was betrayed by one of his Tibetan helpers and nearly captured. He had a harrowing time.

I was, of course, looking for information about the Morning Tree. Mr Ravensburg didn't mention the book specifically until 1967. He had until then been focussing on divination and psychic powers generally. But in that year, an unnamed lama told him (in Cardiff of all places) about a secret order guarding a treasure worth more than all the exchequers and arsenals of the world. This treasure was not material but spiritual information in the form of a book – information that could transform the well-being of the world. The communists would never get this book, the lama told Mr Ravensburg, because it was no longer in Tibet. The lama didn't use the title the Morning Tree, and Mr Ravensburg didn't link it to the book mentioned by Lama Kunchen to Massingberd all those years before, but he was extremely interested in what he was being told.

I can only guess how Mr Ravensburg came to meet this lama in Cardiff, or why the lama revealed so much. I suspect the latter had something to do with money. There were several references in his notebook to sums, some of them coming to hundreds of pounds, given by Mr Ravensburg to individual Tibetans or Tibetan organisations. He had already admitted to me that he'd procured what information he could. And Tibetans who had recently fled their country would have an urgent need to fund themselves in exile. But what made this lama reveal so much?

The lama's information didn't end with what he'd told Mr Ravensburg about this special book. He gave him the name of another lama – a Ponchen Chortzig – in Ladakh, India, who was worth contacting. He then told Mr Ravensburg he couldn't divulge any more. Again, I don't know why this lama was being so helpful, but Mr Ravensburg appeared to trust him, because he left for Ladakh within days. The lama didn't say where in Ladakh Ponchen Chortzig could be found, but after a painstaking search Mr Ravensburg tracked him down.

He asked him about this book, with information so valuable it could transform mankind. Ponchen Chortzig tells him that it is called the Morning Tree. There is a furious scribble in the notebook at this point as Mr Ravensburg at last connects it with the Morning Tree mentioned in Massingberd's notes. You can see he's angry with himself for not making the connection sooner. He is told it is a collation of esoteric knowledge about the true consciousness that mankind is heir to, a consciousness that would indeed transform people's attitudes and the way they lived. It is guarded by a secret order – Ponchen Chortzig all but admitted he was part of this order – and it would be released when mankind was ready. There was great danger though. This book was being sought by dark forces – he called them the dark lodge – who wanted to stop mankind moving forward. The dark lodge would kill to find the book.

But where was the book? Ponchen Chortzig said its location was a closely guarded secret; all he could say was that it was not in Tibet. Mr Ravensburg asked if he could see the book. He was told it wasn't available to be seen. He asked if one could know the contents of the book in more detail. No, was the reply.

I was excited. The information was identical to that relayed by Thaza. And it corroborated there were dark forces, as Lama Kunchen claimed, and both he and Thaza experienced, seeking to destroy the book. But wasn't the first lama that Thaza saw – the one who sent him to Lhasa – called Chortzig? And wasn't the lama who first told Jim about the Morning Tree also in Ladakh? Were things coming together at last?

I still didn't know why this Lama Chortzig was being so communicative – it didn't seem right if he were part of the secret order – but then Lama Kunchen had told Thaza all this and more.

I carried on reading Mr Ravensburg's notebook. He was now focussing his efforts on finding the Morning Tree. Like Jim McField, he had a frustrating time. No other source was as revealing as Lama Chortzig. In fact, no-one else Mr Ravensburg met admitted to knowing anything about the Morning Tree. He was hampered by bouts of illness – mostly respiratory problems – which he put down to overwork, but which I wondered might be like Jim's mysterious virus deflecting him from getting close to the book. He also suffered threats, blackmail attempts and three assaults that terrified him. And there was an unexplained two year gap in the notebook where he seemed to do no work at all. I suspected these were the attacks by the dark that he didn't want to talk about.

As a result, in the latter years Mr Ravensburg slowed his search. But he didn't stop. He began to comb all the texts he could find. He started to see hints, nuances and references to the Morning Tree in a wide range of material, and collated them all. The last part of the notebook – really covering the last twenty years – was textual research. I couldn't see much use in the mass of references he'd assembled.

As I say, I spent two weeks going through these notebooks. At the end I confronted Mr Ravensburg.

"You told me there would be information here that would help me find the Morning Tree," I said, "but there's nothing. There's useful corroboration of the book's existence, and the order guarding it, but there are no clues to actually finding it."

"Those notebooks are the most detailed account of esoteric knowledge," countered Mr Ravensburg, "garnered at great personal cost to myself."

"But they don't tell me where the Morning Tree is!" I replied. "Either you have information on where it is, or you haven't. And if you haven't, then you've seen Thaza's manuscript under false pretences."

He looked at me over the top of his glasses and pursed his lips. "I never said the information I had about the whereabouts of the book was in the notebooks," he snapped. "Some things are too important to write down."

"Well then, what—"

"Next time you come, I will give you the information you need. You will see for yourself how valuable it is."

With that I was dismissed.

I was tempted to discount Mr Ravensburg's claims. He knew about the Morning Tree certainly, but did he really have an idea about where it might be? But I had come this far, so I might as well see what he had to say. So I arranged one more visit for the following week and left his house.

It was a Friday afternoon in the beginning of February. I didn't feel like returning to SOAS so I went straight home. I was in a grey mood from Mr Ravensburg's shenanigans and didn't register at first when I got to the flat that the door was on the latch. I thought Karen must be home. But then I knew she seldom came back before me, and all the lights were off. I pushed open the door to the sitting room and saw, in the gloom, an unexpected mess. It was only when I turned the lights on that I realised what had happened.

Papers were tipped all over the floor. A vase of flowers had been knocked down and soaked the carpet. My camera and iPod were gone. So was a silver picture frame. The drawers to my desk were all open, my DVDs scattered everywhere. I'd been burgled.

I was very upset. Feeling sick, I looked around the flat trying to see what else had been taken. I cursed the bastards who'd done this. I felt defiled. Eventually I rang the police. I'd never dialled 999 before, and when I did I received the further humiliation of being told that my burglary wasn't an emergency and I was to contact my local police station. I found their number and called them.

Then Karen came home. She was shocked too. I accused her of not locking the door properly that morning. We had another argument – just what I didn't need. Only the arrival of two police officers half an hour later stopped us. The officers were polite, said robberies often took place at dusk, but they didn't actually promise to do anything. I suppose they didn't think it was a serious case. I had by now worked out that very little had been taken. The police said I'd probably surprised the burglars coming home when I did. Maybe. But I was still upset and still felt violated.

Once the police had gone, and Karen and I were talking to each other again, we tidied up. I felt unclean and morose. Why had this happened to me? The police had said that several properties in the area had been burgled; it was just a fact of life. Perhaps I shouldn't take it personally. I had a long shower and finally went to bed.

I awoke in the night, my heart thumping. I hadn't been burgled by chance! It was the dark trying to get at me. They knew I was after the Morning Tree and wanted to stop me. It was suddenly so obvious. I didn't need to know how they knew – Lama Neto knew about Thaza, didn't he? – they just did. I was on their radar, and I was in danger. Now I felt the truth of everything Lama Kunchen had said to Thaza about the dark. I even understood what Mr Ravensburg was talking about when he said he didn't want anyone – the dark – to know he was involved in finding the book.

I got out of bed and went into the sitting room. I had a lump in my throat from fear. This wasn't anything I could tell Karen. She hadn't liked my interest in the Morning Tree from the start, and certainly wouldn't appreciate being told dark forces were after me. But that didn't make it any less true. The dark could be anyone, anywhere; how could I fight them?

But, strange to relate, knowing the dark were after me, also gave me new resolve. The fact that they had bothered to burgle me showed that the Morning Tree was important. They did want to prevent its release. The Morning Tree was then, as my heart knew, worth fighting for. I wasn't brave, but I couldn't give up. If I could help it, I wouldn't let the dark win again.

Chapter Five

True to my word, I didn't tell Karen the reason we'd been burgled. She'd only have got alarmed and told me to stop this nonsense with the Morning Tree. Instead I told her I wanted to see my parents for the weekend. She was surprised at my sudden decision, and said she couldn't come with me because she'd arranged to see some friends that evening. I knew she had, and was hoping she would stay behind. I just wanted time on my own. My parents were surprised too when I phoned them, and doubly so when they found Karen wasn't coming. I could hear the anxiety in their voices.

I spent that weekend walking the dog across the fields and thinking. I hadn't had any material to do with the Morning Tree in my flat – my copies of Thaza's account and whatever notes I had were in my briefcase or at work – so whoever had burgled me hadn't found anything. Maybe they'd think I wasn't involved with the book after all. But whatever they thought, I knew I had to find the Morning Tree as soon as possible. But here I kept coming up against the same problem: the book, whose existence was deliberately being kept secret, could be anywhere in the world outside Tibet. I know Mr Ravensburg had said he had information that could help find the book, and Jim had said he was working on it, but the odds were stacked against me.

And that was without reckoning on the dark – whoever they were – trying to stop me.

My parents could see something was on my mind. After I'd reassured them about Karen, I told them a little about the Morning Tree. My father glowered and said it was all tomfoolery: I should be careful before putting my name to such nonsense. That's an accountant for you, I suppose, never willing to believe anything that can't be reduced to facts and figures. But my mother was more encouraging. I even told her something of the book's subject matter.

I went to bed on Saturday night as unsettled as when I'd arrived. But that night I had a dream. I saw Lama Kunchen again. He was smiling at me. We were somewhere in London in the present day. He was showing me something. Although I couldn't see it, I knew it was something to help find the Morning Tree. The dream wasn't clearer than my usual dreams, it was as strange and jumbled, but the feeling in the dream – one of strength and love – was definitely different. It was so wonderful to experience that when I woke up I knew it had been a message for me. Yes, I know, I didn't believe in psychic phenomena, but this, and the vision I'd had in my flat, were so true that I had to accept there was another reality I'd previously been unaware of. I woke up then with hope, even certainty, that the Morning Tree could be found. But in London? Was the message in my dream accurate or had I got it wrong?

I read the Sunday papers before returning to my flat. They were full of doom and gloom about the state of the world. I could suddenly see that people were unconsciously asking for another way of living. My father, whose papers I was reading, was complaining that we needed a change of government.

"Maybe not," I said, half to myself.

"What do you mean?" he snapped. "You don't support this lot, do you?"

"No. I mean, maybe we need a change in consciousness."

"A change in what?"

"If we knew more about ourselves and the purpose of life, then maybe the world wouldn't be so full of problems."

"What are you talking about?"

I didn't want to explain – I didn't know that I could explain – so I let it drop. But my mother said quietly, "That's interesting, Daniel."

271

I returned to SOAS on Monday morning in a much better frame of mind. The first thing I did was secure Thaza's manuscript and my copies in a locked filing cabinet in the departmental office. I figured if the dark came looking again, they'd search my room rather than anywhere else, so with luck the documents would be safe in Ann's office.

The next thing I did was to look for Claire, to tell her what had happened. I heard her laughter in the corridor and went out to see her. But she was holding Milo's arm, talking to him about something. I hadn't realised she was that friendly with him. As I was standing there, Professor Thurgood came up behind me and slapped his large hand on my shoulder making me jump out of my skin.

"Ah Daniel, just the man I wanted to see," he said. "Come with me."

I followed him to his office where he asked how things were going.

I told him what I'd learnt from Mr Ravensburg's notebooks and that Mr Ravensburg had promised to reveal more, specifically on where he thought the Morning Tree might be. Professor Thurgood was impressed.

"Good, good," he said. "I wasn't sure what Ravensburg would have – he is a strange fellow – but I'm glad he's been helpful. It's too early to conjecture, I know, but if you could find this text Daniel, it'd be a major academic event."

"And maybe more than that," I murmured.

"What?"

"It might," I ventured, "help show us how to live in a better way."

Professor Thurgood raised his eyebrows. He was silent for a moment. "Indeed, there is wisdom in Tibetan culture. But more practically Daniel, to unearth this book, you may have to travel."

I hadn't thought about this, but Professor Thurgood was right (unless, thinking about my dream, the book was in London...).

"I've managed to secure some funds for you. Don't look so surprised. It doesn't mean you can swan off whenever you want to;

you have to convince me of your reasons for going. And, of course, you can't neglect your teaching duties. But you should have enough to do what is necessary."

I was amazed. It was unheard of for a head of department to lobby unasked for money on behalf of a junior academic, and especially one on as unlikely a quest as mine. Normally, they jealously guard what little money there is. I was astonished Professor Thurgood was being so supportive.

That afternoon I went to hear what Mr Ravensburg had to say about the whereabouts of the Morning Tree. As I set off from SOAS, I noticed the first daffodils had appeared in Russell Square. Mr Ravensburg's manservant let me in, and I was shown again into the library. He had the curtains open for once, and a shaft of strong sunlight was dazzling on the polished wooden floor. Mr Ravensburg was in his usual chair. He was holding out his hands.

"I don't have Thaza's manuscript with me," I said. "You've told me you have information on the whereabouts of the Morning Tree. If I am to find it, you must tell me what you know."

Mr Ravensburg dropped his hands. "Very well," he said. "But before I begin, I need you to swear once more that you shall divulge nothing of what I am about to tell you."

This nonsense again. "And if I find the Morning Tree?" I said. "How am I to explain how I found it?"

"Make up whatever you want. Just don't mention my name."

"All right," I sighed, "I agree."

"You swear?" He thrust a book into my hands. "You swear on the Kangyur?"[82]

"I'm… I'm not a Buddhist… All right, I swear. On the Kangyur. I swear not to divulge what you are about to tell me."

I had no option. I needed to know what he knew. I didn't consider my oath binding; I was just playing this man's games. Mr

---

[82] The Kangyur is the equivalent of the Buddhist bible. It consists of the words of the Buddha in 108 volumes.

Ravensburg seemed relieved though. He rang his bell and ordered refreshments.

"You have seen how much information I've collected," he began. "A genuine seeker of truth doesn't shy away from doing what is necessary. I put my body on the line for knowledge. I suffered ill health and considerable discomfort in my travels; I have the effects still today. I also pressed my bank balance into play. There was no sum I wouldn't pay to get the right information. I have no qualms about this. However spiritual a man is, he still needs to eat. I know I helped a great number of people with my money, some good, some not so good. But if they gave me information, I would give them money.

"I realised quite soon in my quest for the Morning Tree that I wouldn't simply be told where the book was. If the order guarding it was in any way honourable – and I had every hope that it would be – they would never reveal the book's whereabouts to an outsider, however well-intentioned or well-heeled. I needed another way to find where the book might be.

"One of the most valuable pieces of information I ever obtained was how to do a series of hand and head gestures. Unseen to a normal person, these could identify the doer as a member of the secret order to another initiate."

"Like a freemason's handshake?" I put in.

Mr Ravensburg wasn't pleased to be interrupted. "Yes," he replied irritably, "if you want to put it that way. But these gestures are far subtler than a freemason's handshake." He gave me a quizzical look and then shook his head. "Not that you'd know about a freemason's handshake.

"I was very lucky to get hold of this information," he continued. "The monk who told me – quite an ordinary man, not a lama or anything like that – was desperate. It was the Cultural Revolution, and the Chinese were smashing up the monasteries in Tibet, so there was an increasing flow of refugees at the time. He had had a dreadful experience; I could see it in his eyes. The amount of money I offered would have enabled him to see out his days safe in India. He took the money, and taught me the gestures. He didn't know where the book was, of course, he was too junior, but I'm sure he was part of the secret order. I suppose not all members are of the calibre of Lama Kunchen."

"Could you show me some of the gestures?"

He waved his hand curtly as if I'd asked an impertinent question. "As I say, I was very lucky to get hold of this information, although at least I had the presence of mind to know whom and when to ask about the Morning Tree and its order. I spent days practising the gestures."

"But," I said, "even assuming you could identify a member of the secret order through these gestures, they still won't tell you where the Morning Tree was, would they?"

"You don't get it, do you? I learnt these gestures not so that I could identify a member of the order, but so that I could pass myself off as one of their order. If a member thought I was a member, there would be a greater chance they would reveal something about the whereabouts of the book. You see, I had come to realise that the secret order, like all secret orders, didn't have a central list of members. That would hardly make it secret if the list were uncovered. No, very few of the members would know who other members were. That way, no one member could compromise the whole organisation. That is why they had to have the hand and head gestures as a way of recognising each other. If anything, learning about these gestures confirmed my theory that most members lived in ignorance of each other. And if that was the case, then I could pass myself off as a member too, in the hope of tricking someone into revealing all."

"But you're a westerner, not Tibetan."

"Yes. But the Morning Tree was outside Tibet, wasn't it? And didn't Lama Kunchen say that the guardianship of the book and its knowledge would pass to the West? So it could be that westerners might be members too. Of course, I didn't know at the time that Lama Kunchen had indicated that the responsibility for the book would pass to the West. But don't forget, I wasn't an ordinary westerner: I spoke fluent Tibetan and already knew more about the Morning Tree than most high ranking lamas, so the idea that I might be a member is not as farfetched as you think. I was sure I could pass myself off as one of their order, and so find out where the book actually was."

He paused to take some tea that had been delivered while he was speaking. He was concentrating so hard he was looking drained. I didn't know if it was because he was trying to get a complicated story correct or if it still grated to tell an outsider so much of his closely guarded secrets.

"Armed with these gestures, I tried them on every Tibetan I met. All to no avail. Until one day in France."

"France?"

"Yes, France. Tibetan exiles went there too. If I got a report of a group of lamas somewhere, and they seemed interesting, I would travel to meet them. I had a good feeling about this trip before I set off. There were three lamas. They'd been invited by the French government to found a monastery there. It was the mid-1970s and France, like other countries, was trying to assuage its guilt for not having protested louder about the rape of Tibet. I met them at an old abbey near Combourg. I think the French government thought that, as they were monks, they would appreciate a 15th century monastery. In the event, the lamas found it unsuitable and nothing happened. The head lama, Tensing Dorjee, had originally come from Mindroling lamasery,[83] noted for its study of the more esoteric branches of Buddhism. He was an intriguing man. Peaceful, comfortable in himself and clear sighted. He agreed to meet me at the small hotel in Combourg where they were staying. I did the gesture of welcome. Without a flicker, he made the correct response. I made the follow-up, and he the follow-up to that. He dismissed the other two lamas, and we were alone.

"'Brother, how goes it?' he asked.

---

[83] Mindroling, Place of Perfect Emancipation, is about 35 miles from Lhasa. It was founded in 1676 and is one of the main monasteries of the Nyingma school of Tibetan Buddhism.

"'Well enough,' I replied. 'But I lack the comfort of true service.' This was a phrase I'd been taught with the gestures. It is a statement of one's willingness to serve the order in whatever capacity.

"'We all lack that comfort,' he replied. 'Ever since the red mist smothered the white lotus.' I take it you are following this?" Mr Ravensburg said, arching a look in my direction.

"Yes," I replied. "He was talking about the Chinese invasion of Tibet."

Mr Ravensburg continued. "We talked. He told me the monastery he'd been shown was unsuitable and he would like a more secluded place. Then he said, 'We need somewhere to house various treasures away from prying eyes. One treasure in particular,' he added looking straight at me, 'our book of faith.' I could barely stay still; I knew he was talking about the Morning Tree. 'How will you transport the treasures to the place you will find?' I asked him. 'If we find the right place that is secure enough, then from Darjeeling we will go to Calcutta and then by plane,' he said. This was more than I could expect."

"Darjeeling? Then—"

"Yes, the book is in Darjeeling! You have no idea how excited I was when I read Thaza's account to find that was where he'd taken the book in the first place."

He was right. I had no idea. He'd murmured and twisted in his chair occasionally while he'd been reading Thaza's manuscript next to me, but generally he had remained as crotchety as ever. I looked at him and noticed beads of sweat had appeared on his thin forehead.

"But... but if you know where the Morning Tree is, why haven't you tracked it down?" I asked, trying to take in all this information.

"What do you take me for!" he snapped. "Of course I've tried to track it down! Tensing Dorjee told me no more, and I deemed it wise not to push my luck. He'd already told me more than I'd expected. I took my leave and returned to England. I immediately made arrangements to travel to India. I arrived in Darjeeling at the end of May. I stayed there all summer, searching. But where could it be?

Obviously, in one of the Tibetan monasteries there. There were quite a few in Darjeeling, and some more had sprung up to house the growing numbers of Tibetan refugees. I started making contacts, spreading my money around. The most promising leads came from Ghoom Monastery.[84] I couldn't identify any member of the secret order, but it seemed to me they were guarding some important artefacts.

"I don't know what it was," – at this point he suddenly sounded weary – "but doors started being shut, for I began to meet a wall of silence. To me it was confirmation I was getting close. But monks who had been friendly were suddenly unavailable. No-one needed my money. Then I saw Tensing Dorjee. He had returned from Europe by then. When I say saw, I mean from a distance leaving Ghoom. I sent notes, but he refused to meet me. He blanked me on the one occasion I saw him leave the monastery to go into town. Of course I persisted. But eventually the police were called. A restraining order was put on me by a local judge. I wasn't allowed within fifty feet of any monk or Ghoom monastery. For once, my money didn't help. In fact, I was told in no uncertain terms that I should leave Darjeeling. I don't know what it was, but the Tibetans held more sway with the local authorities than I did. So I had no choice but to leave."

"When was this?"

"1975."

"But how do you know the book hasn't been moved since then?"

"I don't!" he snapped again. "But I did still pay for information about the monastery to be sent to me. That is why I know Tensing Dorjee has since died. My informants did not tell me that anything important had left the monastery. On the contrary, various treasures have found their way there."

"When did Tensing die?"

"Ten years ago."

"And you haven't tried to go back now that he's out of the way?"

---

[84] Ghoom, or Ghum, Monastery is five miles south of Darjeeling. It was founded in 1875.

"I can't. It's not the restraining order. I'm sure that's forgotten. I can't fly, and I can't be at altitude. Not any more, not without imperilling my health. My lungs were never very strong, you see, and my earlier travels took their toll on them. You've no idea how frustrated I have been! To know where the Morning Tree is but to be unable to get it! I'd never thought of asking somebody for help. But then you came along."

"So you think the Morning Tree is in this lamasery called Ghoom in Darjeeling?"

"Yes."

"But I can't just walk in and take it, can I?"

"I said I'd help you find the Morning Tree, I never said I'd hand it to you on a plate! How to get it is for you to work out."

By now it was early evening and quite chilly. I made my way back to SOAS. It had been a long day, so much information, so much to take in. And so much progress. The Morning Tree still in Darjeeling where Thaza had delivered it. This was tremendously significant, the break I'd been looking for. I was deep in thought as I made my way to the Underground.

Chapter Six

I wrote up my notes from my meeting with Mr Ravensburg, and for once heeded his request not to divulge his information to anyone else. I wanted time to absorb what I'd been told.

It all made sense. Thaza delivered the Morning Tree to Darjeeling. There were Tibetan monasteries there to safeguard it. And Mr Ravensburg's lifelong pursuit of esoteric knowledge had finally paid dividends. Of course, I still had the problem of how to prise it from its keepers. But with so many years having passed – indeed, according to Lama Kunchen, with us now entering a new period in human history, one in which the Morning Tree might finally be released – maybe a solution could be found.

I say I didn't want to tell anyone yet about my discovery, but I did want to tell Claire. I'd always found talking to her very easy, but I wasn't running into her at SOAS anymore. Well, I saw her a couple of times, but she was with Milo both times and I didn't want him to know about my business. Karen had guessed something important had happened – she knew I'd been to see Mr Ravensburg, and I had been very thoughtful on my return – but I refused to be drawn. She made a snarky comment about me being uncommunicative. But it would have been too much to tell her, especially as she'd never really been interested in the Morning Tree. Certainly it was a turning point in my research. It meant that everything I'd hoped might happen after coming across Thaza's manuscript was closer to being fulfilled.

I would have beaten the dark too. That was another reason not to be too talkative about my newfound information.

I suppose I felt like someone who's just been told by a beautiful girl that she loves him, but it was a secret between the two of them for now. I was certainly smiling to myself for days afterwards. I'd definitely have something dramatic to tell Jim when he arrived at the end of the month – just two weeks away now.

I was working one morning in my office a few days later when Claire came in.

"Hey Daniel, how are you?" she asked. "Listen, are you free this evening? We should go out."

At last! I'd be able to tell her everything.

"Milo says he knows of a fantastic restaurant."

"Milo?"

"Yes. Trust him to know the best places to eat. Sichuan apparently. He'll meet us there at seven thirty. I'll see you downstairs and we'll take the Tube."[85]

"Milo will be there?"

"Is that a problem? No? Good. I'll meet you downstairs at seven."

I was waiting for her at the entrance at the appointed time. She was ten minutes late, looking flushed and wearing some lovely and probably expensive scent. She took me, not to Leicester Square as I was expecting, but to Queensway. She led me into a stylish restaurant where a receptionist took our coats and we went downstairs. I could see Milo at a table, drink in hand, laughing with a tanned looking man in a smart suit.

"Ah Daniel!" cried Milo when he saw us. "Welcome. Have some wine. You know of course our guest."

I didn't. At least, I didn't until I looked again. It was Sonam Prasang.

"Sonam!" I exclaimed.

"What's the matter Daniel, didn't you recognise me without my robes?" he laughed.

"No," I replied sitting down. "I mean, not at first."

---

[85] Londoners' name for the Underground.

"I don't wear them all the time. People stare. It's easier sometimes to dress like everyone else."

Except he wasn't dressed like everyone else – he was in what looked like a very good suit.

Claire gave me a big smile. A waiter came to ask if we wanted drinks. As he was taking our orders, she leant over and whispered, "You said you needed to talk to Sonam but Professor Thurgood didn't want you to, so I thought if you bumped into him outside work, so to speak, it might help."

"You mean, you—" but the waiter was leaving and she cut me off by touching my arm and nodding in the direction of Milo and Sonam.

"I didn't know I'd be meeting you," I began to Sonam.

"Nor I you, Daniel," said Sonam.

"Daniel and I were going to do something this evening," said Claire. "Then Milo said he was meeting you here and asked if we wanted to come along."

Milo was beaming. He enjoyed complicated situations. He was Italian. "Come, let us eat," he said waving his hands. "The food here you won't believe."

He was right. He'd pre-ordered – God knows how much it must have cost – but dish after dish was brought to our table. I couldn't recognise most of it, but it was delicious and fiery. I noticed Sonam was having a difficult time. As a vegetarian, he only ate the vegetables and rice, and he wasn't drinking either. But we had a good conversation. We discovered that he'd been born to parents in exile, tutored as a monk from a small boy in Dharamsala, and then sent to the West as a young man to join the Kagyu Samye Ling monastery at Esk in Scotland. He went from there to London, which is where I met him as an undergraduate. As the evening wore on, he was the only one maintaining his dignity. The rest of us were eating and drinking far too much.

Finally, it must have been ten thirty, Milo said he had to go. He had another group of friends he was meeting in the West End. He settled the bill, refusing any contribution from us, and ordered one more round of liqueurs for Claire and me.

"Enjoy," he said, waving a hand in benediction as he finally left.

I looked at my drink. I didn't want it as I'd already had too much. But at least the alcohol and the pleasant evening had removed any awkwardness in now addressing Sonam.

"Sonam," I began, "when we last met, you said something about... about the Morning Tree." He gracefully inclined his head. "You said it was dangerous. Why?"

"I didn't say the book was dangerous. I said involving yourself with something you didn't understand was dangerous. But Daniel, are we talking about the same book?"

"You tell me."

"The Morning Tree. A record of man's true powers. Priceless information on the spiritual course of the planet. A key to a new golden age."

"Yes, I think we're talking about the same book."

"But Daniel, how do you know about it? This book represents the most secret knowledge in Tibetan Buddhism. It has been the most closely guarded – the most successfully guarded – secret for hundreds of years. Only a handful of people really know about it. I'm not even one of those people."

"Then you're not part of the secret order?"

Sonam shook his head. "No. I know something about the book. I've studied with very spiritual lamas, and I am an expert in this area. But I am not part of the order responsible for its safekeeping. The fact that you even know about that! I wonder if even the Dalai Lama is a member or knows who they are. My suspicions were raised when you asked me to translate those passages. Where did you get them? Do you have the Morning Tree?"

"No, no, I don't. I'm looking for it. I didn't even know it existed until April/May last year when I was translating a document that had come to SOAS." I told him about Dr Ram's bequest and Thaza's manuscript.

"Are you sure this document is genuine?"

"Yes. I mean, the paper and ink look as if they come from the period. The details of daily life in Lhasa, and even the political figures it mentions, tally. I've since uncovered some information that corroborates parts of the text. But above all, the way it came into Dr Ram's hands, the fact that it lay unnoticed for what, over thirty five years, all point to it being genuine."

Sonam was silent for a while with his head bowed. "From the subject matter you've already shown me, I'd say it was genuine too," he said at last. "An amazing discovery Daniel. Probably the most information available on the Morning Tree known to anyone outside the order."

"Would you like to see Thaza's manuscript?"

"I would be most grateful."

"I'll send it to you. But Sonam, did you mean it when you said dealing with this book was dangerous?"

He nodded. He was looking concerned. "As I say, the book itself is not dangerous. Although, I have heard that if you get too close to it – and you're not meant to – then certain powers will ward you off. No, the danger lies in the forces seeking to destroy the book. There are people who do not want the Morning Tree to see the light of day. People who will stop at nothing to get hold of it, or at the very least prevent its release. These people have been called the dark lodge."

The dark lodge – that was the phrase told to Mr Ravensburg by Lama Chortzig in Ladakh, one of his few contacts to give any useful information on the Morning Tree.

"They'll stop at nothing?"

"I'd say they've already killed. And will kill again. Don't look so shocked Daniel. I know this isn't the sort of thing you'd expect a humble lama to say in a fancy restaurant, but I'm sure this is the truth."

"How do you know the dark are killing people? Do you have proof, or is it just a feeling?"

"It's not a feeling. Look, I don't know if I should tell you, but I do know there have been thefts of certain artefacts that are linked to

the Morning Tree. One of the thieves was caught and interrogated...
but the lama questioning him was brutally murdered shortly
afterwards."

We were silent. Rather, my heart was thumping loudly, so loudly
I thought the others would hear it. Sonam was repeating information
told to Thaza by Lama Kunchen and to me by Mr Ravensburg.
Information I had experienced at first hand when I was burgled. But
being burgled was one thing; being killed was another. Suddenly I
needed that last drink. The idea of cavorting around Darjeeling asking
for the Morning Tree wasn't so appealing now.

"Who are these people?" I asked.

"The dark lodge? They're not what you'd expect. A few are
conscious of who they are and what they are doing. But even these
few don't necessarily have evil written all over them. Most are
overshadowed by the dark. They're ordinary people with a propensity
to negativity. They will be motivated to lie, steal and obstruct in any
way they can. They will be used by higher powers to destroy the
book."

Again, Sonam's information matched what Lama Kunchen said.
"Then the dark, they could be anyone. But why do they want the
book?"

"Because Daniel, when the Morning Tree is released, their power
will go. At the moment people are confused. They don't know their
true status. Misinformation is the key. This misinformation allows all
the abuses in the world – the misuse of power, exploitation and
injustice. When the book is released, and people are at last clear about
what is right, this confusion will go. And with it the power the dark
have over them."

Again, wasn't this just what Lama Kunchen told Thaza? "But
surely the book is safe with the secret order?" I said.

"I don't know. In fact, I don't even know if the secret order is
still operating as it should. The Chinese have destroyed so much.
Although there are a good number of Tibetans in exile, still there are

not many. That is why it is so important to find the book. Any information you might have…"

I'd already told him I'd send him Thaza's text. And I certainly had more to add, not least the fact that the book may be in Darjeeling. But I was remembering Professor Thurgood's large head telling me not to have any dealings with Sonam, so I kept quiet for now. But I had one more question.

"Do the dark know about Thaza's manuscript?"

"I can't say. I think the dark know something is afoot. That is why they are stirring."

There didn't seem anything more to add. It was also late. Sonam sensed this too. He thanked me for what I'd told him, was gracious to Claire and left. Claire smiled at me.

"Quite an evening," she said.

"Yes," I replied, not telling her what I was really feeling. "Thank you for setting it up."

"I knew you wanted to see Sonam, but you couldn't make it obvious. So I asked Milo to arrange this dinner. He's a good friend of Sonam's, as you know."

I was impressed at Claire's dedication to my project. At least that was one good thing to come out of the evening.

"Don't worry," she continued, squeezing my arm. "I'm sure it's not as bad as Sonam makes out."

"I don't know. Fighting evil. I'm not Indiana Jones."

"Sadly, no. But I'm sure it's going to be all right."

Claire hadn't been burgled. Nor, perhaps, did she appreciate just how difficult finding the book might be. But I couldn't blame her for not being aware of the dark forces surrounding the Morning Tree. I trudged home later trying to think of Claire rather than the dark in an effort to keep my spirits up.

Chapter Seven

I must admit, I spent the following days imagining every other person I saw was a member of the dark lodge. I even made sure I didn't stand too close to the edge of the Underground platform. It would be so easy to shove me from behind as a train was coming into the station. I also contacted Ian Gervois and asked if the library had a safe to store important documents. I wanted somewhere more secure and less obvious than the departmental office to keep my papers. But he didn't have a safe, only locked cases and storerooms.

I sent Sonam a copy of Thaza's original manuscript. He sent a courteous note in reply to say he'd received it. I wondered what he'd make of it.

So much had happened since the beginning of the year. I certainly had a great deal to tell Jim when he at last came over, which was only a few days away now. Karen wasn't keen on him coming to stay with us, but I'd promised he could, so we wasted several hours arguing why he couldn't stay somewhere else. Finally, the Friday of his flight arrived. Claire asked if she could come with me to meet him, so we took the Tube together to Heathrow.

We cut through the throng of people in flight arrivals. I hoped we weren't going to be late as the flight from Chicago had already landed. We burrowed to the front of the barrier and there he was, pushing his trolley out of Customs, slowly looking around. I waved and caught his eye. He broke into a smile when he saw me. He was looking older than I remembered. I pointed towards the exit, and we went to meet him.

"Danny!" he cried, when we at last found some space among the trolleys and people. "Good to see you!" He gave me a bear hug. Then he turned towards Claire and cupped her hands in his. "And you must be Karen," he declared. "Hey Danny, she's more attractive than you said!"

"No, that's Claire," I replied.

"Claire? I thought you said her name was Karen."

"My girlfriend's name is Karen. This is Claire. She's helping with the project."

He was confused for a moment. "Claire. So you're helping Danny with the project. *The* project? OK. Sorry for the mix up. It's something we academics do a great deal. It's good to meet you. So, how do we get out of this place?"

We took a taxi back to my flat. On the way Jim kept turning in his seat to peer out of the window. It was a typical grey day but he was pleased with everything he saw. He loved the close, crowded streets we passed as the taxi navigated through Earl's Court and Chelsea on its way to cross the river. When we arrived I showed him his room.

"It's a bit small, I'm afraid."

"Hey Danny, it's fine. Remember I wanted to be a monk once. I don't need much. I hate those over-heated hotel rooms. That's why I asked to stay with you."

That, and the fact we'd have more time to talk about the Morning Tree. I thought I'd let him initiate the conversation; then I'd know he was ready. But he didn't say anything beyond asking, when Claire was out of the room, "You didn't tell anyone I was coming, did you?"

"No," I replied. "Only Claire and Karen."

He didn't seem to mind that Claire and Karen knew. Once he'd got that question out of the way, he was in good humour but jet lagged. He was flagging by evening.

"That was a great supper, Karen," he said with a stretch. Karen had cooked her standard dinner party dish of boeuf bourguignon. "I think I'll turn in now. Be ready for the big day tomorrow, hey Danny?" And with that he went to bed.

He was up before us the next morning. Karen groaned when she heard him banging around the kitchen. She didn't like not being able to wander around in her pyjamas. I went in first and found him looking for porridge. We didn't have any so I went out to get some. Once he'd had two bowls and a cup of strong coffee, he smoothed his plaid shirt and announced, "Are you ready to go to the Tibet Office?[86] There's something there for us."

"But... but it's Saturday," I stammered, surprised at what he'd said. "It'll be closed."

"They're expecting us." He spoke so decidedly that I finished my breakfast and got ready to go.

"Karen coming?" he asked when I reappeared at the kitchen door.

"No. She, um, isn't keen on this project." He looked as if that was what he wanted to hear, and we left.

Once outside, I asked him what was there for us at the Tibet Office. He shook his head sternly and carried on walking. He was deep in thought and not the happy, disorganised Jim I had known at Northwestern.

We arrived at the Tibet Office in Culworth Street. As I'd thought, it was closed. But Jim boldly opened an unmarked door two buildings along and walked straight up a darkened staircase to a first floor landing. The floorboards creaked as we reached it. Just then a door opened and a Tibetan's head peeked out. When he saw us, the door opened wider and he ushered us in.

"Honourable Jim," said the Tibetan. "Welcome."

Jim gave the man one of his old smiles. "Tenzin, old friend, good to see you." He didn't bother to introduce me. "Have you got it?"

Tenzin nodded and handed Jim a piece of paper. He unfolded it, read it, smiled and thrust it in his pocket.

"Thank you friend," he said. "Come Danny, let's go."

---

[86] The Office of the Government of Tibet in Britain in Culworth Street, London.

I waited until we were back outside then I grabbed his arm. "Jim, what's going on?"

"Danny, I'm sorry, I should have filled you in. Let's walk over there and talk."

We crossed the road and entered Regents Park. He set off at a brisk pace. "It's the Morning Tree, Danny. We've got to find it! You've no idea of its true importance. I know you think I get carried away sometimes, but this time I'm right."

I was going to say I agreed with him, but he continued before I could speak.

"I've always been looking for spiritual truths, for some new spark to light our souls. You know how often I'd go on about the state of the world. Things haven't gotten any better. In fact, I'd say they're a heck of a lot worse. Humanity's going round and round in circles going nowhere. The Earth is complaining. We need *change. Spiritual* change. I know people think I'm a new age nut. I guess it comes with the territory of studying Tibetan Buddhism. But I'm not mad. I knew as soon as I met that monk in Alchi that the Morning Tree was what I'd been searching for all my life. I suppose I buried that feeling for years because I couldn't make any progress finding it. But Danny, when I got your call and read Thaza's manuscript – it all came back. I know this book is the key to mankind's future. It's vital!" He said the last word with urgency. "That's why we've got to find it. You know that, don't you Danny?"

"Yes," I said.

"It's not just to illumine some forgotten area of Tibetan Buddhism. It's for mankind's spiritual development."

"I know," I said.

"And it's not just that," he added darkly. "We've got to find it before others do."

"I know that too."

"I don't mean your academic rivals. I mean people who don't want the Morning Tree to see the light of day." He stopped walking and looked at me. "Evil people." He started moving again. "God, you've read Thaza. If you believe the half of it, you've got to believe there are dark forces out to destroy the book. Hell, they nearly took Kunchen's life and damn near did the same to Thaza!"

"Jim, I know!" I interjected. "I know there are dark forces out to get it. Really, I understand. And I know the Morning Tree is important – spiritually, not academically."

He stopped. "You do?" He took hold of my shoulders and studied the look on my face. "You do," he said with more force. "My God, Danny, that's great! I wondered if I'd have to fight you some of the way, but we're on the same page! What a relief. But tell me, how come? You used to disagree with me about these things."

"I don't know. Thaza's account. There's something about it. There's information in there that just feels right. You couldn't make up what Lama Kunchen says – it's one of the reasons I believe Thaza is telling the truth. And if what Lama Kunchen is saying is true, then this book must be important."

I didn't tell Jim about my insights or dreams, and I didn't tell him about my burglary or the warnings I'd had from Ravensburg and Sonam, but I must have spoken with conviction for Jim slapped me on the back happily.

"Attaboy Danny! So you're not just the logical academic that I used to know. It's good to be with you. We'll find this damn book and change the world. Even Philida[87] thinks I've gone too far this time. Taking off to London at the drop of a hat to hunt down a book no-one's seen. But I'm right, Danny. This is the most important thing. And you know it too."

We walked on in companionable silence for a while, both of us reflecting on the task ahead. A cold wind blew across the park. I turned up the lapels of my coat.

"Let's go somewhere else," said Jim.

"There'll be a coffee bar nearby," I replied.

"To hell with that. Let's visit one of your pubs."

---

[87] Philida McField, Jim's wife of thirty years.

I didn't want a drink at that time of the morning, but I let Jim have his way. I was just pleased to have a new ally in my quest for the Morning Tree, and a friend at that. We headed back towards Culworth Street and eventually found a pub. We were the only customers at that time of day. We got our drinks and sat down at a table by a window. Jim was fascinated by warm bitter. I was going to ask him what had happened at the Tibet Office, but he asked first about Claire and Karen. I told him Claire was a PhD student at SOAS who'd been helping me with the Morning Tree. And Karen, well, Karen was my girlfriend.

"She's very pretty," said Jim.

"Yes. We met through mutual friends—"

"I meant Claire."

Before I could reply, he burst out laughing. "Don't worry Danny, I won't pry any further. It's your life. But she does seem a bright button. You're lucky to have her helping you."

He went to get another drink. When he returned I asked him about the incident at the Tibet Office.

"OK, I will tell you. But we've got to do something first. Let's finish up here and go to the British Museum."

He'd always been like this. Active, unpredictable. I remember at Northwestern turning up at his office never sure if he'd be there or if he'd whisk me somewhere else on a whim. So I was used to his ways. I'd just have to wait. But so would he.

"The British Museum? All right. But I said to Claire we'd meet up around lunchtime. She wanted to spend more time with you. Let me call her. We can meet near the Museum and go there together."

Jim raised his eyebrows but didn't object, so we met Claire at a café in Museum Street for lunch. Jim toyed with his sandwich. I don't think he was aware of what he was eating; he was clearly impatient to get to the Museum. At least he was well mannered enough to smile every now and then. Finally we made our way into the British Museum and went straight upstairs to the East Asian section. Jim was searching for something. Claire and I hung back looking at exhibits here and there.

Suddenly Jim waved his arm and called out, "Over here!"

We joined him in front of a large ornately carved gold and silver bowl with a blue stone in its base housed in a glass case. I edged round to read the notice accompanying it.

Tibetan religious bowl given to Colonel Younghusband in Lhasa, 1904. On loan from the Younghusband family.

Jim was beaming. "Look!" he said excitedly, peering closely at it. "It's amazing! Guys, tell me what you see." We were both quiet for a while. "Come on," he urged, "tell me what you see."

Claire started. "There are figures, they look religious, in a long line leading up to a Buddha at the top surrounded by… by animals it looks like, only they seem to be in the sky. There are buildings, and mountains, and… here, at the bottom, there are what looks like devils being cast out. Then there's Tibetan writing."

"Danny?"

"It's as Claire says."

"What does the Tibetan say?"

"'Dawn'… 'new dawn'… no, I've got it, 'After the dawn comes the morning.'"

"And?" said Jim, gesturing to the words on the other side.

"'Then the tree of… of rightness will grow.'"

"So what does it say?" asked Claire.

"'After the dawn comes the morning,'" I replied. "'Then the tree of rightness will grow.'"

"Yeah, 'grow', 'flower', 'come to fruition' – any one of those will do," put in Jim still staring at the bowl. "And 'rightness', I guess that could mean a bit more. I'd say 'spirituality' but you're on the right tracks. Well," said Jim letting out his breath, "that's terrific!"

He was beaming as if he'd just won a million dollars. My brain was slowly cranking into life. The words 'morning' and 'tree', and the implication that spirituality would bloom – surely they were indicating the Morning Tree. But in what way?

We stayed staring at the bowl. Jim was humming – with joy it seemed. Eventually he stood up and announced:

"Let's go."

"Wait," I said, still peering at the exhibit. "Look. Inside the bowl. There's an engraving and some more words."

Jim stood over the bowl and looked down. "Why, yes," he said. "I hadn't seen that. What do you make of it?"

"Well, you might think I'm seeing things, but the engraving inside the bowl – it looks like the sun rising over the mountains. It looks like the emblem Thaza describes as being on the cover of the Morning Tree."

Jim slapped his thigh. "Danny, that's excellent! I think you're right! That's a real bonus."

"And there are words. They say… 'The seed is planted here.'"

"Yes! 'The seed is planted here,'" said Jim looking at the words himself. He repeated them a few times. Then he broke into another smile. "If I had any doubts, I don't anymore! This is fantastic! Fantastic! Well done guys."

By now my pulse was racing. I didn't have a conscious understanding of what was going on but knew it was something significant to do with the Morning Tree. And hadn't Lama Kunchen in my dream shown me something important in London to do with the book?

"What's this all about, Jim?" asked Claire. Jim put his arms round both our shoulders and gave a strong squeeze.

"Let's go to Danny's apartment and I'll tell you."

Jim could barely contain himself on the Tube home. He kept humming, shifting in his seat and tapping his fingers on his knees. Every now and then he'd turn and beam at us. When we got home Karen, who looked as if she'd been waiting a long time for us to return, made tea.

I was desperate to know how, what we'd just seen in the British Museum, was linked to the Morning Tree, but thought I should help Karen make tea first. She asked why we'd been so long. I told her it was Jim, he'd taken me here and there, always a bundle of energy. She then mouthed Claire's name. Why was she here? Because she's part of this project, I replied in a low voice. Karen frowned and looked like she was going to say something when Claire walked in and asked if she could help. We assured her we were all right and finished making the tea in silence.

We brought the tea through. Karen poured everyone a cup and I sat down.

"So, Jim, what's this all about?"

"It's a breakthrough, Danny, a real breakthrough. This is all better than I expected. But I guess I better start from the beginning."

He stirred a sugar lump in his tea and then continued. "As soon as I read Thaza's manuscript, I knew I had to find the Morning Tree. But where could it be? I read and re-read Thaza's text to see if there were any clues. But there were none I could find."

"Except that bit about the pebbles,"[88] I put in.

"Pebbles?" asked Karen.

"Yes. Thaza asks where the Morning Tree will be hidden, and Lama Kunchen in turn asks Thaza where he would hide a pebble. Thaza says in his pouch. Lama Kunchen says the pebble would stand out in his pouch and that the best place to hide a pebble is with other pebbles – that way it won't be obvious."

"Right," said Jim. "But what does that tell us? Not much. Then one day I was reading the text in the original Tibetan. You did a fine job, Danny, making sense of it all. I was reading the bit when Kunchen says the book has to be taken out of Tibet, so it can be safe from the dark, resting in a place until a future time when its treasures can be revealed.[89] At least, that's how you'd translated it Danny. But the Tibetan words are shorter than the English and more opaque. You know how these Asian languages are. Lama Kunchen was actually saying the Morning Tree has to be taken out of Tibet so it can be safe

---

[88] See page 167 in Thaza's account.
[89] See page 98 in Thaza's account.

from the dark in the resting place of future treasures. At least, that's how it came across to me."

I remembered the passage, and yes, very often there were several interpretations. But translating it as 'in the resting place of future treasures' didn't make sense to me.

"It's OK Danny, translating is never easy," continued Jim. "You got the right sense of the passage. But to me the phrase 'in the resting place of future treasures' was the *name* of the place where the Morning Tree will be kept once it is out of Tibet. It's the only way that passage makes sense. I mean, most Tibetan place names are descriptions rather than just names, like Lhasa means Place of the Gods and Sera means Wild Rose and so on. The Resting Place of Future Treasures was clearly a place name to me. And if it was, then Lama Kunchen was actually giving us the name of the place where the Morning Tree was!"

I had to concede I hadn't found that passage very clear, and a place name could make sense. "All right then," I said, "if it's a place name, where is the Resting Place of Future Treasures?"

"I couldn't find it. I looked at all the place names I could find on Tibetan maps. Trouble was, there weren't many Tibetan maps of the outside world made at that time, and not one had a place called Resting Place of Future Treasures. I was beat, I can tell you. I was sure I was on the right track, but it was leading nowhere. I didn't know what to do. But those words. The resting place of future treasures. They haunted me. I was sure I'd seen them before."

We were all listening intently to Jim. My tea had gone cold, and no-one had touched the biscuits Karen had put out.

"Then suddenly it hit me," continued Jim. "They'd been in a book – A History of Dharamsala[90] – that I'd reviewed for the Northwestern Historical Review about six months earlier. I still had a copy, so I searched it out. And there it was. 'The Resting Place of Future Treasures'. Only it wasn't a place, but a gold and silver bowl with a blue stone – the gold and silver bowl with a blue stone we've just seen

[90] A History of Dharamsala by Edward Lukes, Oxford University Press 2008.

296

in the British Museum – given to Younghusband when he went to Lhasa in 1904, and called 'The Resting Place of Future Treasures'."

"But that's not how it was labelled in the British Museum," said Claire.

"No," said Jim, "but it's the same bowl. Look." He pulled out a slim hardback from his briefcase on the floor and opened it at a full page black and white picture of a bowl. It was definitely the same bowl.

"Turns out," said Jim, "that Younghusband had been given the bowl in Lhasa. I know he'd been an invader, but he was courteous, and the Tibetans warmed to him, and as was the custom in those days, gifts were exchanged by both sides. This bowl was one of many gifts that he was given. Younghusband was told its name was 'The Resting Place of Future Treasures'. And he was told that the place where he kept the bowl would one day also house a great treasure that would help free the world. I kid you not. These were the exact words."

"But how do you know?" asked Claire.

"It's all in this book A History of Dharamsala," said Jim waving the copy in the air. "It seems that Younghusband's parents had lived in Dharamsala in the 1850s, and his uncle had lived there for longer as a tea planter. Younghusband visits Dharamsala in 1905. We don't know why. It was a summer retreat for the British, and he might have known it as a kid, so maybe he was on vacation. Anyway, he tells the local British official, a George somebody,[91] that he's come there to donate the bowl he'd been given in Lhasa the year before. He tells the official what the Tibetans had told him – that where the bowl is housed, there will be a great treasure that will save the world. He says that, as he's a serving soldier, he has no home, and he certainly doesn't want to keep such a valuable object in the steaming heat of Calcutta where his barracks are. He adds that Dharamsala is one of the most beautiful places he knows, and he'd like to house the bowl there in the government residence where he can be confident it will be safe. The official agrees. And so the bowl comes to rest in Dharamsala. All this

---

[91] George Manly, British sub-commissioner, Dharamsala 1903-07.

is recorded by the official, which is why we know about it, and it's in this book."

"Hang on," I interjected. "You said the Resting Place of Future Treasures was a place name but in fact it's the name of Younghusband's bowl."

"Yes," said Jim excitedly. "And the Tibetans told him in 1904 that where Younghusband keeps that bowl, there will be a great treasure that will save the world!"

"So... so you're saying that where the bowl was kept by Younghusband, in Dharamsala, that's where the Morning Tree is?"

"Exactly! To me, the similarity between Kunchen's phrase for the book when it is taken out of Tibet and the name of this gift given to Younghusband was striking, especially given what Younghusband was told about the gift. There's no doubt in my mind: the place where Younghusband kept the bowl is in fact telling us where the Morning Tree is!"

He looked round the room triumphantly. We were trying to take in what he was saying and made him repeat what he'd just told us. Colonel Younghusband is given a gold and silver bowl by the Tibetan government in 1904. He's told the bowl is called 'The Resting Place of Future Treasures', and that where Younghusband keeps the bowl will one day house a great treasure that will save the world. In 1905 Younghusband takes the bowl to the government residency in Dharamsala and asks the local official if he can house it there. Years later Lama Kunchen uses exactly the same phrase when telling Thaza where the Morning Tree will be kept once Thaza has taken it to India. So, linking these two pieces of information, the Morning Tree was in Dharamsala.

Jim continued. "When I pieced all this together, and then read that the bowl was currently on display in the British Museum, I couldn't wait. I didn't email you about it Danny because I wanted to see the bowl for myself before getting your hopes up. And seeing it today exceeded my expectations. You saw the relief Danny – mountains with a Buddha – that was surely a pictorial reference to

Dharamsala. Those lines 'After the dawn comes the morning' and 'Then the tree of spirituality will grow', must refer to the Morning Tree and the spiritual truths it will release!"

I picked up the History of Dharamsala that Jim had put on the floor and looked again at the picture of the bowl. I couldn't make out the words clearly but it was the same bowl we'd seen in the Museum.

"And Danny, the emblem you saw on the inside – the sun on mountains just as Thaza describes the cover of the Morning Tree – and those words 'The seed is planted here' – it can only mean one thing!"

I instinctively knew that Jim was correct, and doubly so as I knew from Mr Ravensburg that Younghusband had been admitted into some of the Tibetans' esoteric secrets. More than this, I knew that Lama Kunchen had met Massingberd in 1911 and told him openly of the Morning Tree. If Lama Kunchen was important then, it was very likely he'd been involved with meeting Younghusband too. Younghusband – Lama Kunchen – the Morning Tree – these threads were all coming together in this bowl. I know this countered what Mr Ravensburg had said, that the book was in Darjeeling, but Jim's theory was more exciting and more believable.

"But why would a bowl be used to say where the Morning Tree was?" asked Claire.

"I can answer that," said Jim. "About twenty years ago now, I attended a lecture on the way in which pre-literate societies recorded things. Really, this is relevant. It was given by this elderly Scottish guy from Aberdeen University. Basically, in societies where they didn't write things down, they would use objects to record ideas or events, so where we see a figurine, for example, they would see the representation of a deity or a ruler, and any attendant details, like objects that figurine may be holding in its hands, would hold a wealth of other ideas and associations. In other words, objects convey information. He said it didn't just happen in pre-literate societies, but in ancient civilisations – he quoted ancient Egypt – and in secret societies. He gave an example of a sceptre used by the Knights

Templar in the Middle Ages. If you were one of the Templar Knights, that thing would tell you a great deal, but if you weren't, the inscriptions and markings would be near meaningless. This was an example, he said, of using objects *instead* of writing to convey information, especially information that you wanted to keep from outsiders.

"It's an idea that appealed to me at the time, I don't know why. But when I read that bit in Thaza where Lama Kunchen gives that lama in the Potala that bronze object,[92] I just knew that Kunchen was relaying some specific information to his colleague – just like the Knights Templar did."

"So you think Lama Kunchen or his secret order made the bowl as a marker, as a map, to show people in the know where the Morning Tree was?" said Claire.

"Exactly!" said Jim.

"But how did the Tibetans know Younghusband would take the bowl to Dharamsala?" she continued. "What if he took it to England? The relief of the Buddha in the mountains wouldn't work then, would it?"

"This book deals with powers we don't yet understand. They either knew he'd take it to Dharamsala, or at least made him take it there in some way. Either way, the bowl went there and the book is there. I'm sure. And it makes sense too: keeping the book in the same place as the Dalai Lama.[93] It's likely to be the safest place."

Karen asked the next question. "I don't understand. Why would this secret order need a map or object to tell people where the Morning Tree was? Surely they'd know where it was?"

"I'm guessing most people in the order wouldn't know where the Morning Tree was," said Jim. "That'd be the safest way to protect it. So they would need something, like this bowl, to guide those who needed to find it. I'm convinced it's a deliberate clue to the Morning Tree's location."

---

[92] See page 148 in Thaza's account.
[93] The Fourteenth Dalai Lama's official residence is in Dharamsala.

We were quiet for a while. I realised we'd made the most important breakthrough. It felt right. It wasn't just Jim's infectious enthusiasm. There was something in me that knew that what Jim was saying was correct. But where in Dharamsala was it?

"That's the $64,000 question, Danny. But I think we have some clues. The relief on the bowl showed monks."

"So it's in a monastery."

"Most likely. Or in the custodianship of monks. And if you remember what I was told back in San Francisco in 1975 by that monk from Oregon, one of them will be called the Keeper."

I asked Jim one more question. "Is there anything else that links the bowl to the book? Anything else that makes it undeniable that the bowl is a map to the Morning Tree?"

"Undeniable?" replied Jim. "That depends on your point of view. But there is one more link I have found between the bowl and the Morning Tree. I wanted to check where the bowl was made as that might throw more light on it. I knew that when Tibetan craftsmen made things, they marked the name of their workshop on the object, but I didn't know anything about the marks they used to indicate which workshop. That's where my friend Tenzin comes in. He does know. So I asked him to find out where the bowl was made. I said nothing more, so as to make sure I gave out no clues. He travelled to London and God knows how, but he looked at the craftsman's marks on the bowl and found out."

"And?"

"See for yourself." He took out the piece of paper he'd been given by Tenzin that morning at the Tibet Office. I opened it and read one word.

Chakpori.

Chapter Eight

I didn't sleep well that night. I was too excited by what Jim had told us. I was sure he'd located the hiding place of the Morning Tree. I could feel the book within my grasp. I tossed and turned for hours, images of the book flashing through my mind, an agitated feeling churning my stomach.

Unlike Jim. His loud snores were painfully audible through the walls and would have kept me awake even if I hadn't been so excited. They certainly kept Karen awake. She sighed irritably for a good part of the night. So we were both a bit ragged the next morning.

Again, unlike Jim. He was up before us, making porridge, and managing to make a mess of the coffee percolator. He greeted us with a big smile when we finally shuffled into the kitchen. Karen took over and we had breakfast together.

Jim had shared his information with us. Now it was my turn to share with him. Over breakfast, and for hours afterwards, I told him about Mr Ravensburg, his notebooks and his meeting with that lama in France. Jim was surprised that someone else knew of the Morning Tree, and suspicious at first.

"Ravensburg? A Tibetan scholar? Hey, it's a small field Danny. I'm sure I'd have heard of him, but I haven't. Are you sure this guy's kosher?"

I told him Mr Ravensburg was definitely a Tibetan scholar, but he was exceedingly reclusive and shunned all publicity, which is why Jim had probably never come across him. I added Professor Thurgood had recommended him in the first place. This mollified Jim somewhat.

As I continued relaying what I'd learnt from Mr Ravensburg's notebooks, Jim became increasingly interested and then eager.

"Wow, so Younghusband was told spiritual truths? That just strengthens the link between the bowl and the Morning Tree! That's amazing!"

He was equally thrilled to know that a Lama Kunchen had told Massingberd about the Morning Tree among other things. He slapped his thigh. Like me, he was convinced the two Lama Kunchens were the same person. But when it came to Mr Ravensburg's meeting with the lama in France who told him the Morning Tree was in Darjeeling, he was dubious.

"It doesn't add up, Danny," he said. "Thaza specifically mentions giving the book to an Indian. Why would this man take it to a Tibetan monastery in the town?"

Jim had a point. But could Mr Ravensburg's efforts be dismissed that easily? The academic in me needed to be satisfied, so I played devil's advocate.

I told Jim that if it didn't make sense for an Indian to take the Morning Tree to a Tibetan monastery in Darjeeling, it didn't make sense for the same man to take it to a Tibetan monastery in Dharamsala. Jim countered that there weren't any Tibetan monasteries in Dharamsala in the 1930s, and that the book was probably kept safe somewhere until the Tibetan refugees arrived in the 1960s.

"But the lama in France told Mr Ravensburg that the Morning Tree was in Darjeeling," I said.

"Did he though," Jim shot back, "did he really say that?"

"I have Mr Ravensburg's word for it," I replied. "That is what he said the lama told him."

Jim made me consult my notes. I had to admit the lama never actually mentioned the Morning Tree: it was only Mr Ravensburg's assumption.

"There you have it," said Jim, "Mr Ravensburg's assumption. And can you trust Mr Ravensburg's assumption?" he asked, driving his point home.

I had one last go. "His notes," I said, "provide valuable and believable information."

"*Massingberd's* notes do," said Jim, "not Ravensburg's notes."

He was right. Mr Ravensburg had been given some pivotal information gathered by Massingberd but, with the exception of the meeting with Lama Chortzig, he had not materially added to it. All his work had been ineffectual. I suspected Mr Ravensburg knew this subconsciously; that was why he was always puffing up how important his notes and discoveries were.

I was greatly relieved. It meant I could discount everything Mr Ravensburg had told me, beyond the useful corroboration of the Morning Tree and Lama Kunchen supplied by Massingberd, the unsung hero of all this. It also meant that, if I found the Morning Tree in Dharamsala rather than Darjeeling, I needn't share it with Mr Ravensburg. A part of me felt mean, but the less I had to do with the man the better.

That left only my dealings with Sonam Prasang to pass on. But I was feeling tired from our long discussion, and Karen was decidedly bored, so we took a break and went for a walk in Battersea Park. Spring was definitely in the air. It was one of those mild days, the first at the end of winter, when the sun shines, the birds sing more loudly and you can feel the earth beginning to stir. Karen even had an ice cream from an opportunistic vendor who'd parked his van near the entrance. Jim was amused to see the Buddhist pagoda in the park. It made me wonder about Lama Kunchen's prediction that Buddhism was going to fade away.

I remember that Sunday afternoon as a special time, the last of the good times, before the difficulties that came my way. We spent a pleasant evening talking about Chicago, and how Karen and I got to know each other, and even how Jim courted his wife Philida, as we shared two bottles of wine that Jim had bought on our way home. I went to bed happy that night, promising to see Jim on my return from work on Monday evening. Jim was planning to revisit the British

Museum on Monday to see the Younghusband bowl again before returning to the US on Tuesday morning.

I went to work on Monday earlier than usual. I got off the Tube at Russell Square and went to walk up the stairs. I know there is a sign at the bottom warning the unwary commuter there are 175 steps to the surface, but I often climbed them as a deliberate form of exercise. I've never liked going to gyms, don't play competitive sport, but want to stay healthy. Keeping fit while going to work is ideal for someone like me.

So I started to climb the stairs. After a while I heard footsteps and voices coming up behind me; I couldn't see who they belonged to because the stairs were spiral. It was unusual, I suppose, for a group of people to be climbing the stairs because I rarely met others walking up. It was also unusual that they seemed to be hurrying. But I thought nothing of it at the time. I was aware that the group were catching up. Then suddenly I heard a shout, felt their presence and my coat was yanked from behind. I missed my footing and fell backwards into about four men. Their faces were covered, their clothes black. My head was buried for a moment in a foul smelling leather jacket. I still didn't realise what was going on; I even thought the men were helping by catching me. But then they let me crash painfully onto the stairs. One ripped my briefcase from my hand, another kicked me hard, and I saw the steel of a knuckleduster.

It was then that bewilderment gave way to fear. I started bellowing and covering my head to protect myself from their kicks and blows. The force of them was rolling me down the stairs. I felt a sharp pain in the right side of my body. I actually wondered if I was going to die. But then I suddenly felt Lama Kunchen. And I felt safe, still and removed from what was going on. Then I blacked out.

I was told later that a member of the Underground staff had come down the stairs at that moment and surprised my attackers. When they saw him, they pushed past to escape to the surface. He saw my unconscious body and immediately radioed for help. Eventually, an ambulance arrived and I was put on a stretcher, carried upstairs and taken to University College Hospital. I came to in the ambulance, a paramedic holding my arm. When he saw me open my eyes he told me everything was all right. He had a Welsh accent, I noticed. I lapsed back into unconsciousness.

I came to again in a bed in Accident and Emergency. I had a thumping headache, and it hurt when I moved. I found that my head was bandaged, as was my right arm. A doctor came to check on me. He told me I'd been concussed and had stitches in my head, severe bruising on my right forearm and bruises on my chest. He asked me some questions and seemed satisfied that I was all right mentally, though he advised me to rest. He then ushered in a uniformed policeman.

The policeman asked me to describe what had happened. He told me what the member of the station staff had told him. He then made me check my belongings. All there – wallet, phone, keys – everything except for my briefcase. He asked if I'd seen my attackers, if I'd done anything to attract attention to myself on the Tube, if there was anything of value in my briefcase. Only my students' Tibetan translations, I told him.

The policeman was puzzled at first. He said there were a number of unusual aspects of the case, including the time of the assault and the manner of the mugging. He then became suspicious. Was I in any trouble? Did I owe money? I assured him I was an ordinary person, a lecturer at SOAS, nothing untoward. He eventually left promising to get in touch if there were any leads.

I lay back on the bed, my head still throbbing. I was wondering how long I should stay in hospital when Jim came in. He was looking around agitatedly and broke into a stride when he saw me.

"Danny!" he cried. "I came as soon as I heard! Good God, you look awful. What happened?"

He pulled up a chair as I described the attack. He listened intently. When I finished, he shook his head. "I knew this was a possibility, but I never thought it'd happen – not so soon anyway. You know who did this to you, don't you Danny? The dark. No, it's no good protesting.

They know you're after the Morning Tree, and they're out to stop you – or worse, wring from you what you know."

I wasn't protesting. I had guessed my attack had been orchestrated by the dark. But it was too frightening to admit. Being mugged was a random event. Being beaten up by the dark was a deliberate one. I was too shaken to cope with this now. But I did tell Jim I agreed with him, and I did tell him about my burglary a few weeks earlier. Now he was even more alarmed. He demanded to know what they'd taken. Nothing, I told him, at least nothing to do with the Morning Tree. He said we had to get my material safely locked up before it was too late.

Then he added, "I'm staying here Danny. I'm staying with you in London to sort this mess out." He didn't care that his students would be left in the lurch, and he was even more dismissive about his employers. "It won't be the first time I've gotten into trouble."

We made a list of all my material relating to the Morning Tree. Apart from the translation of Thaza's manuscript and my notes from Mr Ravensburg and Sonam Prasang on my laptop at home, all the documents were in the locked filing cabinet in the departmental office where I'd put them after the burglary. I hadn't even had anything in my briefcase that had been ripped from me that morning. Jim took the key for the filing cabinet from my jacket and went over the list one more time. He was surprised when I told him about the information from my meeting with Sonam Prasang.

"Danny!" he said somewhat sternly. "Why didn't you tell me about this? You've got to tell me everything! How can we help each other, how can we find the Morning Tree, if you're withholding information?"

I told him I wasn't withholding anything. I just hadn't got round to telling him. Jim had the complete list by now, and said he was going to SOAS immediately to gather everything together. I was about to ask him how he was simply going to waltz in and grab all the documents, and where he was going to take them, when my phone rang. It was Karen. She was in tears, asking if I was all right. I told her

I was, that it was just a mugging and they hadn't taken anything. She told me she had a meeting scheduled later in the morning, but she'd cancel it and come to the hospital. I was going to tell her not to worry, but she'd already rung off. Once the call was over, Jim said he'd take care of things and left.

I don't know if it was the pain killers or my inability to grasp just exactly what sort of danger I was now in, but I felt numb. I'd been burgled and now beaten; it could be worse next time. I didn't know who my attackers were, or when they might strike next. I should have been terrified. But I was just numb. I lay in that hospital bed thinking and not thinking about my predicament.

Then Claire came. She was very concerned and held my hand while I told her what had happened. I said my mugging was the dark trying to stop me getting hold of the Morning Tree. She said she thought so too, especially after what Sonam had told us the previous week. I added that Jim had already been to see me and it was certainly what he thought.

Claire sat up. "Jim? How could he have been here? How did he know what'd happened to you?"

"What do you mean?"

"Well, when the police phoned SOAS, they said we were the first people they'd contacted. I was in Ann's office when she took the call. She was very upset – we all were. But I heard her thank them for getting in touch with us first. Ann even said she'd contact Karen and tell her what had happened, which must mean that the police hadn't phoned her yet. And I left not long after Ann had finished the call. There's no way Jim could have known about you before us."

"So what?" I said.

"So how did he know about your attack?"

"I don't know. I didn't ask him." But I was suddenly alarmed. "What… what are you trying to say?"

"Nothing. Forget it Daniel. Let me—"

"Are you trying to say that Jim is the dark?"

She looked at me, alarmed herself. She shrugged her shoulders. "Well, how else did he know what had happened to you, unless he was somehow in on it?"

"Jim? The dark? I…" I was temporarily robbed of thought. My heart was beating double quick. I felt hot. I swung my feet over the side of the bed and sat up. Moving made me dizzy, but I couldn't stay still.

"Jim can't be the dark," I said weakly. "I mean, he's practically told us where the Morning Tree is."

"Maybe it was a ruse to get you to tell him everything you know."

Maybe… he was hard on me for not telling him about Sonam. And right now – good God – he was gathering together everything I'd discovered about the Morning Tree. But Jim, the dark? That man was my friend, in some ways like a father. I'd only ever known him to be decent and genuine.

"But his theory that the Morning Tree is in Dharamsala feels right. If he really is the dark, why bother telling me? Why doesn't he just go after it himself?"

"Maybe he will. That wouldn't stop him wanting to see what you know first. Or even getting you to actually find it for him in Dharamsala. Look Daniel, I'm not saying he is the dark. I'm just saying… I'm just saying he could be." Claire was beginning to sound desperate, as if this was all too much for her.

I was beginning to feel desperate too. My life was in danger. If Jim was the dark, then all my basic assumptions about good and bad would be turned upside down. And even if he wasn't, there were still evil forces closing around me.

"I can't stay here," I said, standing up. Claire looked at me questioningly. "I've got to go home."

"But Jim will be there."

"Well then, I'll find out one way or another."

"Are you sure?"

I was. Claire looked at me for a moment and then nodded. She got up and marshalled one of the nurses to tell them I was leaving.

The nurse was surprised, but gave me some pain killers to take home, and told me to go to my doctor if I felt in any way concussed. As this was happening, Karen came in. She gave a sideways glance when she saw Claire. She asked how I was, and then asked about the attack. Claire took her cue and left while I told Karen what had happened. Karen was very uneasy, and tried to mask it by fussing around me and getting me something to eat and drink. She was startled when I told her I wanted to go home. She said she didn't know if she had time to take me as she had to get back for that rearranged meeting. I told her it was all right, I wanted to go home by myself. I knew if I didn't get straight back onto the Underground I might never get on it again. Karen didn't protest. She gathered her coat and bag, told me to be careful and left. I followed her out soon afterwards.

I had to go home gingerly. I was weaker than I realised. Now was just the time to attack me, I thought grimly. When I let myself into my flat, I heard Jim on the phone.

"Yes, I know I should be home teaching... I understand Philida... but some things are more important... no, I know the Dean won't see it that way... yes, this book is more important... no, not than you Philida, you know that's not what I mean... OK... I don't know when, but I'll call... Philida...? Hello? Hello?"

He put the phone down with a sigh and turned round. When he saw me, his face lit up. "Danny, you're back! How are you feeling?"

"Weak, but I'll live. Everything all right?"

"You know the score. Our nearest and dearest don't always agree with what we're doing."

"You told Philida you were staying in London?"

"Sure. I cancelled my flight. Danny, I got to stay with you. We can't let the dark get hold of what we know."

"Have you got everything together?"

"Yup. You were very clear where everything was. I've got it all here. There was no-one in the department office, and the filing cabinet wasn't even locked, so I just took it. You Brits are too easy going." He held up a large plastic bag filled with papers with one hand and waved my laptop with the other. "Thing is, where shall we keep it all?"

I didn't know. Not at the flat. At least, not for long. "I'll think of somewhere," I said.

"Let me make you some tea or something," said Jim. "I think I can manage that." He disappeared into the kitchen. I heard the kettle being switched on. Jim was being his usual self. Was he hiding anything?

"Jim."

He didn't hear above the noise of the kettle.

"Jim!"

His head appeared around the door. "Yeah?"

"How did you know I'd been mugged?"

"Oh, I was lucky. I was going to the British Museum again, stopped to get some coffee and thought I'd call Raymond[94] while I drank it – we're sort of friends, as you know. As we were talking his secretary came in with the news that you'd been attacked. I overheard her say which hospital you were at. Of course Raymond told me about it as well, seeing as how I know you too. As soon as I finished the call, I jumped in a cab and came to see you. As I say, I was lucky." He went back to the kitchen to finish making the tea.

Why had he decided to call Professor Thurgood when he'd been so insistent that I tell no-one about his visit? It didn't make sense. But then so much of what Jim did didn't make sense.

My heart was beating loudly by the time he came back with the tea. He was a large man, a passionate man, and even though he wasn't suited to physical violence (he'd dodged the draft for the Vietnam war after all), he could still have snapped me in two at that moment if he wanted to.

"Jim," I said, "thank you for helping me."

---

[94] Raymond Thurgood, head of Tibetan at the School of Oriental and African Studies.

"Hey Danny, it's the least I can do. Hell, after what you've gone through. But Danny, we'll get the Morning Tree, you'll see, and then everything will be all right."

"You're right."

"And Danny, I couldn't think of a better person to have on this quest. You've always been a friend."

I took a sip of tea. I don't know how you can mess up putting a tea bag into a cup of boiling water, but Jim had managed it. Jim didn't ask any more questions about my attack. Either he was being sensitive or he didn't need to know any more. I didn't probe Jim either; dark or not dark, I had to wait until things became clearer. Besides, if he were dark, I reckoned (hoped) there wouldn't be much point in harming me right now. He would have me where he wanted and be able to monitor my every move, so getting rid of me would not be necessary for the time being.

We chatted about the old days until Karen came home in the evening. She was distraught and prickly at the same time, upset by my attack, and not able to deal with the mix of emotions she had. Jim was very good, looking after her as well as me, and even managing to make us laugh. I don't know how Karen and I would have been if we'd been alone together.

I returned to work the following morning. Both Jim and Karen told me I should rest at home, but I wanted to be doing something. Ann and Professor Thurgood were surprised to see me. My quip that Tibetan didn't teach itself fell on deaf ears. They all but ordered me out of the building. But I stayed put. I had to be active. If finding the Morning Tree was so dangerous, I needed to find it sooner rather than later.

Claire came to see me when she'd heard I was in. She gave me a comforting smile. She was the only one not to criticise me for being at work. She asked how I was, and asked if I was nervous about being attacked again.

"No," I replied.

"Are you sure?"

312

"Yes. And I'll tell you why. It stands to reason that if the dark knew where the Morning Tree was, they'd go straight to it and destroy it. Since they are bothering with me, it can only mean that they don't know where the book is and they are, like me, searching for it. That's why I was burgled, and that's why my attackers snatched my briefcase – to find out what I know.

"If ever I do know where the Morning Tree is, and the dark wrench that information from me, then I'd be dispensable. But as long as they don't know where the book is, and think I might lead them to it, I'm safe. Well, safe beyond the odd mugging or burglary."

"Yes," Claire commented, "that makes sense."

"But I'm not happy," I continued. "I want to find out who the dark is. I want to discover who is actually responsible for attacking me. Then maybe I can take them out of the game."

Claire thought for a moment. "OK," she said, "but who do you think is responsible for attacking you?"

"It has to be someone who knows me, or how else would they know I was looking for the Morning Tree? That means it could be Professor Thurgood, Jim, Mr Ravensburg or Sonam Prasang. There are any number of arguments for and against each of them. I can't reason my way to the culprit. But maybe I can flush them out."

"How?" said Claire.

"Do you know Ian Gervois?"

"The librarian? Yes. He's obsessed with keeping things neat and tidy."

"He's also in charge of the CCTV system. I need to find out how it works, and how I can get hold of the tapes."

"Why?"

"I intend to place some papers in one of the locked storerooms in the library. I'm going to make a song and dance about them, tell Ian they're very important, but that no-one, apart from me, is to look at them. Then I'm going to tell Thurgood, Jim, the others, that I've found something very significant to do with the Morning Tree, but I can't tell them what until I've gone through it properly. Whichever

313

one of them wants the book for themselves will want to steal that information as soon as possible. If they do, I'll need the tapes to identify them."

Claire thought some more. "It could work," she said. Then she smiled. "Can I help?"

"Yes. I'd like you to find out from Ian how the CCTV system works, and how I can get hold of the tapes."

"I'll find a way." She got up to go. When she reached the door she paused and turned round. "Hey Daniel, what if it's me? I know you're after the Morning Tree."

"That'd be terrible," I answered. "I'd have to tie you up and try to make sure you change your evil ways."

She raised her eyes to the ceiling and left.

Chapter Nine

I spent an uncomfortable week waiting for Claire to get back to me. I couldn't plant my papers in one of the locked storerooms until she'd cracked Ian Gervois. So I had to go through the motions of living a normal life as best I could. I know I'd reasoned I was safe until the dark knew where the Morning Tree was, but I was still apprehensive of another calamity befalling me.

I also had Jim to reckon with. For once Karen wasn't complaining, although he was staying for longer than planned. I think she was reassured by his presence, and of course we couldn't argue as much in front of him. He busied himself during the day revisiting the British Museum and working on his laptop. I checked his laptop occasionally, when he was out of the room. He was emailing mostly and writing what looked like a paper on the Morning Tree.

Of course, I wrestled constantly with the fact that Jim might be the dark. If he was, what store could I put in his theory that the book was in Dharamsala as revealed by the Younghusband bowl? It still felt right. In fact, it still felt exciting. I couldn't come to a conclusion, I just had to wait and see. As for Jim doing me harm while he was staying with me, I basically felt that he'd get other people to do that if it came to it. Even so, it wasn't easy juggling these conflicting emotions.

Then at last, about a week after our conversation, Claire walked into my office with a big smile on her face.

"I'm in," she announced. "Ian's given me all the information we need."

I was impressed. I didn't think he'd warm to her. "How did you manage it?" I asked.

"The key to someone like Ian is flattery," she said. "I told him some friends of mine desperately needed advice on a CCTV system. I'd noticed the one in SOAS was so good. Could he help? He was reluctant at first, but I played the little girl, and eventually he opened up. Then it was just a question of gushing praise on him and the way he runs the library. He told me more and more. Would you believe the room in which he stores the tapes is always unlocked? And he's the only one who sets the system, so anytime he's not in you could go and view the tapes yourself. It's quite easy, by the way. He's showed me what to do."

This was the news I'd been waiting for. Later that day I took a bundle of papers down to the library and started looking round the storerooms. It didn't take long for Ian to come and ask what I was doing.

"I've got some very important papers," I told him. "Actually, they are extremely important. I need somewhere safe to keep them while I go through them. They're going to create quite a stir."

He asked why I couldn't keep them in my office. Before I could answer, he said he understood: he'd heard about my mugging; of course he'd look after the papers for me, they'd be much safer with him. I declined his offer saying that these papers had to be really safe, not just kept in a room somewhere. He sighed and led me to a small windowless room with bookcases and cabinets. He told me this room was always locked and constantly monitored by his CCTV system. A number of valuable books were stored there; my papers would be perfectly safe. I impressed on him that I was the only person allowed access to them. He agreed and held out his hands. I made a play of hesitating before handing the bundle to him. I told him that when I finally published, and the true worth of those papers was recognised, then he'd have to find somewhere much more secure for them. I gave a parting look, much as a father of a toddler would give to an untried babysitter, and left.

It had taken me some time to get those papers ready. I reckoned that if they were stolen by the dark, I might as well try to lay a false trail to put them off the scent. Even if it didn't work, I still had to make the papers look genuine otherwise they might suspect it was a trap. Then they'd know I was on to them. So, I spent painstaking hours assembling a convincing case for the Morning Tree to be in Darjeeling.

I know Mr Ravensburg had already suggested this, and Jim had rejected it, but whoever out of the four was the dark would have read Thaza's story and have known that he took the book to Darjeeling. It was the right starting point. It would confirm Mr Ravensburg's prejudices, and to help convince Jim, I put in an obscure reference to 'The Bowl of False Trails', describing something very like the Younghusband bowl, and hoping (if he were the dark) that he'd conclude that the bowl in the British Museum had been a deliberate ploy by the secret order to confuse things. I even found some old paper and a typewriter to create the main document which I then folded and carried round with me for several days to give it a worn look.

Once I had the document ready, I sent a series of emails to other Tibetan scholars asking if they could answer questions or verify certain information. It was all to do with the false trail that I was trying to lay about the Morning Tree being in Darjeeling. I had wondered for some time whether the dark was tapping into my emails. It was just a feeling, but they had been playing up recently. The IT department couldn't solve the problem. If it was the dark, these emails would add veracity to the fact that I was on to Darjeeling as the location of the book.

Finally, I checked the CCTV system for myself one evening after Ian had gone home. It was just as Claire had said. The monitoring room was never locked, and never manned except by Ian. I even managed to find the tapes covering the room storing my papers. Now I was ready to tell the others.

I started with Professor Thurgood. I burst into his office the following morning and told him, as excitedly as I could, that I'd just come across something vital to do with the location of the Morning Tree. He asked me what. I said I wasn't in a position to tell him yet, I needed to check a number of things, but most likely I would now be able to secure the book. The crucial document leading me to the book was safe in the small storeroom in the library. He looked at me seriously.

"Fine Daniel. Excellent work. Tell me when you're ready. But Daniel, don't overdo it. You've been through a lot recently, all right?"

I told Mr Ravensburg in a telephone call. He was agitated, wanted to know more at once, but I was resolute that I needed to check my sources before being more specific. Again, I made a point of telling him where the document I had discovered was being kept.

I sent Sonam an email. He sent a brief reply. *Very interested. Tell me more when you can.*

That just left Jim. I'd decided on a different approach with him. He would be suspicious if I told him that I'd just uncovered a vital document but didn't show it to him. So I told him that Professor Thurgood had recently received what looked like crucial information on the whereabouts of the book. I reminded Jim that Professor Thurgood had made enquiries about the Morning Tree on my behalf, and now it seemed that another contact had come forward. Only I couldn't see the information yet because the contact was insisting that only Professor Thurgood looked at the material.

"Oh come on," said Jim, "surely Raymond will let you see what he's got?"

"Professor Thurgood has a sense of honour," I replied. "He will respect another person's wishes."

"Does that mean you'll never see it?"

"Professor Thurgood is checking with his contact to see if he can show it to me."

"Where is this guy?"

"India, I believe. And he doesn't use emails. Professor Thurgood told me to be patient."

"Where is the material anyway?"

318

"I haven't seen it. Professor Thurgood told me he recognised its importance at once. It could after all show us where the Morning Tree is. So he's put it in the small storeroom in the library at SOAS."

"Like it's safe there," said Jim.

I know I was taking a gamble because Jim knew Professor Thurgood. But I reckoned Jim wouldn't bother him. I was sure that Jim would see that, if Professor Thurgood wasn't going to show me this material – material that could bring glory to SOAS – then he wouldn't show it to a sometime contact from a rival university. And anyway, asking Professor Thurgood about this document would break Jim's cover that he was searching for the book himself.

Now I had nothing to do but wait. I did take my genuine papers to my sister and brother-in-law's house. They lived nearby off Wandsworth Common and had a safe, so at least my research couldn't be stolen from me. I hadn't committed Jim's theory about the Younghusband bowl to paper, so that couldn't be stolen either. I only kept a copy of Thaza's manuscript. That didn't matter as each of the four suspects already had copies themselves.

I did suggest to Jim that he return home. He wouldn't hear of it. He said the dark were after me and would strike again. We were stronger if we stayed together. Besides, he said, he appreciated having the time to write his account of the Morning Tree. He told me I wasn't to worry: I could publish my account first once we actually found the book. He didn't need the fame. He even said he didn't mind if he was fired from Northwestern and never worked again.

"I don't need much to live off," he said. "In fact, I really could be a monk."

I didn't ask him what Philida would think of that.

It snowed at that time. Although it was now the beginning of March, winter had one last throw and six inches of snow fell during the night. To Jim living in Chicago it was nothing, but to the transport system in London it was worse than the Blitz and everything ground to a halt. It meant Jim, Karen and I spent a happy day lazing at home, scuffing the melting snow in the park and enjoying afternoon tea (a novelty for Jim) at a local café. Jim told us about his belief in psychic powers. I'd always known he believed in the paranormal, but never knew exactly what it meant. He'd had experiences as a boy where he saw beings, heard voices and just had an inner knowing.

"It was like I was a grown up when really I was only a kid," he said. "Boy, would I liked to have met Lama Kunchen."

These experiences had stopped, but he still had his lifelong interest in this area and his hunches.

"I just know certain things are going to happen," he said. "Like I just know we're going to find the Morning Tree."

Karen was absorbed by what he had to say. I never knew she was interested in these things.

The snow only kept me from SOAS for one day. Every day I borrowed the storeroom key from Ian Gervois and checked if my document was still there. I even placed one of my hairs on the side of the document so that if anyone else took it out of the drawer it would fall off. But every day the carefully placed hair and the document were in the same place. Part of me was pleased. It might mean I'd been wrong about one of the four being the dark. But really, I needed to know who it was.

Jim didn't just spend his days writing in my flat. He also began spending time with Claire. He was interested in her PhD thesis as he had lived through the period she was researching. He had been prominent around the time of the Cultural Revolution in 'Free Tibet' organisations in America and had met several senior Tibetans in exile as a result. Of course, he was punished for his stand by the Chinese authorities, who consistently refused him visas to visit Tibet, a punishment he bore stoically. Claire was apprehensive at first, wondering if Jim was the dark trying to prevent the Morning Tree being found. But she came to think like me that if he were, he'd want to monitor what we were doing rather than get rid of us for now. Besides, she admitted, she couldn't conceive how someone like him could be dark.

And then it happened. It was a Tuesday. I'd had a tutorial that morning, then went before lunch to check the storeroom. The document wasn't there. I searched the other drawers and cabinets with rising panic. There was no doubt about it. It was gone. Had the bait really been taken? I had to find out. Part of me was elated that my plan had worked, but part of me was terrified. It meant the dark was up and running and closing in on me.

I rushed to find Ian. He was on his way out to have lunch. I grabbed his lapels.

"Good God!" he said, trying to brush me off. "Dr Clifton, what are you doing?"

"My document! It's gone!"

He was puzzled at first and then gave a little laugh. "Impossible, it can't—"

"It is, you fool! Come and look!" I dragged him down to the storeroom. "It was in there. Now it isn't. You promised me it was safe!"

"Well, I..." He started searching. "Well, it seems it's not... Are you sure you didn't take it away?"

"Of course I didn't!"

"Then someone else must have."

"Brilliant. It didn't bloody walk out by itself, did it?"

"Now calm down Dr Clifton, there must be a perfectly rational explanation."

"There is. Someone stole it!"

Ian was clearly uncomfortable. He pulled at his immaculate shirt collar and suggested we go upstairs and look at the CCTV tapes. On the way he asked when I'd last seen the document, how valuable it was, and who else knew about it. I gave him as short answers as possible, impatient to get to the tapes. We reached his monitoring room and Ian fussed with the computer. He was unsettled and not his usual efficient self. I had to hold myself back from pushing him out of the way and taking over. At last he found the right tapes and started to go backwards and forwards between Monday and Tuesday.

"There!" I shouted. "No, back. Yes, there!" And there was a shadowy figure moving jerkily on the time lapsed tape into the storeroom, bending and searching the drawers and cabinets. At last it pulled out my sheaf of papers, studied them and then plunged them inside his coat. The figure made a play of putting the drawers back into place. Then it calmly walked out. I made Ian rerun the tape over and over again, and in as slow motion as possible.

"Who is it?" asked Ian.

"I don't know," I said. "A man at any rate."

But there was no doubt about it.

It was Sonam Prasang.

I weighed everything up. I guess I had thought it would have been Mr Ravensburg or one of his hired henchmen. I hadn't really considered it would be Sonam. But now I knew it was him, I felt chilled. He was so accomplished, so graceful, so holy for God's sake! If he was the dark then truly anything bad was possible. But at least it wasn't Jim. A great weight fell from me. Jim, my friend. Jim the genuine seeker of truth. He could help me now cope with this new information.

I had to get away. I told Ian this was theft of university property and the perpetrator had to be found. He looked despairing, but I left before he could fret about what he should do. I raced back to my office and grabbed my phone to call Claire. She answered.

"Claire, where are you?"

"I'm at home. Daniel—"

"The document I've planted – it's been stolen. Oh Claire, it's not Jim!"

"I know," she replied in a small, cold voice.

"How do you know?"

"Because Jim's dead."

Chapter Ten

I was speechless. I couldn't take in what she'd said. I stood there uncomprehending.

"Dead?"

I still couldn't take it in. Blank thoughts raced around my head. How could Jim be dead?

"He called this morning," said Claire, her voice unsteady. I had to concentrate on what she was saying as my mind was still unfocussed. "He said he wanted to see me. I told him I was working from home, so he said he'd come over. I was at my desk. You know the window looks onto the street. I saw Jim come down and cross the road. All of a sudden, he was rushed by three men. Jim was startled. He tried to fight them off but it was no good. They pushed him to the ground, they were kicking and punching him, and then they started to go through his pockets. Just then a woman shouted, and a van screeched to a halt and two men jumped out. The attackers ran off and the men and woman went to Jim."

"What, those men *murdered* him?"

"Not quite. I rushed downstairs and went to him. But he was already dead. We didn't understand it. There was no blood, no wound. It was terrible. I've never seen a dead body before, Daniel. We had to wait for the ambulance. I held his head in my lap. Oh God, I really liked him."

"What happened?"

"The paramedics came. So did the police. They started cordoning off the street. It was frightening. Everyone was confused about Jim's death until one of the paramedics found some pills in his pocket. He said they were for the heart. Did you know he had a weak heart, Daniel? They said he probably died from a heart attack brought on by his assault."

I sat down heavily. There was no doubt this was another attack by the dark – by Sonam. He must have known Jim was helping me and had him followed. Did Sonam attack Jim to scare him, or to see if he had any information on him, or to kill him? It didn't matter. He had attacked him and Jim was dead. Wasn't I now really in danger?

"Can you come over?" said Claire, still on the phone.

"Of course," I said, forcing down my fear. "I'm on my way."

That afternoon was a nightmare. I went to Claire's flat and was immediately interviewed by the police. They wanted to know who his next of kin were. Oh God, Philida. I rushed home to get her address and phone number. I had no choice but to call her; I thought she should hear the news from me rather than the police. It was the most dreadful call I've ever made. It took a while to make her understand. Then she was distraught. At one point she shrieked with grief and I just had to wait until she calmed down. I couldn't help thinking Jim's death was my fault.

I also phoned Karen. She couldn't cope with the news either. After a long shocked silence, she said she was going to stay with a friend that night – she couldn't bear to go back to the flat and see his things. She just couldn't cope with anything right now. She didn't know when she'd come back.

I knew how she felt. I looked round the flat. Jim's laptop was on the coffee table, his opened briefcase on the floor beside it and his discarded sweatshirt on the sofa. I couldn't believe that just a few hours ago his living, moving body had been using those things and now… now he was gone. Never coming back. Finished. And the worst of it all was that it was so final. There was no chance of his coming back.

I was numb. And trembling. I didn't want to stay there any longer than I had to. I did have the courage to gather his things and put them in his room. But then I fled back to Claire's.

The police were still there. They reckoned that Jim's death was most likely due to a heart attack; the post-mortem would confirm this. There was an incredible amount of paperwork to go through to register Jim's death, and more because he was from overseas. There would be a Coroner's inquest. And the body could only be released to Philida. And so on. Eventually, the police cleared away and Claire and I were alone by the evening.

She didn't want me to leave. And I didn't want to go. I couldn't return to an empty flat with just myself and Jim's things. It was too grim. We sat in Claire's sitting room in silence for a while.

"It was the dark, wasn't it?" she began.

I nodded.

"They killed Jim."

"Yes."

"We can't let them win, Danny. We've got to find the Morning Tree before they do. We can't let Jim die in vain."

"I know. But look, I've been mugged. Jim's been killed. It's too dangerous, Claire. This isn't your quest. You should step back."

She narrowed her eyes. "Not my quest? What do you mean? I've been in on this since the beginning! The dark probably know who I am. I'm not safe, even if I did step back."

She was right, but I didn't want the possibility that she might die as well. "Claire—"

"You can't do this by yourself."

It was true, I did need her despite the danger to her. If she left I'd be completely on my own.

Claire looked down. I could see she was trembling. Then she burst into tears. I moved next to her and put my arm around her shaking shoulders. Loud gulps were coming from her as tears rolled down her cheeks. I didn't cry, but was going through a gamut of emotions. Jim was gone. Sonam, who had already told me the dark would kill to get the Morning Tree, was responsible and on my trail. And death... it was so difficult. How does one face death? I just felt this great black gulf in front of me.

Eventually Claire's sobs quietened. I went to get her some tissues. She looked flushed but better. She blew her nose and wiped her eyes.

"So, who did steal your document?" she said, scrunching up her tissue.

I suddenly realised I hadn't told her what had happened in the library. "Sonam Prasang," I replied.

"Are you sure?"

"I saw him on the tapes with my own eyes."

She gave a silent laugh. "And I helped you meet him."

"Yes. But he already knew I was looking for the Morning Tree. You didn't do anything to endanger me."

She was thoughtful. "It figures it was Sonam," she said after a while. "He's the only one who hasn't helped you find the book. Thurgood, Jim, even Ravensburg have all offered you information or advice. All Sonam has done is ask you what you know."

She was right. I suppose it was obvious in retrospect. Claire was once again showing how I needed her.

"So, how do we find the Morning Tree?" she asked.

"There's something we've got to do before that," I replied. "We have to throw Sonam off the scent. We can't get rid of him, but I assume he's watching us, so he'll track whatever we do. We've got to persuade him we're no longer interested in the book."

"Why?"

"To protect us. And buy time to follow up Jim's lead."

"How will you do it?"

I threw up my hands. "Maybe by telling him that I'm so upset by Jim's death I'm dropping my research. I mean, it's almost true. And make sure that for the next few weeks I do nothing."

"Will that work?"

"It's our only chance. When we think everything has settled down, then I can go to Dharamsala."

"Then *we* can go to Dharamsala."

I sat up. There was only one light on in the now darkened room, but somehow I could see Claire's every feature. I took hold of her arm and squeezed it. She smiled and squeezed my arm back. I bent my head forward. She did the same. It was all the encouragement I needed. We kissed. I leant back to look at her face. She was so beautiful.

"Oh Danny," she said.

We made love. I guess we both needed a respite from the problems pressing in around us. But actually I was deeply happy. Claire had been wonderful from the start and everything felt so right with her. She was not only helping me find the Morning Tree, she was also perfect for me. I felt truly restored being with her.

I stayed the night. Early next morning I got up to go.

"Hey Danny," she called softly from the bed as I was leaving. "You're more like Indiana Jones than you know."

The next few weeks were extremely difficult. I had to act as Jim's next of kin until Philida arrived to collect the body. There was a delay in the paperwork, so Philida had to stay for two weeks. She didn't actually accuse me of causing Jim's death, but I'm sure the thought was never far from her mind. It's certainly what I believed. If I hadn't asked Jim about the Morning Tree, he'd never have come to London, and he'd still be alive. Claire told me I wasn't to blame – Sonam was – and somewhere inside me I knew that was true. But I still felt guilty and was unable to give Philida much support. It was very difficult escorting her around.

And even if she hadn't been in London, I would still have found it difficult. I had never really faced death before. Well, my grandparents had died, but I hadn't been close to them, and they were either ill or too old to live life as they had, so their death was in some ways a release. But Jim was different. He was a friend. We had grown close, even with my reservations about him being the dark. We were going to find the Morning Tree together. He meant something to me. Every now and then I'd be overrun with grief. I'd suddenly bend double at the realisation that Jim had gone, and have no answers as to where he had gone. I didn't know how to cope. Death was awful. I thought of my own parents then, and their deaths that would surely come – and immediately put the thought out of my mind. How do people cope with death?

Then there was Karen. She told me she wanted to break up. She said that when she heard about Jim, she realised she didn't want to turn to me for comfort. It was a sign we weren't right together. We both knew we argued a lot. We'd had some good times, but now we should end things. She added that ever since I'd become involved with the Morning Tree our relationship had gone downhill. I agreed with everything she said. But I couldn't find the words to express myself. It was bad, I know, but I was mostly silent while she talked. I wish I had told her that I respected and admired her. She only asked if she could stay at my flat while she found somewhere else to live. And she asked if I could stay somewhere else for the time being. I agreed. And Claire agreed I could stay with her.

I took several days off work. Everyone had heard about Jim by now and were suitably sympathetic. When I returned to SOAS full time, I found an email from Sonam. The audacity of the man! He was asking about my research and offering his help. But at least the fool had given me the pretext to tell him I was no longer interested in the Morning Tree. I replied saying I'd suffered a bereavement and was dropping all my work. I even apologised for not trying to locate something that was obviously important to him and Tibetan Buddhism. I also offered to send him Mr Ravensburg's notes to help him. They wouldn't tell him anything he didn't already know. In fact, they would confirm the Darjeeling theory and could lead him away from Dharamsala. I did though make sure there was nothing in my notes to give away Mr Ravensburg's address or identity. He was a crotchety old man, but even he didn't deserve to die.

To make my story more real, I told the same to Professor Thurgood. He looked at me intently, almost disappointingly, as a father might look at a weak-minded son. "Are you sure Daniel?" he asked. "I know McField's death has been a shock, but life goes on. Think of the progress you've made. Let's give it a few weeks and see how you feel then."

I repeated the story to everyone in the Tibetan department. I hoped news of my decision would reach Sonam's ears, maybe through Milo, to confirm that I had stopped looking for the book.

And in a way, I had stopped looking. I just didn't have the energy. But not Claire. One evening she brought back an armful of maps of Dharamsala.

"Don't look so worried, Daniel," she said. "My thesis is to do with the Tibetan government-in-exile, so it's quite normal for me to have maps of the town." She smoothed them out on her dining table. "Now, are there any clues here?"

I joined her at the table. We marked the Tibetan government buildings and the different lamaseries in highlighter pens. Suddenly I had an idea. I rushed to get Jim's copy of A History of Dharamsala and opened it at the picture of the Younghusband bowl. I squinted at it, and then looked at the maps. I did this repeatedly.

"What are you doing?" asked Claire.

"It's only an idea, but look. You see? The relief on the bowl sort of matches the map. You have to hold it at the right distance to get the scale right. But there… they're lined up."

Claire took the book and moved it backwards and forwards. "I don't… oh yes, I see." She held it like that for some time. "What does it mean?" she asked.

I took the book and lined it up with the map again. "See here. That big Buddha lines up with the Dalai Lama's residence. And there, that monk with a halo, matches the State Oracle. Those people are those government offices. And those monks line up with Kirti lamasery, and those with Nechung lamasery."

"And the Tibetan words?"

"The words 'After the dawn comes the morning' line up with those buildings at the bottom of the town. And the phrase 'Then the tree of spirituality will grow' falls outside the main part of the town. I admit that doesn't make much sense. But at least we can identify the principal parts of the town from the bowl."

"Do you think the words indicate where the Morning Tree actually is?"

"Could do. In which case it's in the lower part of the town, or simply that it's not in the main part of the town. But at least the bowl lines up with how Dharamsala is today."

"But that means the people who made the bowl – when, 1904? – they knew what the future Dharamsala would look like."

"Why not? They knew Tibet would be invaded, they knew the Second World War would happen. As Jim said, we are dealing with powers we don't fully understand."

I snapped the book shut. We had discovered something valuable here – meaningless without the bowl – but vital with it. I put the book back with my belongings. I certainly wasn't going to commit this information to paper either.

That was an example of our research going well. A few evenings after that Claire and I tussled with the scant clues in Thaza's text about where the Morning Tree would be kept once it was outside Tibet. As far as I could tell, Lama Kunchen only says it will be with similar objects, either hiding in plain sight or in a concealed place (a pebble placed with other pebbles, perhaps at the bottom of a stream, as he told Thaza). We tried to make a list of the places where a spiritual book would be – I think we only managed to write down a monastery or other type of religious building. When we got to listing where the book could be hidden, we started to argue. It was our first argument. The truth is, I was angry – angry at how opaque these oriental 'sages' can be, angry at Jim's death, angry at the danger I was in, angry at how difficult it all was. I just wasn't being reasonable. We did make up afterwards, but I still had this anger inside me.

I played out the last days of that term before the Easter break going through my normal routine. I had a feeling that Sonam had taken the bait and believed I was no longer interested in the Morning Tree. Either that or I was getting over the shock of Jim's death.

Whatever, I was finding the energy again to think about the Morning Tree. Then one weekend during the Easter break Claire and I were visiting one of her friends. I was turning over the problem of locating the Morning Tree in my mind – actually, I was still feeling frustrated that Lama Kunchen's references to where the book might be were so obscure – when her friend asked what I did. I told her I was a lecturer in Tibetan.

"Oh how interesting," she said. "I love all that stuff." She went into her bedroom and came back with a copy of the Tibetan Book of the Dead. "I don't understand it all," she said flicking through the pages, "but I think it's great."

"Don't understand it all is about right," I replied. Claire arched an eyebrow. "I mean," I continued, "I don't understand it all either."

"But you can read it in the original," said her friend. "That must be fascinating."

"Fascinating, but not very useful."

"Surely you must have gained something from reading it?"

It was too late now to admit I'd never actually read the Tibetan Book of the Dead but I was still riled about how difficult it was to unravel the clues to find the Morning Tree. "You'd think you'd gain something, wouldn't you?" I continued. "But how can you gain anything if the text is wrapped up in obscurities?"

"What do you mean?"

"Well, ask a question: 'Where is the book?' Answer: 'With other books.' Brilliant. Except it doesn't really tell you anything. I'm fed up with all this oriental wisdom. 'Don't look for the ice cream in the oven, it'll be in the fridge.' Of course it will, except they don't bloody well tell you where the fridge is! I mean, where would you find a book?"

Claire was looking at me with concern. Her friend was looking uneasy.

"In a library?" said her friend.

"Eh?"

"Well, you'd find a book in a library," said her friend uncertainly. "Wouldn't you?"

Claire and I shot each other a significant glance. Then she grinned. I did too. It was suddenly clear.

"Of course!" I exclaimed. "Pebbles!"

"I beg your pardon?" said Claire's friend.

"Pebbles! If you want to hide a pebble, you put it with other pebbles! If you want to hide a book, you put it in a library! The book is in a library!"

"I'm sure it is," said her friend nervously.

"What's more, didn't that lama tell Jim the book was with the Keeper? Well, I'll need to check, but the word 'keeper' in Tibetan can also mean librarian! The book is in a library in the safe keeping of a librarian!"

"Daniel, that's brilliant!" said Claire, ignoring her friend. "But which library?"

"Well, there's only one I know of in Dharamsala – the Library of Tibetan Works and Archives.[95] That must be it!"

I was sweating, and breathing faster. The pieces of the puzzle all pointed to one place. Could it really be this simple? Well, yes. Wasn't simplicity the key to Lama Kunchen's approach to life? The Morning Tree was in the Library of Tibetan Works and Archives in Dharamsala. I was feeling as if I'd just won the lottery.

But if it was this simple, wouldn't the dark find the book too? I tempered my feelings for a moment. For the dark to put the pieces together, they'd need to know about the Younghusband bowl which put the book in Dharamsala, and the fact that the book was with the Keeper (or librarian) – both clues provided by Jim. I was sure they didn't know about either – if they did, they wouldn't have broken into SOAS to steal my false document. No, we knew where the Morning Tree was, they didn't.

Claire had started talking to her friend now to divert her from our strange behaviour. I sat back with a warm glow. At last, my way was

---

[95] The Library of Tibetan Works and Archives in Dharamsala was founded by the Fourteenth Dalai Lama in 1970 to house the religious and cultural books and artefacts being smuggled out of Tibet. It has since become the most important repository of Tibetan religion and culture in the world.

clear. I was anxious to leave her friend's house so I could talk to Claire about our discovery. I shifted in my seat, tried to attract her attention, and made let's-go signs when she looked my way. Eventually, Claire made her excuses and we were out on the street.

We were both very happy on the way home and for several days afterwards. Everything felt so right. We started to think where in Library of Tibetan Works and Archives the Morning Tree might be. We presumed we couldn't just walk in and ask to borrow it. We found the names of some of the librarians; maybe one of them was the Keeper.

It was nearing the end of the Easter break. Claire and I had been out for the evening and had taken a taxi back to Claire's flat. As the taxi turned into Claire's street, we saw five men milling around outside Claire's door looking up at her building. One of the men turned round to talk to the others. It was Sonam.

"Drive on!" I shouted to the driver.

"But I thought—"

"Drive on!"

The cab went past Sonam and his men. Claire and I hugged the interior. It was dark, I was sure Sonam hadn't seen us. I risked a glance through the rear window and saw that he was still looking up at Claire's building. I felt cold inside. I was sure he had believed my story that I was no longer after the Morning Tree. But there he was, with thugs, looking for us.

"Where to then?" broke in the cab driver in an irritated voice. I gave him another address. I could feel Claire's fear. We held hands as the taxi made its way to Chiswick. We eventually got out in front of a large house, paid off the cab and rang the bell. I could hear some muttering as locks were pulled back and the door opened sending out a pool of light into the street.

"Daniel?" said Professor Thurgood, standing in his dressing gown. "And Miss Hoskyns, I believe. This is a surprise. I had heard you two might be, em, seeing each other, but I'm not licensed to perform marriages, you know."

"P... Professor Thurgood, I'm sorry..." I stammered.

Professor Thurgood began to take in our distressed situation. "Good God," he said, "you two look terrible. Come inside."

"Who is it dear, at this time of night?" came his wife's voice from within.

"Dr Clifton, and one of his friends," he replied loudly. "I think they need something hot to drink. Now, what's going on, Daniel?"

We sat in his warm study while I told him about Jim's visit, the Younghusband bowl, the breakthroughs that Claire and I had made, and the fact that we thought we had identified the Morning Tree was in the Library of Tibetan Works and Archives. I then told him about the dark, how they had burgled and mugged me, killed Jim, and stolen the document I'd planted. I ended up with Sonam being outside Claire's flat this evening. Professor Thurgood listened intently.

"You probably think these tales of the dark are the work of my oversensitive imagination," I concluded, "but they're not! The dark exists, and they mean business. And we're in danger right now."

Professor Thurgood was thoughtful. "You forget, Daniel, I too have read Thaza's account, and for the most part I believe it. So I do believe there are forces seeking to destroy this book. As for Sonam, it doesn't surprise me."

"Why did you warn me about him in the first place? Did you know?"

"That he was likely to be a murderer? No. But I didn't trust him. I always thought he was riding on the back of other people's work. Trouble was, the man's a monk. Can't call them immoral to people's faces – you simply won't be believed. I just made a point of having as little to do with him as possible."

"But what should we do?" asked Claire despairingly. "I can't not go home. I can't live in permanent fear. That man's got to be stopped!"

"Hmm, well you can't go to the police – you've no evidence. You've got to find the Morning Tree. Once you have it, and made it available, there's nothing more he can do."

"We'll go to Dharamsala, then," I said.

"Yes, Daniel. But if Sonam really is following you, you'll want to do what you can to cover your tracks. Don't go directly to Dharamsala. Just go to Paris or something. A romantic weekend away for the two new love birds. Once there, book a flight to India. It might put him off the trail. Of course I can't sanction this."

"What?"

"I can't as head of department let you leave your post in the middle of the academic year. And I can't lie to our employers pretending you're on sick leave or something. I'll do what I can, Daniel, but the less I know about this officially the better."

I looked at Claire. She was more shaken than I realised. I suppose she felt violated by seeing Sonam and his men outside her flat. I thought of all that I'd gone through. I didn't know why I had found out about the Morning Tree or why I now had to find it, but I knew in my heart that I had to find it, whatever the danger. That vision I'd had in my flat when I'd been shown the two routes mankind could go down came back to me. Why should we continue down the wrong path? Why not change and go down the right one? My course was clear.

"To hell with Sonam and everyone like him!" I said. "I'm fed up with the dark and this endless fear they seek to put on everyone. He wants the Morning Tree? Well, he can't have it. It's not his to have. It's our turn now. I'm going to find this book and give it to everyone. Then people can come into their true power and the dark will have no more sway over us. And if he wants to kill me after that, so what? But I'm not going to kowtow to him or his kind anymore."

I wasn't angry. I was certain. The dark had had their day. I might be in danger, but I shouldn't bow down to them anymore out of fear. The time had come for the light to win, for everyone to have a better life. The tension of the past weeks started to drain away. Suddenly I wasn't frightened anymore.

Professor Thurgood was looking at me trying to assess my mood. Claire was sitting up looking at me as well. I didn't care what anyone

335

else thought. I wasn't thinking about myself anymore. I just knew it was time to stand up and do what was right.

I had no more to say, so I made to go. Professor Thurgood stopped me.

"Wait Daniel," he said opening a drawer in his desk. "You'll need some funds. I can't get the money I've wrung from the university for you, but I can give you this." He tore off a cheque and handed it to me. "For your travels."

"I—"

"Think nothing of it," he said. "Although there'll be hell to pay if anyone finds out; it'll prove I've known what you were doing. One more thing." He scribbled something on a piece of paper and gave it to me. "When you get to the Library of Tibetan Works and Archives, ask for him. You can mention my name." I looked at the paper. It said Lobsang Yeshi.

We left in an entirely different frame of heart than when we arrived. Claire didn't mind going back to her flat now. If Sonam and his men were still there we'd call the police or kick up a fuss until someone else called them. In the event, the street was clear and we accessed Claire's flat safely.

The next two days were a whirlwind of booking our tickets, packing and making sure no-one knew what we were really doing. As Professor Thurgood had suggested, we went to Paris. In fact, we'd made a point of telling a few people (Ann, Milo) that we were going. It would explain our absence, at least to begin with. On our trip over, I started trying some of the energy exercises that Lama Kunchen had taught Thaza to see if we were being followed. I don't know if I did them correctly, but it was a relief to be doing something to protect ourselves.

We got to Paris, and managed to book our flights to India, so that by the end of that week we were boarding the plane to Delhi. We actually took separate flights in case Sonam was checking the airports and his henchmen were looking for us as a pair. We met up in flight arrivals in Delhi and negotiated our way through Indian passport control and customs. Eventually we emerged into the crowded halls that make up the public parts of the airport.

It was night time, but there were throngs of people (mostly just looking at the arriving passengers as far as I could tell) and a glaring sense that we were somewhere foreign. The unexpected warmth of the night, the faces of the people staring at us and the smells wafting around were distinctly different.

I could scarcely believe where I was. A week before I'd been in London thinking of the Morning Tree as some distant prospect, but here I was in India, a short flight from Dharamsala and most likely the book itself. I felt grungy from the flight, and strange in this new place, but excited as well.

Claire led the way out of the airport and got a cab. I was going to be in her hands for the next few days. She'd visited Dharamsala the year before as part of her PhD and knew, insomuch as any visitor to India can, her way around.

Chapter Eleven

Claire booked us into a small and surprisingly clean hotel. We picked at a late supper. I was nervous about the food – I'd suffered from unknown bacteria in my year in Tibet – but I had to admit the hotel's late night buffet was tasty and fiery. Then to bed for a disjointed night's sleep.

The next day we braved the crowded streets to book our journey to Dharamsala. I was dazzled by the light, the heat, the colour, the pollution, the crowds, the squalor, the riches and the fact that the city worked at all despite the apparent chaos. I was also terrified by the driving. I squirmed as our cab weaved in and out of the mess of pedestrians, cyclists, people on motorcycles, motorised trishaws and other cars – some of them looking as if they'd been made in the 1950s. And I squawked as crowded buses and brightly painted lorries came straight at us honking loudly – and somehow missed. I had been told that you needed to be in India for at least three weeks before you relax. I could well believe it.

We eventually managed to book our flight to Dharamsala and a guest house for when we got there. The flight didn't leave for another two days, so we spent our time sightseeing. But I wasn't really in the mood to enjoy myself. The summer term started the day we were to fly to Dharamsala. My absence would be noted. What would happen then?

At last we flew to Dharamsala. The aircraft looked as old as the cars we'd seen in Delhi. But the view as we reached the foothills of the Himalayas was breathtaking. I was relieved to finally arrive. The air was so much fresher and cooler than Delhi, and the place felt welcoming. I was excited too to see Tibetans in the crowds at Gaggal airport. We took the bus from the airport to McLeod Ganj[96] with our luggage on our knees, and then it was a short walk to our guest house.

For the first time in a long time I was happy. I was in a place I liked with a girl I loved and about to complete a vitally important task. I almost felt as if I were on holiday instead of trying to stay one step ahead of someone who would kill me to get what they wanted. The guest house was cool and calm. And when I opened the shuttered windows and saw the Kangra Valley stretching out below, I whistled at the beauty of it. I gave Claire a big hug.

"Let's go and get a pizza," she said. I had a double take but didn't question her. So once we'd unpacked she led me to an Italian café in the main street. The pizzas had the usual names but a definitely foreign taste. A welcome sign that globalisation can never really make the world identical.

As we sat looking at the street, I felt contentment. The town was not only pleasant but seemed familiar. I'd pored over so many maps of Dharamsala, and as the Tibetan part McLeod Ganj was not large, I almost knew the layout by heart.

The next day was sunny. After breakfast we made the short walk to the Library of Tibetan Works and Archives. The white walls and bright prayer flags of the Tibetan style building looked fresh and welcoming. Claire and I glanced at each other and then went in. Our plan was to check out the Library before contacting the man suggested by Professor Thurgood. Claire went to the English language section; I browsed the larger Tibetan section. I wasn't expecting to find the Morning Tree in the catalogues, but I looked all the same. After a couple of hours, Claire and I left for a quick lunch. Then we returned and asked to see Lobsang Yeshi. After a fifteen minute wait a slightly dishevelled man with stubble on his chin came up to us. I wondered

---

[96] McLeod Ganj is the name of the older, upper part of Dharamsala, where the Tibetan community is based.

if we'd disturbed his after lunch nap. He gave us a pleasant smile, nevertheless.

"You want see me?" he said in broken English.

"Yes," I replied in Tibetan. "Professor Thurgood has said we should ask for you. He said you could help."

"Ah, Professor Thurgood," said Lobsang Yeshi, smiling broadly. "He is a good man. A friend. Of course, I should be happy to assist you."

"Can we talk privately?"

Lobsang led the way to a small office in the back of the building filled with papers and books. Some of the papers were flapping up and down as a precariously balanced electric fan whirred round. He pulled out two none too clean teacups from under some papers and poured us butter tea. Claire and I sipped ours and winced. I have never been able to get used to its frankly rancid taste.

"How can I help you?" Lobsang asked.

"We are looking for a sacred text," I began, "and we believe it may be here."

Lobsang waved his hand and smiled. I noticed he had a couple of blackened teeth. "You are welcome to look at our catalogue," he said, drawing a keyboard to him. "We have everything on computer—"

"This is a special text," I said. Lobsang paused, his fingers over the keyboard. "So special that it wouldn't be in your catalogue. It is called the Morning Tree."

I watched him closely. He was hard to read. He tapped something on his keyboard, looked at the information that leapt up onto the computer screen, and then closed it. "Professor Thurgood wants to know about this text?" he asked.

"He does. And we do."

"We have a restricted section," he said. "It's not permitted for outsiders to see without special permission." He looked at us steadily; he seemed to be weighing something up. He glanced at his watch. "It's too late now," he said. "Come back tomorrow morning at nine a.m."

340

We left the Library elated. Lobsang hadn't said anything, but he had definitely signalled he was going to help us. We walked back to our guest house in the afternoon sunshine, pausing to browse in the shops and eventually have a couple of long cool beers. I knew we were on the right track.

We were back at the Library at nine the next morning. Lobsang was waiting in reception. As soon as he saw us, he took my arm and propelled us upstairs to a small whitewashed office. Moments later a tall lama walked in. Lobsang jumped to his feet.

"Honourable lama," he said, bowing slightly. "These are the people. The man understands Tibetan."

The lama sat behind the desk and looked at us with an impassive face. "How do you know about this text?" he asked eventually.

"The Morning Tree?" I replied. "I came across it in a manuscript that was donated to SOAS. I believe you may have the book?"

"What do you know of this book?"

I told him what I knew, and how it was now vital to release it, as those safeguarding the book intended.

"And how do you know this text is here?" asked the lama.

I hesitated. I briefly wondered if this man was like Sonam – one of the dark. I scanned the lama's energy as I'd been practising. He didn't feel wrong; in fact, I got a positive feeling, to my surprise, as he didn't seem a sympathetic person. Part of me marvelled that I was making such an important decision on the basis of a feeling, but I had to decide within seconds, so I decided to trust him. I told him about the Younghusband bowl and Jim's information about the Keeper and how Thaza's account suggested that the book would be kept with other books in a library.

There was a tense silence as the lama considered what I'd said. Eventually he stood up. "You may tell them, Lobsang," he said and left the room. We turned to Lobsang.

"Your request is being looked into," he said. "Come back next week."

"Next week? Surely—"

"Looking at books in the restricted section is a serious matter. This Library is under the personal direction of His Holiness. The lama you have just spoken to has to talk to his aides. Everything has to be considered properly. We will contact you when we have an answer."

We left with conflicting emotions. We were so close! Yet there was nothing we could do but wait. I itched to be able to talk to the Dalai Lama's aides – even to the Dalai Lama himself – to persuade them to release the book, but Claire counselled caution. If we pushed too much, she said, we could get a negative reaction. I knew enough about Asian customs to know she was right. So we had to wait. We spent our time visiting the various Tibetan centres in the town, shopping, taking side trips in the area and hiking on nearby trails. All the while I was on edge waiting for their answer.

I had a dream on one of those nights. I was suddenly in this quiet space. I knew there were other people there but I couldn't see them. These people were definitely high beings. I had a book in my hands; it had a wooden cover. And I suddenly felt sunlight break over me. I definitely felt warm. I couldn't see anything more. But I woke up feeling really good, and really good about finding the Morning Tree. I couldn't have asked for a better sign that all was going to be well.

It was exactly a week after our interview with the tall lama. Claire and I were having breakfast outside in a café. I saw Lobsang on the other side of the road heading towards our guest house, presumably to find us. I hailed him. He turned round, acknowledged me and made his way over. He picked his way through the people and tables. I noticed he was sweating. We offered him refreshment, but he shook his head and clutched the back of a chair.

"I can't give you an answer," he said in Tibetan.

"Haven't they decided yet?" I asked.

"They've decided to have no more communication with you."

"But why?"

"I can't say. I really don't know. But as I've said, there is to be no more communication."

"But Lobsang—"

"I've paid you the respect of telling you this in person. I didn't need to. Please, ask me no more." And avoiding our eyes he hurried off.

I was dumbfounded. We were so close, we couldn't be turned away now! The colour must have drained from my face because Claire asked what was wrong. I told her what Lobsang had said. She was shocked. I pushed away the food in front of me.

I couldn't accept this turn of events. They had given every indication they knew about the Morning Tree. I was sure they were trying to safeguard it. But I also knew that the book had to be released now before an increasingly active dark lodge got their hands on it. I told Claire that we had to find the tall lama and persuade him. She said he probably worked at the Tsuglaghang Complex;[97] it was where the senior officials and the Dalai Lama's personal aides were usually based. So we made our way there.

It was crowded and difficult to find the religious administration offices. We were stopped a couple of times by monks asking what we were doing. I mumbled something and pushed on. Suddenly we saw the tall lama walking across a small compound and disappearing round a corner. We raced after him.

"Honourable lama!" I cried. He didn't seem to hear. "Honourable lama!"

He slowed and turned round. His impassive face broke into a look of surprise, and then anger. "Who let you in here!" he thundered.

"Honourable lama, please give me a moment. It's vital we release the Morning Tree! There are people after it who mean to destroy it!"

He wasn't listening. He was talking urgently to an assistant who ran off. He towered over us while we caught our breath. "Please, lama, we mean you no harm. On the contrary—"

Just then two police monks ran up. The lama spoke to them in a dialect I didn't understand and they yanked us away. The lama's assistant followed as they marched us out. "Never come back here!"

---

[97] Tsuglaghang Complex is the main Tibetan temple and seat of administration in Dharamsala.

he hissed as the police monks roughly pushed us forward. "You know not what laws you are transgressing!"

And with that we were thrust back into the public area. The police monks stood with their arms folded watching as we threaded our way unsteadily through the throng of people.

I was feeling hot, confused and angry. How could they just throw us out without listening to what we had to say? What were we going to do now? I wondered if we would be forced to break into that damned Library and steal the book.

And there he was. Near the entrance. Standing with a small group of other monks. Sonam. It required all my strength not to turn and run. But I had to face him. His kind had had their day, whatever they might think. But how had he known we were here? Was nothing secret from him? Sonam was watching us with narrowed eyes. We had to go past him to get out, so we moved forward. I stopped some feet from him and stared. He edged away from his group.

"You're not very bright, are you Daniel?" he said to me in English. "Did you really think I wouldn't know where you were?"

"I try not to think about you Sonam," I replied.

"That's not very clever of you either, Daniel. Although I must admit you nearly fooled me with that document about Darjeeling."

"What are you doing here?" I retorted.

"Same as you, Daniel. Looking for the Morning Tree. I have to thank you, you know. We really had so little to go on until we met you. And now, here we both are, in the same place." He smiled. "I take it you haven't found the book yet? No? Please Daniel, let's talk. I'm sure it'd be better for both of us."

"I'll never talk to you! Not after you killed Jim! And you're supposed to be a monk!"

"Ah, Jim. He had a weak heart, didn't he?"

"You can't get away with killing people!"

"You want revenge? How brave. But I don't think you want to make a scene here. Assaulting a monk? It wouldn't look good."

"Too right, Sonam. But you don't want to make a scene here either. It's too crowded, isn't it? You can't touch us or else you'll be noticed." A tiny flicker crossed Sonam's face, and he moved imperceptibly from the monks he was with. "Oh," I said, grasping the situation, "your friends don't know who you really are, do they? I'm sure they'd be very interested to find out."

"Please, Daniel, don't flatter yourself. Do you really think they'd listen to your deranged accusations? Watch your step. We are certainly watching you." With that Sonam turned to rejoin his friends. I heard him exclaim I was an acquaintance from London. His friends gave me a polite nod as they moved off. I watched them go. Then I grabbed Claire's arm and we shot out.

We headed towards the main square. Being on the normal streets surrounded by locals and tourists was at least reassuring. We found a café and ordered drinks. Claire was ashen faced. I was worried too. With our summary dismissal from Tsuglaghang Complex, we were further away from finding the Morning Tree than we had been in London. And our unwelcome meeting with Sonam showed he was closer on our heels than ever before. How could everything have collapsed in one morning?

"What shall we do?" asked Claire.

"About Sonam – nothing," I said. "He still doesn't know where the book is. He still needs us. He won't harm us until he thinks we know where the Morning Tree is."

"And then?"

"Then we'll have to be careful, but I can't think of that now. Right now we've got to find the book."

"But how?" asked Claire desperately.

"I don't know," I groaned. I felt a surge of despair. I didn't know whether to cry or smash my drink on the wall opposite. My insides tied themselves in a knot. If I had been with Karen we'd have started to argue; with Claire things were better. At least that was something good. But it didn't help with the Morning Tree. We sat in silence for I don't know how long. Claire hung her head in her hands, but at length she reached out and touched my arm.

"I have an idea," she whispered. "Someone who might be able to help. Give me some time." She took her bag and walked off. I was going to call out "Be careful," but the words died on my lips. I didn't know what she was going to do, and I didn't want to know. I didn't want my hopes raised only to be crushed later.

I spent the rest of that day in the guest house. I mooned about the garden, stared at the unfamiliar flowers and peered at the countless insects engaged in their life and death struggle – anything to pass the time and not think about how we could find the Morning Tree. But thoughts of the Morning Tree were never far away, and I ended up reflecting on the path that had brought me here. I had started as a not very ambitious (admit it, lazy) academic hoping for a quiet, reasonably well paid life in a university, marrying at some point and, I suppose, having a family. But I'd been taken out of my comfort zone, exposed to visions and feelings I'd never had before, forced to face danger, found a new girlfriend, and now here I was absent without leave from my secure teaching post. More than that, I had found a new purpose, and had begun to change in ways I couldn't understand. I was beginning to have feelings, intuition, dreams that were significant, even if my old mind was uncertain about what was going on. Even if we never found this book, it had changed me profoundly.

I waited for Claire to return. She came back at dusk, drained and dusty. But she was smiling.

"Tomorrow at noon," she said. "We meet someone. Don't ask anything now. Wait and see."

She had always been on my side. Without asking for her support, she had always been there to help me. I wondered at my luck, not only to have met her, but also to have won her. I followed her instructions and bided my time.

Next morning Claire told me to be ready by eleven thirty. She led me out and down to the lower part of the town. We scanned ahead and behind to see if we were being trailed by Sonam or his accomplices, but we seemed safe. We entered a quieter, more residential part of town, passing people's houses, playing children and women hanging washing out. We could hear the bangs and shouts of families going about their business. Eventually, we came to a bench under the shade of a tree. There was a middle aged monk sitting there. I looked at my watch. It was noon. Claire went up to the monk respectfully and indicated my presence. She then motioned for me to sit next to him.

"This is Pemba Gephal," she said. It took a moment for me to recall the young monk who had befriended Thaza. The man who had taken Thaza's manuscript out of Tibet. I blinked in surprise.

"How...?" I began.

"The Tibetan government keeps a record of refugees who leave Tibet," she answered. "I managed to find Pemba's details and track him down. At the very least, I thought he might be able to tell us more about Thaza, and even the Morning Tree itself. I think he understands why he is here. It's been difficult to communicate as I don't speak Tibetan."

I turned to look at him. He seemed a little uncertain. But here was someone who had known Thaza. An invaluable find! I squeezed Claire's arm in gratitude and then addressed him.

"Pemba Gephal, formerly of Yerlang monastery? You had a friend, a Mongolian, called Thaza." He sat up and looked at me surprised.

"Thaza? Yes, a difficult man," he said. "I haven't thought of him oh, for years. I respected him. He was old, and I felt he had been through an ordeal. How... how do you know of him?"

I told him how Thaza's manuscript had come to SOAS and I had translated it. I don't know if he followed everything I was saying, but once he understood what I was interested in, he was a mine of information.

He told me about life at Yerlang, how Thaza was considered odd by the other monks, and how he had spent his time caring for the yaks and the few ponies that were in the area. Indeed, peasants would bring their animals to him if they were sick. He had befriended Thaza, he didn't know why, he just felt this respect for him. Not that Thaza was nice to him; he was crotchety to everyone. Indeed, Pemba thought he deliberately distanced himself from the other monks. Most people thought it was arrogance, but Pemba felt Thaza had been through something that removed him from normal life. Thaza just couldn't be bothered to get on with other people. He was in another place inside himself most of the time. Pemba reckoned he was thinking of his past in Mongolia. The only times he would be pleasant were when he talked about his homeland or a lama he had known in Lhasa. Pemba even described him to me. Not tall, but broad shouldered, with a care-worn face, rough hands and a scar on his forehead. He was clearly a strong man despite his limp, and one with an inner heat (Pemba's words); you just felt warmer sitting near him. He was old, and one day he just seemed to give up the will to live.

No-one else wanted to tend to him, so Pemba stayed by his side for the three days he took to die. He became delirious towards the end, talking about things he had done, and telling Pemba about a manuscript he had written. He told Pemba where the manuscript was hidden, and made him promise to give it to a senior lama he could trust. On no account were the Chinese to get hold of it. Thaza had grabbed Pemba's arm and dug his nails into it until he drew blood. On no account were the Chinese to get hold of it, he repeated, and he made Pemba swear an oath to this effect. After he'd died, Pemba unearthed the document from its hiding place in the stables, and kept it about him. Did I know that none of the lamas wanted to conduct a ceremony for Thaza? Pemba had to drag his body out himself and break it up for the vultures to eat.

It was a time of fear, Pemba said. The Chinese were burning and looting lamaseries and killing monks. Pemba was young. He was also an orphan, and had no family to go back to or worry about. He decided with a few of his fellows to escape to join the Dalai Lama in India. He'd had his share of difficulties on the journey, but they made it to Dharamsala. He had taken Thaza's manuscript with him. He had read it, and had no doubt of its importance. He approached the Dalai Lama's staff and gave the manuscript to an official, conscious that he was fulfilling Thaza's wishes. About three months later he was summoned to see Nawang Lingar, one of the Dalai Lama's secretaries. He had no idea why until, in a private meeting with Nawang Lingar, he had been asked about Thaza's manuscript. He was grilled, in fact, about Thaza, the manuscript and its contents. He feared he might have done something wrong because the questions were so tough. But eventually he was asked to testify that the document was genuine, and he was released.

We had been talking for so long that Claire had gone off to get some food and drinks. We eventually had a break for a late lunch. The academic in me was excited; here was incontrovertible proof that Thaza existed and that he was the author of the manuscript. But my spiritual side was even more excited. I sensed there was a nugget to be uncovered, but I wasn't sure what.

I questioned Pemba about his meetings with Nawang Lingar. There had been several, Pemba said, each was with Nawang himself. Pemba was just a chela, in no position to ask questions, even though he was curious about the high level of interest that was being shown in Thaza's account.

"Did Nawang Lingar speak specifically about the Morning Tree?" I asked.

"Oh yes," said Pemba, before catching himself.

He then added he'd been told by Nawang not to divulge anything about the Morning Tree or his interviews with him to anyone, even to other monks.

"Did Nawang admit to the book's existence?" I persisted.

"Yes," said Pemba with difficulty, but he had insisted Pemba didn't talk about it and really he shouldn't be talking about it now.

I could see Pemba was feeling awkward but I had to continue.

"Did he tell you where the Morning Tree was?" I asked as lightly as I could.

Surprisingly Pemba smiled. "Yes," he said in a quiet voice, looking either side of him as he spoke.

He had even seen it. I was startled. I double-checked what he was saying. He had actually seen the Morning Tree, once, when Nawang had visited the Keeper. For some reason, he'd allowed Pemba to go with him. My mouth was dry. Where?

Pemba was silent. I had to accept I was in his hands, and that if my premonitions about the Morning Tree were real, its location would come to me.

Eventually he said, "I can't tell you where, just that it is nearby. I don't know why I'm even telling you this."

"Nearby? You mean, nearby here?"

"I can't tell you any more."

"But do you mean the book is near where we are sitting now?"

He nodded.

Of course! Hadn't the Younghusband bowl indicated the Morning Tree might be in the lower part of the town? That is where the words had been inscribed. And here was someone who had actually seen the book telling me that was where it was!

I was about to ask him where nearby when I saw that he was looking extremely uncomfortable. I left my question unasked. I had got more than I'd expected. A crucial step forward, but... but maybe another dead end as I couldn't just search every building in this part of town. I had a choice to get frustrated or rise above it. Logic said I had no chance, but that part of me, beyond my mind, knew that if I opened myself up I might just find it. So I thanked Pemba (really, I was very grateful), offered him some more refreshment, and he went on his way.

I turned to Claire. Poor girl had had to sit for hours not understanding what was being said. I knew she'd been looking out for any sign of Sonam. I realised that I'd been sweating, not so much from the humidity but from excitement. Even so, I hugged her and told her everything Pemba had said.

"The Morning Tree is nearby?" she exclaimed. "But where? Why didn't you press him?"

"He'd already told me more than he should," I replied. "Pressing him might not have helped. But I know he's given us a real clue. If only I can recognise it."

I started looking around that small square. There was nothing to see but the sides of people's houses. Slowly we got up and walked back to our guest house. I continued peering at all the buildings we passed to see if any of them might be housing the Morning Tree. Nothing seemed obvious. But I knew – I just knew – there must be a clue.

We reached the guest house none the wiser. I kept turning over every possibility in my mind, but nothing felt right. I was silent at supper for thinking so much. Eventually, I got a dull ache in my head. I was trying too hard. Better relax. I watched some Indian television, read a book and then turned in. I couldn't stop myself thinking about it though. Where was the Morning Tree?

It was that night I made the breakthrough. I had gone to bed still turning what Pemba Gephal had told me over and over in my head. I had eventually fallen into a troubled sleep. In my dream I was searching for the Morning Tree, somewhere in Dharamsala, but getting nowhere. Then suddenly everything shifted. There was peace. And the words 'Lower Stream Buddhist Rest House' were seen in front of me. Not only the words, but the building they were on.

I woke up. It was two a.m. I was feeling calm and clear. I remembered my dream perfectly. And I knew where that building was. It was just around the corner from my talk with Pemba that afternoon.

I knew then that was where the Morning Tree was being kept. I don't know how that dream had come to me, but I knew it was showing me where the book was to be found. The Rest House was nearby, as Pemba had said. Although it wasn't a monastery, it was at least connected with Buddhism. There was no doubt in my mind. It was there.

Moments later a big grin spread across my face. Hadn't Lama Kunchen said he'd place the pebble he wanted to hide at the bottom of a stream? Well, the word 'bottom' in Tibetan was interchangeable with the word 'lower'. So when he'd said 'bottom of a stream' he'd given Thaza the phrase 'Lower Stream'. Then he'd added that the pebble (the Morning Tree) could rest there safely.[98] So he'd actually said the words 'Lower Stream Rest'. The crafty old man had indicated the name of the place, even the address of, where the Morning Tree was to be found! The clue had been there all the time, if only I'd had the nous to understand what he was saying. I had to laugh.

I felt a great sense of peace. I even managed to fall straight back to sleep.

---

[98] See page 167 in Thaza's account.

Chapter Twelve

I told Claire my insight first thing the next morning. She yawned and ran a hand through her hair. She always looked good in the mornings, but always hated it when I said so. She wasn't as positive as I expected. But then, I too was wondering if what had seemed so clear in the middle of the night would prove to be right in the light of day.

Straight after breakfast we made our way back to the lower part of the town. It took a few minutes to locate the Rest House, but there it was: the Lower Stream Buddhist Rest House, a nondescript two storey building and a compound. We entered the front door and found an Indian sitting with his legs up on an old bar stool. There was a faded notice in English, Tibetan and Hindi saying 'Lower Stream Buddhist Rest House, Place of Rest and Contemplation, Home for Retired Buddhists, Funded by the Indian Society for Buddhist Studies 1975'.

"Do you have a library here?" I asked the man in English.

"Yes sir," he said, uncurling his legs. "But only religious books."

"We are looking for religious books," I replied.

"One moment please," said the man, and he disappeared through a door. A little later he reappeared with an agitated looking Tibetan.

"Book here for resident," said the Tibetan in broken English. "You go big library in town."

"We are looking for a book that isn't in the big library," I replied in Tibetan. "We are looking for the Morning Tree."

The Tibetan seemed surprised. He looked at us more closely, his brow furrowed. He looked at us one more time, then turned and went back through the door. Claire and I exchanged glances. Moments later he reappeared.

"What book are you looking for?"

"The Morning Tree."

He disappeared again. And returned a minute later. "Do you have the password?"

Password? Oh God, I wasn't expecting this. Thaza had mentioned nothing about a password – no-one had. Surely I hadn't come this far to fall at the final fence? Claire could see the wrought look on my face so I whispered to her what I'd been asked. She was shocked. I racked my brain to see if I could come up with anything. Password. What could be the password? I couldn't think of anything. I was about to confess in despair that I hadn't a clue when an idea came to me.

"Sunlight on mountains," I said swallowing hard. I was sweating by now in the close atmosphere of that stuffy entrance hall. If this didn't work, I wouldn't know what to say. The Tibetan said nothing and disappeared back through the door. He was longer this time, but when he returned he said:

"Follow me please."

I let out my breath. If I had been asked for the password again, I wouldn't have known what to say. I clutched Claire's hand as we went through the door. My heart was beginning to beat strongly. We were conducted down a dimly lit corridor to a room at the back of the building full of light. The room had doors leading onto a small courtyard. The doors were open, with sunlight and the sound of a stream rushing down the hill coming into the room. An old – I'd say very old – lama was seated cross legged on the floor by the doors.

"Your visitors, venerable lama," said the Tibetan softly, while he bowed. He gestured to us to sit on the floor, then backed out of the room slowly. He shut the door and we were alone.

The lama wasn't looking at us. Indeed, his eyes were closed. But he was definitely aware of us. I was sure he was checking us out – how, I don't know, but he was feeling into us. He radiated peace and strength despite his age. We sat in silence for some minutes. I was now nervous and excited, but for once having to sit cross legged wasn't making me uncomfortable. The sound of the stream and birdsong were clear in the room.

"I have been waiting for you," said the lama at last. A breeze blew in, cooling me. I shook myself. It was only then that I realised he'd addressed us in English. He opened his eyes. "I am glad you have come."

"You... you knew we were coming?" I stammered.

"I didn't know you were coming – I don't even know your names – but I knew someone was coming."

"You know why we have come?"

"For the Morning Tree."

"And you have it?"

"Yes."

I didn't dare move. I waited for him to say something more, but he was silent. Eventually I continued, "And we can have it?"

"You can."

I stared at him. His eyes held mine. I was aware of a new type of energy coming into me.

"Really?"

"Yes. I have waited a long time for this. It is my duty to pass the Morning Tree on. As you can see, I won't last in this body much longer."

Claire and I shot each other glances. I don't think we could believe what we were hearing. But a flowering inside at that moment, not only took my breath away, but also confirmed what I knew in my heart. We had come to the end of our quest.

"And you are...?"

"The Keeper."

I was washed by a wave of energy. The agitation and tension of the previous weeks was beginning to drain from my body. I felt a heightened sense of awareness.

"You're not surprised we're westerners?"

355

"I was expecting westerners," replied the lama. "That is why I am speaking English." He chuckled. "I have had a long time to learn the language. It is good to put it to use at last. The fact is, the knowledge in the Morning Tree now needs to go to the West. Some of my colleagues would say that's because the West is in dire need of spiritual guidance. It is in fact because the West will now take up the torch of spiritual change."

"And you don't mind we're not Buddhists?"

"What is Buddhism but truth seen from one point of view? Religions are still useful, for they can help to guide people. But the time is coming when religions can be replaced by direct spiritual knowledge. Buddhism will gently fade away, as will all religions in time, and the world will be better for it. I serve a higher truth, not just one religion."

"But… but how do you know we're the right people?" I asked. "How do you know we should have the Morning Tree?"

"I know."

I waited for him to say more. After all, I could have been Sonam asking for it. He must have sensed this because after a while he said:

"Trust me, I know you are the right people. The fact that you've even asked that question proves it."

I let out my breath. Claire was smiling. A part of me still couldn't believe what was happening. But it was. Against all the odds, we had found the Morning Tree. I felt relief, happiness and achievement. More than that, there was a settled rightness, a balance that was more meaningful than the celebration I was also feeling.

"Can we see it?" I asked at length. "Can we see the Morning Tree?"

"All in good time," replied the lama. "But first, please, tell me how you found me."

So I pieced it all together – how I found Thaza's manuscript, how it interested me, how I contacted Jim, and met Mr Ravensburg. How Jim came to London and showed us the Younghusband bowl. How he died. How Sonam Prasang pursued us. How we realised the

Morning Tree was in a library. Our trip here, our approach to Lobsang Yeshi, the incident at the Tsuglaghang Complex, and how Claire tracked down Pemba Gephal who had told us the Morning Tree was nearby. I mentioned how lucky I had been to meet people who had known about the Morning Tree, but the lama said, "It wasn't luck. Your willingness to look created the next step for you to move forward."

When I got to the dream I'd had last night that led us to the Rest House, I felt sheepish – surely a dream couldn't have shown me the final clue? – but the lama simply said, "Sometimes dreams can be a door to higher consciousness."

When I finished, the lama was silent for a while.

"So many clues we had to lay," he said eventually. "But it worked. I did sometimes wonder if the jigsaw could be put together. But you have done well. Very well."

"You mean, you planted those clues?"

"Not me, but our order."

"But… but the Younghusband bowl was made over a hundred years ago! And Massingberd was told about the book in 1910. And Jim was told about it by that monk he met in 1972."

"Yes. A lot of planning went into this. Colonel Younghusband was most helpful."

"But he invaded Tibet!"

"He did. But, even though he wasn't consciously aware of it, he was there to help us. As, paradoxically, were the Chinese. Because the good consequence of these invasions has been that Tibet's knowledge has been revealed to the outside world. And with the Morning Tree, Tibet's real jewel will be handed on. There were powerful forces in Tibet to keep Tibet's treasures to itself. But we have to share what we know. Perhaps we should have done this a long time ago, but maybe the world was not ready then. It is now."

We sat for a while. I was still coming to terms with the fact that we were in the presence of the Keeper, we were going to receive the Morning Tree, and we had beaten Sonam.

Sonam! He was still out there, and still a danger. I suddenly wondered if this old man had taken on board everything I'd told him.

"We may have done well, as you say," I said, "but the dark are still after us, after the Morning Tree. That man – that monk – Sonam Prasang may have followed us here and be waiting for us outside right now. He must be stopped!"

The lama sighed. "Sadly you are right. We cannot allow this. Now that we know who he is, we will take care of him." He rang his bell.

"Take care of…?"

"He won't be harmed, but he will be stopped. In the past, we would not have been able to act like this, but today we are stronger. He will not bother you anymore."

Claire and I looked at each other. "Really?"

"Yes."

The lama's attendant came in and bent his head close to his master's. The old lama spoke quietly but firmly. His attendant nodded. The lama spoke again. The attendant bowed and left.

As I watched, my spirits soared. Almost as much, I think, as when the lama had admitted he was the Keeper. I didn't realise how deep my anxiety about being pursued by Sonam had been.

The lama turned to us again. "Don't think ill of him," he said.

"Don't think—but he killed a man!"

"Death is natural. Don't worry about your friend dying."

"But—"

"Your friend had his part to play. He gave you the vital clues. That was his job, and he succeeded. Once he had given you the clues, he could move on. You might not understand now, but you will."

I didn't understand. Nor did I understand his next remark.

"I dare say that man Sonam Prasang helped you too."

"He what?"

"Would you have been here so soon if it hadn't been for him?"

"I…" But the lama was right. We were only in Dharamsala now because Sonam had pursued us. He'd pushed us to come sooner rather than later. And he'd made me face situations I'd never have dreamt of. Even so, the fact that Sonam might have helped wasn't something I wanted to consider for the time being.

"This is enough for now," said the lama. "It is good to have met you. Tell my assistant where you are staying. And return here tomorrow at ten in the morning. Just you," he said looking at me. "You will have a different task to perform," he added to Claire.

We unwound our legs and got to our feet. We bowed like the lama's assistant and moved slowly to the door. At the door I paused.

"The password I gave," I asked. "Was it correct?"

"It wasn't incorrect," smiled the lama.

I wasn't sure what he meant, but he was content. We met the assistant in the entrance and told him where we were staying. Then we broke outside into the sunshine.

We'd done it! We'd found the Morning Tree! Amazingly we'd found the book and been told it would be handed to us! I felt a deep sense of achievement, and a deep sense of well-being. But at the same time, I had a feeling that I wasn't at the end of my quest. There was more to do? This doubt jostled with the happiness and satisfaction.

Claire had a big smile on her face. She slipped her hand into mine as we walked back to the main part of the town and squeezed it. I stopped and spun her round.

"Thank you," I said. "I couldn't have done it without you."

"That's OK, Indie," she replied. "I knew you needed some help."

Claire and I spent the afternoon going over what the lama had told us. I wondered if I should contact Professor Thurgood and tell him about our progress. But I wanted to see the Morning Tree – hold it in my hands – before announcing our success. And what would our success mean for the rest of the world? I couldn't fathom that until I had read the Morning Tree for myself. Oh, if only I could see the book now! We celebrated that night by going to the best Indian restaurant we could find and ordering a blowout. I half hoped we would bump into Sonam so we could tell him we'd won, but we didn't see him. Maybe the lama had already got to him.

At ten a.m. the next day I was back at the Rest House. I told the attendant I had come to see the old lama. The attendant looked displeased.

"But he asked me to be here," I said.

"He shouldn't have asked you," the attendant replied. "He should know better to rest for his health. But he never thinks of himself. Here I am, charged to look after him, but how can I if he never listens to what I say?" He led me down the corridor into the lama's room. He bowed to the lama, motioned me to sit opposite him and left.

The lama was sitting straight backed on the floor. I could see he really was old, at least in his nineties. I understood what the attendant meant about his health: he seemed well, but he was frail. I had a chance to look around the room. It was very simply furnished with a bamboo bed, a chest with a few religious objects and three low tables. The sound of the stream running down at the back of the courtyard was ever-present. It was very peaceful. Just then the attendant returned bringing tea and plates of delicacies. He poured butter tea for the lama and then, thankfully, Indian tea for me. He bowed again and left.

"Please," said the lama, "have some refreshments. Tea and something to eat."

I helped myself to what looked like sugared petit fours on one of the plates. The one I tried was very fragrant and chewy. I'd never had anything like it before. I took another. And then another.

The lama was laughing. I was too busy eating to notice at first. But his eyes were moist and he was definitely laughing.

"I see you still like sweetmeats," he said.

So that's what they were. I paused, a sweetmeat in hand en-route from plate to mouth. But what did he mean, I *still* liked sweetmeats? I'd never had them before.

"You always loved them in the past," he continued. The lama really was very amused, and he really did have tears in his eyes.

"I…"

I was confused. I didn't know what the lama was talking about, yet I knew he was right – I had always liked sweetmeats.

360

More than that, something was going on inside me, some movement of energy that I knew was significant. Yet, I still didn't know what was happening.

"What do you mean?" I asked.

"You're Thaza," he replied.

I was silent. It must have been several seconds. Yet in that silence everything was happening. I couldn't remember being Thaza, yet bizarrely I knew that I had been. I felt a rush inside, as if layers were falling away.

"I'm… Thaza…"

"Yes," said the lama. "You are the reincarnation of Thaza. You've come to finish off what he – or you – started."

As I say, I couldn't remember being Thaza – I had no flashbacks – but I just knew I had been him. I had travelled to Lhasa, I had studied with Lama Kunchen and I had taken the Morning Tree to Darjeeling. Now I understood why I'd snatched Thaza's manuscript out of Dr Ram's collection in the first place. Why I'd translated it. And why, quite against my personality, I'd pursued this crazy quest to find the Morning Tree. I had taken it out of Tibet. Now I had to reveal it to the world.

Perversely, despite the shock I was feeling, I also felt ashamed. Thaza hadn't been very likeable (God, he'd even killed people). And it had taken me a long time as Daniel to understand the Morning Tree's true importance. I didn't feel I had covered myself in glory.

These feelings were profound, but they took just seconds to go through me, and I felt in a completely different space. As if someone had just told me that the people who'd brought me up weren't really my parents but some slightly disreputable, more exciting couple were instead. I felt as if something very important had just been explained to me, and a lot of things just outside my conscious grasp now made sense. I had been Thaza. I knew it as surely as I was sitting in that room. But how did that lama know? I took a gulp of tea.

"Lama, how do you know? How do you know I was Thaza?"

He tapped his forehead. "I have a certain sensitivity," he replied smiling.

"You mean your third eye is open?"

"Yes. The Keeper is usually psychic to some degree. So it was with Lama Kunchen. So it is with me."

Lama Kunchen? I caught my breath. Had this man known him? I was being given surprise after surprise. "Lama, did you know Lama Kunchen?"

He nodded.

"Then... who are you?"

He smiled broadly. "I'm Jigme."

"Jigme?" It was a common enough Tibetan name, but something was nagging me.

"From Chakpori."

This floored me. I hadn't mentioned Jigme's name in my description of Thaza's account to the lama. He hadn't, as far as I knew, read it either. How could he know the name of the young lama who'd been with Thaza and Lama Kunchen at Chakpori?

"You're..."

"Still alive. I got out in the Dalai Lama's retinue in 1959. I've moved around since then. But now I'm here. Till I pass over."

Jigme. It made sense. If he'd been in his twenties in the 1930s, he'd be in his nineties now. And if he'd been Lama Kunchen's assistant then, why not his successor as the Keeper today?

"I'm... amazed," I said, my heart beating faster at everything that was being revealed. "To think that you are still alive. And that you knew Thaza. You helped train him. You can verify his story. Although... you never liked him," I added uneasily.

"I was young then. I admit I didn't agree with Lama Kunchen's plans for you and the Morning Tree. But I have come to realise he was right and you had qualities I didn't see at the time."

I was still taking all this in. I was feeling hot and sticky, my mind in a whirl, yet there was a distant clarity that knew, however strange all this sounded, that what Jigme was saying was true. Jigme realised the state I was in and suggested I go outside for a moment. I went into the courtyard and let the sun and the breeze refresh me. My heart was still racing and I had to wipe sweat from my face. I stamped my feet on the ground to reassure myself that I was still me, Daniel, alive, here, today.

I was still Daniel. But I had been Thaza. I suppose I'd always accepted that reincarnation existed. I'd never consciously thought about it, but I knew it was a fact for Buddhists and Hindus, and a lot of people in the West believed it too. I realised that I'd always just thought it made sense. But now I'd been given proof of it. Still in a daze, but needing to know more, I went back into the room.

"Are you feeling better?" asked Jigme. "If not, I can recommend some herbs that will help."

"I'm all right," I replied. "Well, surprised. But all right." I settled myself. I was calming down but there was still a lot to take in. "So, I was Thaza," I continued. "I can't remember being him, but somehow I know that what you're saying is true. Can you tell me more?"

"I told you about being Thaza only to assist you with the Morning Tree. I think in your case it will help you to understand what is going on. Why the Morning Tree can now pass to you."

"But I'd like to know more about who I was."

"You can open yourself up to impressions, if you like. But it is far more important to focus on what you need to do with the Morning Tree now, than to know what you may have been in a past life."

"Really?"

"Yes. In many ways, what you were is unimportant. What you are now is important. And especially what you are to do with the Morning Tree."

I reflected on Jigme's words. I wanted to know more about being Thaza, but I was here for the Morning Tree. Maybe he was right.

"The Morning Tree," I asked, "can I see it?"

"Not yet. There is still more to do before I can show it to you. You wouldn't sit in the cockpit of an aeroplane and try to fly it without first being trained. I can't just show you the book without training you either."

"Oh. Do I have to join your order or something?"

"No. You're already part of our order."

"*I'm* part of your order?"

"Yes, just as Thaza was."

"But you distrusted him all along! And he had no idea about religion. In fact, he despised monks!"

"Yes. But he correctly identified a bowl that had been his in a previous life – a life in which he had been a high lama. In fact, a life in which he had been the head of our order."[99]

"He did! He identified a bowl. But he doesn't appear to have any idea what it signified."

"No, he didn't consciously know what he'd done when he chose that bowl. But he was in fact a tulku. It was a good thing he didn't know. It would have confused his personality and lessened his test."

"So Thaza was a member of your order. And I am too."

"Well, if he was, you are, because you and he are the same. This shouldn't surprise you. Why else would Thaza's account come to you? And why else would you be so interested in the Morning Tree?"

"And Claire? And Jim?"

"Yes. They are part of our order too. But the young woman, she doesn't need to know it. She has done very well to help you. She provided you with some clues, did she not? But why was she willing to help? Because she too was with us. But please, don't read too much into this. Everyone dedicated to the truth, to helping the world move forward, is in a sense part of our order. If your inner sight was more developed, you could see for yourself just how many people there are helping the world move to more spiritual times."

---

[99] See page 85 in Thaza's account when Lama Kunchen asks Thaza to choose a bowl from a number laid out on a table. Dalai Lamas and tulkus (recognised incarnations of high souls) often had to identify objects from their past lives. The correct identification would confirm that they were the reincarnated souls of the previous owners of the objects.

At this point the attendant came in. He fussed that Jigme needed to rest and take his medicine and later have his lunch. Jigme succumbed to this nannying with equanimity. He told me to go to the dining room and join the other retired Buddhists for my own lunch. I was to return in three hours and we would carry on talking. I did as I was told and had rice and dhal with six old men – presumably worthy Buddhists who were now living out their days in this home. I resisted the temptation to go back to our lodgings and find Claire; I still wanted to absorb what I'd been told. So, after lunch I hung about in, what I took to be, their common room trying to process all the information I'd been given.

I returned at the appointed time. Jigme was looking rested. I sat down opposite him again.

"Do you have any questions?" he asked.

I did.

"So, I was Thaza," I said, "and now I'm to receive the Morning Tree. But out of all the people in your order, all the people who want a better world, why me?"

Jigme smiled. "You made a promise thousands of lifetimes ago to be of service," he said. "You have had hundreds of lifetimes of training since then to bring you to this life so that you can fulfil your promise."

"Why did I make that promise?"

"You were, how shall I say, on the dark path. Another soul showed you there was a better way. To make amends you decided to be of service."

"You mean, because I was bad, I had to do good?"

"Because you were very bad, you had to be of real service." Jigme was amused – his eyes were twinkling – but I was uncomfortable. I had always felt I was a good person and, I suppose, doubly so for risking so much to find the Morning Tree. But now I was being told that it was only because I had been so bad in the past...

"You don't need to look so upset," said Jigme. "It's natural. A soul starts out unconscious, not knowing right from wrong. Just as a child left to its own devices is likely to be selfish, so is a young soul. But having experienced selfishness, an evolving soul senses there is another, better way."

"You mean people are only good because they've been bad?"

"In a way. If you have built up a great deal of dark light, there is a need to balance it with the same amount of white light. In your case, that meant a promise to help us. All saints have been sinners in the past. It is why they are saints."

"And you?"

"I am not dissimilar to you." He was still very amused, but I was struggling.

"Then… then that means all the dictators and crooks and bad people, like Sonam, they're doing what they should because it's helping them to become good?"

"Eventually, yes."

"So we should let them be as bad as they want? It doesn't make sense."

"The 'bad' people, as you call them, are gaining experience. Unless you have experienced the dark, you won't know there is a better way to live. It is the way to create a better world. A butterfly has to be a grub first."

"But the rest of us have to suffer."

"Don't forget those 'bad' people accumulate karma. If they hurt someone, they have to make amends to that person later. They do not get away with anything."

"But surely it's better they don't hurt people in the first place?"

"Maybe. But don't forget as well, that these so-called bad people also perform a useful role. They help to test those they oppress. If it had been easy for you to find the Morning Tree, if Sonam Prasang hadn't threatened you, you wouldn't have been here so soon, and you wouldn't now know how courageous you really are."

"So a dictator killing thousands of his subjects is all right because he'll make amends to them later, in the meantime he's helping them to see how good they might be, and whatever happens that dictator is on his way to becoming a saint!"

Jigme sighed. "Sometimes a young soul will incarnate as a dictator so that it can experience what it is like being dark as a way to becoming something more. Sometimes a highly evolved soul will incarnate as a dictator in order to give others the opportunity to see where they are spiritually. Don't forget, most souls are fast asleep. Currently the usual way to wake them up is through crisis. People pray when they're in trouble, not when they're happy. So sometimes it is beneficial to have problems, and sometimes high beings will come down to do this."

"Then…" My bearings were being torn from me.

"Then you realise you can't judge others," continued Jigme. "Either someone is gaining necessary experience, or they are helping you to awake spiritually. Indeed, the very existence of problems encourages some to stand up, to confront evil, to show the 'bad' people there is a better way. And those who do so gain more light. I know the rest of the world only sees turmoil and struggle, but spiritually speaking, those creating the turmoil are evolving, and those trying to end the turmoil are evolving. Everything is positive when you see it this way."

This was, in many ways, what Lama Kunchen advocated when he refused to move against Lama Neto. It still felt strange, but there was a logic to what Jigme was saying, and it meant… well, it meant that the world wasn't in such a bad state after all.

"But what if the bad people, the dark, what if they win? We won't evolve then."

"That time has passed. Just as a soul that builds up dark light needs to balance it with white light, so collectively, the weight of dark light that has been built up during the Age of Kali has created the need now for a golden age to balance it. The dark can't win now.

"I can tell you something else too," added Jigme, after a few moments of silence. "We are moving to a new way of doing business. One where you won't have to be bad in order to become good. We are nearing the point when enough souls have done it this way to allow us to move on to where we can learn through joy rather than suffering. Where consciousness will automatically show us a higher way. Collectively, we will be at that point soon. It is one of the changes the Morning Tree will herald."

I was wading in spiritual waters, and it wasn't what I was expecting. But before I could ask Jigme anything else, he suggested I leave and return the following day. I knew how frail he was, so I agreed, although I still had plenty of questions. I was Thaza; Claire and I were part of their order; I was the next to receive the Morning Tree; it was Jigme for goodness sake who was the Keeper; good and bad weren't what I thought. What was going on?

Chapter Thirteen

I went back to the guest house as evening was coming on. Claire had been waiting for me all day and was impatient. I was bursting to tell her my news – that I was the reincarnation of Thaza, and the old lama was Jigme who had been with Thaza in Lhasa. I don't know if I related this badly, but she didn't take it too well.

"You're Thaza?" she said peering at me.

"I know it sounds strange," I replied, "but it feels so right, and it makes sense."

"But Thaza?" she continued, wrinkling her nose. "He wasn't very nice…"

"I know! I don't think he was very nice either. But maybe you needed someone like him to take the Morning Tree to India."

"He killed people, he cheated on women, he was so angry."

"I know."

"He killed *lots* of people."

"I get the picture. But I'm not Thaza now. I'm Daniel. I couldn't kill anyone." Claire still looked uncertain. "I mean," I went on, "we don't know who you were in your previous life. You could have been Lorga."

This was the wrong thing to have said. I was trying to say that although she might have been someone unpleasant in a past life, it didn't mean she was unpleasant today. Instead she just thought I was trying to say she might have been unpleasant too. The thin walls of our room prevented us from shouting, but this didn't stop us having an intense argument. I really didn't want to argue about what Jigme had said, and I didn't want Claire questioning me, and I didn't want her disliking me. I didn't understand what was going on. Eventually she left to get supper on her own.

I was upset and perplexed. I knew I shouldn't tell everyone that I was the reincarnation of Thaza – most people would find it weird or unbelievable – but I had to tell Claire. Why had she been so angry? And why had I got so angry? I didn't follow her; I stayed in and wrote my notes of my conversation with Jigme. I pretended to be asleep when she finally got back. I needn't have bothered, because she gave every indication of ignoring me.

When I returned to the Rest House the next day Jigme sensed I was unhappy. He asked what was wrong. I told him about Claire. I expected him to say that she was bound to feel uneasy knowing I was Thaza, or that she might find it difficult to come to terms with the fact of reincarnation, but he said something different.

"Daniel, when people move up to a higher level of consciousness, those around them can find it difficult to accept. Finding the Morning Tree, succeeding in this part of your task, has enabled you to move up. You have a new light in you, and you are vibrating at a higher rate. Claire has yet to match you, so she finds it difficult. This all happens subconsciously. You are unaware that you have a new light, although you might feel better in yourself, and Claire doesn't see this light, but she does sense it, so she feels uneasy. She probably won't know herself why she is feeling uneasy. But this is natural. She will become accustomed to your new light, and she will match it herself, but for now you need to show her love.

"Besides," he chuckled, "sometimes an argument is good. It helps earth you after going so high. For finding out who you are, and discovering what your task is, are transforming your energy. If you didn't have an argument, you might have had an accident or something to bring you down."

"Bring me down?"

"Yes. Too much light and we can drop our bodies. We literally vibrate too highly and can't stay in the physical plane. We need to balance spirituality with earth energies. An argument, an accident, a big meal, shopping, doing something you enjoy – all these things can help us stay grounded. And staying grounded is important if we are to be any use down here."

Now he was telling me that sometimes an argument or even shopping was good for you. I couldn't fathom it, but I did love Claire, so I would show her love.

Jigme then stood up and walked slowly to the door. He motioned me to follow him. We went down a corridor and into an L-shaped library. His attendant was waiting for us with a pile of books on a table. Was the Morning Tree there? It didn't seem likely as these were relatively modern looking. We sat at the table and the attendant started handing Jigme the books. He showed each one to me, asking me to tell him what they were about. They were Tibetan religious texts, some I knew, but most I didn't. I simply read the titles or passages on the pages that were open.

"I'll say one thing," he said after about an hour of this. "Your Tibetan is better in this life."

He then asked me to tell him which books I thought were the most important. I hadn't a clue, as I'd never been very interested in Tibetan Buddhism. Not knowing what else to do, I quickly scanned the books and pointed to four or five that jumped out at me. Jigme peered at the ones I'd chosen.

"Very good," he said rubbing his chin. "Very good." With that he stood up and started to walk slowly back to his room. I glanced at his attendant, who gave me a noncommittal look, and then followed Jigme out.

"Lama, what is all this about?" I asked as I caught up with him in the corridor. He ignored me and carried on to his room. I followed him in, shut the door and sat down opposite him. He was arranging his robes and looking at the floor.

"There is knowledge in you that has to be activated," he said, still folding his robes. "Knowledge from previous lives. By showing you the texts, you are reconnecting with the frequencies you once had. I dare say you won't consciously recall all that you once knew, but it is inside you all the same. It's all part of preparing you to receive the Morning Tree."

I wasn't sure I understood.

"You haven't been particularly spiritual in this life, have you?" he said. He didn't seem to be criticising me, but I felt it as criticism. "No matter. You have had lives of spiritual importance in the past. These need to be activated now."

"So I can receive the Morning Tree? But why do I need this?"

"Energy is a real thing. The energy contained in the book would burn you unless you are properly prepared. Oh, you could hold the Morning Tree, even read it. But as you are now, it'd probably make you feel uneasy. You might find yourself getting ill, or your life wouldn't work in several ways. You wouldn't connect this with the Morning Tree, but it would be the result of very high energy burning into you. As I said this morning, your partner was upset with you because your energy is higher than hers right now. The book's is higher than yours. That's why I need to bring you up so you can engage with the book properly."

"And this means reconnecting with my past lives of spiritual importance?"

"That is half of it. The other half is to bring through your future self."

My future self? I mouthed the words. Jigme knew I was confused for he smiled and said, "It will become clear. For now, please just relax and humour me."

At this point the attendant came in. It was time for the lama's lunch. The attendant was displeased with me for taking so much of Jigme's time. He told me I could have lunch again with the other men down the hall and all but shooed me out. The old men in the dining room didn't seem perturbed to see me again, although I was when I discovered it was rice and dhal for the second day in a row. Still, at least it wasn't tsampa. For all the romanticism of Tibet, Tibetan food is unpalatable. I chuckled when I realised that's exactly what Thaza thought.

Thaza. I couldn't remember being him. I couldn't remember anything apart from what I'd read in his manuscript. Yet I could feel him. It was as if I was in a cinema watching a film. I wasn't actually in the film, but I was observing the film, following it, and feeling it. In some non-verbal way I knew everything about Thaza. But why couldn't I remember being him?

I asked Jigme this question when I returned that afternoon.

"Ah," he said, "that is not allowed. The emotional energy from your most previous life is usually too strong. If you could remember who you were, it would destabilise you. That is why a soul reincarnating on Earth passes through the ring-pass-not, a band of blue energy around the planet. This strips you of your memories and enables you to concentrate on the life you are about to have, rather than the one you have just had."

"But," I countered, "it would help me to know about Thaza's life."

"Would it? Imagine if you were a pauper but could remember being a king. You would find it much more difficult being a pauper. What if you passed someone in the street and remembered them torturing you? You would dislike them for what they had been rather than for what they are now. What if the beautiful girl you were about to make love to had been your paedophile father in a previous life? She wouldn't be so beautiful then. If you could remember your past lives, it would make your present life difficult, and it would mean you weren't addressing what is in front of you in this life. The life you are in is important, not a previous one you may want to know about. Oh, sometimes we can have impulses from past lives, but only if they assist us in this life. It happens all the time with relationships. You will instinctively be drawn to someone with whom you have had a strong past life connection. It happens in other ways too. In your case, you had an impulse to look for the Morning Tree. But full recollection of what you were – that would not be helpful."

373

"But we can have impulses?"

"Yes, especially with relationships."

Suddenly I wanted to know something very important. "Lama!" I said. "If I was Thaza, who else from that life is around now?"

Jigme smiled and considered for a second. "I can't tell you everything," he said. "It would not be helpful, for the reasons I've explained. But you may as well know that your friend, the American, the one who died, he was your companion in your previous life."

"Norchen?" I asked.

Jigme paused. "No, your other companion, the difficult one."

I thought for a moment. "Not Jorchin?"

"Yes," smiled Jigme.

"J…" The word died on my lips. Thaza's resentful companion, who obstructed him at every turn, who risked the Morning Tree at the end, and whom Thaza had had to kill. How could that be Jim? Jigme read the confusion on my face.

"It is not as strange as it sounds. Yes, that soul hindered you in that life. But that created an obligation for him to help you in this life, and especially to help you find the Morning Tree. It wasn't an easy task. He had to endure great difficulties searching for the book, and of course, he has only been allowed to help you find it but not actually see it for himself, as he so wished. I would say that he has made amends for his past behaviour."

Jim. That nice, eccentric, kind man – my friend – had been Jorchin. I suppose it showed that if you had once been bad you had a need to do good. Even so, I was shaken that a man I had genuinely liked had also, in the past, been someone I certainly didn't admire. But if I was surprised at this, it was nothing to what Jigme said next.

"Lama Kunchen is in your life at the moment."

I was astonished. Lama Kunchen was a truly spiritual man. I'd been moved reading what he'd said. He came across as the best example of a human being I had encountered. I just didn't know anyone of that calibre in my life today. I searched my mind for who he could be.

"No idea?" asked Jigme, amused at my discomfort. "He's your boss."

At first my father flashed through my mind, and then Claire, but neither was my boss. Then a foggy idea formed.

"Professor Thurgood?" I ventured.

"Yes!" said Jigme happily.

I was truly bemused. How could Professor Thurgood, nice though he was, be the reincarnation of Lama Kunchen? I mean, Lama Kunchen had been head of his order, his third eye had been open, he'd behaved with true humility, and he understood, probably more than anyone else, the future spiritual course of humanity. Whereas Professor Thurgood, I knew for a fact, voted Conservative. Apart from the detail that they both spoke Tibetan, I couldn't think of anything that linked them.

"How can this be?" I said. "Professor Thurgood didn't jump when I first mentioned the Morning Tree to him. In fact, he thought it might be a hoax. How can he be Lama Kunchen?"

"But was he supportive? Did he help you?" asked Jigme.

I had to admit he had helped, perhaps more than I realised. He had after all hired me, allowed me to research Thaza's manuscript, suggested I try to find the Morning Tree, said this would be to my benefit and given me money so I could be here today.

"You have to understand," continued Jigme, "that he is bound by the same laws as us all – he is not allowed to recall his previous lives. He is also not the only one responsible for the Morning Tree, others must be given the opportunity to be of service, so he had to step back from the book in this life. After all, his job as Keeper passed to me, and soon it will pass to you. Since he does not have responsibility for the book in this life, he is unlikely to jump, as you put it, when he came across it. You jumped, because the responsibility will soon be yours."

"Even so," I persisted, "Professor Thurgood, well, he's nice, but he's not exactly holy. I mean, I've never heard him complain about the state of the world."

"Maybe that's because he knows the light is winning and the problems today are evidence that things are being sorted out. If the economy is based on the wrong principles, wouldn't a global financial crisis help demonstrate what was wrong? If we are living in a harmful way, wouldn't a natural disaster help us to think differently? And things are moving now in the right direction in so many ways."

"But surely someone of Lama Kunchen's standing, surely they'd reincarnate as someone important?"

Jigme laughed. "People always get confused about these things. Being spiritually evolved doesn't always mean that you are outwardly spiritual as the world understands it. Lama Kunchen was outwardly spiritual in that life. He was consciously sentient to a degree, and he safeguarded the Morning Tree. But you can do important spiritual work without being religious or holy."

"How?"

"It is all to do with frequencies. If you have high frequencies, then you automatically challenge the lower frequencies of negativity and despair. You make changes wherever you go. People who come into contact with Professor Thurgood, as you presently call him, will be brushed by those frequencies. They won't know it, but they will be helped just by being near him."

"So... so he helps the people he meets. But that's not many."

"It is more than that. Frequencies know no barrier in time or space. He could be challenged by negativity in one person but, in that small incident, in fact be dealing with negativity on a larger scale. Similarly, he could look at a map of the world and irradiate the right frequencies into the whole planet. He could even get angry at something and his anger could remove a block in humanity. As long as he focuses correctly, he could have a great impact. As it is, his interest in Tibet is enormously helpful for us and the country."

"But Tibet still isn't free! How can he be helping?"

"He is enormously supportive in ways that can't be seen. Remember, water takes a long time to wear down stone, but one day the stone breaks and then it is obvious what the water has been doing. So it will be with Tibet."

I shook my head. This was still hard to understand.

"One can be a high lama or a road sweeper," added Jigme. "One's external status does not determine spiritual standing. The frequencies, energy or light one has does. In fact, the more spiritual one is, the less one needs one's status to be acknowledged. The highest beings very often are the least obvious spiritually in a conventional sense."

I had to reflect on what Jigme was saying further. But I was beginning to see that the idea that Professor Thurgood had been Lama Kunchen wasn't so strange after all. Not only had he helped me with the Morning Tree, he'd also never liked Sonam. This was making more sense than I realised.

Suddenly I had another question.

"Lama, please tell me, who was Claire?" I was hoping he was going to say Sarangerel, the girl Thaza had truly loved. My heart was suddenly beating faster. Jigme narrowed his eyes and looked at, or beyond, me for some moments.

"I can't tell you everything," he said at length. "Some things you need to work out for yourself."

My shoulders dropped. I wanted to know. Why hadn't he told me? As if reading my state of mind, Jigme added, "Your feelings for her are all that matter, not who she might have been."

I was sure Claire was Sarangerel. I certainly felt a great love for her, and it would be wonderful if she was. But even though Jigme wasn't telling me, I had one more question about Sarangerel.

"It's been bothering me," I said. "Thaza says Lama Kunchen promised that if he delivered the Morning Tree to India, he would be allowed to marry Sarangerel. And yet he couldn't. It rankled with him for the rest of his life. Why did Lama Kunchen say Thaza would marry her when he didn't?"[100]

Jigme paused, as if trying to recall the incident. Then a smile broke across his face. "Yes," he said, "I remember. I was there. I was

---

[100] See page 99 in Thaza's account.

shocked that Thaza was negotiating with him. But he did say if Thaza delivered the Morning Tree he could marry Sarangerel."

"But he didn't marry her! Lama Kunchen lied."

"He didn't lie. He just didn't say it would be in that life."

"But that's cheating!"

"It's good practice. If Lama Kunchen had told Thaza what would befall him, do you think that would have helped him? As it was, he didn't lie. 'Thaza' will marry 'Sarangerel', just not in that life."

So would it be in this one? That would be for me to find out. Suddenly I was impatient to get back to Claire. I made to leave. Jigme was surprised. I think he expected me to stay longer. But he didn't stop me. He just told me to see him again the following day.

I went out into the late afternoon sunshine and walked quickly back to our guest house. I passed a flower stand on the way and bought a bunch for Claire. Backpack and flowers in my hands, I pushed through the door of the guest house into reception and hastened down the dim corridor to our ground floor room. But the manageress – a stout, sometimes stern woman – called out my name.

"Dr Clifton, your companion, she left this afternoon."

I stopped.

"Left?"

"Yes, with her luggage. You haven't fully paid for your room. Please do so before leaving."

"I… I'm not leaving," I said, confused, and trying not to appear so.

"Are you sure?" The manageress arched her eyebrows.

"Where did she go?"

The manageress still looked at me as if she was weighing me up.

"All right, how much do I owe you?" I paid her, and paid for another week. "Now, please, tell me what happened?"

"Some men came. They waited while she packed and then they all left. She handed in her key."

"Which men? Who?"

"Tibetans. I don't know who."

"And she said nothing else?"

The manageress shook her head. I sat down heavily in one of the wicker chairs in reception. A cold fear was creeping over me. Had she left me? We had parted on difficult terms, but I didn't think they were that bad. And who were those men? I knew she had contacts in Dharamsala, but why leave with them?

"One of them was a lama," said the manageress.

I leapt to my feet. "About so high?" I asked, indicating Sonam's height. "And with a more pointed nose than usual?"

The manageress nodded.

"Did she leave willingly?"

"I must say, I didn't think she looked happy."

How could Sonam still be free? And why had she left with him? The world suddenly felt black and dangerous. I cursed the book and all it had brought. What did I care about it, and why couldn't I be left in peace to live a normal life? I had to see Jigme at once.

I raced back through the early evening streets to the Rest House. I hammered on the door until, finally, one of the old men opened it. I demanded to see Jigme's attendant but the old man didn't grasp my meaning. I pushed past and made for the reception area. I put my head round the door into the room leading off reception and saw the attendant in his vest and underpants with his feet up on a chair smoking a cigarette. He was paying rapt attention to an overloud television. He was surprised and then irritated to see me.

I told him I had to see Jigme. The attendant just waved his hands not listening. I had to shout over the noise of the television which was making a bad situation worse, so I barged past and turned it off. A welcome silence filled the room. But not for long. The attendant was furious, and I couldn't understand half of what he was saying. I explained again I had to see Jigme. But the attendant was adamant Jigme couldn't be disturbed: he was meditating, and after that would go to sleep. I was killing him with my daily visits as it was; whatever I wanted had to wait until morning. I flirted with the idea of ignoring the attendant and breaking into Jigme's room, but something held me back. Much as I didn't want to, I left the Rest House and returned slowly to my lodgings.

I still couldn't make out why Claire had left. Either she had been forced to leave – which was chilling – or she was so fed up with me she decided to throw in her lot with Sonam – which was even more chilling. Then I stopped dead in the street. What if she'd been with him all along? She had asked how I would feel if she was the dark. What if she'd been dark all this time?

And if she had been, this would mean there was still danger and the Morning Tree wasn't safe.

I ducked into a bar and ordered whisky. It was foolish, I know, to blunt my senses with drink, but at that point I couldn't think straight and wanted to block out the frightening thoughts that were crowding in. I got back to the guest house hours later, worse for wear, but with the presence of mind to lock my door, jam a chair under the handle and bolt the windows.

I was late getting to Jigme the next day. The attendant let me in without a word.

"I hear you wanted to see me last night," said Jigme, once I'd sat down.

"Yes," I said emphatically. "Claire's gone! I think Sonam's taken her."

If Jigme was surprised, he didn't show it. He merely asked me to explain in more detail. When I'd finished, he asked me what I felt.

"I don't know what I feel! You said you'd take care of Sonam and you haven't. Claire probably hates me. And I'm fed up with everything! I just want to go home."

"I mean, what do you feel about the situation? Do you really feel she has gone with the dark?"

"How do I know? I'm not a mind reader."

"Feel."

"It's too confusing, I can't work it out."

"I said 'feel' – don't use your mind."

"Look, shouldn't you be stopping Sonam? I want to find Claire!"

"*Feel.*"

I looked into his eyes. They didn't waver from mine. I still didn't want to do what he said, but my resistance crumbled. Reluctantly I closed my eyes and a silence spread inside me. I did as Jigme had asked and started to feel if Claire really was the dark. I didn't feel that she was. But then my mind jumped in with the thought that she'd been with Sonam the whole time and I felt cold and bitterly cheated. I opened my eyes and told Jigme.

"Which of those two feelings is more real?" he asked.

"The first one…" I said slowly. "The one that says she's not dark."

"And do you feel she left with Sonam?"

I was in a different space now. I felt into Claire's departure the day before. I know I hadn't been there, so couldn't know what had happened, but somehow I could see, if that's the right word, that she hadn't left with Sonam. He hadn't been there. She'd been unhappy, but he hadn't been there. I opened my eyes, puzzled.

"How…?"

Jigme was smiling broadly. "You are just using your other senses," he said. "Senses you don't know you have, but which you possess – which everyone possesses – if you'd but let go and let it happen."

"You mean, like Thaza was taught to read energy?"

"Yes. There are many words for this. Psychic powers, sixth sense, intuition. It is in fact as natural as our other senses, just less developed at the moment."

"But surely I can't trust this sense? I mean, I can't live my life by it."

"Why not? You've just demonstrated how you can do it. And how useful it is."

"But how do I know I am right? Are you telling me Sonam really has nothing to do with it?"

"I can promise you he had nothing to do with it. He's not under lock and key exactly, but he certainly was nowhere near your guest house yesterday. As to how you know you are right, you just know."

"But how can I just know? I get conflicting feelings."

"Then wait until you get calm, as you did just now, and choose which of the feelings feels more right."

"But what if I make a mistake?"

Jigme laughed. "We all make mistakes. All you have to do is review them and you will learn how to discern what is right from wrong. You don't think I just woke up one day with my powers, do you? You can become like me. All you have to do is recognise these powers are there, let go and trust."

I'd never thought that Jigme had once had to learn what he knew, or that I might one day be like him. It was a tantalising thought.

"And never listen to anyone else," he added. "If you do, you let their energy dominate yours. They might not be wrong from their perspective, but they are not you, and only you are right for yourself."

I was feeling much better now. Claire wasn't with Sonam – I wondered how I'd leapt to that conclusion – although she wasn't with me. I wanted to see her. Desperately.

"OK," I said, "but where is she? Where's Claire?"

"You tell me."

"I... well, I don't know where she is, but she left to get away from me."

"And?"

"It feels like she hasn't left the town. But where is she?"

"Will you see her again?"

"Yes."

"Do you know what to do now?"

"No..."

"Then don't do anything for the time being. Wait until you know how to act."

"That's easy to say, but I want to see her!"

"You have to respect her journey."

A silence fell between us. Absurd as it seemed, I did feel she still liked me and all would be well. As I sat, this feeling grew. Suddenly the horrors of yesterday evening were gone. I stared at Jigme. What magic had he worked here?

"You can go."

Jigme's words started me from my reverie. I could go and find Claire. Only I didn't know where to look. As he'd said don't do anything until I knew what to do, I carried on sitting.

"Or you can trust your intuition and stay."

I knew what I wanted to do.

"I'd like to stay."

He rang his bell and the attendant came in. Jigme asked for refreshments. Suddenly I wanted to receive more from this man.

Chapter Fourteen

I waited until the attendant had finished with the tea and sweetmeats. Then I asked Jigme a question. "Lama, when can I see the Morning Tree?"

He surprised me with his answer. "Now, if you want."

"I'm ready?"

"Not to read it. But you can see it."

He rang his bell again. The attendant returned, a mix of humbleness towards Jigme and wariness towards me. Jigme spoke to him in a dialect of Tibetan; if I hadn't known he was asking for the Morning Tree, I might not have grasped what he was saying. The attendant seemed almost as surprised as I felt, but he remained silent, bowed and left the room. I waited expectantly. Jigme was unperturbed. He motioned for me to have more tea and sweetmeats. After about five minutes – it seemed much longer – Jigme slowly got to his feet and left the room. I followed him out. We went down a long corridor that turned right and into a small windowless room. And there, on the table, was an oversized oblong book.

The Morning Tree.

I felt such a settling inside me, as if something lovely had just fitted into place. I felt at peace and right.

More than that, the Morning Tree was… friendly. I know that's a strange word, but it was as if I had just been greeted by a friend, someone I was only now remembering I knew. Someone on my side who empowered me and was happy to see me.

In fact, it felt like the Morning Tree was gently but indelibly showing me that I was not the uneducated peasant I had assumed I was, but a prince who should accept his inheritance. I was not a grotty human with all my failings but something much, much purer. And what was true for me was true for everyone else. It was a wonderful realisation of the perfection at the heart of life. There was no need for anxiety, struggle or worry anymore.

I looked at Jigme. He was smiling. I was cleaned, balanced and happy. I didn't feel the need to say anything. My human side was surprised at what I was experiencing, but at peace with it all. My soul (or so it felt to me) was beginning to understand who it really was.

I focussed on the Morning Tree again.

It had a dark wooden cover with the engraving of sunlight on mountains as Thaza had described – the same engraving as on the inside of the Younghusband bowl. Jigme was standing back smiling. Without asking his permission, I touched the cover. Again, there was that feeling that everything was deeply right, and I didn't need to feel tainted because in essence I was an incorruptible purity deep inside. The wood was smooth, even soft. I lifted the cover to see an ornate title face with the words 'Morning Tree'. The paper was surprisingly white, thick and fresh. I tried to open the pages somewhere in the middle, but they weighed too much and flopped back. Jigme stepped forward and restrained my arm.

"It's the only copy," he said. "Let's leave it for now."

I closed the cover, looked at it one more time, then followed Jigme out. I felt as if I'd just had an audience with a spiritual being – one who had transformed me – rather than simply seen a book. We walked back to Jigme's room in silence as I was trying to work out what had happened.

"The Morning Tree," I began when we'd settled ourselves down again. "It's made me feel peaceful. As if I am more than I thought – as if everything is more than I thought. It's not because of anything I read in it… I didn't read anything… I just feel lifted up by the book."

"It's energy," replied Jigme, with a smile. "The Morning Tree has an energy of its own. Because it deals with esoteric truths, that energy is very high. In fact, because that energy is dedicated to moving creation up, it will, if you are receptive, lift you up too. However, if you are not that receptive, the book can make you feel uncomfortable because it is so bright."

If I had any doubts of the Morning Tree's importance, I had none now. I was surprised at its effect on me, but it proved it had the power to move the world.

"When can I read it?"

"Not yet," said Jigme with a chuckle. "You still need to be better prepared. Be patient. Your training is going well."

My training? All I was doing was talking to this old man. I was about to ask Jigme what he meant when he continued:

"The next step in your programme is to know more about reincarnation."

I sat up. I knew I had been Thaza. Yet I didn't know much about reincarnation beyond the idea that if things don't go well we might be someone's cat in our next life.

"Reincarnation is a gift because it enables a soul to grow spiritually," began Jigme. "A soul's original state is as an indivisible part of God. It is the Father. It is conscious, because it is God, but it is not aware of itself as God because it has not experienced anything else. So it exists, if you like, in a state of unconscious bliss of being God, but not being fully aware of what that means. So it begins a journey to discover its true nature.

"Like a drop being skimmed off the ocean, a soul is separated from the divine and it begins to fall. This is a bit like the fall from grace as Christianity has it, because it is a separation from the Father. As it falls, the consciousness it had as God diminishes. In fact, the soul falls asleep. It continues to drop away from God, leaving more and more layers of the divine, until it hits Shadowlands. That is creation as we know it, called Shadowlands because it is literally in the shadow of the divine.

"The soul continues falling until it hits the mineral kingdom. For the purposes of this discussion, the mineral kingdom can be seen to be the furthest point from God. Here the soul is fully asleep – that is to say, it has now forgotten that it ever was a part of God. But, although the mineral kingdom is the furthest point from God, and although the soul is asleep, there is a form of consciousness, a limited awareness of where the soul now is. Believe it or not, the mineral kingdom – rocks, minerals and the earth – has consciousness. It is just very slow. But it is a start. The start of the soul garnering an awareness of itself.

"So the soul moves through the mineral kingdom, identifying itself as mineral and gaining in consciousness, until it enters the plant kingdom. Again, it moves through the plant kingdom identifying itself as plant and growing in consciousness until it comes to the animal kingdom. Here, through countless lives, identifying itself as the animal it currently is, the soul moves up through the animal kingdom becoming more and more aware of itself and its surroundings. A dog, for example, is ruled by instinct, yet it has a limited idea of itself as an individual and a limited form of personality.

"Finally, the soul enters human form. As a human, it has a hundred per cent consciousness in a lower way, that is, it knows itself to be a separate living being, although it still has animal instinct. At this point, the first goal of creation has been achieved – that of achieving consciousness of yourself as a separate being, separate from other aspects of life and from God."

"You mean," I put in, "I've been a rock?"

"Yes," said Jigme. "And plants, and insects, and fish and all sorts of animals."

"Can I be an animal in my next life?"

"No. It's a common misconception. One of the jobs of reincarnation is to help a soul build consciousness. Once you have achieved a hundred per cent awareness as an individual human, you don't go backwards. I would add though, in all this, you will experience life on other planets."

"As an alien?"

"Yes. Although it is not much different to being here. It is just another body form to help a soul build consciousness and gain experience. And gaining experience is the second gift of reincarnation."

"Experience? You mean so a soul can know what it's like to be rich one life and poor the next?"

"That, and much more. There are so many aspects to the human condition that one life can't possibly contain them all. Being rich and poor is part of it, as is being fat or thin, popular or unpopular, beautiful or ugly, a success or a failure. Being able to experience these different states – and lifetimes can be given to each – helps satisfy a soul's natural curiosity. But gaining experience means something deeper. Over countless lifetimes, souls build insight, courage, strength and understanding. All souls will have significant lives where they are called upon to demonstrate a growing spiritual understanding, and I don't just mean a lifetime where you might be martyred. I also mean moments – and they can be seemingly insignificant – where you extend a hand or accept a difficult situation in a way that is beautiful in its simplicity and purity. There is always a spiritual reason, in other words, for reincarnating."

Jigme paused. He took some tea. Then he cleared his throat. "And this is the real beauty of reincarnation. However baffling it may be to see someone living a life of poverty, pain or oppression, there will be a positive spiritual reason to it. It may be to pay off karma, or absorb negativity, or learn the difference between right and wrong, or be close to someone else to help them grow spiritually. There will always be a benefit to the soul."

"You mean, all the suffering in people's lives is somehow right?" Jigme had said something like this before.

"It is right for the soul in question, or else the suffering would not be happening."

"So we should just accept the suffering in our lives?"

388

"You should never accept the suffering, but you should accept the lesson it is showing you. As soon as you have seen that, your suffering can go. The world might not be perfect, but it is the perfect place for people to grow through their imperfections. If people really understood this aspect of reincarnation – that their many lives are there to help them become something more – they wouldn't feel bad about their current lives, and they wouldn't criticise other people's lives either. In fact, they'd understand more clearly their own life circumstances and would be able to evolve more quickly. The time is coming when this will happen. Indeed, the time is coming when people won't need to learn through suffering anymore. But whichever way it happens, everything is right and for a beneficial purpose."

I took some tea myself. Jigme was looking tired, and it was getting muggier in the room. It seemed like it might rain soon. But at the same time, he had this glow about him, this energy as I was learning to call it, that was other-worldly.

"You know the way I really like to describe reincarnation?" he continued after a pause. "It's all about love. We all have small groups of souls with whom we revolve life after life, so that we can learn to love each other. So we experience them as mother, brother, lover, sister, wife, father, husband, child, teacher, student, torturer, friend and so on. We experience all the different forms of conditional love until we are able to love unconditionally."

"Torturer too?"

"Yes. Hate is a form of love when you investigate it. It binds you closely to the person you hate. There is an intensity of emotion. And it will eventually, over lifetimes, create a strong love. Hate in this sense isn't wrong. The conditional forms of love are not wrong. They are all stepping stones to being able to love unconditionally."

This made sense. I thought of Jim. I had genuinely liked him in this life, but fought him in the previous one. I suddenly glimpsed a continuing dance between us, weaving in and out of time, leading us closer together. It was the same with Claire. I didn't know whom she'd been to me previously (I still hoped Sarangerel), but clearly I was learning how to love with her.

Jigme was looking at me as I was thinking. When my eye caught his, he started talking again.

"Learning how to love is not the final gift of reincarnation," he said. "The final, and best gift, is that it leads us back to God. A soul, over millions of lifetimes, explores all the aspects of creation. As it experiences more and more of creation – more of everything that exists – it comes to realise that this everything is in fact nothing. It has been rich and poor, it has loved and hated, it has been everything and its opposite, and it slowly comes to accept that it doesn't need to experience anything else. It realises that the myriad of experiences it has had are somehow a fabrication. At that point, the soul realises creation has no more hold over it. The scales fall from the soul and it wakes up to its true nature. That it is, always has been, and always will be, a part of God. At this time the soul becomes consciously aware that it is God.

"Put another way, the soul that was a drop taken from the ocean rejoins the ocean by realising it has been identical to the ocean all along. Only now it is aware of what the ocean is.

"Remember, I said a soul in the beginning is in unconscious bliss. Well now, having experienced itself as mineral, plant, animal and human, having experienced itself as something separate from God, at the end of the soul's journey, rediscovering that it is God, it does so consciously. That is to say, it can compare not being God to being God and it knows at last what God is. It is in conscious bliss.

"This is the whole aim of life. This is the goal that reincarnation supports. After being separated from the Father, and garnering consciousness of itself, then absorbing so many aspects of life, a soul comes to realise that it is not a part of creation but it is in fact God. This is God realisation, and when this happens the soul leaves the reincarnatory programme and goes home to the Father in a state of conscious bliss. Thus the wheel of life, from unconscious bliss to conscious bliss, has been turned."

Grey clouds had, by now, come in making it dark outside, and a breeze had got up cooling the room. Inside the room itself was a peace I had never experienced before. Jigme seemed deeply happy. We sat in silence for several minutes. I just felt this constant opening of a peace inside me. Then Jigme nodded to me. I gathered my belongings and got up to go. I bowed to him before I left.

I let myself out and started to walk back up to the town. I wasn't consciously thinking of all that Jigme had just told me, but the whole of what he had said was simultaneously in me. The low clouds and the breeze were welcomingly refreshing. Soon a few large drops of rain thudded into the dry ground, their dark circles contrasting with the lighter brown of the road. The first rains were coming, earlier than expected. I quickened my pace and just made it to a café as the rain started to hammer down in earnest. I sat at a table under a billowing awning enjoying temperatures that, at last, were as cool as a British summer. I ordered tea and buttered toast over the noise of the rain, and drank in the dank smell of water refreshing the earth while I waited.

As I sat there, I glanced at a neighbouring shop. There was a knot of Indian workers sheltering from the rain. They were speaking their incomprehensible language, picking at their dirty feet and one was chewing and then spitting this black liquid onto the ground. Ordinarily I would judge them, and recoil at how they looked and acted. But I found myself feeling open towards them. I might be one of them in my next life, I now realised, and almost certainly had been something like them in a previous one. How could I judge, especially as I had no idea of their spiritual path? I simply smiled at them and felt at peace.

My mind wandered to my life in London when I travelled on the Tube. I was constantly assaulted by the parade of humanity shoved onto the Tube with me. I usually felt affronted by the men who didn't wash, the sloppy looking youths, the overweight adults who should know better and the countless other odd people. I could see now that I was always criticising them, and always feeling uncomfortable in myself. And yet they must be living lives that were right for themselves, they would be completely different in future lives, and (strange though it felt) I could well be like them in lives to come. I laughed to myself as I realised I shouldn't judge them at all.

Then I saw a beggar sitting under the awning. I realised I didn't know how he'd got to that point, but he wasn't there for me to criticise. Perhaps more importantly, there was no need for guilt. When I'd passed beggars in Dharamsala or London, I'd always felt a pang of guilt. Wasn't it wrong that they should be beggars and I wasn't? I'd feel bad if I didn't throw them a few coins, and bad if I did, thinking I was being taken for a ride (I'd read stories in the press about how much these 'beggars' can make in a day). But now I was free from all that. I simply saw a soul in a beggar's body gaining experience, who had been more prosperous in a previous life and who would be more prosperous in a future one. He wasn't there for me to pity.

Just then the waiter brought my tea and toast. He was skinny, had a big gap in his front teeth and smelled of garlic. Amazingly, I didn't shut myself off from him or wish he hadn't eaten so much garlic. I simply smiled and was happy. He was just another soul with me on this journey called life. I even enjoyed my tea and toast. I had drunk tea and eaten bread, I realised, millions of times before. Curiously, knowing this made me savour this latest experience more fully. Catching all these insights about reincarnation was making me see the world in a different way.

The rain eased and then stopped. A few moments later sharp sunlight hit the ground, and steam started rising as the newly revealed sun began to burn off the recently fallen rain. I paid, and carried on walking back to the guest house. People were emerging from their temporary cover and resuming their briefly interrupted lives. I seemed to be seeing everything for the first time. Housewives shopping; market traders slyly serving their customers; children playing amongst the stalls; a group of toughs gathering outside a shop; an anxious man wheeling an overloaded bicycle; a young couple on a motorcycle threading in and out of people; ones and twos of western tourists buying souvenirs; and more beggars sitting sullenly or clamouring for money. I seemed to be sensing the cares and comforts of all them. I understood what Jigme meant when he said the world might not be perfect but it is the perfect place for people to grow through their imperfections.

Then I stopped in my tracks. If reincarnation was true – if it was really true – then what of death? Death would only mean the end of one act and the beginning of another. It would mean, well, it would mean there wasn't death, not as we understood it. There would still be loss – I would miss my parents when they died, for example – but they wouldn't be dead. I thought of Jim. He'd been Jorchin, and then Jim. He wasn't dead, he was presumably getting ready for another life. Had I known this, I need not have been so upset when he died.

I got to the guest house in a good frame of mind. I even saw the manageress and felt kindly towards her. We were all in a cosmic dance together trying to move forward. Even if she was crotchety from time to time, I knew from Jigme that we were all in some sense here to help each other. I spent the rest of the day writing up my notes and emailing Professor Thurgood (at last) to tell him I had not only located, but also seen, the Morning Tree. It was funny, knowing he'd been Lama Kunchen. I certainly didn't feel so ambivalent about him anymore. In the evening I went round the restaurants Claire and I had been to in the hope of seeing her. I still felt that all was well, even though she'd run off. I didn't catch sight of her, so I stayed at the last one for a solitary supper.

I woke up the next morning feeling unaccountably happy. The sun was shining, the air was fresh and the world was full of potential. I didn't even mind that my eggs were runny or the guest house's coffee was too weak again. I was just happy. I had a new sense of peace within me. All those judgements I'd made about other people and the state of the world were unnecessary. From what Jigme had told me, each soul was on its own journey back to God, each life was a stepping stone to that, and there was a positive reason to everything that happened. If there were people I didn't like or things I didn't approve of, well I'd have to put that down to my ignorance of not knowing why those people or situations were as they were. Certainly, I didn't need to criticise.

But it was something else. Perhaps for the first time in my life, I felt at peace with who I was. Jigme's explanation of reincarnation meant that I had had millions of bodies and personalities. As a result, it suddenly didn't matter that in this life I wished I were better looking, or less insecure, or brought up somewhere more exciting than the home counties. Most likely I had been a hero, an artist, a beggar, a prostitute and a saint (and probably everything else I could think of) in previous lives; I was on my way to being, and becoming, everything in future ones; so I simply needn't worry about the niggles in this life. In fact, for the first time I could see myself as I really was – and it wasn't as bad as I'd thought. I was me, and it was good enough, because I was here for a positive reason. Suddenly this constant low level of anxiety about myself that I'd always felt melted away and in its place was acceptance.

It was a great relief. I wasn't proud of myself. I just accepted myself. I even saw that the aspects of me that weren't right were part of my evolution to help me get better.

In fact, a whole layer of fear was slipping from me. I saw in an instant that most of my life I'd felt compelled to behave in a certain way. I'd had to do well at school, find a safe job, one day get married, buy a house, have children and achieve financial security – all because I thought I didn't amount to much and life wasn't on my side. But I was all right. Life was actually set up to help me move forward. And my failings were parts of me being worked on. We were all in the same boat together (even the animals, rocks and trees, if Jigme was correct). Perhaps best of all, I had all the time in the world. The phrase 'you only get one life' simply wasn't true! I'd never realised just how much negativity about myself, others and the world I'd had inside me.

Even finding a surprisingly thunderous email from Professor Thurgood didn't upset me. He crackled that I was absent without leave, my students had to be reallocated, their exams were coming up and I was in serious trouble. I knew this was mostly an act on his part, but I guess I hadn't fully appreciated how much trouble I might be in. But instead of recoiling in fear, I just felt even and on the right timeline. I would sort everything out when I returned with the Morning Tree.

Jigme hadn't asked to see me that day, and curiously I didn't feel the need to see him, so I decided to have a day off. I remembered reading somewhere that time by yourself is as important as time doing something. I hadn't understood it then, but it made sense now.

So I stretched myself out on my bed, ready to reflect on life, when the door opened. I was about to tell the maid that I didn't need my room cleaned today when Claire walked in. She was looking emotionally battered. I jumped up and held out my hands. She looked at me uncertainly, doubt in her eyes. I sat back down on the bed. Eventually she sat down some distance away.

"I'm sorry I just left," she began, staring at the floor. "We'd had that terrible argument. That lama was telling you such strange things. You were different. I was confused. I suddenly wondered why we were together. I understood helping you find the Morning Tree – that was important – but what now we've found it?"

She looked at me with sorrowful eyes. Then she looked away again. Her hair fell in front of her face. "I left the morning after our argument to walk off my unhappiness in the town. I bumped into Joe. It's not his real name, he's Tibetan, but he calls himself Joe. He's a contact of mine in the Tibetan government. He didn't know I was in Dharamsala. He was very happy to see me. He told me he'd just finished building his house in Talnu[101] and really wanted me to see it. I thought why not? Some space was what I needed. So I checked out and went with him. I tried to write you a note but I was too confused."

I was listening to what she was saying. I wasn't anxious about this Joe character whisking her away to his house in the hills. I just knew that she was in my life to help me, and I was in hers to help her. I also knew we had all the time we needed. This life, a future life, it suddenly

---

[101] A village about seven miles from Dharamsala.

didn't matter. If she was confused about us now, I didn't need to fear I might 'lose' her. But I did need to love her.

"How do you feel now?" I asked.

"I don't know," she replied. "I can't give you any answers. If you're angry, I understand. But I don't know what I want. I was taken up with the excitement of finding the Morning Tree. And then Jim died, Sonam pursued us and then I was in Dharamsala with you. Don't get me wrong. I like you, Daniel. But maybe things have gone too fast. And, well, finding out you're Thaza, and that lama telling you so many things, it's weird."

"It hasn't been a run-of-the-mill relationship," I agreed.

She turned to look at me. "Are you upset?"

"Not at being with you."

She was so soft and beautiful, I wanted to reach out and touch her. But she needed space so I stayed where I was.

"I've been very happy with you," I continued. "You've helped me in more ways than you know. But I understand what you're saying. If you need time to sort things out, then take it."

She swept her hair back and looked straight in my eyes. For a moment we were one. Then she looked away.

"Would you mind?" she asked. "If we take a break?"

"Not if it's what you want."

She was quiet for some moments and then nodded her head. The tension seemed to be draining from her. Then she looked at me with a half-smile and sat up.

"Thank you."

"Shall I book your ticket to London?" I asked.

"Yes, yes. I need to get back to my research. But what about you?"

"I have to get the Morning Tree. As soon as Jigme gives it to me, I'll return."

"When will he do that?"

"I don't know. He says I need to be ready to receive it. I'm not sure what he means. But I am seeing a number of things. Good things.

I know he's giving me some strange information, but there's a ring of truth to it all."

She held out her hand. I took it. She squeezed mine and then let go. She was much more relaxed now.

We spent the rest of the day booking her ticket and going out. We had a good time. I actually felt there was a new, stronger space between us. By which I mean I felt we were operating on a deeper level than before. I wasn't trying to protect myself, or ensure I had what I wanted, or act in a certain way to please her. I was just with her. I can't say how she felt, but she seemed freer and happier too.

Chapter Fifteen

Claire's flight didn't leave for a couple of days, so we had more time together. She was recovering her old self. Even so, I was surprised when, the next day, she said she wanted to see Jigme before she left.

"Only once," she explained. "Look upon it as some sort of closure."

So later that morning we made the now familiar way to the Rest House. I explained our presence to the attendant who told us to wait in the hall while he spoke with Jigme. The attendant returned and said Claire was to follow him. I got up too.

"Not you," he said.

I watched them depart and then sat down again. And got up and walked around. And sat down. And waited some more. After some time I went to look for the attendant, but he was nowhere to be found. I thought of going to Jigme's room but decided against it. If he wanted me, he'd send for me. But what was going on? I listened to see if I could hear anything. There was only a deep silence throughout the Rest House. So I sat down again and literally twiddled my thumbs.

I don't know how long it was – more than an hour – but eventually I heard movement and the attendant came into the hall.

"Now you," he said. I followed him into Jigme's room. It was full of light and air after the stuffy, dark hall. Jigme was sitting in his usual place on the floor, the door open to the courtyard outside. And there was Claire. I checked to see if she was all right and nearly fell backwards when I saw her face. She was beaming, a big smile on her lips, brimming with cheerfulness. I had never seen her like this, not even in the good days. I looked at her questioningly as I sat down, but she just gazed at Jigme. He was looking at me though.

"I see you are changed too," he said after reflecting on me a while. "Quite a lovely light."

Jigme seemed like a father delighted with his son. I didn't know how to take his comment. Claire flashed me a beautiful smile. The attendant came in with more tea and sweetmeats. I was surprised as it was about Jigme's lunchtime and I was expecting us to be shooed out. But Jigme seemed to be enjoying hosting us. Certainly, his attendant made no attempt to tell Jigme what time it was and what he ought to be doing.

As soon as the attendant left, Jigme got up and served us tea. He wouldn't let us do it for him. "I know what I'm doing," he said firmly in response to our protests. He then gave us sweetmeats. All the while he just seemed really happy.

"Claire and I have been talking," he said. "I think we have cleared up a number of things. She's in on this too, you know. She was, I believe, very helpful to you in finding the Morning Tree. I have asked her if she can do one more thing. She has agreed."

I shot her another glance, but she was still smiling at Jigme. "I am deeply grateful to her," he added.

I settled myself and took another sweetmeat. I began to take in the peaceful atmosphere in the room.

"We've also been talking about reincarnation," continued Jigme. "I have been telling Claire how it works. The time is coming when people will know reincarnation as a reality. Then their lives will change, as yours are changing now. If people knew the positive reasons for their lives being the way they were, they would be able to move forward more quickly.

"Perhaps the biggest change will be that people will no longer fear death, for reincarnation means there is no death. This fear of death is one of the most misguided thought forms in the world. When someone dies, people feel bound to have grief, they think they are not human unless they are sad, they think they should feel bad about the whole situation. Even people who believe in life after death or reincarnation feel this way. Why? Has God decreed we should feel sad over something as natural as death? No, it is simply misinformation."

Yes, I was beginning to see this myself. If reincarnation was true then death wasn't real.

"It is misinformation to keep us in fear of life," Jigme continued. "This fear clogs our emotions so that we are uncertain and then plunge down when faced with death. It prevents us from living properly. It is a tool that has been used by the dark lodge to keep people down. Happily, as with so many other things, this will change as people come to know reincarnation is real, and then the fear of death will fade. Life will become so much more fulfilling as a result."

"We really needn't fear death?" asked Claire.

"Absolutely not. The point of death is always painless, however dramatic or violent it may look. And the person who 'dies' goes to a much better place where they rest, review their past life and plan their next one. The person who has 'died' is always much happier than when they were on Earth, for in truth this Earth is a school where we learn our spiritual lessons. Home is upstairs, where we come from. In fact, there is only one birth – when you come into creation – and only one death – when you become God realised. The rest is only life. The rest is only life after life representing evolution and growth."

"But... but where do you go when you die?" I asked. "What happens?"

"The person who dies will feel peace come over them. If they've been ill or in pain, this goes, and they leave their body. They look at their dead body, can see people in this world fussing over them, but they do not feel anything but peace. Then they will be met by someone they have loved who has died before them. It can be a parent, spouse, brother, sister, friend or lover. It can even be a group of people. Whoever it is, they have come to pick them up, so to speak. They engage the person who has just died in conversation. They point out they are dead. Usually the person who has just died won't believe them, but seeing their dead body, seeing the person who had died

400

previously in front of them, convinces them that yes, they are dead in the sense they are no longer in the body they used to occupy."

"What if you don't have anyone close to you who has died before you? What then?"

"You are always met. In that case, the soul will be met by a sympathetic person who will show them they have died. Being met is a gentle transition from this world to the next."

Jigme paused to rearrange his robes. Then he continued. "When the person who has just died realises they are dead, this world fades and the soul and the people who have met them go up to the astral or mental levels, depending on the soul's evolution. The energy here is peaceful, clean and entirely energising. The soul gradually ceases to worry about the people and life they have left behind and becomes engaged with their new surroundings. They often have a period of rest to recuperate from the incarnation they have just had."

"What does it look like, this place they are in?" asked Claire.

"Mostly like Earth but without any of the dross," replied Jigme. "The astral levels more closely resemble life down here. And people usually choose to inhabit places similar to those they have just come from or wished they could have lived in. They don't need to eat or drink, but some do when they first arrive. But remember, the colours, sounds and feelings are so, so much better than on Earth.

"After a time, the soul will review its most recent life. It will go through everything it has done while in that body. It will then judge whether or not it did well. It is important to realise the soul judges itself, no-one else does.

"This is usually a chastening experience! But no matter, for however badly a soul may have done, it will have gained experience, and all experience leads to eventual success. The soul, armed with knowledge about how it has done, will then meet guides to work out what it does next."

"You mean, its next life?"

"Yes, but first they will discuss what the soul wants to do while it is upstairs. Souls don't just sit around on clouds doing nothing, there is always useful work to do."

"Like what?"

"Helping others. This can be through music, literature or plays for those who are less evolved than you. You can also look after the souls of animals. There are many useful things you can do. But then – it can be after minutes, months or years, for time is different up there – you plan your next life. You decide the lessons you want to learn, you review the karma you have and then you search for suitable conditions down here to fulfil what you want to experience. You have guides to help you with this too. Eventually you choose your future parents, you claim the sperm and egg that will be your next body, and then you sort of feel your eyes close up there – you go to sleep, if you like, upstairs – and then you wake up down here as a baby being born.

"Of course, if you are a more evolved soul, you go into the mental levels, everything is more refined and you are not as bound by the human form as you are in the astral planes. But even the highest souls who are still incarnating plan their next life and reincarnate in the same way."

I felt taken by what Jigme was saying. I didn't consciously know the information he was relaying, but it felt right. It felt, well, sensible. As if it was all obvious once it had been explained. Jigme sipped the butter tea beside him. He looked down and then cleared his throat.

"I would add," he continued, "that in the future, when all this is known, people will die consciously. At the point of death, they will know what is happening and will embrace the wonderful new world they are stepping into rather than having to have it explained to them. In fact, people will be able to choose their time of dying simply by consciously going from this world to the next. Currently, people need illness or old age as a way of persuading the animal in them to let go of this life. In the future, when death is properly understood and there is no fear of it, pain or creaking bodies won't be needed. Death will become an easy transition from this world to the next."

I looked at Claire who seemed absorbed as I was. We sat in silence for a while. Eventually she stirred.

"Do you fear your own death?" she asked.

"Absolutely not! I am curious about my manner of death – dying in my sleep seems too boring – but I am not frightened by it. I know I will be moving on to something better. And, you know, I could do with a rest."

"But what about the people who are left behind?" I sensed Jim was in that happy place Jigme was describing, but his wife had been distraught at losing him and I missed him too.

"Of course people close to the person who dies miss that person," said Jigme. "Grief in this sense is natural. But be clear: this grief is for themselves, for what they perceive they have lost; it is not for the person who has moved on. As I have said, that person is always in a better state, even if they died young or in the prime of their life. If someone misses the person who has died, then it is for them to come to terms with their 'loss'. Yes, they will have lost something, but remember, life gives and life takes away. If life has taken away, there is always something it will give in return. You just have to see what it is.

"But if those left behind can realise that the person who has died is happier – if they can actually touch the happiness of that person – then in reality they need not feel grief at all. Really, the true reaction to death should be to feel happy for the one who has gone to a much better place."

This was certainly a new way of looking at death. We were all quiet for a while as we let Jigme's words sink in. Suddenly he chuckled.

"Actually, shall I tell you a secret?" he said. "When someone dies, the world moves up. When someone dies, the negative energy in their body is transmuted. We all build up negative energy. If we have been ill, we absorb a great deal of this energy, for illness is merely negative energy seeking conclusion. When we die, and especially if we die violently or in an accident, we clear this negativity. It is a soul's tip for the life they have led. At the same time, as the soul leaves the body

403

and reaches up to the light, a link is created to higher realms. This allows purer energies to connect with the Earth in that moment. It's funny, people always choose unhappiness when they witness death. But really, the point of death represents a great clearing, and an influx of higher energy. If you could see what was really going on, you'd realise it was beautiful. One day people will come to know this truth about death and see it for what it really is. You will help them do it."

Now Claire looked at me. I could see all her anxiety from the previous days was gone. I smiled back. We waited for Jigme to continue, but he stayed silent. Claire and I didn't move. The silence built and built. It was silence, yet it was also active. I knew Jigme was doing something, but I couldn't work out what. So I just sat there and let it happen.

After some time, the door opened and the attendant came in. He was quiet and, for a change, respectful to us. It was hard pulling myself back from the active silence I had been in, but I became aware the attendant was beckoning us to get up. Claire and I stood up stiffly, smiled at Jigme and followed the attendant out. I thought it was our cue to leave. But to our surprise Jigme got up too and followed us. We made our way slowly to a room I hadn't noticed before. The attendant ushered us in and bade us to sit down at a table laid out with food. Jigme sat down too. When we were all seated, the attendant took the lids from the dishes and served us. It was rice, vegetables and, to my surprise, curried chicken. We started eating.

Jigme didn't have any chicken, but Claire asked him about eating meat. He explained that he didn't eat meat out of choice: he'd seldom had it before entering Chakpori, and never had it since, so he just didn't feel the need for it. But, he said, in this round of existence most people needed the minerals in meat, so it was all right to eat it. However, the time would come, in about 400 years, when we could get all the minerals we needed from other sources, then we wouldn't need to eat our younger brothers and sisters. He added that the world currently was predatory: every creature or organism ate other creatures or organisms to live. Even picturesque coral reefs were actually eating each other to survive. Our eating meat was just another example of this. But eating others was in truth a form of spiritual exchange. When we eat a chicken out of need, we are giving the chicken an experience of the human spirit which adds to its evolution. We are also in debt to the chicken for having given its life so we may live, so we have a duty to help that soul in the future. So even predatory mayhem was not as it seemed.

It was a delicious meal – simple, but full of freshness and flavour. Jigme was still in a good mood, very happy that he could give to us. He asked about our lives in London, our families and our plans for the future. He astonished us when he said he'd been to London – and Paris and New York – some years ago as part of the Dalai Lama's retinue. We asked about the future of Tibet. It would be all right, he told us. We protested it seemed anything but all right, there was still oppression and a fundamental denial of human rights, but he said the course was set to peace and freedom for his homeland.

He then started talking about the world in general. He said it did not seem in such good shape. Claire agreed volubly, saying there was greed, corruption, poverty and a woeful denial of climate change – and she was only talking about Britain, she hadn't started on the rest. But, said Jigme calmly, these crises were signs that things were better than people thought. For crises help break the old and bring in the new. This used to be done by war, but was now being done through social, political and environmental upheavals. These reveal what is going wrong and help show a better way. As the tide receded from a banking crash, for example, it would be possible to see how wrong it was to build up so much debt and how we can live more straightforwardly.

Indeed, the focus on problems was evidence that negativity was being tackled. As people identified things that were wrong, negativity was drawn to the surface. As it was revealed, it could be removed. There were more stories in the press about paedophilia nowadays, he pointed out. Paedophilia had always existed; the heightened focus on it now was so that this twist could at last be taken away.

Political systems will change, he continued. It may seem like an upheaval, but the old has to go and sometimes you need dramatic events to make this happen. However hard it may be to believe, new frequencies will be coming in as change occurs.

Natural disasters perform a similar role. These were likely to grow in number for a while. They too draw out negativity and transmute it. The aftermath of an earthquake was always clean and calm, he pointed out. The planet and its weather system is a being with its own intelligence, and it too was responding to the changes that need to happen. It may be unpleasant to be in a natural disaster, but we should always remember we needn't come to any harm, and it will be happening for a positive reason.

Humanity usually marks time for thousands of years experimenting with a set of frequencies, as we have been doing in this Age of Kali, he explained. But at special moments there are turning points where everything alters. We were in one of those special moments now. Mankind hasn't done anything wrong, and we were definitely not to think the world was on the road to ruin. On the contrary, we were at the dawn of a new light path. Life could get difficult in the coming years as the change is made. But it will never be more than people can bear, and it will lead to something much better.

Of course, people won't see what is happening as positive. In many ways, this is how it should be: people only pray when they are in trouble, so some pain and suffering was helpful in focussing people onto higher ways. But they needed to be reassured. Here Jigme paused and fixed us with his gaze. "Your job," he said, "and that of others like you, is to give hope."

By this time we had finished eating. I had never been as political as Claire, never as worked up about the state of the world, but even so, this was a novel way of seeing what was happening. I could see Claire was thoughtful as well.

Jigme led us back to his room. There was fresh tea waiting for us. Claire asked him about his life. He told us he had been born into a well-off merchant's family in Lhasa. Although he was the elder son, his mother had been very religious, and had persuaded his father to send Jigme to a monastery. So, at eight years old he left home to go to Chakpori. He was less than a couple of miles from his home, but he never returned. His parents would come to see him at religious ceremonies, but he was never alone with them or his brothers and sisters. He was nine when Lama Kunchen became his master. He then endured ten years or so of rigorous training to become a medical lama and be initiated into Lama Kunchen's secret order. Of course, this wasn't by chance; Jigme had come down in this life to be the Keeper after Lama Kunchen. Even so, he said quietly, he had to earn the right through hard work and study. He had just passed his lama's exams, he said, when he met me.

I was temporarily confused until I realised he was talking about Thaza. Jigme said he was sorry he'd been a little proud and suspicious back then but I hadn't been an easy person to get on with.

I asked if he had known if Thaza had been successful in taking the Morning Tree to India. He said he hadn't known at the time, but Lama Kunchen had. I asked if he'd been aware that Lama Neto had pursued Thaza.

"Yes," said Jigme. He had been quite worried, but Lama Kunchen had told him Thaza could handle it; it was one of the reasons he had been chosen. In fact, Jigme added, he'd always thought that Lama Kunchen could have stopped Lama Neto going after Thaza, but he never did. I asked him what he meant. Jigme said he thought Lama Kunchen could have asked the Dalai Lama to keep Lama Neto in the Potala for longer when Thaza left Lhasa. But Lama Kunchen indicated to the Dalai Lama that he could release Lama Neto early. I shifted uncomfortably in my seat. Why would Lama Kunchen want Lama Neto to follow Thaza?

Claire asked what would have happened if Thaza had failed.

"Sometimes you have to risk everything on one throw of the dice," was Jigme's reply. "We had done what we could to make the dice roll the right way. We had to show trust as much as Thaza did.

And he didn't fail. Just as you haven't failed in this life, for here you are."

Jigme said Lama Kunchen dropped his body in 1936 – three years after the Thirteenth Dalai Lama died. It was then that he became the Keeper. He'd always known that one day he would be following the Morning Tree out of Tibet. He had resisted the idea – he didn't want the Chinese to invade – but he had come to recognise how, in the bigger picture, it was right. Claire started at this, but Jigme said that Tibet had to offer its spiritual treasures to the outside world, and invasion was the only way to break down the barriers in Tibet to relations with foreigners. The Chinese invasion had forced a large number of Tibetans into exile, including the Dalai Lama. It had focussed people's attention onto Tibet and what it represented. At the same time, the material condition of life in the country was slowly improving.

"But the destruction of Tibet's culture!" protested Claire.

"It was painful, but the essence has been retained, and there were many things in Tibet that needed to change," replied Jigme.

Jigme told us that he arrived in Dharamsala with the Dalai Lama in 1959. He was active with the Dalai Lama in religious and political affairs for several years, but then a different feeling came upon him. He began to long for quiet and contemplation. So he asked for permission to leave and went to live in several remote monasteries. His work as the Keeper was coming to the fore. It was in this period that he came to understand so much – and so much of what Lama Kunchen had told him years previously began to make sense. He knew then that he had to learn English, and he had to prepare himself to hand the Morning Tree to a westerner. So he returned to Dharamsala in 1975, studied English, and came to live in the Rest House. He was reunited with the Morning Tree then and kept it with him in a special section in the library. He'd been waiting for me ever since.

"How did the Morning Tree come to Dharamsala?" I asked.

"The Indian to whom Thaza gave the book had instructions from his master to travel to Dharamsala and lodge it with the family of another of his master's followers in the town. That family looked after it. Actually, they were local solicitors. The Morning Tree was in their vaults with other documents. Lama Kunchen had told me that the Morning Tree, which deals with natural law, would be kept by worldly representatives of the law, so when I was ready, I went round the established firms to locate it."

"And they gave it to you just like that?"

"Yes. They had been given instructions all those years ago that they had to hand the Morning Tree on, and to a monk."

"But what if a member of the dark lodge – a member of the dark lodge as a monk – had asked for it?"

"They would have had to have had the correct password. It had been given to the family, and of course Lama Kunchen had told it to me. In the event, I was the only person who ever asked for it. I would add that you inflicted a heavy defeat on the dark lodge when you refused to give them the Morning Tree and took it to India. Their link to the book was largely severed then. They tried to find it – as you know, they have been trying to find it until very recently – but their power was ebbing. They didn't know where to look. The simplicity of that family's love for their master also shielded the book from view. And who would think to look in a solicitor's vault full of papers for the Morning Tree?"

I had a number of other questions about the book, the secret order and what I was to do with the Morning Tree, but I refrained from asking them because Claire was there. This was her time with Jigme, and she seemed to be enjoying it. By now it was late afternoon. The attendant came in and started clearing the tea things. As he was doing that, Claire reached out and touched my hand.

Jigme must have seen, for he said, "You two have been together a number of times. It hasn't always worked, but you are learning. The most important thing is to respect each other's wishes and remember why you met in this life."

Claire and I looked at each other. The attendant reappeared and Jigme said, "I am told I have to rest a while. It has been my honour to see you," he said to Claire. "Always remember who you are." With that he bowed his head to her and we left.

We didn't really talk about our time with Jigme. We were both absorbing what had happened. Although I did ask Claire what she thought Jigme had meant by people like us giving hope.

"Telling people that death isn't real," she said, "but reincarnation is. Telling people that life has a spiritual purpose and there is always something positive to what happens. Showing them that despite the turmoil, the world is moving to a better age." There was a new timbre in her voice as she spoke.

Claire spent the rest of the day packing while I wrote up my notes. We went to the pizza place we'd been to on our first night. And the next morning I went with her to the airport to help her catch her flight to Delhi and then London. We were both very different from when we had first arrived. We hugged goodbye and I told her I would see her back in the UK.

But when would that be? When I got back to the guest house there was an official (I'd say officious) email from the Dean's office summoning me for a disciplinary hearing at SOAS the following Monday. If I failed to appear, I would be constructively dismissed. If I was given the Morning Tree in the next day or so I could just about make it. But I had no idea when Jigme would give me the book.

I tried to compose an email in reply, but found I couldn't. I couldn't explain why I'd had to leave so suddenly and without giving any reason; I couldn't prove my life had been in danger; and I couldn't say I'd told Professor Thurgood because that would compromise him. I didn't want to ruin his career as well, especially as he was so close to retiring. But I didn't want to lose my job either. As a result, I spent an uncomfortable night, doubly so, as with all the insights from Jigme I'd hoped I'd be past such fearful feelings.

I returned to Jigme the next day but was told he was unavailable. I didn't believe the attendant, and demanded to see him. In the end, I was shown Jigme's empty room and told that he'd gone to the Dalai Lama's residence. I asked if I could wait, but the attendant said Jigme would likely be there the whole day and would need to rest when he returned. I had no option but to leave and spend the day kicking my heels around town.

Finally, the following day, he could see me. He asked about Claire, and then said that now she was gone we had more time to work together.

"But lama!" I blurted out, "I don't know how much more time I have." I told him about my disciplinary hearing at SOAS and how I needed the Morning Tree today if I was to get back to London on time.

Jigme sighed. "It seems you have a choice," he said. "Either go home without the Morning Tree and save your job. Or lose your job and wait for the Morning Tree."

"Then let me go and come back," I said.

"Your training can't be interrupted. I don't have much time left."

"But a few weeks?"

Jigme was unmoved. I felt like Thaza, helpless in the face of his master's insistence on sticking to a timetable that he wouldn't reveal. I tried one more time.

"Lama, surely you don't want me to lose my livelihood? If I am the next to receive the Morning Tree, why can't I receive it now and go home?"

"The Morning Tree embodies higher purpose. We bend our lives to serve that purpose. We don't twist it to fit into our lower purpose."

"But surely there's a way I can go to London and still complete my training?"

"I know what is needed, you don't. You still have free will. You can leave if you want to. But if you choose the Morning Tree, then you must stay."

I had to decide. I wanted my job, definitely: there were so few openings for people like me, I was at the most prestigious place for the post I had, and if I was fired from SOAS, most likely, I wouldn't work teaching Tibetan again. Then what would I do? And what would I do for money, not just in the future but next month?

But then could I return home without the Morning Tree? That felt like something I would regret for the rest of my life. I suddenly realised I felt right with the Morning Tree; I felt strong and fulfilled. But without it, back in my job, well, it just felt indifferent. But, protested my mind, I can't be stupid and give up the job and income I was so lucky to have! But equally, could I go against what the energy was telling me?

I looked at Jigme again, searching for help, but he was impassive.

"I'll stay," I said. I half winced as I said it, but at the same time I detected a new strength. I would stay for the Morning Tree and take my chances.

"Then I'll see you tomorrow," said Jigme.

I winced again. Why couldn't he carry on with my training now? But as I had the thought, I realised I was still trying to dictate what happened. I had made my decision. If I really meant it, I should give up my old life and trust this man's plans for me. So, without saying anything, I got up and left.

As I was at the door Jigme spoke softly. "You will be looked after," he said. "If you focus on higher purpose, your lower purpose is always taken care of."

Chapter Sixteen

My new resolve was sorely tested over the next few days. I reported to the Rest House every morning at nine a.m. Jigme would see me, but only to ask me to do certain things, never to talk to me as he had before.

He asked me to read Tibetan tracts. Not all of these were religious. Some were just newspapers, and old ones at that, and some were just descriptions of Tibet. I felt at the time it was ironic, since I probably wouldn't need my Tibetan once I was thrown out of SOAS.

He made me clean religious artefacts. These could be gold Buddhas, silver prayer cups, prayer wheels and even wooden bowls. I was aware Thaza had picked out his bowl from a previous life, and that selecting objects like this was one way a tulku was recognised, but I can't say I had any significant feelings as I cleaned them.

And he made me do housework – sweeping floors, washing dishes, weeding the compound (I startled a small black snake while I was doing that which nearly gave me a heart attack), and he even made me clean the bathrooms and latrines. Worst of all, I was under the command of Jigme's attendant for these chores. He enjoyed my forced labour. I disliked having to do his work while he ate or watched television or had friends round, all of them grinning at me as I toiled at my tasks. It was hard not to resent the apparent senselessness of it all.

My resolve was further tested when I received an email from the Dean's office to say I had now been fired from SOAS for wilfully abandoning my job. I understood their decision – from their point of view they had little choice. The old me found it hard not to defend myself, it felt as if I had let Professor Thurgood down, and it still gnawed at me about what employment I could have when I finally returned. But the new me realised that there was a positive reason for what was happening. I was sure far worse things had happened in previous lives. And really I was all right for now. Besides, hadn't Jigme said if I served higher purpose my lower purpose would be taken care of? Who knows, once I had the Morning Tree and published it, SOAS might see what an asset I actually was, or maybe I'd be snapped up by another university.

I did tell Professor Thurgood by email about my progress. He replied saying he had tried to stave off the inevitable sacking (*I even lied Daniel and told them you were one of the best linguists we had*, as he delicately put it), but he hadn't been able to prevent the authorities taking action over my absence. Still, he was encouraging about finding the Morning Tree (*a true scholastic achievement, and one bought at no little cost to your own safety, as I know*), and he urged me to secure the book and bring it home.

I appreciated Professor Thurgood's acknowledgement of what I was accomplishing, but knew the Morning Tree was more than he (as Professor Thurgood in this life) realised. I still didn't know what the book said, but I was certain it would bring about the changes Jigme and Lama Kunchen had promised. I was actually free to publish the book as I saw fit now I'd been fired from SOAS. That was the silver lining in my dismissal, and an example of there always being something positive.

I told Claire what was happening too. She'd emailed to say she'd returned safely and was picking up the reins of her old life. But I never got a reply to my message because shortly after sending it SOAS stopped my email account. I didn't think they'd be so efficient.

Jigme's new regime continued for three weeks. It was now the beginning of June. I wondered how much longer he'd be before giving me the Morning Tree, not only because I was impatient, but also because I was running out of money. On more than one occasion I nearly asked him. But I held my tongue. I had to show obedience.

Then, one afternoon, I was summoned from cleaning the kitchen floor and asked to appear in Jigme's room. He had shut the doors to the courtyard and drawn the curtains so the room was dark. He had also lit several sticks of incense. I was surprised. It seemed like a religious ceremony.

Jigme was seated on the floor as usual, but he'd placed a large gold Buddha behind him. I sat down and he rang a bell – not to summon his attendant, but to start the ceremony. He began by intoning prayers in Tibetan. He was speaking more and more quickly and loudly. I could feel an intensity rising in the room. Suddenly there was a bang – it wasn't a noise he'd made but more a bang inside me. Then he rang his bell again and there was silence – a clear, growing, dark silence. I felt the silence surround and physically hold me. Then he spoke in English.

"Feel a point of light in the distance. See its brightness. See this light full of love coming closer. It stops some way in front of you and forms into a figure. It beckons you to come forward. Go up to this being and receive its light. This is your future self. It has completed its journey; it knows everything. Ask it anything and wait to receive its answer. Ask it to give you a message, one word that will serve as a tuning fork for you in this life. Receive this word. Now open again to its light. Allow it to merge with you. In truth, time does not exist. Become your future self, your higher self. Feel your success, your completion, the Father's plan for you and creation. Become all. See the being give you a touch. This touch is a white rose. The white rose will now guide you in all that you do. The being bows as you acknowledge its presence and then with a smile it withdraws. Now, slowly come back to your body. Merge with your body and reengage with the here and now."

This might have taken moments, but it felt like ages. Jigme was silent for some minutes. Although he had told me to come back, I kept my eyes closed. I had followed his meditation, felt all he'd described, glimpsed the images he'd painted, and felt something significant that I couldn't put into words. I had been present and not

415

present at the same time. It was hard to say what had happened, except that something had.

And the word he had asked me to receive. A word had come. It was 'trust'. Trust what is being given. Trust all is well. Trust my higher self. I had also clearly seen the white rose Jigme had mentioned. In fact, it had come with the word trust. I was definitely in a different space.

He rang his bell again. Each chime felt as if it was playing the atoms in my body in a delightful way. My cells were alive with this wonderful spirit. Literally, I felt another type of life – a divinity – infuse me.

When the chimes stopped I opened my eyes. I felt very comfortable, if a little bemused. Jigme was looking tired. I waited for him to speak. Eventually he said I could go. I went back to the kitchen and continued cleaning the floor. Obviously I was the same, yet I felt completely different. Although I was doing the chores as before, I was in another dimension. After I'd thrown away the dirty water and rinsed the cloth, I put everything back and looked for the attendant. He was nowhere to be seen. The Rest House was completely silent. So I made my way back to my lodgings.

I was unperturbed, quiet. The car horns, the throng of people, the rickety chair I sat on during supper, even thoughts of SOAS – nothing disturbed me. Everything just passed through. The headlines on the evening paper, the mother slapping her child, the beggars in their usual place – I saw it all but knew there was nothing to worry about. I hadn't a clue about my immediate future, but I didn't need to worry about a thing. It was as if everything had been completed and was all right. I just smiled. When I went to bed that night, even the lumpy mattress I'd put up with for the past two months was a perfect place to lay my head.

The next day I returned to the Rest House and got on with the chores I knew I'd be asked to do. I was sweeping the kitchen floor when the attendant came in and asked me to go to Jigme's room. I felt no ill will towards the attendant for the niggles between us in the last few weeks. I made my way to Jigme's room, not wondering for once what he might have in store. I entered, bowed and sat down. Jigme was smiling. He studied me for some moments and then said:

"Your frequencies are completely different. I don't know if you are aware of it, but you have completely changed. You are ready."

I didn't feel a surge of excitement – which, in retrospect, is surprising. Hadn't I been involved with the Morning Tree for the last year and a half? And given up my job and old life to get it? I just waited. Jigme rang a bell – one I'd never heard before, with a different chime. Moments later five monks came into the room. They bowed to Jigme, then two of them helped him to his feet. They walked either side of him as he left the room. The other three didn't move, and I realised I was to follow Jigme. So I did. The three monks then fell in line after me.

We made our way to the back of the building and into a small chapel. There was a funny smell – it took me some moments to work out it was charcoal. Then I noticed a burning brazier through an open door leading to a courtyard outside. On what I took to be an altar (although Buddhist chapels don't have altars) was the Morning Tree. Again I felt a lovely energy coming from it. I wondered briefly how I was to get it on the plane – it was too big for hand luggage yet I certainly didn't want to check it in – but then I was pulled back to the present by Jigme and the monks who were now sitting in a circle, on cushions, on the floor. There was one cushion inside the circle facing the altar, so I sat there. Jigme rang another bell and the five monks started intoning prayers in Tibetan. I caught some of what they were saying – they were stating the importance of the Morning Tree and their commitment to looking after it – but I wasn't really listening. I found myself focussing on the book in front of me. Focussing and still inside.

At various points in the service one or more of the monks would take up the litany, or light sticks of incense, or ring a bell. By now, I wasn't paying attention to the words or external events; I was just becoming more and more aware of the Morning Tree itself. Tendrils of light from it wrapped round me, and a strong, clear energy washed through me. Then suddenly, I was standing in tall white flames in the middle of the Morning Tree. The flames didn't burn, but they touched the essence of my being. At this point I saw and heard everything in creation. The reason for existence, for all that had happened and for all that would happen, was shown to me in that instant. And it was, simply, for us to return to the Father.

The service was carrying on, but I was in another space, imbibing another reality. Then slowly the images faded and I became more aware of myself. But I was so much bigger and cleaner inside than before.

Then, in what seemed to be the end of the service, Jigme, followed by each of the monks, got up and touched the Morning Tree. Jigme sat down again, but the five monks lined the back of the chapel. Was this the moment the Morning Tree was to be passed to me?

Jigme was silent for several minutes. I was still absorbing what had happened, but at the same time I couldn't help pick up a strange sense of sadness. I didn't know where it was coming from. I waited. As I did, I felt the sense of the book and the white flames come back, but this time it was different. Instead of standing in the Morning Tree's flames, the Morning Tree and its flames were inside me. I could still feel everything in creation, but now I was a vessel holding creation. In fact, the Morning Tree was like a baby inside me. I was now looking down at the book as a father would to a new born, but how could this be? Then I felt a kick from the Morning Tree, as if it had grown all at once to an adult, and I knew then that I had merged with it completely.

Still Jigme was silent, but I moved. I got up and stood in front of the Morning Tree. No-one tried to stop me, and I knew I wasn't breaking any sacred protocol. The Morning Tree was mine now. I touched the wooden cover and felt its energy course through me. The book suddenly felt familiar. And I knew I was equipped to look after it. At last, I could read it and know what it said.

The next thing I noticed was Jigme standing the other side of the altar. When our eyes met, he addressed me in English. "Let us take the Morning Tree outside."

The five monks lifted the Morning Tree off the altar, and we followed Jigme into the courtyard. Jigme turned to face me. He had a cup in his hand. He dipped his fingers into it and sprinkled me with water. "Receive the treasure of life," he intoned. "Safeguard it with your life. You are now in service to the higher truth." He then nodded to the five monks.

They still held the Morning Tree between them. I wondered how they would hand it to me and if it would be too heavy for me to hold. But instead of moving towards me they went to the brazier. I could feel its heat from where I was standing.

Then they heaved it in.

Wordless screams sounded in my head. They were burning the Morning Tree – *my* Morning Tree – the sacred text I had struggled to find and had to release to humanity! What were they doing?

I quickly looked at Jigme. He was impassive and obviously at peace with what was happening. I rushed to the monks and tried to break into the circle they had formed around the brazier. They blocked me with their backs and carried on prodding the burning book with iron rods. Moments later I pushed through only to stagger back as the flames and heat from the fiercely burning paper scalded my face. I shielded my face with my hands and looked to see what I could salvage, but it was hopeless. I watched with incomprehension as the Morning Tree crackled into ash before my eyes.

Fumes were in my nose, ash was floating from the brazier, and some was falling onto my hair and clothes. I stank of smoke. By now the monks had put all of the Morning Tree into the fire and were standing back. I stared at the brazier mesmerised and confused. When the flames had died down, although the embers were still red hot, I turned to face Jigme. It was no use being angry, but I couldn't help it.

"What have you done?" I cried. "You promised you'd give me the Morning Tree, but you've destroyed it! What sort of Keeper are you?"

Jigme looked compassionate. "I have given you the Morning Tree," he said. "Just not in the way you expected."

"Rubbish! The book is burnt to cinders! I never even read it!"

"But you did. In the chapel. I saw you. You read the Morning Tree and absorbed it all."

The images and feelings I'd had during the service. "But what use is that?" I demanded.

"More than you can imagine. Come inside and let me explain."

I stood my ground. I was fed up with these games! I stared at the brazier, unable to pull myself away from the remains of the Morning Tree, yet ready in a heartbeat to leave that Rest House once and for all. But something in Jigme's manner blunted my temper. I waited – still angry, still shaken and still confused. Then I followed Jigme back to his room. It didn't seem so hallowed now that he'd burnt the Morning Tree. Jigme was sitting on the hard floor as usual. I grabbed a cushion from the side. I didn't see why I should be uncomfortable anymore. I also didn't wait for Jigme to speak.

"I'm at a loss…" I began.

"No," he replied, "you have gained."

"But how? All I wanted was the Morning Tree. You said it would be mine to look after. I've lost my job, run out of money, had my girlfriend bale on me – all for the Morning Tree! I needed to bring it home, to show others it existed, to tell them about it, to use its wisdom to help humanity. Lama Kunchen said all the answers were there. We *need* it. We're not all holy monks who can impassively accept suffering. The rest of us need help. Surely the Morning Tree could have done that? And all you've done is burn it!"

"The Morning Tree is all you say," replied Jigme evenly. "And it will help humanity, but not in the way you imagine. I have told you enough for you to know that this is an important time in the spiritual history of the planet. It is actually the most important time, for it marks a decisive and irrevocable change in ways even the Morning Tree didn't fully explain. Suffice it to say, the past is over and a new and amazing future is beginning, one where all of creation can at last evolve towards perfection. This changeover is happening now. When a sperm fertilises an egg, the mother is not consciously aware of it, but it is definitely the start of a new life. It is the same with this time of spiritual change. Most people are not consciously aware of it, but it is definitely the start of something new, and it is happening now. Souls are aware of this change, which is why there are so many people on the planet today. Of course, externally things don't look rosy – there is economic turmoil, bitter conflicts, overcrowding, unhappiness, natural disasters and more to come. But spiritually – in the womb, so to speak – the most important change is taking place. A new life is being born, not just for humanity but all life forms, which will eventually make the divine a reality and consciousness a truth. This has not happened in creation before. And it will transform everything.

"The Morning Tree talked about this change. But the book represented old natural law and the old way of doing things. It was esoteric knowledge, known only to a few, and acquired only after lifetimes of painful study. It was right for its time, for humanity then was not ready to accept the information in the book. But it is not right for the new age that is beginning.

"This new age has a new way of doing things, a new natural law. This new natural law, the spirit of the divine, isn't going to hide in monasteries anymore but is going to reside in every person in their normal lives. And it is not going to be filtered through the mind, as old natural law was, but lived directly – it will become a lived experience. You've glimpsed this with reincarnation. To you, now, it is more a reality than an idea. But this is only the beginning. All of humanity will one day know reincarnation, the truth of life, the breath of the divine and so much more consciously, directly, as an experience. It will be as real to people as being hungry, or being in love, are today.

"People will in fact become sentient. That is to say, they will understand the divine reason for life, and see the divine in all life.

421

"These experiences, this sentiency, will not come through words but through frequencies. Frequencies are energy charges. They inform and create our reality. Higher, more spiritual frequencies mean we will experience higher, more spiritual lives. You have the frequencies of the Morning Tree inside you now. That has been happening all the while you have been with me, and it happened completely just now in the chapel. I think you felt it too. But more than that, the new frequencies which the book said were coming – the frequencies that will make the divine a reality, the frequencies which are actually an aspect of the divine – have entered you as well. You might not recognise it, but they are there. The Morning Tree, in giving itself up, has transformed itself into the new. But it is not something like the old book that you can pick up and study. It is more powerful than that. It is the new frequencies containing the answers that will reveal themselves now and over the coming generations.

"These frequencies do not suffer from having to be interpreted by your mind. They just reveal themselves in your life. You cannot lose them. They cannot be corrupted. They are there now, untainted forever. And as you have them, you will irradiate them to other people; in fact, to all life forms. Frequencies are passed on by those who have them to those who do not – like a virus, only in this case a good virus that everyone will catch. This is what you will now do.

"In burning the book, we released the old and allowed the new to come in. You may lament you do not have the Morning Tree to show people, but that is just the old way talking. You have something much more powerful, for you have the frequencies that people need inside you. You said the world needed the Morning Tree; the world still has the Morning Tree, but not in the form of words which can be misunderstood and argued over, but as divine frequencies that will lead to direct consciousness. I burnt the book deliberately to mark the end of the old and the beginning of the new, and to help show you the new way of doing things. Your anger and confusion are understandable. Indeed, you are not the only one to feel this way – I have faced opposition from others inside the order. There will even be a sense of sadness at what has been lost. But in time you will come to appreciate how much better the new way of doing things is."

I'd followed everything that Jigme had said, but I still didn't understand. "But everything was explained in the Morning Tree," I countered. "Why couldn't we have the words in the book to help us?"

"Because words don't work. You can tell anyone about reincarnation, but if they have the frequencies of an un-evolved soul the words won't mean anything. They may understand the words, but they won't believe them, and they won't act accordingly. Millions today say they believe in reincarnation, but still they act as if this is the only life, the only thing that is important, rather than feeling the truth and beauty of reincarnation and the fact that there is no death, only another life, another opportunity to work your way back to God. Give people the words of the Morning Tree and they may know more about how life works, but without the right frequencies they will be just as unhappy as before, just as selfish as before and just as despairing as before."

"And these frequencies," I said, "they really are better?"

"Yes! They govern how we experience life. They condition what we are able to do. All matter, all thought, all emotion are vibrations or frequencies. In the Age of Kali, the frequency range is low and restricted, hence the wars, depression and anxiety. Higher frequencies were available only to a few. But today higher energy is coming into the planet. As I said, it is actually divine energy. As a result, people will have better and more beautiful experiences. Over time they will become sentient. They will have a direct understanding of the divine spirit that has always existed but has never been recognised. Words mean nothing without the right frequencies to inform them and make them real. If you want to change the world, you need to work with frequencies – that is what the higher beings charged with overseeing humanity are doing. So, yes, it is much better to focus on frequencies than words. And frequencies are contagious. If you walk into a room of old people depressed about death, you will soon feel depressed yourself, even though you might be in the best of health. Conversely, if everyone is happy because their team has won the world cup, you will feel uplifted even if you don't like football."

I pondered a moment. "Then... then I don't need to talk about what has gone on... or publish anything?"

"You can if you want, but as I've said, words aren't the key, frequencies are. If you write or talk, people will probably disbelieve you, or argue with you, and you will waste a lot of energy. But they can't disbelieve or argue over frequencies they subconsciously pick up and then manifest without knowing. It's like a growing child – they are not aware how they might be changing physically or emotionally, they just grow."

I shook myself. This was all new. Jigme continued:

"There is in fact no need to publish anything at all as you have the new frequencies inside you now. You are the Keeper. You will irradiate the Morning Tree's frequencies – these new frequencies of divine understanding. You will overshadow other people with them. You will cause a shift in consciousness, not just in the people you meet, but in governments, companies, organisations. Anyone who opens up – and there are others like you – anyone who catches what you and these others are giving – can help to bring about this shift in consciousness."

I was beginning to realise that perhaps there was a strange logic to what he was saying. Just as we still don't fully understand how, for example, our bodies, cells and DNA work, so we don't fully understand how frequencies or energy actually govern our lives. What Jigme was saying made some sense, but still there were so many questions.

"But I'm only me," I said. "How can just one person make such big changes?"

"Frequencies have no barrier in time or space. But they do need to be anchored in the physical plane. Now that you have absorbed the Morning Tree, you are the first anchoring. You have the frequencies. You will now irradiate them. You won't be able to stop it. And the frequencies you broadcast won't be able to be stopped. If you walk into a bank, you irradiate into the whole banking system. If you watch a football match, you link into all the other people watching that match. If you read an article on politics, you are connected to the whole political system. If you smile at a child you pass in the street, you smile at all children. We are all – everything is – interconnected. I think you know that really. And each person you influence, and in the beginning especially, each person you meet physically, will catch something of the new frequencies. So yes, one person can make big changes. But you are not alone. As I've said, there are others like you, doing things like you, with spirit like you. They are not connected to the Morning Tree as you are, they deal with other aspects of the divine plan, but it is all happening now."

This was a lot to take on board, but hadn't he said something similar about Professor Thurgood working in this life? I began to realise I wasn't fighting the information Jigme was giving me, however much I still had to come to terms with it.

"Will I be aware of what I'm doing?" I asked.

"Not at first. And that is how it should be. If you knew exactly how much you were doing, you might be tempted to be prideful, or direct what was going on. Higher beings have arranged matters this way because human personalities, which are necessarily flawed, because they cannot but reflect the old law from which they come, are not yet strong enough to see the truth of what is happening. One day they will be – one day soon actually – but not yet.

"But no matter. People might not be aware of what is happening but the new frequencies are here now and they are all important. They will make the changes. The changes will be little at first: changes in attitude, then behaviour and then actions. It is not sensible to change too much in one go; human systems might find that stressful. But as time goes on, the changes will accelerate. Higher frequencies coming in will allow even higher ones to come through. Advanced souls will then be able to come down and make further changes. And then the golden age that the Morning Tree talked about will be here. In about 700 years, people will be as interested in spiritual matters as they are in survival and materialism today. That will be a significant change, especially as human nature hasn't really progressed in the past few thousand years. This change starts with you."

I was feeling more settled now. I still stank of smoke, but I was no longer rattled. I was really just trying to open up to what Jigme was saying and feeling the truth of this new information.

"But if this is the case," I said, "if it's frequencies that matter and not the book itself, why did you all work so hard to preserve the Morning Tree? Why did you ask Thaza to take it out of Tibet? Did you know it would end like this?"

"At the time, the Morning Tree was the most important collection of esoteric knowledge in the world. In the wrong hands, it could have opened up powers that would not have been beneficial to the world or even to those who exercised them. It was vital to protect it from darker forces. Even if these darker forces hadn't used the knowledge in the book, they could have still destroyed it. That would have been a loss of hope, for the one thing the Morning Tree did was to proclaim the golden age that is now coming. So it was definitely worthwhile to work so hard to protect it.

"Should we have asked Thaza to take it out of Tibet? Absolutely. It meant we could have today's ceremony to mark the beginning of the new. If the Morning Tree had stayed in Tibet, we would not have been free to act as we have. Moreover, Thaza's effort to safeguard the book built up an energetic charge that earned you the right to be here today and to carry the new frequencies. Believe me, you Thaza – Daniel, as you are today – have made a difference.

"As for whether I knew the book should be destroyed, I didn't when I saw you as Thaza. I didn't when I first came here. My true understanding has only been revealed to me in stages over the last twenty years. But I am very clear now on what should be done."

So, the Morning Tree was burnt because it was the old way of doing things. I had the Morning Tree inside me now as divine frequencies which would change everything. And these frequencies are automatically broadcast to others. I made a soundless chuckle.

There I was thinking first that I would publish an academic article that would make my name, then that I would publish the book as a spiritual text that could rescue humanity, and now I had nothing to publish at all!

"So I'm to do… nothing?"

"Just live your normal life; the work will be done. You might feel motivated to see someone or go to a particular place. If so, follow your intuition; it'll be an aspect of the work, even though you might not be aware of exactly what is going on. But whatever you do, you will be sowing the seeds of new law."

"Just like that?"

"Yes. You have earned the right to carry the new divine frequencies, and they will broadcast themselves through you."

"And no-one will know what is going on?"

"People may be aware something is going on, but your work will be done without acknowledgement. That is how true spiritual work is carried out – in silence without others knowing what you are doing."

Jigme paused, looking at me. Then he continued:

"Others may not know what you are doing, but you will have a growing consciousness. That consciousness will be your reward."

I hung my head. Such a different scenario from the one I'd been expecting. And yet I sensed some relief, even a deep sense of rightness. Then I chuckled. Jigme looked at me.

"It's nothing," I said. "It's just that when Thaza had his third eye opened he was told the impressions he was receiving would subside. And now you're telling me my consciousness will grow. It's just the other way round."

"Or turning full circle to completion."

A silence fell between us for a moment. I was finding that, bizarre though it might be, what Jigme was saying was beginning to make a great deal of sense.

"Any special instructions?" I asked.

"Be happy. You can be unhappy and do the work. But it is much better if you are happy. Just remember, your path has been mapped out by your own endeavours. There are higher beings watching you, helping you. They want you to be happy. The universe actually guides one to happiness if one but knew it. So be happy, for everything is being taken care of. If you do what makes you happy and excited, you will be doing what you should."

I didn't move for some time. I reflected on everything Jigme had said. Or rather I let it come into me. My mind couldn't grasp it all, and I didn't try to grasp it either. I just let my being understand. Curiously I felt renewed. I didn't have a single idea what to do now, my old life was falling apart, but I did feel a clean energy I had never experienced before.

Then I let out a laugh. I saw that I had come to Dharamsala so full of importance and worldly status, but now I had been stripped of everything and had nothing to show for what I was doing!

I looked at Jigme. He was suffused with peace and strength – a peace and strength that I was beginning to feel.

"Remember," he said, "you are doing this for others. You are broadcasting the new frequencies to all life forms and especially to the people you meet or think about. Your job is to give, without judgement, to others the divine frequencies you now know are inside you."

I looked to the floor and then back up at Jigme. Strangely, although I respected him more now, I didn't feel he was some guru at whose feet I needed to sit. He felt more like a very good friend. I smiled at him and he smiled back. We were in this together, and perhaps always had been.

Chapter Seventeen

So, I had the Morning Tree (so to speak). It was time to return home. The next day I booked my flight on my overcharged credit card and settled my guest house bill. I couldn't email Claire to tell her I was coming back because I hadn't managed to set up a new address, and explaining what had happened was too much for now, so I had to wait until I got back to London.

As I went about my business I did have a consciousness that 'something' was happening. The waiter who served me breakfast, the man at the grocery store where I bought my water, the people I passed in the street – I felt an interaction with them, an expansion of energy, another dimension at work, which I took to be the frequencies that Jigme had talked about being broadcast to others. I even felt it with some dogs I passed and some trees I saw – I could sense some quickening going into them too. If that was the way my life was to be, then so be it. It wasn't earning me a living, but I would follow this path.

At one point during the morning I stopped. Jigme had also said that as time went on I would have growing consciousness. But what would I be more conscious of? He hadn't said, and I wanted to know. I'd have to ask him the next time I saw him.

I carried on with my tasks – then suddenly it came to me. I'd be more conscious of the divine. Of the divine reason for why life is the way it is. For why life is undeniably worth living. With this, would come peace, trust and an undimming happiness that would literally, quietly and spectacularly transform my life. I saw that this consciousness would be the new frequencies becoming a reality in me. It would be a direct experience of the divine.

I don't know how I saw this. It just came in and touched me. And I had certainty. I realised I didn't need to ask Jigme my question anymore. Perhaps that growing consciousness was already coming in.

Nevertheless, I wanted to see Jigme one last time. I wanted to thank him, and tell him I was leaving. I got to the Rest House about lunchtime, but he wasn't there. The attendant said he had gone to see some religious officials and would be back later. But, he added, Jigme had mentioned that if I wanted, I could meet him in the market square and walk back with him to the Rest House. I didn't realise he could cover those distances on foot. I did want to see him, so I made my way back to the main part of town.

I got to the square and scanned it. No sign of him. It was hot and sultry; the monsoon would be arriving soon. I was glad I'd be home in London by then, but knew part of me would miss Dharamsala. I had been too preoccupied with getting hold of the Morning Tree to appreciate the town's charms, but they had seeped into me, nevertheless. I felt quite at home there – maybe due to past lives in India. I hung around the square, watching people come and go, and trying to find some shade from the strong sun. After about half an hour I succumbed and bought some tea from a nearby vendor. Normally I was careful not to drink anything other than bottled water to avoid getting diarrhoea, but I'd been all right so far, and had come to appreciate how tea can be refreshing on a hot day. I was fumbling with some tatty notes to pay the man when I saw Jigme coming through. He looked so humble, yet I knew him to be one of the greatest of all people. I felt a surge of affection. I really was glad to see him. As I was looking at him, he caught my eye and acknowledged me. That feeling of being great friends came back.

Finally, the vendor had my change. I thrust the money into my pocket and picked up my glass of tea. It was far too hot. I put it down instantly and waved my hand to cool it down. I looked again at Jigme. He was making his way towards me. I smiled… and then noticed something puzzling. A beggar sitting on the ground was suddenly remonstrating with Jigme and waving his arms. He got up and I saw the flash of a knife. For some reason, the significance of what was happening didn't penetrate my brain. I just stood next to my too hot tea watching. Then the beggar plunged the knife into Jigme's back. Jigme staggered and collapsed to the ground. The beggar stood over him shouting obscenities and then plunged the knife into him again and again.

By now I was moving. So were astonished bystanders. Some men grabbed the beggar and pulled him off Jigme. I raced to his crumpled body and turned him over. But as soon I touched him there was... nothing. He was inert, his open eyes were completely blank, and although his body was heavy in my hands there was no life in it. Surely he couldn't be dead? But he was. I searched for vital signs, but there were none. Although I swear there was a contented smile on his face. Warm dark blood from his wounds oozed onto my shirt as I held him.

How could this be? And couldn't I have prevented it? Why hadn't I gone to him as soon as I'd seen him instead of buying that tea that deep down I knew I shouldn't have had?

By now there was a huge commotion. Three men were sitting on the finally subdued beggar and shouting. Others barged me out of the way to seize Jigme's body and were shouting at him too, as if that would revive him. Everyone else around us was making a noise and gesticulating. A harassed policeman was trying to make his way through to get to the scene.

I stood up and retreated to the edge of the crowd. I heard a woman exclaim that the old beggar was always being rude to monks. He was mad, she said, but no-one ever thought he'd actually harm someone. No-one was paying attention to me, so I slipped further back. I had a lot to take in.

I sat on a low wall at the edge of the square. Jigme was dead. I was shocked. And yet didn't it make sense? His task was over once he'd passed the Morning Tree (or at least its frequencies) to me. Hadn't Jim died once he'd accomplished his task? More than that,

Jigme had said he didn't have much time left, and that he was looking forward to dropping his body. The manner of his death was surprising, but perhaps the fact of his death was not.

As these thoughts passed through me, I felt a clearing inside. There was no need to be upset. Jigme had done what he had come to do and wanted to move on. He wasn't dead, he was alive in another place. And, by Jigme's own account, in a much better place than this one.

I laughed. Reincarnation was real. The soul that had been Jigme was going on to a higher dimension before reincarnating into another body. There was certainly no need to feel sorry for him. He had met a violent death, but he had said the point of death is always painless, and I had seen the smile on his face. He was moving on, just as his soul wanted.

I stopped. Surely I should feel grief? Certainly the crowd around him were upset. A wave of grief did sweep through me. But what was I grieving for? The fact that I wouldn't see him anymore? I wasn't going to see him anymore after tomorrow anyway. The fact that I hadn't thanked him or said goodbye? We had acknowledged each other, and in that moment recognised each other's true worth. Even if this wasn't the case, it was selfish to want to end in a certain way with him. Where he was now, he knew exactly how I felt about him. And if there was unfinished business between us, well, wasn't that what future lives were for?

I admit, I still felt the shock of Jigme's death. And there was still a sense of loss because he'd gone. But Jigme had gone to a higher reality, and it was possible to come to terms with whatever loss I felt. Really, there was no need to feel grief at all. I smiled. The truth of Jigme's words – that the true response to death should be happiness for the one who has gone to a better place – was becoming real.

So I sat peacefully, oblivious to the slowly quietening scene around Jigme's body. I focussed on him – on Jigme as I'd known him over these past weeks – and stirred. As I focussed, I saw him. At least, I felt him, as real as anything. It was as if I'd suddenly been given access to where he now was. And it was such a high, beautiful, happy place (those words don't do justice to what I experienced), and he was so resplendent, that I knew for a fact that death was not real. This feeling swept through my system, impregnating it with this knowledge. I was elevated, balanced and at peace.

I even ran through how I would feel when my parents died. I'd always shied away from thinking about their deaths, even though my father was retired and not in robust health. But now I saw clearly there was no need for grief. If my father died, he'd move on to a wonderful reality. I may not have been an ideal son, and there were many unsaid things between us. But I could see the sacrifices he had made for me, feel the love we had for each other and knew there was a strong bond between us. My mother would be alone, but her grief, although understandable, would be for her loss, not for where he would be after 'death'. And if she truly knew that he was in a better place, that they may meet up when she died, and that most likely their relationship would be picked up in a future life, well then, she might be able to bear her loss without so much pain.

So, Jigme was now in a wonderful place. He was all right. What about me? I paused. Surely this was a selfish thought? But even though I realised that the rest of the world would see it as selfish (as I would have done a couple of weeks ago), now I knew it wasn't. He was definitely being looked after; it was all right to think about my well-being.

An ambulance and several more policemen had arrived by now. The crowd had finally become still as the beggar, talking to himself and shaking his head, was led away and Jigme's body was lifted onto a stretcher. I didn't need to waste several weeks of my time being ground through the mill of Indian bureaucracy as a witness to Jigme's death so, since no-one was paying attention to me, I slipped back to the guest house.

I left Dharamsala early next morning. I still felt good about Jigme; he was where he should be and I was where I should be, even if I was uncertain about my next steps. I caught the bus to the airport. As I pressed my nose against the window and saw the now familiar scenes pass by for the last time, I wasn't sad I was leaving. On the contrary, I had a sense of completion. But neither was I excited to be returning home. I was just neutral. I did reflect ruefully for a moment that my luggage didn't contain the physical Morning Tree, but then I felt a glow, a spirit, inside that I knew was the Morning Tree in me.

Getting to the airport and then to Delhi to catch my flight to London was a shock. The real world was returning to me in stages. Landing at Heathrow was a bigger shock. Although it was mid-June, the sky was grey and the wind was cool, and my old (now unattainable) life was presenting itself to me. I couldn't believe it had only been four months earlier that I had been at Heathrow to pick up Jim.

I felt apart from everything around me, almost as if I was seeing things for the first time. It was momentarily strange to be surrounded by British people and British things. As the Underground rattled into London from Heathrow, with my luggage between my knees, I felt like an empty vessel being shaken from side to side. It wasn't unpleasant. In fact, it was preferable to worrying about what was going to happen. I trudged the nine minutes from the Underground to my flat and opened the door. I had to push a pile of post aside, and was nearly knocked over by a stifling heat. I'd forgotten to turn the central heating off back in April and the flat, with the windows shut and the summer sun occasionally pouring in, was as hot as Dharamsala. I turned the boiler off, flung open the windows and sat down.

I saw the mail on the floor and noticed letters in red ink, presumably utility companies getting anxious about their bills being paid. I also saw letters with SOAS' stamp on the envelope – the official notice of my dismissal. The message light on my phone was flashing. I hadn't told my parents or non-SOAS friends that I was in Dharamsala until I'd been there for several weeks, and hadn't contacted them at all after that. I wondered if they, especially my mother, were worried.

I surveyed my flat from where I was sitting. It wasn't big, but it suited me and it was mine. But not for much longer. I calculated I'd probably defaulted on my most recent mortgage payment, knew I had nothing in my bank account, and no prospect of a salary soon. A salary! There was a challenge – what on earth could I do for a job? No university would touch me now I'd been fired from SOAS. I had no other professional qualifications, wasn't a businessman and was no good with my hands.

And then there was Claire. Or rather, was there Claire? We had left on good terms but not as girlfriend and boyfriend. I had to get in touch and see how she was. I should prepare myself that she probably wouldn't want things to be as they were… another part of my old life that was going.

I felt a surge of despair. And yet, at the same time, there was something different inside me. My old self was panicking, but another part was calm. At that moment I felt the Morning Tree. I saw it as I had seen it, but also felt it as it now was – this new, strong, assured, forward looking energy that was unperturbed at what was happening. I wasn't special, but I did have this special energy inside me – on loan, it felt, but there nonetheless – and this energy knew that everything was all right. I understood what Jigme meant when he said, despite the turmoil, the world was moving forward to a golden age. Everything was all right, no matter how things looked externally. I shook myself to make sure that what I was feeling was real. It was. The more I connected with this energy, the more it flowed into me, and the more I felt looked after. I just had to go with the energy, follow where it was leading, and the right things would happen. Didn't Jigme say be happy? Bizarrely this is what I was feeling now. I had my life to live, my work to do, so let's get on with it.

I suddenly had the motivation to start sorting things out. I piled the post on the table, unpacked, showered and then gave the flat a long overdue clean. I went out to get provisions. Instead of seeing this as a chore, I enjoyed the simple experience of choosing my food and paying for it at the checkout. I noticed the flowers in the gardens I passed on the way home, and the strong purple of the buddleia now blooming, not only in gardens but in every place it could find to grow.

There was a message, I thought: something of beauty growing on wasteland and cracks in the walls. Beauty was winning through now.

Once home I ploughed through my post. The hysterical demands for money, the curt letter from SOAS, the pile of circulars plying me with special offers – none of them bothered me. I saw it all as the clamouring of a world that need no longer be mine. A better future was assured and, although it wasn't here yet, its first rays were beginning to warm me. I laughed. My mind couldn't find reasons why it should be happy, but my system (soul?) knew there was every cause to be happy and no need to worry. Jigme was right about frequencies being all important.

I slept well that night, and not because I was exhausted from jet lag. This new, calm, happy space was there inside me. It existed with other aspects of myself – my old self and its preoccupations – but I could choose which space to be in. And it worked every time.

I spent the next morning going through my phone messages. They were several months old as the inbox had quickly filled up. My parents had been worried about me and, despite their relief when I finally called them, told me off for being so neglectful. I'd have to tell them I'd been fired later. As soon as I'd finished that call, I was ready to contact Claire. I dialled her number.

"D… Daniel? Where are you?"

"Home."

"When did you get back?"

"Yesterday."

"With the Morning Tree? Why didn't you tell me you were coming?"

"I couldn't. I don't have email at the moment, and I couldn't call. But there is a lot to tell you."

"Come over. I'm at SOAS. I'll be free for lunch."

"I'd rather not go to SOAS, if you don't mind. How about your flat this evening?" She was quiet. "No strings attached. It's just it'll be easier to talk somewhere private."

"OK," she said. "Come at seven."

I was looking forward to seeing her. I knew things weren't as they had been, but she was wonderful, and the only person I could really talk to about my experiences with the Morning Tree. I turned up at seven p.m. She opened the door in a T-shirt and shorts. She gave me a hug. I could smell pasta cooking in the background.

"You're looking good," she said, as I went in. "Tell me everything. Where's the Morning Tree? Do you know, I've never even seen it? What are you going to do with it? Why were you there for so long?"

We sat down and she handed me a glass of wine. I told her that Jigme had made me choose between going back to London or having the Morning Tree when he judged I was ready. I wanted the Morning Tree, so I stayed. But things hadn't turned out as I'd expected. I then told her about the ceremony, and the burning of the book. She didn't comment at that point, so I carried on. I gave her Jigme's explanation that the frequencies of the Morning Tree were now inside me, and that frequencies were more important than words understood through the mind. I told her I was now the Keeper, but in a completely new way. Although I didn't have the physical book, I did have its essence, and that essence is broadcast wherever I go.

Claire was thoughtful. To my surprise she reacted not with disbelief but understanding. "So, you are the Keeper now. It makes sense. Words are always misinterpreted. I guess if you had the book and translated it, people would only have argued over its meaning. But now you just irradiate the higher frequencies of the book?"

"Yes. I mean, I feel I should be doing something, but in truth the Morning Tree's message is sent out and people pick it up."

She nodded. As I say, I was surprised. As an ambitious academic, I'd expected her to want papers, books, something to show her peers that could be reviewed and tested.

"Jigme told me to expect something like this," she said. "He told me you would become the Keeper but in a new way. He told me oh so many things. I had an experience Daniel... well, I can't really explain it..."

"I understand. I've had something similar. You don't need to explain."

"It's changed me, Daniel. For the better. But I sometimes wonder if life wouldn't have been easier if I'd never met him. I mean, I see life in a completely new way now. It's not all about a struggle for survival – which, in our world, meant scrabbling to the top of the academic heap – it's about… about something more beautiful. I can't put it into words, but I feel I'm in unchartered waters. It's Jigme. He showed me this. How, I don't know, but he did."

Jigme. I hadn't told her he'd been murdered. Again she surprised me with her response, for she just smiled and said, "I guess it was his time to go. He had lived a long life, and passed the Morning Tree on to you. He deserved a rest."

I agreed. But what she said next surprised me even more. "Of course, you knew he was going to die like that."

"Eh?"

"As Thaza. Don't you remember?"

"No…"

"That bit in Thaza's account when he and Norchen went to some strange underground room and Thaza held a crystal ball. Hang on, let me get my copy."

And there it was. Thaza was holding a crystal ball and having visions. *Then I saw Jigme, only it wasn't him because he was an old man. I knew I was around too, but I couldn't see myself. Suddenly I saw a skinny man with hardly any clothes flash a knife and kill him. I felt a pang of guilt because I was sure I could have stopped him being killed.*[102]

"My God," I breathed. "I had completely forgotten."

We spent the rest of the evening talking about what I was going to do, where she was with her research, and how people at SOAS had reacted to my disappearing without explanation.

"Most can't believe what you've done," Claire said. "Milo says he always thought you were a puppy, at SOAS to do as little as possible and have as comfortable a life as possible. He says you've shattered

---

[102] See page 108 in Thaza's account.

438

his faith in his ability to read other people's characters. He hopes you've gone mad or won the lottery, as those are the only things he can think of to explain your behaviour."

I asked her about Professor Thurgood. She looked sad. "He... I think he got into trouble with the Dean for trying to protect you. Of course, they can't fire him, he's too close to retirement, but I think they gave him a formal warning."

Professor Thurgood. At the very least I owed him an explanation. I said as much to Claire.

"But you don't have the book, Daniel," she said. "He might not understand."

"He might," I replied. "And I've an idea how I can prove it to him."

Claire gave me supper. I was enjoying her company and the conversation was easy. After the dishes had been cleared, we sat on the sofa with cups of tea. Claire turned towards me. There was a moment of silence. Then she said:

"I still need time."

She spoke softly and her eyes looked into mine. She was beautiful.

"That's all right," I replied, "do what you need." If reincarnation was about moving towards unconditional love, as Jigme had said, then I had to take another step on the way by respecting her wishes. She smiled and sipped some tea.

As I was leaving at the end of the evening, Claire touched my arm. "Why do you think we met in this life?"

"To help each other."

She nodded. "You've certainly helped me."

I stepped out of her flat, and she shut the door.

Chapter Eighteen

I went to see my parents for the weekend. I told them everything that had happened. For the first time, I didn't sublimate my behaviour to try to please them; I just told the truth. My mother was supportive and my father, amazingly, was emollient. For once he didn't criticise or indicate displeasure. Instead, he told me I'd done the right thing to jeopardise my job to try to get the Morning Tree, if I'd thought it was that important. He even said he'd wished he had followed his heart more in his life.

I returned to London on Monday. On my way home I stopped at a convenience store to get some milk and bread. I was looking to see if I needed anything else when I heard a commotion. I turned round to see three youths with hoods pulled over their faces. They were shouting at the storekeeper, and one was waving a knife near his face. A woman and a child were cowering at one side. The storekeeper was shouting back, clearly afraid. For some reason I felt calm. I stood there and caught the eye of the youth with the knife. He harangued me with swear words and threats, but I was unmoved. He edged backwards. The storekeeper hadn't handed any money over, and was making no attempt to do so. One of the other youths urged the one with the knife to hurry up. The youth with the knife pushed his friend away and looked at me one more time. Then, with some more oaths, he took off, the other two racing after him out of the shop. The storekeeper, with shaking hands, dialled the police. I was still standing where I had been when the incident began.

"Thank you," said the woman with the child to me. "Oh thank you. You were so brave."

I shook myself out of my reverie.

"You saved us!" the woman continued.

"I didn't do anything."

"Yes you did. You… you changed their minds. I saw it."

Once the police had taken my statement, I walked home. I picked up a newspaper on the way. The headline was about trouble in the Middle East. I suddenly saw the conflict in the Middle East, the attempted robbery I had just witnessed and my weekend with my parents all in one go. I saw that it was all a dance of souls in matter, working their way through their lives to achieve greater levels of consciousness and understanding. My parents were on their journey, just as I was. The three youths were trying to cope with life and would one day realise they shouldn't harm others. And the conflict in the Middle East was a crucible in which the past was being hammered out for a better future – the souls in that region were doing this on behalf of mankind. Jigme had said I would get impressions of the work that was going on. I didn't realise they would come so quickly.

When I got home, there was a brown envelope with HM Revenue and Customs stamped on it. I opened it half expecting another problem but instead found a tax rebate for £2,900. I'd completely forgotten I had a dispute with the taxman, which now seemed to be settled in my favour. It wasn't much, but it meant I could pay my immediate bills. Hadn't Jigme said if I followed higher purpose, my lower purpose would be taken care of?

I contacted some friends and arranged to meet them. I wanted some normal company and a good time. We met up that evening and it was all I hoped for. We laughed about the past, and about one of my friends' problems with his girlfriend. While I was with them I suddenly felt a burst of love. Not for them as personalities, but for the souls I was going through life with. It just seemed obvious we were helping each other. And I swear I saw my friends catch some of this:

441

the light in their eyes become brighter and they sat up straighter inside themselves.

After our drinks we had gone to a restaurant. As I handed my payment to the waitress at the end of the evening, I knew that wrapped up in the money was also new spirit that she was receiving on a soul level. I knew then that the frequencies Jigme had said were now in me were broadcasting themselves to others, as I could see they had done to my parents over the weekend and the youths in the shop that morning. I certainly wasn't doing anything, but something was happening.

I also spent the next few days making phone calls. I wanted to set everything up before I went to see Professor Thurgood. When I was ready, I contacted him. The academic year had all but ended and he was winding everything up before going for a month to his house in France.

"Daniel!" he said when I called him, "I wondered when you'd be back. There are some things here of yours that you might like to collect. They're in my office, but I can leave them with Ann if you prefer."

"I'll come and collect them from you, if that's all right," I said. "I can come in this afternoon."

"Right. What time?"

So it was at four thirty that I entered SOAS. I always preferred it in the holidays; the place was more accessible without hordes of students wandering around. I knocked on Professor Thurgood's door.

"Ah, Daniel, right on time. There are your things. Had to pack them myself, hope you don't mind."

It was strange seeing him and knowing that he'd been Lama Kunchen. Strange too knowing that I knew but he didn't.

"Sit down. Tea? I can rustle some up if you don't mind it black – there's no milk."

When he returned with two mugs of tea I started. "Professor Thurgood, it's been difficult, I know. I want to thank you—"

"Daniel, no need for thanks. We all did what we had to."

"Yes. But you were particularly helpful. You supported me, you gave me money, you tried to stop me being fired."

"I was just doing my job. Frankly it was a godsend that research of yours. Something different for a change. Something potentially useful."

"But you were suspicious of the Morning Tree at first."

"Yes. It took me a time to realise what was in front of me. Too many years in the same job doing the same thing. But when I read Thaza's manuscript, well, there was something in it that bit me. I must say, I'd never have thought you would have gone for something as risky as that. Always took you to be more cautious. But I'm glad you did. It's what true scholarship is about – discovering something new and worthwhile. By the way, what did happen with the Morning Tree? Do you have it?"

"Not in the way you'd think," I replied, and I told him what had happened.

He furrowed his brow as he listened. "Hmm, that's bad luck," he said when I'd finished. "I was hoping you'd have the book and publish something. Help make your name in this field. But I think I can understand what that lama was saying. Words in a book are not as important as the spirit that animates you. I dare say charismatic people have the impact they do because of some special energy they possess, rather than what they might say."

"I don't know that I'm charismatic."

"Maybe not, but you do look changed, Daniel. It seems that lama has done you a power of good. Still, it's a shame you can't publish anything. It would have been satisfying to have proved the existence of this text, and to have seen what it said. I was very keen to know if it was all true."

"We can do something to prove it's true – or rather, you can."

Professor Thurgood put down his tea. "Me? Do what?"

"Past life regression."

He looked uncertain.

443

"It's hypnotism," I continued. "A way of getting in touch with previous lives we've had. I've found someone from University College who's an expert in this field and he's willing to try it on you."

"But what good will that do? Look, I understand the idea behind reincarnation – Lord knows, I am a professor of Tibetan – but that doesn't mean I was one, or that I know anything about this book of yours."

"I can't tell you why it might help. I can't give you information that might influence what happens. But I have been told things about the Morning Tree that you don't know. If you relate similar information under hypnosis, I promise it will prove the book and what we believe about it is true."

"So… so you think a past life of mine contains information that is relevant to the Morning Tree and you want to see if I relay this under hypnosis?"

"Yes. And if you do, you'll have corroboration that the Morning Tree is what Thaza says it is and what I know it is."

"Hmm, well, it's unorthodox, quite strange really, but I can see what you're driving at." He leant back in his chair and rubbed his chin. "You really think this will work?"

"It could," I replied.

In the past I'd have put money on Professor Thurgood dismissing the idea, but now I was hopeful he would succumb.

"I don't know, I have to go to France, I've a lot to do before I go. But, well, if you think it will help… But just one session mind."

I left to make arrangements with the expert at University College, a Dr Sampson. Because it was the end of term, he was able to see Professor Thurgood early the following week. The session would be conducted in Dr Sampson's office, so I picked up Professor Thurgood on the way to University College.

Dr Sampson greeted us at the entrance. He was bearded, bookish and busy. He talked all the way up to his office, going into fine detail about how he hypnotises people, but not managing to convey anything very understandable. Maybe he was trying to put Professor

444

Thurgood at ease, but I suspect he was irritating him. Needless to say, I had briefed Dr Sampson about the session, but hadn't told him everything. I didn't want him to give anything away to Professor Thurgood.

"Now," said Dr Sampson, in his cloying voice once we'd reached his office, "it's all quite simple really. As I've said, you sit there and I will talk to you and bring you into a state of hypnosis. When you are, ah, under, I will ask you some questions. You don't need to worry about anything for at that stage you won't be consciously aware of what is happening. You'll be quite safe though. I have never had any problems with any of my patients."

Professor Thurgood winced at the word patient. "Well, let's get started then," he said gruffly.

"Ah, right. Let me adjust the lighting." Dr Sampson pulled the blinds and turned on a small lamp. "Now, just relax, close your eyes and listen to my voice."

He took Professor Thurgood through his routine. In a remarkably short time, Professor Thurgood's large frame slumped as he went into a deeper state of consciousness. Dr Sampson fussed around Professor Thurgood, checking his breathing and vital signs, and then he turned to me and whispered, "He's ready."

I nodded to Dr Sampson to continue.

"Imagine yourself rising up," Dr Sampson began. His voice had taken on more authority. "Go up above the roof. Look down and see the buildings below. Now come back down. Come down, down, down. You touch the ground."

Professor Thurgood grunted.

"Now look at your feet. What are you wearing?"

Professor Thurgood's breathing became deeper. His body shifted in his seat. His face made a slow movement.

"What is on your feet?" repeated Dr Sampson.

"Felt boots," said Professor Thurgood slowly, in a voice that wasn't quite his own.

"And what are you wearing?"

"A robe. My robe."

"What colour is it?"

"Red. It's faded though. And thin. I should get a new one."

"Where are you?"

Professor Thurgood kept his eyes shut, but he moved his head as if looking round a room. "Chakpori," he said. This time he said it in a voice that definitely wasn't his. He said it in a Tibetan accent that I'd never heard before.

Dr Sampson looked at me for instruction. I nodded vigorously to get him to continue.

"What year is it?" he asked.

There was a pause before Professor Thurgood replied, "Year of the Iron-Sheep.[103]" He was speaking in Tibetan now, and in the same accent as before.

Dr Sampson looked confused. Obviously he didn't understand Professor Thurgood's answer. "Maybe we should bring him back?" he said, looking at me.

"No!" I hissed. "I'll take over. You're recording this?"

"Yes, yes, but I'm not sure he's—"

I held up my hand to silence him, and turned to Professor Thurgood. "What is your name?" I asked him in Tibetan.

There was a pause. Professor Thurgood smiled.

"What is your name?" I repeated.

"Pem-ba," he said slowly, "Kun-chen."

"What are you doing?"

"Teaching."

"What are—"

"You."

I stopped. His eyes were closed, he really did seem hypnotised, yet he was interacting with me in an unexpected way. Dr Sampson was watching us without understanding what was going on.

"Me?" I asked.

"Yes. Thaza."

---

[103] 1931.

446

It was getting hot in the room. The windows were closed to shut out the noise of the traffic. I wiped my face. "What are you teaching me?"

"Manners," he replied, chuckling. His voice was deeper and his Tibetan accent was hard to follow. It was like seeing television clips from the 1950s – the people speak English, but in an accent you don't hear anymore.

"Do I need to be taught manners?"

"Yes!" he said with a rich laugh. "You are so arrogant! But we tolerate it. You need to have a certain strength if you are to succeed."

"Succeed at what?"

"Safeguarding the Morning Tree."

"Are you the Keeper?"

"Yes."

"Who else knows this?"

"Very few. Jigme. The Great Thirteenth. One or two others. My job is to make sure people don't know who I am."

"Have you ever met any Europeans?" I thought a change of tack would either throw this connection or confirm it was real.

"Some."

"When?"

"Several times."

"When was the first time?"

"Year of the Wood-Dragon.[104] When the British invaded Lhasa."

"Who did you meet?"

"Younghusband." He gave his Tibetan name.

"Why?"

"He was a high soul."

"But he invaded Tibet."

"He was still a high soul. It was my duty to meet him."

"What did you tell him?"

"As little as possible. But he was there to help us."

"How?"

---

[104] 1904.

"He was to show the way."

I waited. I didn't want to lead the witness, so to speak. Professor Thurgood was silent, but at the same time I could see his eyes were moving rapidly behind his lids. I watched him closely. I wasn't sure what was going on, and would have to speak if I felt he was coming back. Dr Sampson was beginning to get fidgety in the silence, looking repeatedly at me and Professor Thurgood. I caught his eye to tell him to wait. He ignored me and was about to get up when Professor Thurgood spoke.

"He was to show the way with the Morning Tree."

"Did he know about the Morning Tree?"

"Not consciously. But he was one of us."

"Have you ever left Tibet?" I thought another change of tack would help.

There was another pause. "Once."

"When?"

"Year of the Iron-Dog.[105]"

"Where did you go?"

"To India with His Holiness. We had to escape the Chinese."

"Did you like India?"

"No. It is busy and crowded. It wasn't an easy time. But we had to go."

"Who did you meet there?"

"Lonchen Bell.[106] And a military man.[107] He was one of us too."

"Lonchen Bell?"

"The military man. Lonchen Bell was a friend."

Professor Thurgood's voice suddenly sounded tired. Dr Sampson noticed this too. He leant over and told me in a low, urgent voice that

---

[105] 1910.

[106] Sir Charles Bell 1870-1945. He was a British Political Officer who first met the Thirteenth Dalai Lama in India in 1910. He subsequently formed a close relationship with him and the Tibetan government and was the first member of a European government to be invited to Lhasa. He stayed in Lhasa for several years. The Tibetans called him Lonchen Bell.

[107] Presumably Brigadier Massingberd.

he thought the session should be concluded. I begged him for more time, and carried on before Dr Sampson could act.

"How do you know it's me?" I asked.

"Ha!" Professor Thurgood replied, this time with more life, "I would recognise you anywhere. Our lives have been intertwined more than you know. This is not the first time we have met. But you have always been so disrespectful! Still, you were a good student. And I did test you. I am sorry about Lama Neto." I sat up. What did he mean? "I could have stopped him following you, but I deliberately allowed him to go after you when you had the Morning Tree."

"Why?"

"I had to allow Lama Neto to exercise his free will. And I admit I was interested to see how you would cope. I had placed a bet on you to succeed."

"And if I hadn't succeeded?"

"You did. A great deal was achieved when you won that bet. Especially when you refused to give the Morning Tree to him. So much of your karma was wiped out. And the light took a great step forward then. You helped speed up the golden age that is coming."

"Do... do you have anything more to say?"

"You did well with the Morning Tree. It was kept from the dark. And you have done well with it now. You will give it to everyone."

I was silent.

"One more thing." His voice was picking up as if our session was coming to an end. "You will have a happy marriage, but to whom and how may not be obvious. Also, there is someone willing to help you. Look in an unexpected quarter."

"What—"

"And be happy. You have succeeded. The Morning Tree is inside you now. One day it will be inside everyone. The light is winning. The turmoil the world is experiencing is just the birth pains of a new and better life. Never worry. Hope is growing into certainty."

I felt a peace filling the room. It was as other-worldly and profound as anything I'd experienced with Jigme. My mouth was dry, and I was soaked in sweat.

"Thank you," I croaked. It was all I could manage. Professor Thurgood didn't hear me. He just slumped further in his chair, started breathing heavily and then his head jerked. Dr Sampson quickly took over.

"Become aware of your body," he commanded, as he began to bring Professor Thurgood back. After some guidance from Dr Sampson, Professor Thurgood stirred and then opened his eyes. He blinked awhile and shook his head.

"It's awfully hot in here. Is that it? Anything happen?" He was speaking in his normal voice. He pulled at his collar and shifted in his chair.

"I can't tell you," said Dr Sampson. "You were speaking a strange language. The session should have been stopped some time ago, if you ask me, but your colleague—"

"We have everything recorded," I interjected. "I'll play it to you later."

We left that stuffy office. I opened my arms to fan the breeze of the warm afternoon around my body. Professor Thurgood was sweating, but he didn't loosen his jacket and tie. We stopped at a water fountain on the way out to refresh ourselves, and went back to SOAS. I told him the experiment had been a success. I waited until we were in his office and he had settled himself before outlining what had happened. I then played the recording. He listened intently, without comment, but taking it all in.

I then told him that under hypnosis he had, as Lama Kunchen, revealed that I was Thaza, confirmed that Lama Kunchen had gone with the Dalai Lama to Calcutta, and divulged that Younghusband and Massingberd were part of the Morning Tree – all significant facts that he hadn't known as Professor Thurgood but which had been vouched to me. I added that he'd even answered Jigme's confusion over why Lama Kunchen had allowed Lama Neto to pursue Thaza.

450

I showed him the parts in my notes that backed this up. He rifled through my papers, reading the passages I pointed out. He said everything I was telling him seemed right – he certainly wasn't resisting the idea that he had been Lama Kunchen – but he added what really impressed him was the Tibetan he had been speaking. It was an accent he could never have made up because he had no idea it existed.

I sat back in silence as Professor Thurgood looked again over the passages I had pointed out to him. I guess he was feeling like me when I had been told I was Thaza. He had a whole new concept of himself to take on board – that he had been Lama Kunchen and central to the Morning Tree. He was keeping an even keel, but he was clearly dealing with a significant change.

As he read, a deeper certainty began to spread through me. Not that I was suddenly safe and sorted in my life – there were still so many uncertainties – but that there was a higher plan and all I had to do was let it unfold. I knew I was being looked after. In fact, there was no 'I', there was just this trust that all is well.

By now I became aware of Professor Thurgood drumming his large fingers on his desk. He was deep in thought. Eventually he cleared his throat and looked up.

"Do you know, apart from corroborating Thaza's account and what that monk told you, that session proved reincarnation is real. I mean, I can't think of another explanation. There is no other way I could have said what I did."

He was silent again for a while.

"So there is no death," he continued. "Only life. And no need to fear death. Or even grieve for the one who's gone."

He looked at me. Then he sat up and said in a voice more his own, "But to what end, I don't know."

Jigme had told me to what end, and he'd known it as Lama Kunchen, but it was too much to explain now. So I simply said, "To learn how to behave and come to a true realisation of what we are."

By now it was evening. Professor Thurgood hadn't stopped being Professor Thurgood, but he had become a friend – the friend, I think,

451

he had always felt I was to him. He phoned his wife to say he would be home late, and we went out for supper. We went to a Spanish restaurant he knew on Charlotte Street.

"I might have been Tibetan in my last life," he quipped, "but I could never get on with the food in this life. Now Mediterranean cooking… To tell the truth, that's where I should have been born. Perhaps I'll put in a request for my next life."

The meal lasted a long time. The Spanish waiters seemed to think that we had come in unconscionably early and it took over an hour for even our starters to arrive. But the food, and the whole evening, was delightful.

At the end, as we stood outside the restaurant, Professor Thurgood put out his hand. "It's been an experience, Daniel. You have given me a lot to think about."

I shook his hand. "I couldn't have done it without you."

"Keep in touch, won't you."

The next day I contacted Claire. I asked her to come and see me so I could tell her in person what had happened with Professor Thurgood. She turned up at my flat later and I relayed the events at University College and afterwards. She was intrigued, and asked if she could see my notes, not just of the session, but of my whole experience with the Morning Tree. I didn't see why not, I wasn't going to publish anything. The Morning Tree might be in me but it was not mine in any way. So I told her I'd give her this account when I'd finished it. It was then she confided that Jigme had asked her to chronicle my whole story. She'd been waiting for the right time to tell me what he had said and ask for my notes. So, the crafty old man was planning something after all. She was looking, if anything, more beautiful. She asked what I was going to do.

"Follow Lama Kunchen's advice," I told her. "Look for help in an unexpected quarter."

She asked me to keep in touch too, and I said I would. I then made a phone call. I'd never have guessed I'd make that call. But I knew with clarity it was the right one to make.

Editor's Postscript

Dr Clifton has given permission for his account of the search for the Morning Tree to be published, along with his translation of Thaza's account of how he came to take the Morning Tree out of Tibet.

Dr Clifton does not seek any publicity himself, and will not enter into correspondence or dialogue about his or Thaza's accounts.

Professor Thurgood passed away unexpectedly in December 2009, five months after his session with Dr Sampson.

Dr Clifton is currently working with Mr Ravensburg. The nature of his work cannot be disclosed.